Praise for Lynda William's Previous Books

"Plenty of action with great world building and well-written characters. This one is a keeper. And made me want more of the Okal Rel universe." - Pam Allan, ConNotations Magazine

"The Okal Rel Saga is culturally complex and politically tangled, an epic tale of clashing civilizations and worldviews. Righteous Anger follows the making of a military hero, Horth Nersal, and is a strong, highly readable installment to this ambitious and far-reaching space opera." - Dru Pagliassotti, The Harrow

"Williams builds a very deep universe that could easily be off-putting in its level of detail, but it is so populated with interesting characters and moves along so breezily that the only problem might be keeping track of all the threads" - Lisa Martincik, VOYA Magazine

"The book is detailed, especially in the description of the many duels and the sword-play. The story takes place on different worlds and in the depths of space. The author deals with everything from race relations and xenophobia to the early sexual maturity of a genetically enhanced youth whose passions come to play much earlier than one would anticipate. We have feuding factions, politics, power plays, religion and tribal warfare taken to a galactic level. ... Recommended." - Ronald Hore, CM Magazine

"In the Rel universe life and land are precious and warring is against accepted practice - differences are solved by duels fought by a single champion- and RIGHTEOUS ANGER provides the story of champion Horth, never accepted by either side of two warring houses. A fast-paced fantasy of action results." - Diane C. Donovan, Midwest Book Review

"Once again I was very appreciative of the depth of the characters and found myself stealing moments to learn more about their struggles and ultimately the life rendering decisions each would make. The turmoil of the characters corresponds with the political turmoil between the two civilizations and builds to an explosive climax that would be difficult for any reader to anticipate or deny." - T.M. Martin, Yet Another Book Review

"I was captivated by the possibilities of living in that time and impressed with Williams' visions of the future and her ability to successfully weave in cultural differences in sexuality and love. I look forward to the next volume." - T.M. Martin, reviewer

AVIM'S OATH

Lynda Williams

EDGE SCIENCE FICTION AND FANTASY PUBLISHING

AN IMPRINT OF HADES PUBLICATIONS, INC.

CALGARY

Avim's Oath
copyright © 2010 by Lynda Williams

This is a work of fiction. Names, characters, places, and
incidents are the products of the author's imagination or
are used fictitiously and are not to be construed as real.
Any resemblance to actual events, locales, organizations,
or persons, living or dead, is entirely coincidental.

Edge Science Fiction and Fantasy Publishing
An Imprint of Hades Publications Inc.
P.O. Box 1714, Calgary, Alberta, T2P 2L7, Canada

In house editing by Richard Janzen
Interior by Brian Hades
Cover Illustration by Lynn Perkins
ISBN: 978-1-894063-35-7

EDGE Science Fiction and Fantasy Publishing and Hades Publications, Inc.
acknowledges the ongoing support of the Canada Council for the Arts and the
Alberta Foundation for the Arts for our publishing programme.

Library and Archives Canada Cataloguing in Publication

Williams, Lynda, 1958-
    Avim's oath : part six of the Okal Rel Saga / Lynda Williams.
    -- 1st ed.

(Okal Rel saga ; pt. 6)

I. Title. II. Series: Williams, Lynda, 1958- . Okal Rel saga ; pt. 6.

PS8595.I562A95 2010 C813'.6 C2010-900160-5

FIRST EDITION
(e-20100723)
Printed in Canada
www.edgewebsite.com

Dedication

For Krysia Anderson

Other Books In The Okal Rel Saga

AVIM'S OATH

Lynda Williams

PROLOGUE

Starting Over

Amel set his shuttle down on Perry's runway behind the old palace of Barmi II, with a feeling of holiday jubilation.

The last time he had seen Perry, weeks earlier, he thought it was for the last time. Now he was returning in triumph—not a prisoner of the Reetions, but the First Sworn of his half-brother Erien.

A liege! he rejoiced in his heart. *I have a liege!*

Admittedly, Erien was a bit odd for a Sevolite, but Amel believed he could serve his Reetion-raised half-brother without fear of being asked to harm anyone he loved. And for once in his life he would have an official place within the status hierarchy of the empire.

I might even be able to organize poetry festivals, Amel thought excitedly. He toyed with the idea of converting Lilac Wedge, below his residence on Fountain Court, into a permanent dance studio, and envisioned a clump of glum swordsmen watching him rehearse. The image raised a liquid chuckle in his throat, and for a moment he indulged himself in fantasies of vengeance on all the hard-hearted people in his life who belittled the sensitivities he cherished. But his appetite for spite, even in so mild a form, was small. As his shuttle ship rolled to a halt, all Amel's thoughts turned to Perry D'Aur.

Memory was a potent force in someone as Demish as Amel. Inhaling, he could invoke Perry's coppery scent. Smiling, he remembered the feel of her in his arms as they lay in bed talking about people dear to both of them. Perry wasn't a beauty in traditional Demish terms. Her aging body was compact and muscular. Her oval face was lined from too many hours of *rel-skimming* by someone who lacked the regenerative abilities of a highborn, like himself, but the laugh lines about her eyes were all the dearer to him for the proof they offered of her resilience in the face of mounting cares.

Amel dropped lightly from his cockpit to survey the empty landing field. He had radioed Perry from space as soon as he'd dropped out of skim at the requisite distance from the edge of the planet's atmosphere. There should have been a small army of friends assembled to greet him.

Amel scanned the edges of the landing field again, his disappointment shading into worry. Then he spotted Perry walking toward him from the back end of the palace and he forgot the unusual reception.

For twenty years, Perry had sheltered him whenever he got the worst end of the power struggles he kept being pulled into at court. Now, for the first time, he was in a position to do something meaningful for her. He was eager to make a hundred promises to ease her stress of living out here, on the fringes of the empire, locked out of the best opportunities for commerce by her lack of representation at court, and forever at risk of a military take-over by the Silver Demish—who refused to accept any nation founded by a liege-killer.

Once, Amel had hoped Perry might be the one special woman he could make his wife, but he had long accepted that he took second place in her heart to Vrenn, the man with whom she shared the hard work of leading her rebel alliance. It was the same with his other *mekan'st*, although in Ann's case his rival was not another man, but her commitment to the Reetion Space Service. What he felt for both Ann and Perry was still beautifully real to him, and Perry—in particular—was family.

Perry stopped and waited for Amel to run over to her.

He hugged her fiercely, satisfied by the firmness of her arms about him. It was only when she failed to respond to his kiss that he realized something was wrong.

"You're angry!" Amel cried, alarmed.

"Worried," she denied his conclusion, and forced a smile. "So much for your alleged powers of discernment if you can't tell the difference."

Amel responded with a nervous laugh, leaving a little space between them as they walked through a machine yard and into the palace via the back entrance. He knew she was put out about something, and betrayed his apprehension by babbling to her excitedly about how Erien had turned everything around for him on Rire.

"Seems to me Erien might have worked his miracle a few days earlier, if he's so amazingly clever," Perry interrupted him with an impatient snort, "and spared you the need to try killing yourself to protect secrets you didn't want the Reetions digging out of your brain again."

Amel stopped short to stare at her where she stood, holding open the door to the little parlor off the ground floor of the palace where she entertained visitors. It alarmed him to be having such a strange conversation in the friendly, faded opulence of the palace, so rich with good memories for him. "You can't dislike Erien!" he pleaded.

"Can't I?" she said. "Your new hero is too Vrellish, too Lorel and too messed up by spending the second half of his childhood on Rire. If he proves to have anything but contempt for Demish people—Blue, Gold or Silver—I'll be damned."

She went into the lounge.

"Erien isn't my *hero!*" Amel exclaimed, scrambling after her. "He saved me on Rire, and on Fountain Court, but I'm not like some kid with dreams of glory idolizing Horth Nersal! I know Erien's not perfect! He's—"

"Cold and calculating?" Perry supplied. "Fixated on technical solutions without respect for the lives they disrupt or the values they undermine?"

"He's practical," Amel reinterpreted her analysis. "You like people who get things done."

"Maybe," she said. Amel could sense her wrestling with herself about whether to go on and left an expectant silence.

Perry sighed, releasing some of the internal pressure feeding her ill humor. "What I am, Amel," she said, "is Blue Demish. That makes me a liegeless nobleborn in an empire that isn't set up to make life easy for people without representation on Fountain Court. And I very much doubt your Erien, or his Lor'Vrellish father the Ava, have any intentions of reuniting the Blue Demish clans who are losing their identity, oath by oath, as their nobleborn leaders find it easier to turn to the highborns of other houses for representation under Sword Law: something they have to do because there is no Blue Hearth anymore on Fountain Court."

Amel blinked at her. "Blue Hearth? But Perry, that isn't Erien's fault!"

"No," she said pointedly. "It's yours."

She might as well have struck Amel with an ax. He stared at her, thunderstruck. He had returned to her feeling like a new man, about to take his place at court, only to discover this was not enough. In one terrible moment the last two decades of his intimate friendship with Perry lost definition for him, and resolved itself into new patterns: she viewed him as a failed liege, not a good lover; she wanted him to be worthy of her oath, not babbling to her about his willing surrender of power to Erien Lor'Vrel. And no amount of love on his part could make up the difference.

Amel slumped down onto an old, familiar couch in the lounge, oppressed by the weight of his insight.

Perry sat down beside him and put an arm around his shoulders. "I understand why you want to serve Erien," she said wearily. "It will be easier than establishing credibility as a Demish prince, given all you've been through." She tightened her arm around him. "You deserve to enjoy life."

Amel would not yield to the awkward hug. Even their habit of speaking in simple *rel*-peerage felt less like a gesture of friendship than an admission that he did not deserve her respect.

He groped for a way to explore the huge feelings of inadequacy she'd raised in him, and was spared by the flamboyant entrance of a young woman dressed in a tank top and work trousers.

"Amel!" the new arrival cried, her bold features blazing with possessive intensity.

"Diff!" He rose to receive her as she dove for him, swinging her up in his arms. "Look at you!" he exclaimed, holding her aloft with perfect balance as he admired her grinning face, damp with sweat. "You're all curves and muscle!" he added with a dash of naïve surprise. He had been out of circulation for months, during which she had sprung into adulthood with all the violent suddeness of a Vrellish child, despite her Demish good looks.

Diff, whose full name was Alivda, adjusted her grip on Amel's forearms, cuing him to shift his weight and dip for lift as she arched herself upward in a handstand, their palms on each other's shoulders, until her body made a straight line above his.

"Stop showing off, Alivda," Perry snapped. "You too, Amel. After two decades of messing around with half-measures, you're about to take your place as a peer of Fountain Court. Act the part!"

"Sorry!" Amel eased Alivda down again, trying to look contrite.

"Lighten up, Gramma," scoffed Alivda with an insolent teenage sneer, reminding Amel of the friction between Perry and her granddaughter when baby Diff had been a hyperactive toddler. Back then, Perry had resorted to caging her whenever her mother, Ayrium, was away. Even Ayrium, as protective as a lioness about her daughters, had agreed to let Amel take Diff with him on his envoy trips rather than continue to inflict Diff and Perry on each other. Now, although he hated to face it, Amel could see the truth in Perry's face: his baby dragon, as he liked to call Diff, was getting out of hand again.

"Life isn't all fun and games," Perry chided her granddaughter.

"Really?" Alivda snapped back. "Then why doesn't Vrenn let me lead the irregulars? I've got the grip. And the skill."

Amel thought of Vrenn as the man Perry would have married if the grim, ex-Nersallian hadn't been too Vrellish for monogamy.

"The grip, maybe, but not the discipline," Perry said testily. "Vrenn has discharged her from fleet service," she added to Amel, "for dereliction of duty."

"It was *ward* duty!" Alivda complained, as if Vrenn had assigned her to slop out latrines. She, too, appealed to Amel. "Vrenn had me flying ward duty out of *Blind Eye Station* for two weeks straight, just to punish me for disobeying his signals in a shake-up with a rogue Vrellish ship." She stopped, then added in a tone as hard as hullsteel. "I nailed the rogue. My tactic worked."

"Vrenn needs to know he can trust you to—" Perry began.

"Vrenn's a frustrated Nersallian wannabe admiral!" Alivda lashed back, feet planted and hands on her hips, looking solid as a rock despite her slim build. "He just likes giving orders and being obeyed."

Perry's face drained of blood. "Get out," she said.

"Perry—" Amel tried to intervene, but she pushed away the arm he extended toward her.

"No problem," Alivda assured him coldly. "I'm getting used to rejection. Starting with my nervous sire, the Ava of the whole venting empire, who won't give me any recognition beyond 'love child.' Why not gramma and Vrenn, as well?" She flashed her wide, bright grin, a sharp glitter in her blue eyes. "I think it's wonderful you're going to take your place as a liege of Fountain Court at last, Amel! I see great things in your future."

"Now she thinks she's a seer," Perry muttered under her breath.

"Exactly!" Alivda tossed her bright head. "A seer knows the future, which is much better than being a clear dreamer, forever looking back into past lives." She grinned at Amel. "So yes, I'm predicting you can cope with Fountain Court!" She winked at him. "Because I'm going to come help, as soon as I wrap up a few things around here."

"You will always be welcome in my hearth," said Amel, unable to withhold the invitation despite misgivings. "But I do have Erien to help me," he pointed out.

"Right, Erien," Perry muttered. "The Reetion-raised kid who provoked a title challenge that would have seen the Red Vrellish charging through Killing Reach on the way to invade Rire if Horth Nersal had lost on the Challenge Floor? That Erien."

Alivda broke the awkward silence by pulling Amel into a sudden hug.

She released him with a last squeeze of his hand and flashed a smile as bright as Ayrium's—except in Alivda's case the effect was more laser-like. "Don't let Gramma Perry get you down," she told Amel in parting. "She's getting old and regretful and tired of the slog out here."

When Alivda was gone, Perry sighed and rubbed her forehead. "She's right, damn her." Age sat heavily on her features, as if a filter had been removed that had prevented Amel from seeing the years that had accumulated there. Perry was not a regenerative highborn, and the long struggle to keep her alliance afloat had taken its toll on her nobleborn physiology.

"When you left here, for Rire," Perry told Amel, "to face the wrath of the Reetions for helping Ann make it possible for them to defend themselves—Amel, I thought you really were too good to live in this mad universe. So I offered you sanctuary if you survived. I figured I could shelter you if everyone else was done knocking you around—including Ann, I might add. She's come as close to getting you killed as anyone has."

Amel tried to take her hand, but she shook her head.

"Don't worry, I'm not converting to *Okal Lumens*," she said, and hunched her shoulders. "It's the opposite, if anything. Hear me out."

He kept still, a knot of worry in his gut.

"I was prepared to take you back, spent and worthless," Perry told him. "Maybe not even sane."

But still able to gift highborns—even to commoners! he couldn't help thinking. Normally, of course, people's interest in his breeding potential gave him nightmares, but it irked him that

Perry wouldn't acknowledge his pedigree as a mitigating perk even though he knew it was, simultaneously, why others might have persecuted her for sheltering him.

Perry reclaimed his interest by laying a hand on his arm.

"If you leave here to follow Erien and his alien agenda for the empire," she told him sadly, "go as my friend and *mekan'st*." She withdrew her hand. "But don't come back expecting to be either, because once you've sworn to White Hearth you will be turning your back on your own. You are Demish, Amel. Blue Demish. And we need you."

He caught his breath with a gulp, looking at her as if he had never really seen her before. Then his expression twisted into anguish.

"Perry—" he began, stepping forward to draw her into his arms.

"No," she said, wrapping her arms about herself instead. "You had better go, Pureblood Amel of Lilac Hearth on Fountain Court. You don't want to keep your liege waiting on Gelion."

Amel did not argue. He knew when Perry was adamant. He felt the weight of all the years of disappointed hope behind her eyes. They did not touch. Did not embrace as lovers one last time.

It was all he could do to hold back tears until he was safely alone in his ship. There, once the door was sealed, he braced his arms on the control panel of the cockpit, lowered his forehead to his leather sleeve, and let himself process his heartbreak in wrenching sobs.

Barmi II had been home for nearly twenty years—the one place where he had believed he was accepted for himself, no matter how inadequate or broken by his past. And Perry had just barred the door.

CHAPTER 1

Sex Ed

Stubbornly, Erien shouldered his duffel bag, ignoring the stares of the Silver Demish men among the honor guard sent by his father, Ava Ameron. All six of the Silvers were highborn men, their uniforms littered with embroidery representing their rights and privileges. Erien was a seventeen-year-old raised on Rire, but he also outranked them and it was very clear they resented his lack of respect for his own lofty heritage, because it belittled their own coveted place in the complex hierarchy of the empire.

Opposite the line of Silvers stood the Vrellish members of his receiving line: the Monatese dressed in green livery and the Nersallians in black. The Vrellish spokesman was a Nersallian woman whose crimson braid declared her a member of the *kinf'stan*: one of those entitled to challenge her liege for his title. She was also the only highborn of the six people on the Vrellish side and—to judge by her profile—grounded by the imminent birth of a child.

"Welcome, Heir Gelion," the pregnant Nersallian greeted Erien. "My liege would have greeted you himself, but he is busy with the shipment he received from Rire."

The Silver Demish members of the honor guard made an extra effort to look unresponsive at this remark, which even Erien—with his paucity of court experience—understood to mean they assumed Horth was slighting him by failing to appear.

"Tell your liege I look forward to seeing him later," he told the black-clad woman, "and I hope his shipment of cats from Rire traveled well."

One of the Demish men was startled enough to blurt, "Cats?"

House cats had been extinct within the empire since the Lorels were exiled after the Fifth Civil War over two hundred years before.

The Monatese exchanged knowing looks, doubtless informed about Horth's acquisition through their own channels.

Princess Luthan of the Silver Demish was the next to greet Erien. She had not stood waiting for him, like the rest, but was fetched from a nearby pavilion.

Luthan was what the Demish called a princess-liege: a female leader governed by her male relatives. The gender bias irked Erien, but the sight of Luthan's wide blue eyes, petite figure and mass of golden hair did other things to him. At sixteen, she was a year younger than him and lacked the breadth of education given him by his Monatese and Reetion foster parents, but somehow she made him feel woefully inadequate in all things.

"Welcome back to court, Pureblood Erien Lor'Vrel, Heir Lor'Vrel and Heir Gelion," Luthan delivered her greeting, keeping her gaze fixed on his chest. Only when she had completed the last word did her blue eyes flick up to meet his gray stare, jolting him with their sweet purity.

"Thank you," was all Erien could think to say. He did, at least, manage to get the pronoun right, down-speaking her by the one birth rank between Pureblood and Royalblood. But he had no sooner said it than he regretted the necessity of implying a superiority he did not feel. She looked so cool and poised in her multilayered, floor-length skirts that he found himself wishing to call forth the girl, met at a court reception, who had complained of pinching shoes.

"I hope you won't be leaving us again for some time," Luthan said, her own acknowledgement of their respective status seamlessly smooth.

Erien nodded stiffly. He knew they were both on display here on the docking floor, and wanted to behave naturally, but something about Luthan's very presence seemed to paralyze him.

She was the first to hear the approach of a new arrival. "Late as usual," Luthan said, in the girlish way Erien had been longing to glimpse in her. "I will leave you to catch up with your Monatese half-brother, Prince Erien, and look forward to seeing you again. Ava Ameron will, of course, be hosting a reception for you in White Hearth? Or will you leave the business of an Avim's Oath reception to your new vassal, Amel? Never mind," she concluded, with a sudden rush of blood to her ivory-pale cheeks. "I'll see you again, I'm sure." She drew back her full skirts in preparation for a stately departure.

"Wait!" Erien detained her, and knelt to rummage in his duffel bag while the assembled Demish made a point of looking elsewhere and the Vrellish watched with open curiosity. "I've something for you."

"What is it, Erien?" Luthan asked as he handed up the package.

"A book," he said, rising again. "I had it manufactured in paper, because I thought the format would be culturally appropriate for you. I translated it into Gelack myself. Was I right? Or would you have preferred an animated Reetion info blit?"

Luthan looked with wonder at the gift in her hands, wrapped in brown paper. "What's it about?" she asked.

Erien made to answer and balked for the sake of their audience. "Something you have expressed a need to learn. It seemed right to me you shouldn't be kept ignorant."

"Thank you," she said, and withdrew with the book clutched to her chest, just as Erien's half-brother Tatt burst upon the scene.

"Royalblood Ditatt Monitum, 104th liege of Monitum," a nearby Monatese herald announced, belatedly, as Tatt plowed through the Vrellish side of the receiving line with a little girl perched on his shoulders.

"Welcome back!" Tatt hailed his childhood playmate with reckless informality, catching Erien in his arms. The child upon his shoulders hung on.

"This is Hemma Lorson of Monitum," Tatt enthused as they separated, swinging the little girl down with one hand. "My most Sevolite offspring to date and hence my named heir."

"It's an honor to meet you," Erien introduced himself gravely, structuring his pronouns to follow Tatt's usage, which told him Hemma was a Royalblood like her father. It was wisest, Erien had learned, to be factual about birth ranks unless one had compelling reasons to do otherwise. His egalitarian upbringing might balk, but his Reetion foster father, Ranar, was also an anthropologist and Erien knew there was nothing simple, in Gelack, about offering peerage to someone of a lower birth rank. If nothing else, condescension could be unwelcome if it implied a false intimacy.

"The honor is mine, Heir Gelion," said the child, whose head came no higher than Tatt's waist. She beamed with a glimmer of her father's irrepressible joy for life. "I've heard a lot about my sire's strange Reetion *ha'brother* Erien."

"Nothing too dreadful, I hope," Erien said seriously.

"Oh, no." She shook her head, lower lip stiffening as she rested her right hand on the hilt of her child-sized sword. "Sire Tatt likes you tremendously! But I have *fem*-kin who say you are going to ruin Monitum by introducing Reetion competition to our nervecloth monopoly, and undermine our brokerage of medical services with Reetion competition, as well."

"Nonsense!" Tatt admonished his daughter, ruffling her mop of dark brown hair. "Monitum is Erien's favorite house on Fountain Court!"

The child gave her father a concerned look. "But if Reetion medical sciences are competitive with those of Luverthan, and he convinces people Reetions can be honorable—"

"I assure you I will take him down myself on the Challenge Floor if he plans to ruin Monitum with his Reetions!" Tatt cried. There was laughter in his bold voice, but the words sent a shiver down Erien's spine at the thought of the two of them facing each other in a serious duel. It wasn't just that Tatt was better than he was with a blade, it was the horror of imagining such a falling out.

"Bringing harm to Monitum is the last thing I want to do," Erien assured the serious-minded little girl.

She pursed her lips then yielded to a nod. "Welcome to Gelion," she concluded with the precocious maturity of Sevolite children in positions of importance.

"Thank you," he answered with equal formality.

Tatt gave his daughter a parting hug and handed her off to one of her mother's relatives—her *fem*-kin in Vrellish terms—reminding Erien of the limited rights embodied in the Vrellish term 'sire,' in contrast to the Reetion notion of fatherhood. Tatt was valued by his house in a capacity bordering on stud, which sometimes troubled Erien's more Reetion sensibilities.

"Let's go," said Tatt, steering Erien in the direction of a car he had waiting. "Ameron gave orders to fetch you soon as you arrived, and I want to get back to the Justice Ministry as soon as possible."

The Justice Ministry was Tatt's calling—his *rel* as Gelacks would put it—just as Erien's was beginning to revolve around the idea of educating Sevolites to create trust in science as a force for progress.

"I've teamed up with Luthan," Tatt explained as he piled into the back of the car beside Erien. "She let me put a branch office of the Justice Ministry—well, the only office to date apart from Green Heath itself—into her orphanage. My people provide security for the orphanage staff, and the orphanage has been around long enough to be trusted as a place to make contact with Sevolites who give a damn about living up to their responsibilities. It's working for both of us. But it's a new arrangement and I like to spend as much time down there as I can. So—" Tatt shifted to look straight at Erien, a hand spread across the back seat behind him. "—listen fast."

"Listening," promised Erien.

"There are two things I must hammer into that unworldly head of yours," Tatt told him. "First, and I want you to say this after me so I am sure you've got it—the Dragon-Lion Accord."

Erien frowned. "I am aware of Ameron's plan to bring the two pillars of his oath closer together."

"Really!" Tatt exclaimed in mock astonishment. "And yet, you left Dorn Nersal on Rire when he's supposed to be sealing the deal by marrying Princess Luthan."

"Dorn was injured," Erien defended his decision. "He needed time to heal. And I wasn't sure how he'd be received, at court, given the Reetion medical intervention required to save him. Besides, the genetic component of the accord doesn't require Dorn, specially." He paused, wrestling with an internal discomfort he couldn't label. "Horth has plenty of other sons."

"Dozens!" Tatt agreed heartily. "But none of them as housebroken to the ways of the Demish court as Dorn was! Besides," he added energetically, "insulted Demish tend to up the ante."

"What do you mean?" Erien asked, with an apprehensive frown.

"Prince H'Us will try to renegotiate for something even better, and it took Ameron long enough to get the current agreement hammered out, given Vrellish and Demish differences concerning modes of procreation."

Erien sighed. "What's the second thing?" he asked.

"Amel, and the women who view him as a signet of passage to power."

Erien's heart sank. He was fed up with Amel's doe-eyed helplessness in the face of predatory females. His jaw locked. He coaxed it loose again with difficulty, letting Tatt's words wash over him.

"Amel was under a cloud when you left court for Rire," Tatt explained. "His connection with Ann of Rire looked suspicious enough to overshadow even his value as a Pureblood. Then a group of *Okal Lumens* lobbied Ameron to rescue Amel from the Reetions on the grounds they believed him to be a Soul of Light, although that still isn't the official line from the Golden Emperor on Demora, and here's the amazing part—" Tatt paused for dramatic effect, a tactic lost on Erien who was feeling more disgruntled word by word "—the *Luminaries* were backed up by Nersallians!"

"I didn't think there were any Nersallian *Luminaries!*" Erien objected.

"There aren't!" Tatt assured him. "But some Nersallians are pretty close to Nesak orthodoxy and believe Amel is what they call a *zer-pol*, which means a sort of holy sacrifice whose persecution points a finger at the bad guys to be wiped out by the righteous—at least according to Di Mon. I checked the Monatese logs."

Tatt's casual mention of his predecessor caused Erien a pang of undiminished grief despite the long years since Di Mon's death. Unlike Tatt, he could take no comfort in communing with his mentor through the notes Di Mon kept during his term in office, nor by appealing to his soul among the Watching Dead.

"The religious groups broke the ice by making it possible to view Amel's bad behavior in an elevated light," Tatt continued to explain Amel's women problems. "Apparently a saint can't be a traitor or a slut; he's sending complex messages to the faithful, instead. And as soon as the charge of traitor vaporized in the glare of possible divinity, three sets of females woke up to the realization there was a very breedable male up for grabs."

Tatt's very Vrellish way of putting the situation sat uneasily with Erien, because his own status as a Pureblood paralleled Amel's. "I suppose you had better tell me more about these women," he admitted.

"Vretla Vrel to start," Tatt obliged him. "Amel is still the only male who has ever managed to get her pregnant, back when he was working as a courtesan, and Vretla wants a child to raise at court as heir to Red Hearth. She expects to be his First Sworn, which would make sense since she's the best sword in the Avim's Oath, as it existed under Ev'rel."

"Go on," Erien told Tatt, trying to sound bored instead of irritated.

"The Goldens have designs on Amel, as well, but even Ameron is getting headaches making sense of them. Think factions. And marriage."

"That's two," said Erien tersely.

"Number three is the Dem'Vrel," Tatt concluded. "With Ev'rel gone, they are breaking up into the rival houses of Therd and Lekker. So it's factions again, but with the Dem'Vrel it's a toss up whether co-opting Amel would mean Vrellish style child-gifting or Demish marriage. I'd bet on child-gifting, myself, because they need highborns in the Knotted Strings as badly as Monitum did before me." Tatt grinned with unabashed pride at his role in restocking his ancestral house with highborns. "I may not have sired as many children as Horth Nersal, yet, but I'm working on it!"

And you don't know most of them, Erien thought unhappily. Erien never wanted to be forced to fight one of his own children, as Horth was when challenged, nor feel responsible for the reckless or malicious acts of any child of his raised without the benefit of his guidance.

"Last but not least," Tatt moved on, "I have a bone to pick with you about the way things went down before you left court for Rire." Tatt paused, an ominous and unnatural act of will in so volatile a personality. "You...didn't...tell...me...anything," Tatt ground out in a tone bordering, for him, on grim.

"There was hardly a chance!" protested Erien. "You were too ill, and everything happened too fast."

Tatt produced a frown remarkably reminiscent of Ameron, the parent they shared. "So tell me now."

"Some of it isn't mine to tell," said Erien.

"Meaning it is Amel's to tell?" Tatt caught on in a flash, looking as pleased as a detective with a clue in hand. "Brilliant move, by the way, swearing Amel."

"It was necessary on Rire—to empower me to act for him politically," Erien explained, feeling wrong-footed.

"Whatever," Tatt said with a shrug, and grinned again. "It very cleverly removed him as a rival for the title of Avim."

"But Amel is Ameron's man much more than he is mine," Erien said. "Even though—"

"Father was prepared to write him off on Rire?" Ditatt finished for him. "That's the odd thing about Amel. The worse you treat him, the harder he sticks. As though he's out to prove his grip."

"I am not interested in treating him badly," Erien said, a little tensely. Ditatt had no idea what unpleasant memories his light-hearted comments evoked.

"I heard the news about Ann of Rire!" interjected Tatt. "A Pureblood Sevolite child-gifting to a Reetion—was that your idea?"

"No!" Erien denied vehemently.

"Father was less than thrilled," said Tatt. "He thought it might have been your idea, given how you feel about the Reetions."

Wonderful, thought Erien. *So now I'm to be blamed for Amel's sexual indiscretions.* "Believe me," Erien said dryly, "Ann is the last Reetion I would have selected for the 'honor' if I'd had a choice."

Tatt gave him a sudden grin. "And how about yourself, Erien? What's your position on child-gifting these days? The promise you made Di Mon is obsolete. You know who you are, now." Tatt gave him a playful punch. "Have some fun. Loosen up. Build yourself a power base. I bet you could get Vretla's oath, easy, if you can get her pregnant before Amel does. She doesn't really care who does the job so long as he can make her a mother. If you're up to it, of course!" He shoulder-checked Erien, making him lurch. "Stop looking so offended!" exclaimed Tatt. "Anyone would think you were still a virgin."

"Tatt," Erien said stiffly, "I am not child-gifting."

Tatt stared at him. "It's not natural for a man to have no children! People start wondering if you are capable of it! And then, maybe, they'll start wondering about other things." Tatt's face colored with embarrassment. "You've been on Rire, you know, and everyone knows that Reetions uh..."

How have we got into this! Erien thought. "Reetions, unlike Gelacks, accept same-sex relationships. It doesn't mean all Reetions are homosexual. And I'm not ruling out having children. I'm ruling out child-gifting. I want to have children in a relationship."

"You mean with a *mekan'st*, right?" Tatt said, sounding worried.

"I don't know," Erien said in frustration. "There are no models for the relationship I want to have, except maybe on Rire. And anyway, Tatt, I'm only seventeen years old!"

Tatt gave him an odd look that made Erien remember Tatt's first child had been born when he was barely fifteen. The Gelacks didn't care that physiological maturity was no measure of emotional readiness.

"Erien," Tatt said, unexpectedly gently, "you're on Gelion now."

"I know," Erien sighed. "And there are things I want to do here. But not become a father. Not yet."

"It might cost you the Avim's Oath," Tatt warned.

"I'm not after titles unless I need one to establish the academy," said Erien.

Tatt perked up. "Academy?" he said, eyes sparkling with excitement, apprehension, or both. "So you're going to get that started, then?"

"Yes," said Erien, "I—"

"Hold on," said Tatt, noticing something taking place on the street as they drove past. He snatched his sword up from the brace where he'd secured it. "Back up!" he ordered their driver. "And stop."

Tatt was out before the car came to a complete halt. Erien hurried to follow his impetuous half-brother.

The ruckus Tatt had noticed was caused by a child and a woman being hassled by a small gang of Silver Demish men who had not yet gone as far as drawing swords. The men's braid identified them as Highlords from some side branch of Luthan's house. They looked like young troublemakers on the prowl.

Recognizing Tatt's braid and liege marks, one of the men slapped another on the shoulder to get his attention and in seconds the whole group of them had turned to confront the new arrivals.

"These two have no business on the highborn docks!" the Demish spokesman greeted Tatt, and pointed at the woman. "She is only nobleborn."

"I'm the highborn!" the child exclaimed, pulling out of the woman's grasp, his handsome face flushed with excitement. "Take back what you said about my father!" he cried in fury at the biggest of the Demish Highlords.

"I merely repeated a rumor I heard on the Plaza," the Demish man said lazily, with a smile for Tatt. "I am sure you know the one I mean, about D'Lekker Dem'Vrel's overly keen interest in collecting pornography featuring Prince Amel."

"I am D'Lekker now," the boy declared in strident tones, barging forward so violently that Tatt gave way rather than confront the seven-year-old. The boy was beside himself, bright tears of anger in his dark eyes. "And I will avenge your slur against my father's honor!"

The woman with the excitable boy took a firm grip on the child's shoulders from behind.

"We do not want any trouble," she insisted, addressing herself to Tatt. "These men accosted me over my birth rank because I appeared to be without highborn company on the highborn docks. Naturally, Leksan came forward in my defense." She indicated her charge with a nod.

Leksan! Erien thought. He was looking at the elder of the late D'Lekker's two small sons: the children he and Amel had risked their lives to protect from a truth even viler than the rumors the Demish men were playing up, because if Gelion learned what D'Lekker had really done, his descendants would be murdered out of a misguided sense of genetic determinism.

Erien's throat locked. He couldn't help identifying with the orphaned child. He, too, had lost a father at about the same age. A foster father, in his case, but one he could not have loved or honored more if he had been Di Mon's natural son.

"And you are?" Tatt asked the woman, whose grammar—in Gelack—pegged her as a Midlord.

"I am Sen Lekker," she replied. "Leksan's regent and aunt. We came here with a Golden Demish escort, but they stopped to commune with the Watching Dead at the Luminary Reverie of the Messenger. We grew impatient and decided to go on, alone, to Lilac Hearth where we knew we would be welcomed by Amel, himself." She paused for emphasis. "I am an old friend of His Immortality, Prince Amel."

"It's him!" Leksan cried suddenly, spotting Erien hanging back, behind Tatt. "The murderer!"

Sen Lekker snatched at her excited nephew and missed. It was Tatt who blocked the boy's charge, deflecting the child's hastily drawn sword. He followed up with a disarming move and swept up the kicking, raving seven-year-old.

"Killer! Killer! Killer!" Leksan shouted, pounding Tatt's arms.

The words struck Erien like knives. *Some people need killing,* Horth Nersal had dismissed Erien's remorse over D'Lekker's death, but Erien could take no comfort in the idea. From a Reetion point of view, the late D'Lekker had been a passionate, troubled man in need of treatment.

Tatt surrendered Leksan into the care of his nobleborn aunt.

"Thank you, Liege Monitum," Sen Lekker said, kneeling beside Leksan with her arms securely wrapped around him. Her eyes met Erien's.

"I have heard, Immortality," she said to Erien in measured tones, "that Prince Amel has given you his oath."

"No!" Leksan cried from her arms. "Amel wouldn't!"

"It was necessary on Rire," Erien said quickly. "It remains to be seen how the oaths will fall out at the Swearing Ameron has called to settle the Avim's Oath."

"Would you like an escort to Lilac Hearth?" Tatt asked, with his usual generosity of spirit.

"No, thank you, Liege Monitum," Sen Lekker told him coolly, as Leksan continued to glare hotly at Erien. "We'll return to our Golden Demish escorts and pass through Golden Gate with them."

"As you wish," Tatt said breezily, and fixed a hostile glare on the pack of Demish Highlords who hesitated only long enough to oblige Tatt to reach for the hilt of his sword. Erien had a bad moment in which he cursed himself for not bringing his own weapon, but no swordplay proved necessary. At a gesture from their leader, the Demish group paid respect to Tatt's reputation on the challenge floor by heading in the opposite direction from Sen Lekker.

"Maybe you should tell me what actually happen in Lilac Hearth to make you kill the late D'Lekker," Tatt said, watching them go.

"No," Erien said with finality.

"Being secretive is a Lorel failing, you know," Tatt admonished him, grumpily.

They got back in the car and continued in silence to Green Gate, where they surrendered the car. Tatt took his leave with a parting clap on Erien's shoulder, saying, "I presume you know the way to the Blackwood Room." He put out his hand for Erien's duffel bag. "But give me that, because the idea of you showing up to see our illustrious father looking like a junior Nersallian officer on shore leave just bothers me. And put your sword on!"

Erien handed over the bag with an odd feeling of reluctance. "Thanks," he said. He strapped on his sword, as well, after waiting for Tatt to detach it from the back of the duffel bag where he had tied it securely.

"I'll be at the Justice Ministry if you need me," Tatt said, and headed off at a brisk walk. Erien let him get a good head start before following him through Green Gate, planning to use the time alone to gather his thoughts. But the walk across the promenade beyond and into the Palace Sector proved too short. He arrived at the Ava's anteroom feeling unprepared.

"The Ava is expecting you, Heir Gelion," a herald said, and showed him into the Blackwood Room, past a waiting mob of envious petitioners.

Ameron was pacing before of the famous mahogany desk the room was named for. He stopped abruptly at the sight of his recently acknowledged son and heir.

"Erien!" Ameron crossed the space between them in a few swift strides, put a hand on Erien's shoulder, felt the absence of a spontaneous response and took his hand away. "Sit!" he said.

Erien considered apologizing for his standoffish character. He realized Gelacks in general, and Ameron in particular, were more physical in their interpersonal relationships than Reetions typically were. Or maybe it was just him. He preferred to maintain his personal space.

"Congratulations, on the whole, for your handling of the Reetions," Ameron got straight to business. "It almost makes me grasp Di Mon's wisdom in fostering you on Rire with his scholarly friend, Ranar."

They were lovers, Erien thought resentfully. *Not friends*. Of course the last thing Di Mon would have wanted was for Ameron, of all people, to know what Ranar had really meant to him. But it irked Erien that the truth of Di Mon's wholesome relationship with Ranar still had the power to wound his living relatives, just as the late D'Lekker's decidedly unwholesome obsession with Amel could have damned Leksan and his little brother.

"Of course, there are things I take exception to," continued Ameron, "starting with you interference in the Dragon-Lion Accord. Do you have designs on Princess Luthan yourself, maybe?"

"What?" said Erien. He had been braced for a very different lecture—about letting Amel child-gift to Ann.

"Dorn, lad!" said Ameron. "Dorn Nersal! He was slated to wed Luthan to give her uncle heirs who share Horth Nersal's blood." He scowled. "H'Us is as taken with Nersal as a giddy tournament fan, although he's loathe to say it in so many words except to go on, at receptions, about how the Nersallians and H'Usians share Demish roots." Ameron rolled his eyes, then fixed them upon Erien with the intensity of lasers. "Do you mean to exploit the girl's interest in you to forge a H'Usian alliance for yourself? It is not a bad idea," Ameron admitted. "But I hope you understand—by now—that males rule Demish houses even when a princess-liege is nominally in charge, and H'Us will be an obstacle."

It took all Erien's self-control to choke his outrage at Ameron's casual presumptions about Luthan's helplessness to make her own choices.

"Princess Luthan Dem H'Us has no 'interest' in me," Erien insisted with cold intensity.

Ameron realized he had made a misstep and stopped, re-assessing Erien with an aloof, calculating air. "I see," he said, at last. "My mistake. I understood otherwise, from Tatt."

Erien gave no answer and Ameron circled behind the Blackwood desk to sit down, the energetic and outgoing manner in which he had greeted Erien moments earlier displaced by an unnatural calm. Ameron was thinking. Hard. And Erien didn't like it.

"There are a few things I need to explain to you," Erien said as blandly as he could. "First, although I need to be here to do what I believe Di Mon and Ranar have uniquely prepared me for—"

"You feel you have a mission?" interrupted Ameron. "Imposed upon you by your upbringing."

"If you like," said Erien, more crisply than he had intended.

Ameron nodded, leaned back and steepled his long fingers in a mannerism painfully reminiscent of Di Mon. *Although,* Erien was forced to admit, *Di Mon was more likely to have adopted the habit because he had read about it in the Ameron biography.* Ameron had always been Di Mon's idol.

"Go on," said the dangerously still and watchful Ava.

"I cannot behave in a typical manner for a Sevolite highborn," Erien explained. "I do not believe in *Okal Rel*, as a religion, and I hate the waste and injustice intrinsic to Sword Law. I do not care about lands and titles beyond the need to have a base to work from. But I will do what you require of me in order to achieve my goal."

"Which is?" asked Ameron, in the mildest of tones.

"I want to create an academy. A sort of university for Sevolites, to teach them about science and redress the prejudice against medicine, in particular."

"Very Lorel of you," said Ameron.

"Your own father, Avatlan Lor'Vrel, believed it should be done," insisted Erien.

Ameron nodded. "My father was a leader among those altruistic but opinionated Lorels who wanted to help the ignorant and suffering masses. They built and operated medical clinics in the UnderDocks." He paused. "Some of those my father trained betrayed the cause for personal gain, and other forces resented his encroachment on their prerogatives. During the Fifth Civil War, my father's philanthropic hospital was burned out and gutted along with the dishonorable Lorel establishments. People cannot tell the difference once their fears are aroused. Or perhaps his enemies among the elite of more than one house were to blame. 'People will behave criminally in defense of wealth.' I believe that is how your foster father, Ranar, puts it, which is a sentiment worthy of a Lorel. In fact, I am coming to appreciate his anthropology as a science not entirely foreign to what I view as the art of ruling the Gelack Empire." Ameron leaned forward, resting one long arm on his desk. "I can't afford a Sixth Civil War, Erien."

For a long moment, Erien held his father's stare, wondering if it was possible to glimpse a canny idealist behind the master politician. Something in the way Ameron spoke of past and present in the same sentence made him wonder if Avatlan's agenda still lived in both of them. The next moment he felt as if Ameron was debating his father when he refuted Erien's ideas, and his dream of an academy to educate Sevolites was part of a struggle he had lived and lost before, in another life.

It is no wonder even intelligent people like Horth are able to believe in reincarnation, thought Erien, before dismissing the uncanny feeling with a dose of cool reason. Such feelings might stem from the artificial nature of Sevolite DNA which made them 'breed true' with respect to certain personality traits, as Di Mon had once explained it to him.

"I will be very careful," Erien assured the Ava.

Ameron sat back with a huffing sound. "It is yet to be determined whether you have earned the right to try, at all. We will talk about it further. First, before Amel arrives, I wish to discuss how we should handle him. His current situation is—"

"Wait!" Erien interrupted, not wanting to hear details he wouldn't be entitled to once he'd relieved himself of what he had to say next. "I have given it a lot of thought, and given my priorities I think it best I relinquish Amel's oath in your favor. I will swear to you, and let the vassals of the Avim's Oath swear as they wish under the new arrangement."

Ameron blinked. "You would give up being Avim?"

"Amel does not share my goals," said Erien. "And, in all honestly, I am loath to get between him and the women who believe he would make a good puppet liege."

"One of you must become Avim," Ameron said in a severe voice. "If you don't, someone else will covet it. A Demoran champion, perhaps, on behalf of the Golden Emperor, or some unsuspected Pureblood dredged up in the wilds of Red Reach. For that matter, there are plenty of Silver Demish who are over 90% Sevolite. Only their own conservative nature prevents them seeing the shortage of Purebloods as a huge advantage to them. As to Amel's women problems, I can help you decide which camp to favor." Ameron halted, seeing Erien begin to bristle. "What is the problem?" he asked in surprise.

"I do not want Amel sworn to me," Erien said, as hotly as he had ever spoken to his formidable sire. "I have saved him twice. I've paid the debt I owe him. And I have business of my own to get on with."

"Then you had better swear to him," said Ameron, in a bantering way that convinced Erien it was nothing but gamesmanship. No doubt Ameron thought the idea of swearing to Amel would rankle on Erien, and it did.

"That would hamper me even more," Erien said stiffly.

"Do you expect Horth Nersal to give you his oath?" Ameron demanded. "Because he won't. I've spoken with him. Not an easy task, but—"

A ripple of cloth from the *gorarelpul* entrance at the back of the room caught Ameron's attention. The supposedly cerebral Ava was up in an instant, a sword draw from a hiding place behind the Blackwood Desk. Erien was up as well, although he had not felt threatened by the movement of the curtain which he presumed to be nothing more than one of Ameron's *gorarelpul* listening in. He had already decided, at an instinctive level, to defend Ameron if the Ava was attacked.

The curtain stopped moving and hung straight again.

"Who is there?" Ameron's booming voice demanded.

CHAPTER 2

In a Man's World

Princess Samanda O'Pearl opened her eyes and blinked up at the face of the transport pilot leaning over her.

"We have arrived, Your Highness," the nobleborn pilot said with an amused smile.

"Oh," said Sam, then cleared her throat and made an effort to drop her voice to match her man's clothing, stolen from her brother's wardrobe at home on another, gentler world. "On Gelion?"

The pilot straightened up. "I certainly hope so, Your Highness. Gelion was the planet I was aiming for. I could go check, to reassure you, although seeing as the other passengers have disembarked and not returned to berate me for setting them down on Monitum or Tark, I feel fairly safe confirming—yes, it's Gelion."

I ought to box his ears for such insolence, Sam thought. A real man probably would. All she said was, "Er, no. Thank you."

The pilot executed a deep bow, irreproachably respectful but still somehow mocking.

Sam struggled out of her seat, avoiding further eye contact.

She was the last of the six passengers to leave the transport and even the servants waiting with her luggage looked impatient.

Sam's suitcase sat on the clean, smooth floor beside her, looking orphaned. For a moment, she did not have the heart to claim it. She looked around instead, at the brightly lit floor of the Silver Demish shuttle port. It's interior was large enough to accommodate twenty passenger transports the size of the one she'd arrived in and the ground floor was filled with a purposeful bustle of life. The second storey, above, was lined with shops.

"Your sword, Your Highness," the elderly servant belonging to the shuttle port prompted her.

"Thank you," Sam got out, gruffly. She took the sword and tried to keep her hands steady as she fixed it in place on her left side, wondering what she was going to do if she was ever called upon to use it because, as adventurous as she had always considered herself for a woman of her rank and position, she had never studied fencing.

She was staring about her, trying to decide which way to head, when a scrawny boy of nine or ten darted from cover to snatch up her suitcase and plant himself in front of her.

"Carry your bag for you, Highness!" the boy cried in a bold voice, looking her in the face with bright, challenging eyes. He looked as if he hadn't washed in days, and his clothes were rumpled.

"Off with you!" exclaimed the elderly servant indignantly, down-speaking his fellow commoner by two birth ranks to convey his contempt. "My apologies, Your Highness," he addressed Sam, correctly, as a Royalblood. "I'll have someone suitable here in a moment if you need a porter."

"I'm suitable!" the boy insisted. "Born and raised a porter, right here in Bell Port."

"Nonsense!" exclaimed the old man. "I know you. Your mother was a cook at Chimes before she died and left you to run wild!" He stabbed a finger toward an ornate storefront on the second floor, where the silvery letters of the word "Chimes" stood out from a wall embedded with half-sunken wind chimes. The motif struck Sam as misplaced, since there was no wind at all in the subterranean city of UnderGelion. The chimes locked into the plaster of the wall seemed like prisoners.

"Having trouble here, Sylvester?" a third voice interrupted with authority.

"This beggar boy is hassling passengers for work," explained the old servant.

The security guard made a grab for the ragged boy, who dodged in Sam's direction to elude him. She shied away, bumping into someone behind her, and her sword detached from her belt where she had failed to attach it properly. It tangled up her feet. She tripped and the boy fell on top of her, one hand landing squarely on her chest. She felt her breast compress beneath her brother's jacket, which she'd padded about the waist and shoulders, and had to repress the instinctive urge to slap the miscreant touching her. The boy's eyes went wide. Then he grinned as he was hauled up.

"We are so terribly sorry, Your Highness," the presiding servant, Sylvester, apologized as Sam scrambled to her feet.

"A beating will teach you some manners," the guard declared, holding the boy by the scruff of his rumpled uniform, which Sam noticed was decorated in chimes like those in the wall outside the restaurant. "And don't worry, Sylvester, I'll dump him on the far side of the Palace Plain when I'm finished. He won't be finding his way back this time."

"But His Highness has already engaged me to work for him!" the boy exclaimed with feverish excitement, hurling masculine pronouns at Sam like lances in an effort to convey a deeper meaning. "*He* knows we already have an understanding! And I can be trusted! If I'm working for *him*!"

Sam opened her mouth and closed it again, dumbfounded.

"Make it a *rel* beating!" advised Sylvester harshly as the guard jerked the boy around and started marching him away.

"I'll tell!" the boy screeched over his shoulder in pronouns cast for addressing a Royalblood.

Sam came to herself with a start. "Wait!" she raised a hand, took a step forward with her heart in her throat, and bumped her foot on her brother's sword. "The boy's right," she said, and interrupted herself to stoop for the sword. She rose again clutching it about the middle in its scabbard, realized the hilt end was pointing down, and tipped it up before it had slithered out more than a centimeter. "He works for me!"

Sylvester looked nonplussed. "Indeed?" he asked, dubiously.

The boy jerked free from the baffled guard to plant himself by Sam's side, firmly in possession of the suitcase once more. "This way, Your Highness," he told her, and set off with her suitcase towards the main entrance.

With a nervous smile at Sylvester and the guard, Sam clutched her sword and hurried after him.

"Put the sword back on your belt," the boy said out of the side of his mouth when she caught up to him.

"Oh, right." She paused to clip it on, and got it right this time. She had decided since her brother almost never drew a sword in any situation outside of fencing classes, she had cause to hope she would not need to, either. It made her hand steadier when handling the weapon.

The boy led her out through wide, transparent doors flanked by shining steel girders and white marble pillars. A row of small carriages drawn by healthy men in crisp white uniforms waited outside. The boy picked a carriage, nodded to one of the pullers, and helped her into the seat, sword and all, before tossing in her suitcase and climbing in beside her.

"I'm Jack," the boy introduced himself, grinning with relief at his success in attaching himself to her. "Who are you, really?"

Sam drew herself up. "I am Prince Samdan O'Pearl, knight errant in the service of the Princess Liege of H'Us."

Jack directed a pointed look at where her breasts lay concealed beneath her padded uniform.

"All right!" she snapped, searched for her gloves, found them in a pocket and flourished them at him. "Samdan is my twin brother who has run off and shirked his responsibilities. My real name is Princess Samanda. I go by Sam. We called him Dan." She stopped, screwed her eyes up and covered her face with a hand, slapping herself with the gloves, which she promptly dropped into her lap. "Oh, why am I telling you these things!" she moaned.

"Because I'll help you pull it off, Your Highness!" Jack enthused. "You'll be grateful you took me on. You'll see—I'm resourceful."

Sam gave him a critical appraisal. "You're dirty!"

"I clean up good," he assured her.

Baffled, Sam looked away out the window of their human-drawn carriage at the people in the bustling square surrounding them. A commotion was underway in the mouth of an alley between buildings.

"I don't know, Jack," she said, her attention distracted by the sight of five people in odd, close-fitting clothing, who were fanning out in a search pattern. "I don't think I can be responsible for the welfare of any commoner at the moment. Especially not a child! But Princess Luthan runs an *Okal Lumens* home for foundlings on the Palace Plain. I could drop you off there."

She watched one of the searchers stop a man and toss back the hood of his traveling cloak to get a look at his face, which was terribly rude! The man reached for his sword, then stopped and took a step back with an alarmed expression.

"But it's me who will be looking after you, Your Highness!" Jack assured her.

Sam lurched back from the window of the carriage, closing the curtain. "Vrellish!" she exclaimed in shock, blinked at Jack and leaned forward again to peek ever so carefully at the searchers. She had never seen Vrellish people before, except in dramas. They were lean, dark haired and sudden in their movements. She was pretty sure half of them were women, although they dressed and acted just like their male companions: pushing and bullying the people they stopped to question. They were all dressed in bright colored slacks with decorated vests on top and no shirt beneath them. Their bare arms were hard-muscled.

"Tell the pullers to avoid those people," Sam ordered, feeling nervous.

Jack leaned over her to get a look out the window, making her frown at further proof of his unsuitability to be her servant. Properly trained domestics would never be so familiar. "Spiral Hall Vrellish!" he confirmed, and whistled. "What are they doing in a Demish district?"

Sam gave him a shove to get off her.

"Sorry, Your Highness!" he sang out, trying to bow inside the little covered carriage. He banged his head, of course, but only grinned at her and tried again with less vigor.

"Never mind!" Sam exclaimed in frustration. She pulled herself up to open the hatch above, and delivered her own instructions to steer clear of the alarming disturbance.

She was just getting seated again when the door on Jack's side of the carriage opened. A sleek shape hopped in and crouched beside Jack.

"It's all right," the intruder said, smiling reassurance at them as the carriage adjusted to his weight and Sam's shift in position as she sat down again.

Jack was staring at their hitchhiker with his mouth open.

Sam couldn't inhale properly. Her lips formed the name 'Amel,' but no breath animated it.

He was dressed in white flight leathers worn under a short black cloak with a hood that hung down his back.

"No harm will come to you for helping me, I promise," he told Jack, speaking in simple *rel*-to-*pol* address. "I'll deal with the Vrellish if I have to. I'd just rather...put it off until I know what my new liege expects of me."

He looked from Jack to Sam and smiled. The impact was devastating. She also became aware of a mild scent of warm vanilla mixed with leather. Vanilla was a scent used by some Silver Demish princesses in honor of the Golden Demish Family of Light, who were said to be naturally fragrant. The evidence was overwhelming. She was sitting in the very same carriage as the Pureblood Prince Amel.

Back home, on Clara's World, Sam had spent hours looking at pictures of Amel during secret meetings at the *Okal Lumens* abbey with her brother Samdan and the prince she had planned to marry. They had pondered the weighty question of what Amel's early experiences as a commoner were meant to convey to those who believed in him as a sacred messenger. Those heady days had also been the start of her life's greatest adventure. But the adventure ended badly, for reasons unconnected with Amel, and by the time she had decided to take her brother's place and go to Gelion to escape her troubles, she had forgotten Amel existed as an actual flesh-and-blood person.

"You look...fluid," Sam heard herself say, in a small voice. She got the pronouns right, up-speaking him with the proper differencing and inflections for an adherent of Amel's order addressing her spiritual leader.

Amel's pale brow constricted, putting a wave in his jet black eyebrows. "Pardon?" he said.

Mad Gods! she thought. *He said something to me!*

She coughed, and covered her mouth with her gloves, trying to mask her blush.

"S-sorry," she said, "I only ever knew you as a picture. I never imagined how you might move, and breath, and everything." His expression told her she was talking nonsense. "Are the Vrellish people looking for you?" she asked him.

"Yes," he said simply. "I slipped back in the old envoy way, instead of announcing my arrival like I'm supposed to these days. But Vretla knows my habits and was waiting for me." His gray eyes laughed. "And I got the feeling her idea of negotiations might get a little rough if I let her catch me alone, if you know what I mean, Prince...?"

"Samdan," Sam got out, brain stalled trying to decode Amel's remark about the notorious Vretla, liege of Vrel. She had the strong impression it was one of those unspoken things men expected each other to 'get' without the kind of explanation she required. "I am Samdan O'Pearl," she went on to introduce herself properly, "knight errant to Luthan Dem H'Us. That is, I will be. I'm new to court."

"Really?" he asked, with mock surprise and a warm trickle of amusement.

A dreadful idea struck Sam. "You don't mean real negotiations!"

Amel's eyebrows shot up.

"You mean a fight!" said Sam, in horror.

Amel's expression relaxed again.

"You can't seriously be considering a duel with the liege of Vrel!" Sam admonished him. "Because you are worth far too much to the universe alive, without any need to prove yourself by conventional, life-threatening—"

She broke off because Amel was getting a funny, uncomfortable look on his face.

"Prince Samdan is a follower of *Okal Lumens*," Jack said quickly, making Sam look at him in bewilderment.

"Oh," Amel said, somewhat mollified, but still vaguely suspicious about something. "You had better get your servant some better clothes before you take him into Silver Hearth," Amel remarked to Sam without making eye contact. "There are plenty of stores in the last few blocks before Silver Gate."

He produced a small handful of honor chips and pressed them into Jack's hand. "For the ride. *Ack rel*, Prince Samdan."

"*Ack rel*," Sam said, hurriedly, feeling an eerie prickle up her spine at this tacit promise to abide by Sword Law when she couldn't even use the wretched weapon!

Amel dropped out of the carriage so lightly it barely shifted.

Jack looked up from the mixture of pale purple and white chips in his hand and said, "Wow!"

"Did I say something to offend Prince Amel?" Sam worried aloud.

Jack chuckled. "I hate to conjecture about something so delicate in the hearing of a princess."

Sam narrowed her eyes at him. "If you are going to work for me, Jack, you are going to learn to tell me anything I need to understand about being a man!"

Jack pocketed the money, looked at her, wiped the grin off his face and said, "He thought you were sweet on him. You know, being all gushy about him maybe getting killed in a duel."

"Well of course I was!" she said, astonished. "Any Luminary who believes in him as The Messenger would—"

"Yeah, but the thing is ..." Jack said, with a grimace that wrinkled his freckled nose, "he thinks you are another guy."

Sam gave Jack as severe a look as she knew how. "Oh, and I suppose you think, like half the stupid universe, that only silly, infatuated women believe in Amel as a Soul of Light sent to bring a message to Sevildom! Well, let me tell you there are also men who think he has been sent to lead us! Plenty of them!"

Jack opened his mouth to reply, turned a little pink in the cheeks and started over. "Never mind," he said. "Let's go make me respectable! Then it's Silver Hearth and good food every day until I die!"

Sam sat back in her upholstered seat. "You are going to take a lot of educating, young man," she said severely, and held out her hand. "Give me the money."

Jack handed it over reluctantly. "We are going to get clothes for me, right?"

"Yes, but we won't need all of this," she told him, studying the colored chips. "And it is time you learned to think about the plight of your fellow, wretched commoners."

"What? All of them!" Jack asked her, wide-eyed.

CHAPTER 3

Acts of Charity

This could be the last time I get away with arriving incognito, Amel thought, standing cloaked and hooded in the midst of the foot traffic on Gate Street at the west end of the highborn docks, looking at Lilac Gate in front of him.

The façade was carved in lilacs of the kind found on FarHome, with the crest of Dem'Vrel overhead: a dart-shaped envoy ship against a stylized sun.

Perry would like it better decorated with a rose and sword, Amel thought. *With Blue Demish story icons on either side.*

He thought about his friends among the Dem'Vrel, as well. His half-brother's hardy daughter, Zind Therd, and the capable nobleborn Sen Lekker, who ruled her clan from behind the geneprint of a child. Half of Amel's adventures in the Knotted Strings during Ev'rel's reign had involved helping Sen save a hapless Lekker from a domineering Therd.

Sen will be bringing Leksan to court, to introduce him as the new D'Lekker now that his father is dead, thought Amel. *And Zind Therd is bound to be coming to the Swearing as well, even though her sister, on Demora, is the titular D'Therd.* Both facts were at least as ripe with conflicts as the meeting he'd evaded with Vretla Vrel, and Amel decided he could use a break before dealing with his mother's vassals in an official capacity.

He was strolling back along his route, looking for a suitable café where he could relax for half an hour, when he heard the sounds of a struggle emanating from an alley between two shops. Amel paused to listen. Two other men in Demish costume passed by with a glance and kept going.

Wisest thing to do, Amel agreed. It was too dark in the alley to make out much from the well-lighted street, and he might have convinced himself to move on if the boy named Jack had not come pelting out of the darkness waving his arms.

"Help!" cried Jack, one sleeve of his brand new clothing torn. "My master's being mugged!"

Amel intercepted the boy and held him firmly by one arm. "Where?" he ordered, loosening the ties of his cloak with his other hand.

"There!" the boy gasped, and pointed with his whole arm.

Amel looked around him for people to enlist but there was no one close at hand. Sevolites who spontaneously gathered to witness fights among themselves were just as good at disappearing at the suggestion of hazard involving only commoners.

I shouldn't be doing this! Amel thought. But he drew his sword and followed Jack into the gloom. Jack had already crashed through the decorative barrier screening the alley from the street. Two body lengths behind this lay a winding path through a shantytown of stacked crates and ragged curtains occupied by houseless commoners. Just what Jack's master had been doing in such a place was beyond Amel, but it was pretty clear Prince Samdan was being roughed up by residents alarmed at being discovered.

Amel reached a clearing built around a battery-powered stove. Three ragged shapes had a man down and were pelting him with frantic kicks as their victim tried to hold them off with an improvised shield.

"Stop!" Amel shouted. He seized the nearest squatter by the scruff of his neck and tossed him aside, onto his bottom, to make his point. "Let the prince up," he demanded in an angry tone.

All three assailants went still as death once Amel's presence registered: one sitting where he'd been thrown and the other two crouched over Prince Samdan, who lay flat on his back beneath his makeshift shield of cheap construction board made with dust from the surface of Gelion. One of the squatters held a bludgeon in his raised hand.

Amel, who didn't count himself a fighter, was pleased with the impression he'd made by showing up armed with a sword. He just hoped he didn't have to use it on the squatters, because he felt nothing but pity for them.

"My master's all right!" Jack reported.

Samdan stood unsteadily, leaning on the boy. "I just wanted t-to...to help them," he said, sounding shaken.

"They aren't supposed to be here," Amel explained. "And you will not report them," he insisted in a cross tone. "Neither the attack, nor the fact they are squatting here. That's the price of my rescue."

"Y-yes," said the hopelessly incompetent Silver Demish prince from some backward, pastoral world.

"Get him out of here," Amel ordered Jack, feeling irritated.

"Yes, Your Immortality!" the urchin boy rapped back, making the three squatters go still as death again at the use of so lofty a title. Only Purebloods were called Immortality.

The man with the bludgeon slowly lowered it. "Ah...Amel?" he asked shakily, awe dawning on his bewildered face.

Amel didn't like the stares. He backed away, covering Jack and Samdan's retreat while keeping an eye on the squatters. Honor chips had spilled on the ground, probably knocked loose in the struggle.

"Keep it," Amel told the squatters, pointing at it.

The man with the bludgeon took a step toward Amel, raising his hand as if to touch him.

A spasm of aversion countered Amel's compassion as he evaded the pathetic fingers reaching for him. There were too many people like this, rotting away in dark places on Gelion. He wished them all well, but just being back in one of the spaces that contained them frightened him. "Use the money to take care of each other!" he called back, before turning to pick his way out of the dark passage, feeling as if his past pursued him.

Bursting into the brightness of Gate Street, Amel shook off memories of helplessness. A couple of people recognized his face, now he had shed his cloak, and stopped to stare at him. He answered their interest with what he hoped was a thoroughly ungentle glare as he sheathed his sword and scooped up his cloak from the street where he had dropped it earlier.

He caught enough of a glimpse of Jack and Samdan to see they were doing all right, and cleared off before they tried to embroil him any further in their affairs, heading briskly for White Gate because it was nearer than Lilac.

White Gate belonged to house Lor'Vrel and was manned by members of the Ava's Oath, sworn to Ameron. In theory, this comprised five hearths. In practice, it meant the Nersallians, Monatese and Silver Demish, since the houses of Lorel and Lor'Vrel were all but extinct.

Nersallians always rubbed Amel the wrong way, so he was pleased to find none of them on duty. He was passed through by a bored Silver Demish prince with a couple of nobleborn Monatese technicians working under him, all of whom were used to dealing with him during his years as royal envoy.

"So," the Demish prince concluded when Amel had submitted himself to standard security scans without incident, "we hear you're going to become divine, officially. A genuine Soul of Light."

Amel gave a startled laugh. "What?"

The prince smiled with the knowing air of someone eager to demonstrate he was better informed than a social superior. "There are two factions of Demorans at court: one set on recruiting you, and one on wooing our own Princess Luthan as their next liege. Word is they want you and Luthan to take part in a contest, on Demora, to decide which one of you is divine. And then both sides will endorse the winner."

"Divine?" Amel exclaimed. "Since when has that been necessary?"

The man shrugged. "There's no making sense of Goldens, if you ask me. Maybe it's dawned on them their emperor needs an heir, and you're his only living descendant. But it could be worse. At least you're going up against our Luthan over who's the kinder soul, and not taking on a paladin in the arena."

The Demish man considered it a good joke, but Amel scowled.

So I'm not much of a duelist, he thought with ill humor. *How many Challenge Floor champions can sword dance half decently?*

He crossed the promenade in enough of a brown funk to ignore everyone who stared at him, by which time he had relegated the guard's remarks to nothing more or less than the usual gossip connecting him with one religious sect or another, from Luminary fringe groups to Nesaks who believed he was supposed to be a holy sacrifice known as a *zer-pol*.

Certainly there could be no question of competing with Luthan for anything! They always cooperated. Like the way she solved his problem concerning the destitute waifs he collected in his travels by co-founding the Silver and Gold Orphanage on the Palace Plain.

I'll discuss it with Erien later, he told himself, and forgot about it.

Once inside the Palace Sector, Amel decided to go up the Lorel Stairs because it was the quickest way to get to Ameron and he wanted to get past the reaming out in store for him over Ann's pregnancy. Then, perhaps, he and Erien could steal a few hours to work out a joint approach to the coming Swearing.

The Lorel Stairs were notorious for messing with the navigational sense of good pilots, causing weird mental side effects, but today Amel felt sufficiently preoccupied to be immune.

He started up the stairs at a good clip, thinking about Vretla Vrel, and wondering why he should be so worried about running into her. All she wanted was sex, which was easy enough for an ex-courtesan to deliver, and now Ev'rel was gone he had no particular reason to be stingy about child-gifting. He had always been afraid, before, of the use Ev'rel might make of his children. He had also feared for Vretla herself, if any transactions between them had roused Ev'rel's jealousy. If not for these twin fears, there were plenty of times he would gladly have agreed to Vretla's invitation to take up where they had left off when he was still a courtesan she patronized.

Of course, I can't child-gift to Vretla, Vrellish style, and become a respectably married Demish prince at the same time, Amel realized, unwisely letting his eyes focus on a section of the wall at the very moment the idea of marriage, as a political expectation, pounced on him.

The universe tipped sideways and inverted itself, most unhelpfully. One moment Amel was bounding up firm steps within an enclosed well decorated in eerily beautiful starscapes, and the next he was tumbling down again, at the mercy of an inward scream of warning from his potent navigational instincts.

Chaos and terror resolved into a jumble of hands and voices at the bottom, as people rushed to help him.

"Ohhh," Amel moaned, feeling himself being lifted onto a stretcher. He made an uncoordinated effort to get up and was pressed down.

"It was the st-tairs," he stammered, trying without success to get his eyes to open.

Since the Lorel Stairs and the Flashing Floor guarded two of the most direct approaches to the imperial suite in the Palace Sector, most people thought the original Lorels created them early in the history of the empire as a defense against Vrellish attacks. More pragmatic minds argued they must have been part of UnderGelion's original, mysterious design, since whatever powered them both was encased in a hullsteel protrusion from the Plaza. The bottom line was that whatever they did, it was beyond the ability of Monatese scholars and Nersallian engineers to figure out, short of measures no Ava had ever been prepared to allow for fear of shattering the hullsteel shell of UnderGelion in an effort to get at encased innards.

Someone laid a hand on Amel's shoulder. "We're taking you up the stairs," he said. "It's the fastest way to get you to the *gorarelpul* nest behind the throne room. Keep your eyes closed."

He recognized the voice of Ameron's medical *gorarelpul*, Drasous, and flinched involuntarily at his touch, remembering events on Rire. But getting his eyes open had already proved as hard as if he were certain they would instantly be filled with piercing knives. He worked on calming himself down by summoning to mind entirely nonspatial poetry full of pretty girls and blooming flowers.

By the time they reached the top, which was easy to deduce in a setting he knew as well as this one, his alarm was giving way to hot embarrassment, and he decided to feign unconsciousness a little longer.

"Keep an eye on him," Drasous told the woman helping him. Amel waited until he heard Drasous leave, then allowed his eyelids to flutter.

The woman touched his brow.

He opened his eyes to find himself staring up at a young Nersallian. Her braid declared her a nobleborn of the planet called Tark.

She helped him as he made a shaky effort to sit up, steadying him against her with typical Nersallian strength and confidence.

"Thank you," he said, voice still rough with chagrin at his foolishness. "Usually I can damp out the effects with poetry," he mumbled, "but I got distracted."

"There is no shame in being taken by the Lorel Stairs," the Nersallian told him.

"Take me to see Ameron," he told her.

"Yes, of course," she agreed at once, and helped him to his feet, continuing to offer her support.

"I'm interested in the Lorel Stairs," the Nersallian said, staying close. "It's astonishing, isn't it? Something so powerful and mysterious right there in our midst for all these centuries and we still don't know how they work or what they're for. My name is Zita, by the way," she added. "I'm going to be an engineer."

"Mmm," Amel said, not feeling conversational. The young Nersallian had the feel of someone bursting with questions, but she managed to keep them to herself as they passed through first a guard room and then the private ready room used by the Ava to brief his *gorarelpul*. Amel was feeling better by the second, and increasingly aware of Zita's sword hilt pressing into his side.

Just as he was disengaging from her, ready to assure her he could stand on his own, his attention was snatched by the sound of voices beyond the heavy curtains screening Ameron's audience chamber from the ready room.

"I do not want Amel sworn to me," Erien's voice was declaring in a decisive tone. "I have saved him twice. I've paid the debt I owe him. And I have business of my own to get on with."

"Then you had better swear to him," said Ameron, like a challenge.

Or a joke, Amel thought. His ears became hot. His skin tingled.

"That would hamper me even more," Erien insisted with typical, stubborn arrogance.

An unfamiliar feeling of rage flared in Amel. *Hamper you, will I?* he thought. The dislocation he'd experienced with Perry happened again. Did he really know Erien? Did they share the bond he thought they'd forged?

I am nothing to him, Amel thought, instead, as his heart sank with shame for his naivety.

"Do you expect Horth Nersal to give you his oath?" Ameron asked. "Because he won't. I've spoken with him. Not an easy task, but—"

Amel lurched clear of Zita, brushing the curtain separating him from the two men discussing him so callously. He drew back again, at once, heart hammering as he heard someone clear a sword beyond the curtain.

"Who is there?" Ameron demanded.

It was Zita who drew back the curtain, taking action like any good Nersallian would. Amel stepped up beside her to see Ameron confronting them, sword in hand. Erien was up, too, but seeing who it was he looked completely unalarmed, which Amel found he resented because—just for once—he wanted to feel to be thought of as at least a bit threatening.

"Amel! Can't you ever come in through the front door!" Ameron exclaimed angrily, as he lowered his sword.

That does it! Amel thought. *This is the last time I'll be taken for granted by anyone!*

"Don't trouble yourselves to make arrangements between you about my oath," Amel told them both, the steel of a new, hot emotion putting strength into the words—even as his body felt hollowed out and robbed of the love for others and the world which was its usual sustenance. "I can make the decision myself. If I decide to swear to either of you!"

Amel whirled, leaving Zita to explain his humiliating tumble on the Lorel Stairs. He fled through the Ava's waiting room and the grand rooms of the palace sector, down Demlara's Walk, and out onto the Plaza, barely aware of the stares he drew and the gossip stirred up in his wake.

All he wanted, very badly, was to go home to Lilac Hearth.

Mira will be there, he told himself. Mira was a real sibling: not by blood, like Erien, but by virtue of spending their first decade together. The bond between them had survived terrible trials of loyalty forced on them first by Mira's controlling father, then by H'Reth and finally by Amel's mother, Ev'rel.

Mira will be an equal in my hearth! Amel thought fiercely. *And her daughter Mona will be raised like the niece of a Fountain Court liege, no matter what anyone thinks about them being commoners! Having them with me will make all of this mean something.*

"Amel!" a rough voice hailed him.

Amel snapped out of his blind grief to register people converging upon him from three directions. The one who had shouted was Zind Therd. She approached from his left, alone. Five of Ameron's royal errants, led by a willow-thin *gorarelpul* named Iarous, were jogging to catch up with him from behind. From his right came a small mob of Golden Demish dressed in the robes of a Luminary sect he didn't recognize. At least he was quite certain he had never seen the device all six wore on the breast of their snowy white robes, depicting a plain looking scroll clasped in a beautiful, opalescent hand. The hand-with-scroll emblem was not even rendered in the usual embroidery, but must have been made out of nervecloth because it looked ever so gently alive.

"Amel!" Zind barked at him again, making him forget the Luminaries. She was dressed in flight leathers, as big and tough looking as her late father, Chad, who had been known at court by his clan title, D'Therd.

Zind was a Knotted Strings power in her own right with a castle fortress in an alpine region of FarHome and the natural leader of clan Therd, who had long acted as his presumed heir. But the late D'Therd had set her aside in the interests of consolidating his dynasty around the daughter born of his prized Demoran marriage. *Which has got to rankle*, Amel realized, with a pang of sympathy for his tough niece from the Knotted Strings.

Zind greeted him with a slap across the cheek with the sweat-stiffened gloves she held gripped in one hand.

"Why weren't you at the docks where we were waiting for you!" she ripped into him, half a head taller than he was and easily heavier. Her mixed heritage had bequeathed her a Demish build with Vrellish muscle. It felt like facing down an angry avalanche. "Don't you know there are people who would like to see you dead, or stuff you in a sack and take you home to use you as a pawn!"

Like you? Amel thought, anger rising in his gray eyes. Every insult Zind's father had ever inflicted on him fueled his sense of affront as he forced his hand down from his hot cheek.

"I need to talk to you about the situation on FarHome," Zind demanded. "Right now!"

Before Amel could decide if he wanted to hit her back or attempt to be reasonable, they were enveloped by an onslaught of Golden Demish in snowy white robes.

"Whoever strikes a Soul of Light strikes us all," declared the leader of the Luminaries. She shoved her hood back to reveal a proud, handsome face with a wide forehead, prominent eyebrows the color of sand and a long, straight nose. Her necklace, worn over the white robe, declared her the abbess of a reverie: a religious retreat devoted to communion with the Waiting Dead. Two men in her entourage shed their white robes to reveal the complex and colorful uniforms of paladins belonging to her hand-and-scroll order. The paladins cleared their swords in unison.

Zind stepped back, alarmed.

The palace errants led by Iarous were still running toward them. Amel could hear their hurried footfalls at his back. The paladins shifted to intervene between him and the palace errants.

Amel was never sure why his skin began to prickle as one of the remaining Demorans moved to his side. All he knew for sure was that he turned in time to see a dagger glint in the man's hand, made a wild attempt to dodge and was knocked down by the intervention of a second man in white robes.

"Abomination!" screamed the assassin.

"No!" cried the man who threw himself in front of Amel.

In the next instant it seemed as if everyone on the Plaza had converged on the failed attempt to kill him.

Zind pulled Amel up off the floor. Iarous and the palace errants claimed the attacker, who begged them to let him finish his sacred task. The paladins tried to extract Amel from Zind, as their leader bumbled into the tangle of people around him, asking in a panic-stricken voice, "Is He all right? Is He all right?" Her choice of pronoun elevated Amel to a Soul of Light, equal in spiritual status to the Golden Emperor.

Amel exerted his Pureblood strength to free himself of Zind's grip and shoved one of the paladins away from her.

"Get Mira!" Amel ordered Zind, fixated on his rescuer who was down and bleeding. "She lives in Lilac Hearth!"

Zind Therd accepted the order and sped away across the Plaza.

Amel plunged through the Luminaries and palace errants, each struggling to protect him in their own fashion, and caught Iarous by the arm. The *gorarelpul* woman was tall, thin and bonded to Ameron. She was busy giving orders to the errants holding the hysterical assailant. Iarous knew Amel, and gave him her attention when he pulled her around.

"Help him!" Amel said, pulling her back with him a few steps to where the man who had taken the dagger for him lay on the Plaza, his white robes soaked crimson surrounding the wound in his abdomen.

Iarous gave Amel a worried look. She was an info tech, not a medic, but Ameron's *gorarelpul* cross-trained.

"Just stabilize him," he told her, "until Mira gets here."

Amel knelt beside his savior as Iarous attempted to apply first aid, and was astonished to recognize the face inside the white hood.

"Ron D'An!" he cried. "The Blue Demish *relsha* I soul touched once, years ago."

The abbess knelt by the wounded man's other side, oblivious to the drawn swords of the palace errants surrounding her. "He is Brother Ron to us," she said, speaking of Ron D'An in *rel*-peerage, although Amel felt certain no abbess on Demora would be a mere nobleborn. "Brother Ron has been a member of our order since its founding," she continued, "and a witness to your sacred nature." The look she fixed on Amel convinced him she was someone who felt deeply. It helped him see past the absurdity of the honorifics she kept bestowing on him.

The abbess took the wounded man's hand, tears standing in her pale eyes. "Dear Brother Ron," she said. "You have saved our order from eternal disgrace in the eyes of the Sacred Dead. Brother Rand must have been a Purist, planted in our midst, and we had no idea!"

Looking past the abbess, Brother Ron's eyes met Amel's with a look of worship more powerful than the fear of death. Amel couldn't have denied him the comfort of belief under the circumstances, even if it had been within his power. He saw Ron's hand move, and clasped it in both of his.

"Thank you," he said, stunned by what the Luminary had done. "Thank you for my life."

"You will unite the Demish in the power of your light," Brother Ron said in a weak voice. "You will lead the strong and teach the wise."

"It's a spleen wound," said Iarous, sitting back on her heels. "He's losing a lot of blood."

Spleen, Amel thought with relief. Mira had pulled Tatt through a wound to the heart! A spleen should be no challenge.

"Can we move him to Mira's med lab in Lilac Hearth?" Amel asked Iarous.

"Blue Hearth," Brother Ron muttered, eyes no longer focusing on Amel but off into the distance. "Yes, let me die in Blue Hearth."

Iarous compressed her colorless lips, watching the blood continue to soak into her makeshift pressure bandages.

Amel felt Brother Ron's grip weakening and decided not to quibble about the name of the hearth he'd inherited. "Yes, Blue Hearth," he said, smiling gently. "I have the best medic on the planet waiting for us there."

Mira should be in sight by now, running toward them with her emergency medical kit clutched in one thin hand. Instead, there was only Zind, panting from her sprint across the Plaza and back again. She leaned over with her hands on her knees.

"Mira?" Amel prompted.

"Not there," Zind said, straightening up.

"Not there?" Amel panicked, imagining Mira's commoner body succumbing to one more *rel*-skimming trip than it could stand on the round trip to Barmi and back again. "No!" he rejected the image. "I'd have been told if something happened to her. She must be...out." He couldn't quite believe this explanation, either. All his memories of Mira located her in a fixed place, out of sight of superstitious Sevildom.

"Not out," Zind told him. "Gone. Your staff said she's working for Liege Monitum."

Near Amel's feet, the man he owed his life to was bleeding to death of a survivable wound. In Amel's heart, the cold shock of desertion once again stripped him of assumptions he had lived with for the last twenty years.

"I...don't understand," he confessed, his skin prickling with dread, because at some level he knew that it made sense. Mira needed to be free of him. She'd told him in so many ways over the years, chafing at the closeness that was life to him.

"Mira's at the orphanage!" Tatt's bold, clean presence cut through the feeling of darkness closing in on Amel.

Iarous rose, deferring to the Monatese medic Tatt had brought with him.

Amel felt lost.

"I heard there was an attempt on your life," Tatt told him, looking grim. "Branstatt and I will take over the investigation."

Tatt's half-Nersallian captain of errants, Branstatt, noticed Amel's eyes well up with tears and looked away, perhaps remembering unsavory scenes in Lilac Hearth he would rather forget.

Amel swallowed down the lump in his throat, looking past Tatt to the wounded man whose care was being taken over by a Monatese team. "Bring him to Blue Hearth, when you can," he said.

Tatt nodded briskly. "I'll need to question the assassin and— To where?" Tatt's political acumen caught up with the name change. "Did you say *Blue* Hearth?"

Amel didn't repeat himself. He shouldered past Branstatt, making a point of giving Horth Nersal's nephew a firm push to force him to make room. He found space to kneel beside Brother Ron opposite Tatt's medic, soiling his trousers in Blue Demish blood, and laid his hand gently along the side of his savior's face. Brother Ron was shivering with insipient shock, but his frightened look gave way to calm as he realized who was touching him.

"I will try to be all you believe I am," Amel told the wounded man, and blinked, shedding the tears he'd been ashamed of under Branstatt's embarrassed gaze.

Brother Ron's eyes shone in eloquent response.

"Immortality..." the medic interjected, hesitant to be forceful. Amel rose and drew back, leaving her room to work.

He found Zind Therd staring at him, thunderstruck. "Did you say Blue Hearth?" she asked. "Blue Hearth! Not Lilac Hearth?"

Her hand went to the hilt of her sword. Two golden paladins reacted with alarm but Amel was closest. He clapped a hand over Zind's wrist, feeling the strength in hers and exerting his own to immobilize her.

"We need to talk," said Amel, looking straight into Zind's stubborn, stony stare so much like her father's. "But I have to talk to everyone before I can make promises. You lead people yourself. You must understand."

"Talk to me *before* Sen Lekker!" Zind said, and jerked away from him as Golden and Monatese honor guards closed in to shield him in a wall of flesh. Out of Amel's sight, but not his earshot, the abbess from Demora was arguing with Tatt over custody of the failed assassin.

Irritated, and unable to think properly about anything but Mira's desertion, Amel didn't want to try untangling whatever theological differences had led one group of Goldens to revere him as a Soul of Light while a member of another faction tried to kill him. He was sick of people being so unwilling to cooperate with each other. He was tired of all the infighting, the jealousies and, most of all, his own stupid refusal to accept there was nothing more to life than this.

"You are the aberration," Ev'rel used to dismiss his distress. "People are just animals. Reward them and they serve you. Punish them and they fear you. Indulge them and they will take advantage of you. It is your need to believe otherwise that makes you vulnerable to them."

Amel couldn't bear the touch of strangers, pressing close around him. He tore away across the Plaza. The paladins pursued him. Palace errants shouted. He ran faster.

"No one will ever see your needs the way that you see theirs," Ev'rel's voice continued to mock him. "Not unless you bray them as rudely as the rest of the world does. No one sees you, at all, except as some means to their own ends."

No, no, no! Amel thought, revolting against Ev'rel's bitter logic.

But the terrible truth was he didn't even want to love people anymore! Blow by blow, his heart grew more afraid to care. Ev'rel would call this freedom. To Amel it felt like a kind of death.

CHAPTER 4

Virtual Men in the Flesh

Princess Luthan Dem H'Us of the Silver Demish sat, fully dressed, on a leather-covered bench in her private bath chamber and closed Erien's book with a heavy thump. One of her ladies was tapping on the door.

"Your Highness?" the woman asked gravely. "Is there something wrong?"

"Wrong!" Luthan exclaimed with a little start. Her heart was pounding and her normally cream-white complexion was red hot. "No!" she squeaked, and cleared her throat. "Why do you ask?"

"The Luminaries from Demora are nearly ready for you," Princess Barbanna said from the other side of the door. "Your uncle will be disappointed if you don't make a timely appearance."

"Yes, yes," Luthan sang out, in a voice more like her own.

"Very good, Your Highness," said Barbanna.

Luthan closed her eyes and swallowed. "Erien...?" she whimpered in a puzzled, tortured tone. She looked down at her slim, white fingers on the cover of the Reetion sex manual so helpfully translated into Gelack for her that lay, like a guilty secret, upon her lap.

What do you mean by giving me such a thing! she wailed at Erien in her thoughts, but with such desperation she could hardly believe it made no sound. *Is it an insult?* she agonized. *Or some crude Vrellish suggestion? Or could it possibly be your strange, Reetion notion of trying to help?*

If so, Luthan had no idea how to make use of the pictures and descriptions she'd encountered in the book. She had never seen a man naked before. Now her previously hazy ideas about

sex were entirely too well defined, mechanically, and it all
seemed absurd and quite horrible. There was nothing warm
and melting about the descriptions in the book; no reference
able to invoke the sweetly painful longing or the delicious
giggles inspired by reading Erien's letters from Rire that Tatt
had shared with her over the years. She was baffled, as well,
by what seemed like incongruous facts. Men were hard and
frightening compared to women. But from what she had thus
far been able to grasp from the sex manual, she couldn't help
feeling their part in the operation was the more fragile and
embarrassing one. And she couldn't quite bring herself to
imagine Erien performing the function as it was laid out in the
manual with anyone, let alone herself. Erien was always so
serious and self-controlled.

A hiccup-giggle escaped her at the attempt to connect her
ideas of Erien with the lessons in the book. She clapped a hand
to her mouth to control herself, and determined to sober up.

"Princess Luthan?" Barbanna called again. "Please, I don't
know what your uncle will think if—"

"Coming!" Luthan called, getting up.

First, she left the book behind her on the seat; then she
snatched it up and cast about her for a place to hide it, without success.

I'll take it to the orphanage this afternoon! she thought. *If anyone
finds it there, they'll never know for certain it was mine. And I might
even be able to look at it again, properly, if I get some time alone.*

The next challenge was how to conceal the book inside her
clothes. Her skirts were long and voluminous enough, but she
had no time to sew it into a petticoat. She settled, instead, for
taking off her little decorative cloak and stuffing the book down
her back. When she pulled the cloak over her shoulder again,
the lump barely showed.

"Prin—" Barbanna broke off her next harangue with a gulp
as Luthan pulled open the door.

"Goodness!" Luthan said with a laugh, catching the older
woman's arm. "How important can these Luminaries be, for
Uncle H'Us to worry so!"

Barbanna patted Luthan's hand, happy to have the obstacle
of the door removed. She was a pleasant enough person, Luthan
allowed, but no substitute for Hillian, the captain of Luthan's
guard. Prince H'Us had assigned Barbanna to be Luthan's new,
special companion after the scene on Fountain Court, leading

up to the recent title duel for the throne, in which he felt Luthan
had played too prominent a role. He had sent Hillian away,
replaced all Luthan's other errants and placed her under the
tutelage of matron Barbanna, a fifty-year-old widow with no
children of her own.

If it hadn't been for Tatt, Luthan's friend and neighbor on
Fountain Court who was a real liege, and a man, not an underage
princess-liege like Luthan, she would not even have been able
to get news of Erien's adventures with Amel on Rire. As it was,
even though Tatt shared everything he knew with her, it simply
hadn't been enough. Now Erien was back, had given her a
shocking book, and she wasn't even free to read it in peace, let
alone ask him what he meant by giving it to her.

Why, for all I know, she thought as she marched along beside
Barbanna, not even pretending to listen to what the matron was
explaining to her, *the book is really just a way to send me some
important message I need to decode.*

But if this was the case she thought Erien might have picked
some less alarming subject like a book of Reetion poetry.

After all, even Reetions must have poetry of some sort! Luthan
was thinking as she entered the stately receiving room where
her uncle met with visitors from other hearths of Fountain Court.
*They can't spend all their time thinking about nothing but science
and voting procedures and—"*

At the sight of the Golden Demish awaiting her, Luthan's
mind went blank.

Before her, decked out in the glittering glory of the full formal
wear of the Inner Circle surrounding the Golden Emperor, stood
two visions of Demoran beauty. The woman was Princess
Chandra of the House of Vesta, the aunt of Luthan's late mother.
Luthan had last seen Chandra at a court reception where the
El Princess begrudgingly condescended to acknowledge her.
Pale eyed, with straight, glistening hair the color of pure gold,
Chandra looked extra thin beside the robust paladin escorting
her. Luthan recognized the paladin, as well, but not by personal
acquaintance. Like many Demish girls, she had once collected
decorative cards with the pictures, lineages and tournament
statistics of Golden paladins on them. Paladins renounced
marriage and children to spare their widows pain, since they
took more risks than other Demish men, and were historically
famous for their exploits over the centuries. But these sacred
warriors of *Okal Lumens* were known to retire and settle down

when they fell in love with the right heroine, which ,together with their sterling reputations for celibacy while in service, made them the idols of many a young girl's daydreams.

The man with Chandra was the greatest living Paladin, Oleander Vesta, and he looked every bit as strong and dignified as his collectible card. He was eighty-five, never married, only twice defeated in tournament duels—once by the infamous champion D'Ander—and the victor of six fatal challenges over his long career as champion to the House of Vesta. Oleander was dressed in a paladin's surplice of pure white cotton, heavily embroidered in the golden house braid of his order about the collar and hem. Beneath the loose outer garment he wore a bright yellow body suit. His near-white hair was pulled back, slick, against a well-formed skull. His jaw was square, his eyes were pale and clear, with frosty eyebrows just a bit too unruly compared to the otherwise complete air of serene refinement he projected.

Luthan was speechless. She considered Chandra a bit of a prig. But just the sight of Oleander made the skin of her back burn with shame where Erien's book pressed against her.

He bowed to acknowledge Luthan's entrance, extending one leg and dipping forward over it in her direction, which was the gesture owed an El Princess.

"Oh!" Luthan said, flattered and astonished. As far as she had been able to make out, her Demoran relatives had no use for her.

Chandra confined her own greeting to a nod.

"Ah, Luthan! There you are," Prince H'Us said, taking her hand. "This is Princess Chandra and Prince Oleander, relations of your mother."

"Yes," said Luthan, glad to be given her uncle's arm to steady her in the face of such an unprecedented visit, but also eager to overturn the impression his introduction gave that she was ignorant of how things stood between herself and Chandra, in particular.

"Princess Chandra and my grandmother were sisters," Luthan said as firmly and clearly as she could. "And by blood rights they were equal in rank, but since Chandra was the elder she stood to inherit the title of Liege Vesta. Then my grandmother married a paladin who had been kept from claiming title to Vesta only while in service to the Vestal Order, and their child—my mother—displaced Chandra as Heir Vesta. That is, until she was bartered away, in marriage, to my father."

"Bartered!" Prince H'Us exclaimed, in shock.

"It isn't my father I blame for it," Luthan said quickly, sorry to have bruised her uncle's feelings. "He was a good man. My mother simply wasn't happy with him."

She turned her attention from H'Us, who seemed mollified if still perplexed by the chronic problems Silver princes had with Golden princesses, and steeled herself to deliver the rest of what she had to say to Princess Chandra, whose haughty treatment had been rankling on Luthan in the months since they'd first met at a court reception.

"I never knew my mother very well," Luthan told her illustrious relative, her voice trembling with the pain of the few memories she did possess of a listless, lonely woman in whom her daughter's childish antics could rouse no more than a benign smile and a light touch. "But I know she grieved for the loss of the life she loved," Luthan continued. "And you did nothing to relieve her distress. I used to imagine you couldn't. Now I've met you, I believe you simply didn't care!"

Luthan finished on a rising note, stiff lipped, with tears in her eyes and her whole body trembling with outrage on behalf of her dead mother. Chandra's face was as unmoved as wax—until Oleander shouldered forward. Then Chandra's expression became one of frozen horror as the legendary paladin went down on one knee before Luthan. His pale, oval face turned up toward her with the rapt expression of a passionate supplicant, reminding her suddenly of seeing Oleander's face looking up at her from a card held in her mother's drooping hand.

"Some of us, Dearest Luthan," he said, with the diction of a poet and the heart of a champion, "cared too much." He lowered his head, his right arm set across his raised knee in a pose of sorrow. "I loved your mother, but I was too proud to let her know for fear it would seem I loved her out of self-interest and because I did not wish to set aside my vows. It was Chandra who agreed to sound out your mother on my behalf, to see if she would wait until I was prepared to marry and unite our claims to Vesta through a child. Instead, as I have lately learned, she told your mother I felt sullied by her sweet love, and convinced her, in her grief, to wed your father for the good of our line. And although Chandra claims to love me, were she but a man, I would slay her for this betrayal!"

Princess Chandra emitted a thin cry at this last remark, swooned and collapsed in a graceful spiral movement.

"Good gods!" Prince H'Us exclaimed in alarm, as Oleander deftly caught his fragile relative before she hit the floor. "You've killed her, man!"

Luthan's heart was in her throat but she swallowed it down, trembling with anger at discovering the cause of her mother's broken heart. "It may be possible to kill an El Princess with harsh words, and it may not," she declared, with contempt for Chandra's swon. "But even if it is, I don't believe it's possible with that one!"

Barbanna, who was thoroughly Silver Demish in her sympathies, raised herself in Luthan's affections by giving her a look of hearty approval behind the men's backs as Oleander laid Chandra on the nearest couch.

Luthan wanted to slip away to process the shock Prince Oleander had delivered, concerning her mother, in private. But Oleander sprang to intercept her.

"No, wait!" he cried. "Chandra played your mother false," he said, looking thoroughly wretched. "But I have been much worse, because I loved your mother, and out of fear of seeming less than I believed myself to be, I failed her. My cowardice betrayed her to an early death, in exile, and I cannot live unless it is to champion the restoration of her blood to its proper place. In short, Luthan, I live to see you succeed to your mother's rightful title as princess-liege of Vesta, acknowledged as a Golden Soul, and made Protector of all Demora!"

"I—I don't know what to say!" Luthan exclaimed in dismay, stuttering at the audacity of being tongue-tied in the face of such a declaration from so legendary a figure. Indeed, the very stuff of legend had been laid out before her: an unrequited love, a deceitful relation, a tragic death in the wake of an unwanted marriage. She should have been reduced to fainting herself, but even as tears welled in her eyes she felt a stubborn, flinty anger at the childishness of it!

"I understand," Oleander said gently, looking into her face with an openness she'd never seen before except, now and then, in Amel. The faint feeling of familiarity about it melted Luthan's heart but she looked for her uncle H'Us, instinctively, needing the reassurance of his presence.

House Vesta was a bastion of purists who did not believe hybrids like Luthan and Amel were acceptable options for the rebirth of Divine Souls. It was the Vestas, Oleander chief among them, who had remained solidly opposed to Prince D'Ander throughout his otherwise successful career as both Protector and Champion of Demora.

Yet here was Oleander, looking at her as if she held the hope of his soul's survival in her hybrid, Silver Demish hands!

"Daughter of Vesta," he said, going down on his knees again to gaze up at her with the dignity of a king and the spiritual intensity of a supplicant. "I beg you to forgive us for past wrongs, and for our present ineptitude—" A thin moan from Chandra, on the coach, interrupted him briefly but only firmed up the set of his mouth, "—in attempting to apologize for them. The Golden Emperor has spoken. He said D'Ander was correct. He said Divine Souls may follow mixed blood. He said we need their vigor. There are those who have taken this to mean we should embrace Amel as our liege, but we of House Vesta have long resisted the horror of believing the Golden Emperor's last living descendant could possibly be divine in any measure! I bear him no ill will, El Luthan. But no Golden Soul could have survived the ordeals he has lived through, let alone a Soul of Light and true heir to the Golden Emperor. You, however, we believe to be a Golden Soul of *Okal Lumens*. But to win the day your divinity must be officially recognized. So I beg you to return, El Luthan, to the world your soul knows as its own. The world your Blessed mother pined for. The family who can understand you."

"Really?" Prince H'Us barged into the conversation, almost nudging Luthan aside in his attempt to interpose between her and Oleander, and then catching her in the crock of his arm to steady her, which was necessary because Oleander's speech had left her dizzy.

"So you would make the princess-liege of H'Us your liege, would you?" H'Us demanded, face set in a mask of Silver Demish pride. "After generations of bargaining away your princesses in marriage and then damning their husbands for accepting them? After snubbing our Luthan, and going so far as to swear to Avim Ev'rel for twenty years just to avoid sharing an oath with the Silver Demish, your natural protectors? In short, after treating us like second rate Demish for centuries and turning my nephew D'Ander against me, your Golden Emperor—supposedly still grief-stunned by the loss of his wife and daughter—suddenly gets talkative, and all at once you expect me to believe you would make Luthan your leader! My little half-H'Usian Luthan? Why? That's what I want to know.

Paladin or not, and whatever you may or may not have felt for her mother, there's more than souls in the balance I'll wager."

H'Us set Luthan behind him. Deprived of his support, she sank into the nearest upholstered chair. The honor Oleander paid her was one she had fantasized about receiving all her life. It lay at the root of her phantom relationship with her dead mother, and her own sense of uniqueness at the Ava's court.

To be a Golden Soul! she thought, only vaguely aware of her uncle's angry voice. *An arbiter of right and wrong!* The idea was deeply exciting to her. Collecting the Demoran oath would please H'Us, but to her it would be one more pleasant honor with no real responsibilities attached to it. Golden Souls spoke their minds and had influence with Luminaries everywhere. The Golden Soul Dar'Cynth of Orchard had once commanded a roomful of Silver Demish princes to accept Ayrium as liege of Barmi, and made them stand down their fleets, too—all because she decided Perry D'Aur's rebellion had been morally justified.

The very idea she might really be a Golden Soul made Luthan want to disown the book pressed against her back, and alarmed her with visions of the scene if it should be discovered. Golden Souls, she was certain, did not skulk about hiding obscene books!

"I'll tell you what this appeal to our Luthan is really about!" ranted Prince H'Us, his big fist raised as if to threaten Oleander, his face flushed beneath his bushy eyebrows. "It's nothing but a transparent attempt to take Luthan from us on the brink of an unprecedented triumph! Or hadn't you heard she is about to forge a bond of blood between us and House Nersal. Yes, that's right! H'Us and Nersal. The two hybrid houses. The two pillars of the Ava's Oath. What do you think of that, Prince Oleander of the Vestal Order! What if we Silver Demish have grown tired of admiring you Goldens in the teeth of your insults and are ready to look elsewhere to enrich our blood lines in more vigorous directions!"

Prince Oleander endured this harangue with a look of grave forbearance, his eyes focused only on Luthan. "House Vesta has hurt you and your mother," he told her, trying to speak past the bulky obstacle of Prince H'Us. "But we are still your blood. Come to Demora. See what your mother lost and understand her at last. Come, and find out if your soul will recognize its home."

Luthan looked up at the spectacle of Prince Oleander Vesta, no longer just a figure on a child's collectable cards but a man in the flesh, and yet every bit as glorious as possible, pleading with her so sincerely she could not bring herself to doubt his motives no matter what her uncle told her—and she stared back, spellbound, feeling her eyes fill with tears.

Just like Amel's eyes do when he's moved, she thought involuntarily, and wished she hadn't because her political instincts were astute enough to grasp Oleander was setting her up against Amel, and in her heart of hearts she suspected Amel was much closer to being a Soul of Light than she was to possessing a Golden Soul: the two categories of divinity for Purebloods and Royalbloods, respectively.

"Sir!" Prince H'Us addressed Oleander with strained patience. "I would thank you to leave."

Oleander remained rooted to the spot, insensible to all but Luthan's stare. Holding his, she found it hard to breathe.

"I said—" H'Us began, laying a big hand on Oleander's shoulder.

The Golden Paladin came to life suddenly.

Luthan blinked.

When she focused again, H'Us had been shoved back three paces and Oleander had his sword out, soulful expression displaced by cold, deadly anger. Chandra had made a miraculous recovery and stood unaided at his back, clutching her shawl.

"No!" Luthan cried in alarm.

"We will leave," Oleander told H'Us bitterly. He shifted his attention to Luthan with an immediate and profound change of expression. "But we will be in Golden Hearth. Just across Fountain Court."

Luthan's mouth had gone dry. She could not speak. She nodded once, instead.

In a swirl of gold and glitter, Oleander marshaled Chandra to precede him, and was gone.

Princess Barbanna was the first to come to life again.

"You were marvelous!" she exclaimed to Prince H'Us.

"Huh!" Luthan's uncle said, squaring his shoulders and shaking off the aftershock of Oleander laying hands on him. "I've been wanting for decades to say a few things of that sort to a Golden who could take them in without fainting!"

Luthan couldn't help smiling at her uncle. It seemed to her as if he had not understood half of what had happened between her and the Goldens right before his eyes, and yet he was a good man in his bluff way, and she knew he cared about her. The day-to-day minutiae of her life once again embraced her, muting the radiance of the dream Oleander had inspired in the lighter, grander quarter of her spirit.

Silver feelings, she identified the old emotions as they settled. *I'm not a hybrid, all evenly mixed. I'm like a salad dressing made of two parts: oil and vinegar. Silver and Gold. Oleander makes the Gold in me rise to the top.*

"Ohh," she sighed as the next thought occurred to her, making Princess Barbanna and her uncle rush to her side to fuss. But she had only been thinking how Silver and prosaic it was to think of salad dressing at such a time.

Amel would have thought of something beautiful, she imagined. And disliked herself for the pang of jealousy it invoked.

"Perhaps you should cancel your visit to the orphanage today," Barbanna said as soon as Prince H'Us had relinquished Luthan into her custody once more.

"Oh, no, that's not necessary," Luthan insisted, waking from her musings to the cold reality of the sequestered book.

Barbanna clucked and worried, making Luthan long for her old companions: real friends in whom she might have been able to confide. She tried, instead, to deflect Barbanna from rehashing the Demorans' unprecedented visit by discussing what she ought to wear to travel to the orphanage on the Palace Plain.

A servant met them on the way to Luthan's rooms.

"Prince Erien Lor'Vrel wishes an audience," the man said with a bow.

Luthan's heart gave a great thump that seemed to resonate right through her chest to the book against her back. She said, "Oh."

"Whatever could the Lor'Vrel want?" Barbanna said disdainfully. "Tell him Princess Luthan is indisposed."

Luthan said nothing. After meeting Oleander, her feelings about Erien suddenly felt frivolous to her.

"In that case," said the servant, "His Immortality, Pureblood Erien Lor'Vrel, begged me to deliver a short message."

Barbanna frowned, but Luthan consented with a distracted nod.

The servant cleared his throat and repeated, "Tell Luthan not to worry about Amel. He survived the assassination attempt without a scratch. Tatt has the assailant, who appears to be a Luminary zealot attached to no particular order. Amel is far more upset about Mira moving out of Lilac Hearth, so if you are going there, you might tell her so, although I don't understand why he opposes her decision to work for Tatt."

Luthan heard the whole message clearly enough, even though her ears began ringing the moment the words "assassination" and "Amel" came together with the proper impact.

"Is there any response you would like me to relate to Prince Erien?" the servant asked.

Luthan struggled for breath, felt a lightness in her head as darkness crowded her vision—and passed out for the very first time in her life, just like a real El Princess of Demora, instead of a vigorous hybrid one.

CHAPTER 5

Sam gets lost and tells her story

"Are you sure Princess Luthan comes here?" Sam asked doubtfully, looking around her with a worried air. She and Jack were seated at a table in the outdoor section of a cafe. Ahead of them lay a plaza covered in a sheet of some material patterned to resemble cobblestones and glued to the hullsteel floor. The orphanage was to their left, a garish, block-shaped building three stories high, painted bright yellow to hide a history of petty vandalism. The cafe lay roughly at the center of the circular compound enclosing the Gold and Silver Orphanage. Behind them, a short street stretched 170 meters back to the gate they had entered by an hour earlier.

Jack swallowed a mouthful of the stuffed bun she'd bought him and shrugged. "We may need to wait a few days, of course," he admitted.

"Days!" Sam straightened up in alarm.

"Unless you've remembered where you put the signet of passage you got from your brother," Jack prompted in a hopeful manner. "So we can get onto the Plaza to reach Silver Pavilion."

"I told you," Sam said miserably, "I don't think I took the signet from my brother at all."

Jack put his bun down on the chipped plate in front of him. "Begging your pardon, Your Highness, but aren't you a Demish highborn—I mean, male or female—"

"Hush!" Sam cautioned.

"—don't you have a better memory than nervecloth?" Jack got to the point. "Surely you know whether or not you had the signet when you left home."

"It isn't that I don't remember, exactly," Sam confessed. "I just don't notice things like signets of passage and other vital details when I'm thinking about something else. Samdan—the real Samdan—had a signet. I just forgot all about it until we were asked for it, at Silver Gate. I must have put it down somewhere when he gave it to me. I was thinking about more weighty things," she added in her own defense.

"Too bad Prince Amel didn't stick around to escort you to Silver Hearth," Jack said with a sigh.

"You may think so," Sam said, drawing courage from her indignation over the alley incident. "I don't. Amel was positively rude to me over those ruffians, when I was the one set upon!"

"Um," Jack said thoughtfully, "well, about you and him, I've been meaning to explain that with you making out you're a man, and coming over all 'ooh, you're Amel' on him in the carriage and all, and seeing as you don't come across as the most manly of princes, I've suspected he might think—"

"Stop!" Sam ordered, going white. The thought Amel might guess she was female made her wish she had put on more of Samdan's cologne and padded her jacket more cunningly. It chilled her to the tips of her toes. "I don't want to talk about Prince Amel," she said roughly. "It would only be dwelling on another mistake in my foolish past. Amel is not a Soul of Light! It's just ridiculous. Why, there is nothing nice about him but his looks!"

Jack subsided with a resigned, "Yes, Your Highness."

Sam hunched her shoulders, trying to shut out their surroundings, which were bleak by her standards, although considered a bright spot on the Palace Plain. They had ridden here by delivery truck, the road getting dimmer as they passed out of the busy commercial zone of the Market Round near the Citadel and docks. The darkness of the unlighted route had oppressed Sam and she'd been relieved to come into the light again as they approached the brightly painted buildings of the Gold and Silver Orphanage. The complex was caged in by a fence that circled the compound and its associated buildings. The fence enclosed a farm, park and greenhouses for raising food. There were also barracks for security guards, whom Jack insisted on referring to as 'toughs,' and some little businesses like the outdoor cafe in which they had stopped to wait for Luthan to pay a visit.

The other highborn patron of the orphanage was Prince Amel, but Luthan came more regularly, wherein resided Jack's hopes of managing an interview with her.

How like a man to claim half the ownership when he puts in less than half the effort! Sam thought furiously, deciding it was shoddy behavior on Amel's part.

"You do have some means of establishing who you are even if you didn't bring a signet of passage, right?" Jack asked her. "Like a letter of introduction or something."

"Don't be silly!" Sam said. "Why, I could have stayed at home and gone to be a weary sister at the reverie if I imagined nobody at Silver Hearth was expecting us to send Prince Samdan O'Pearl to serve at court as errant to the Luthan Dem H'Us." She assumed a firm look of confidence. "Of course she'll know who I'm supposed to be."

"Just so long as you're sure," Jack said, took another bite of his bun and chewed thoughtfully.

"I'm tired," Sam realized moments later, with a hopeless feeling of being out of her depth. "Where are we going to sleep?"

"I'm thinking about it," Jack assured her, with a dose of his unfounded optimism.

"Pendant? Portrait? Souvenirs?" a childish voice piped up by Sam's side. "Princess Luthan. Prince Amel."

Sam turned to find a skinny boy offering her merchandise from a tray around his neck.

For a moment, Sam was intrigued. She dipped a hand into the offerings on the tray to lift out a cameo of Amel with his head surrounded by a glow that was activated by movement. Then she remembered she was bitterly disillusioned with her idol.

"Rubbish!" she said, dropping the icon back onto the tray again.

"Your Highness is not a follower of *Okal Lumens*?" the boy guessed with a disappointed air, and bowed as best he could over his tray.

"I'll buy this for your sake," Sam said, taking the icon, and dropped an honor chip onto the table.

"Thank you!" the child-vendor exclaimed.

Jack put out an arm to delay the boy's departure. "You can give me the change," he said.

Business transacted, Jack's attention reverted to Sam. She shoved the icon across the table until it struck his plate. "You have it."

Jack took the medallion willingly enough and stuffed it in a pocket. "You really are unhappy with Prince Amel," he observed.

"He's a disappointment," Sam said sullenly.

"Disappointment?" Jack prompted, eager—she suspected—to keep her mind off where they were going to sleep until he figured it out himself. "Then you were a Luminary before you came here?" he guessed.

"More than just a Luminary," she said, giving the icon a poke with one finger. "One of Amel's Children."

Jack's eyes opened very wide. "Prince Amel is your—"

"No, no," she said, "not literally! It's a name for people who believe Amel is a Soul of Light and his early life as a commoner is a message to us. Just like the coming of Sweet Lellalee, the Soul of Light reborn as an actual commoner during the Golden Age. The message, you see, is to treat commoners better. To look after them."

"Look...after us?" Jack said, slowly and carefully, as if he might have misunderstood. Then he grinned. "How about making it so we could look after ourselves, Princess?"

"Prince!"

"Sorry!" he corrected himself. "And...now you've met Amel, you've given up being one of the Messenger Cult. Is that it?"

"Cult!" Sam frowned at him. "I am not part of any addle-brained cult obsessed with worshipping the Sevolite of the week!"

"Begging your pardon again, Highness. The Children of Amel, I meant. Here on Gelion, we call them the Messengers."

"Messengers?" Sam made a face. "It makes us sound like page boys or envoys or something!"

"Amel was Royal Envoy for years!" Jack pointed out cheerfully.

Sam's indignation deflated. "I suppose so, yes." She rallied with a deep breath. "If it is going to be a long wait and if you want to know how I became a Child of Amel—" She quickly extracted a leather-covered booklet from a side pouch of her suitcase and sat down again, opening it to the first page. "I will read you a bit of the story I am writing to explain it all," Sam declared.

Jack weighed the situation and asked cautiously, "Could I get more to eat while you do?"

Sam did not appreciate his priorities, but since he was now the only being entirely in her confidence, and hence the only soul she dared to entertain, she set aside her finer feelings to allow for his half-starved condition and lack of literary education.

"Yes," she said.

When he had waved over a waiter and ordered enough food for two boys his size, she applied herself in a determined way to the manuscript, and began to read.

> Dearest Krissa,
> I asked if I could help you cope with death and you said, "Please Highness, tell me your story!"
> What a small thing to ask! And yet how difficult I find it to reach into my past and reconstruct myself and all my loved ones as we were before you knew me by my brother's name. Poor, dear Krissa! Your short, bright journey through life screams its meaning for any Sevolite who dares to hear, and yet it is my story you ask for.

"Who is Krissa?" Jack asked her.

Caught up in the spell of her own storytelling, it was Sam's turn to blink at him. "A servant at Silver Hearth who becomes my bosom friend," she said. "She is dying of something incurable."

"But you haven't been to Silver Hearth, yet," Jack pointed out.

"It's a story," Sam told him. "I made her up, to motivate me."

"So she's not dying, that's good," said Jack and remembering the food on his plate, took a huge bite of bun stuffed with flavored vat protein. "Go ahead," he said around his meal.

Sam dived back into her manuscript.

"The story of how I came to be an errant serving Princess Luthan of Fountain Court is not as grand as the lives of the people it has become my job to serve. My story is the size and texture of Jewel County in the Lakes District of Clara's World. Jewel County is a quiet Demish district with traditions as well-worn and comfortable as the heavy velvet drapes of my grandmother's four-poster bed, so old that even the patches have histories.

Let me start, in fact, with my grandmother's bed. As a child it seemed so large that it was easy for my twin brother, Dan, and me to transform it, in our imaginations, into a grand and mighty battlewheel in which we toured the universe righting wrongs. I was a Golden Soul, and he my paladin. We researched our missions in my father's library, abandoned for as long as I can remember except for our excursions. Dan was always better at describing the cultures we visited on our imaginary battlewheel, although as my brother he took care to shelter me from knowledge of the less wholesome elements in the universe—a detail I now find ironic given the events that have made us both exiles. But my brother strove to be the model prince in those happy days."

"So you don't really have a brother, either," Jack interrupted her again.

"What!" she exclaimed, irritated by his lack of reverence for her storytelling. "Of course I do. Samdan O'Pearl."

"You called him Dan."

"Yes, because Samdan and Samanda sound too similar. My mother always called us Sam and Dan."

"People shouldn't name twins things that sound similar," Jack told her in an accusatory tone.

"Oh! By all the Muses of the Watching—" Sam was in the middle of complaining when a sword-bearing man interrupted.

"You!" the man accosted Jack with a jerk of his big thumb. "What do you think this is—a Monatese hanger? Servants don't eat in the cafe! Scat."

Sam rose with a jolt of anger. The intruder was a solid looking, swaggering man in the livery of a Seniorlord Silver Demish house from the Apron District. Sam was well enough educated in braid and heraldry to pin him within six relatives and knew his birth rank. "This boy is with me," she insisted, downspeaking him firmly enough to have quelled any inferior gentleman on Clara's World who sought to tell her where her servant could and could not eat a meal.

"Fine. You can eat in the back with him," said the bully in *rel*-peerage. "Unless you're game to take the matter up with me," he added, and pulled his sword.

Jack scrambled to his feet. "On my way, Your Grace!" he sang out, flattering the errant through his choice of pronouns.

Sam was flushed with indignation. "I don't have to duel you!" she exclaimed in a squeaky voice, although she managed to reject his grammatical insult and continued to downspeak him properly. "You aren't in my challenge class! You're nobleborn. I'm highborn."

"True," said the errant, with an evil grin. "But I don't think you are even a real man, which makes you less than a Fractional to me."

Sam's heart missed a beat. "H-how do you know I'm..." she stuttered in horror, convinced he had seen through her disguise.

"So I'm right," the bully jeered. His expression turned ugly, as if she disgusted him. She backed up a step, sword still in its sheath; drawing it never occurred to her. She looked for Jack, but he had disappeared.

"It's legal enough to kill a *slaka'st* of any rank," the horrible man declared, and whipped his sword at her.

Sam flinched and turned away, feeling a sting across her shoulder as she let out a frightened shriek.

"Draw your sword!" the man exclaimed. "You fight like a farm girl!"

Sam could barely think. Her mouth had gone dry. Her upper arm screamed about a kind of damage new to her—not the weary, grainy feeling of an overflown pilot, but the hot alarm of a fresh hurt. For all she knew, she might have been fatally struck and was about to keel over dead. She couldn't get breath into her chest.

Then a woman's voice claimed her attacker's attention. "So tell me," the newcomer asked, "do you have lots of experience fighting with farm girls?"

"Who are you?" the bully demanded. But at least he turned his attention elsewhere, encouraging Sam to open her eyes— once she realized she had them closed tight—and stare.

The woman in snug flight leathers confronting them was blue-eyed and blond-haired. She was calm. She was sleek. Her features were as well-proportioned and delicate as a Golden princess's, but her hands were large and capable. Strangest of all, she looked like she was enjoying herself.

"If you like fighting women, try me," the bizarre apparition with no house braid on her leathers said, all with a dazzling grin. "I'm Alivda D'Ander D'Aur Lor'Vrel," the icy vision of lethal beauty introduced herself. "Daughter of Ayrium, Liege Barmi, and Ameron Lor'Vrel, Ava of the empire."

She smiled again. "Nice to make your acquaintance. Short as it is going to prove to be. Now, shall we have this out by Sword Law, since we've got the witnesses? I'm happy to condescend to accept your challenge if you're still game to take on a highborn."

The remark about witnesses made Sam glance around. They had attracted a circle of about twenty people, half of them sword-bearing Sevolites of roughly the same stock as her tormentor, and probably there from the Apron District in the hope of catching sight of Princess Luthan when she put in an appearance, which made her hopeful Luthan was indeed about to arrive.

The bully sized up how much face he might lose if he declined Alivda's offer, and scowled, his breath coming deeper and faster. "I've heard of you," he ground out, reluctantly allowing her *rel*-peerage, which wasn't accurate but was still better than the grammar he had used for Sam. "I've heard you are a wild one, despite your blue eyes. And I've heard your father would be glad to see you safely out of the way."

Alivda considered this. "Possible," she said, neutrally. Then drew her sword with a quick, economical motion. "Decide."

"I accept! It's a pity to kill a woman who looks like you, but I don't like your kind of freak any more than I like his!" he jerked his head in Sam's direction.

"*Ack rel*," Alivda said.

They stepped clear of the table. People closed in. Sam was drawn into the circle, mesmerized by curiosity and still in shock from the slash on her arm. Jack squeezed in past two armed Demish men and tried to pry her fingers from her blood-soaked sleeve to see how bad it was, but she jerked away from him, afraid to take her eyes off the bully who had hurt her or the woman who had so casually agreed to fight him.

The bully feigned. Alivda played to his suggestion, blocking. He grinned, and danced to one side to take another poke. She rotated and answered him again.

The crowd was growing restless. It wasn't hard for Sam to guess some of the men felt they should be standing up for the girl who seemed to be on the defensive, however unconventionally she might be dressed. And while Sam didn't know enough about fencing to be sure Alivda was in trouble, the bully's gleeful expression worried her.

Alivda's next block looked wobbly even to Sam's inexpert eye.

"We should put a stop to this!" a male voice muttered nearby.

"She's Ameron's daughter!" another said.

Alivda heard. Sam could see her mild look harden at her father's name.

The bully went for a lunge, causing half the witnesses surrounding the duel to catch their breath. But Alivda blocked with sudden competence and slid away, elusive as water, from the rebound attack. The bully hadn't gotten it yet, but Sam picked up her cue from the sudden stillness in the more knowledgeable watchers as the murmurs of gentlemanly concern died away.

In three seconds, Alivda drove her opponent back. His defense became more desperate with every block. In five seconds, she bloodied his left arm. Her next assault touched his sword arm but left it unharmed as if she was reluctant to spoil her fun. Her eyes glittered. Her mouth had settled into a relaxed smile. Sam had seen more compassionate expressions on the hunting hawks of her betrothed on Clara's World.

A grasp of his danger displaced the gloating look on the bully's face. He took a deep breath, shifted his grip on his sword hilt and prepared to fight for his life.

Alivda laughed.

She darted in, picking at the periphery of his guard. He turned one way, then another, struggling to regain the offensive. The crowd grew deathly quiet as each clash crippled the bully's confidence a bit more. It became painful to watch. Sam turned her head toward Jack and closed her eyes, listening to the victim's grunts, the crowd's stillness and the clash of swords. She knew it was over when the crowd exhaled as one and broke up into talk.

Opening her eyes, Sam saw the bully lying dead, on his back. Alivda stood watching him with a slight scowl of disappointment. Her sword tip let fall a single drop of blood.

"I presume he has friends to take charge!" Alivda bellowed in a commanding voice.

"Come sit down," Jack said to Sam, and led her back to their table. "I should look at your arm."

Sam felt dizzy. She let Jack take charge until he started messing around with her sleeve, then she cried out. Tears of pain stood in her eyes.

"Do you have a seamer?" Jack asked.

Sam knew what a seamer was. Highborn fighters used them to close shallow cuts and even to do first aid on deep body wounds, trusting to regeneration to sort out the damage later. And she was highborn, even if at sixty-eight percent she was only a middle class princess by courtly standards. But it had never occurred to her to carry a seamer because princesses on Clara's World didn't fight.

Alivda swaggered over, pulled out a chair, handed Jack her own seamer and started helping herself to his unfinished lunch.

Sam was too busy staring at the other woman in astonishment to notice what Jack was doing until she was assaulted by a soft buzz and a fierce smart. She gave a shriek and started, nearly choking on the stench of burned blood. For a moment she was certain she was going to pass out.

"I can't—believe you did that!" Sam blurted at Jack.

"Not from around here, are you?" Alivda remarked, putting down Jack's tankard of weak, flavored gin, which was standard fare for commoners of all ages. "Prince...?" she sounded unconvinced about the prince part.

Sam did her best to rally despite the pulsing mass of pain that had replaced her upper arm. "Sam. Samdan O'Pearl of the Lakes District on Clara's World."

"Clara's World." Alivda narrowed her eyes. "That's outreach in Princess Reach. Silver Demish. Parochial. A nothing-happening sort of place, off the beaten track."

Sam had suffered more insults and humiliations over the last few months than her upbringing had led her to believe she ever would. But this was too much.

"Clara's World is beautiful!" she cried back.

Alivda shrugged one shoulder. "No doubt." She cocked her little finger to flick a bit of Jack's lunch out from between two pure white teeth, smacked her lips and lowered the hand. "I used to think—a lot—about how to lay hands on a world in the Demish net. There are so many of them, relatively speaking, and no Horth Nersal to take out. But the Demish protect their riches in other ways. Contracts and marriages. Rights and honor bonds of mutual defense and service, layers and layers of them. You'd have to take out the whole Silver Demish fleet to break the wall of tradition that shelters those who couldn't defend themselves, one on one, in any kind of fight."

Sam's ears burned with shock. Every hair follicle on her skin stood straight up. "You wanted to *conquer* Clara's World!" she exclaimed in horror. "By *force*!"

Alivda pushed back, lounging in the simple chair. "No, I told you, I figured out it isn't possible."

"But you'd do it if it was?" Sam asked, still unable to believe what she was hearing.

"Sure," Alivda said. "Why not? I mean, I'm not going to get even so much as a measly command handed to me on a platter of any color: white, blue, purple or brown. So I'm going to have to do something unorthodox."

"You were toying with that man you killed, weren't you?" Sam said, putting her uneasy feeling about the duel into words. "You wanted him to be afraid. You liked it."

"There's gratitude for you," Alivda quipped back. She leaned forward with an elbow on the table. "I did make sure he was a bigger monster than me, first. I mean, when I came across all girly, he could have tried to go for first blood, and he didn't."

"I do the moral check-up for Amel," she added with perfect seriousness. "I have to be able to tell him the bastard deserved it."

"You are the...bastard!" Sam told Alivda with passionate indignation, barely able to force out the offending word. "Ameron's bastard by Perry D'Aur's bastard! A bastard two generations deep!"

"Different meaning, same word," Alivda said, sounding perfectly Demish about the linguistic issue but indifferent to the social slur. "But have you ever wondered why 'bastard,' in Demish usage, not only means a child born out of wedlock, but a mean-spirited jerk? Think about it someday. And how all the rights and privileges of ownership flow through legal contracts in the Demish system. So yes, my parents aren't married," she added with a bored expression. "And I'm also a bastard in the other sense, so don't forget it."

Jack had gone still as a frightened mouse since Alivda intruded on them. Belatedly, Sam realized he was probably wise to be scared, and forced down her indignation at the woman's outrageous behavior.

"Thank you for helping me," Sam said in stiffly proper peerage. "Is there something you require in return?"

Alivda considered. "Can't think of anything just yet," she concluded. "Maybe later. I was hoping to see Amel when he checks in down here. Don't suppose you'd know if he's paid a visit since he arrived?"

"Do you know Immortality Amel?" Sam blurted before she caught herself. Alivda had said as much earlier, but her arm hurt her so much it was hard to think.

"Know him!" Alivda gave a sharp laugh. "He's mine."

Sam was close to fainting from the loss of blood and pain in her arm, or felt she ought to be. She wanted her mother. She wanted to be home, sitting in a swinging chair in the backyard with her younger siblings rushing around under the benign sun of Clara's World, with smiling servants who had loved her all her life serving up fruit jellies and lemonade. But she couldn't let Alivda's remark pass without a challenge.

"You mean you are going to marry him?" Sam demanded.

"If necessary," Alivda said cheerfully. "But we're already like this," she held up her right hand, brandishing crossed fingers. "I used to fly with him on his trips, ever since I was a toddler." She swung up out of the chair and stared back down at Sam and Jack, her hands on her hips. "Amel's been pushed around too much by people with their own ideas about what he ought to be. He needs someone strong to protect him. And to help him make the most of what he's got. So I'm going to be his First Sworn and Champion. Admiral of his fleet, as well. Soon as I get him one." She grinned. "Then, maybe we'll come after Clara's World."

Sam was speechless. She had never known such rudeness or heard such unbounded, shameless ambition. She was outraged on behalf of decent Demish everywhere. At the same time, she felt thoroughly intimidated.

"Here comes Her Highness, Luthan," Alivda said, looking past Sam to the courtyard where a half a dozen forerunners of Luthan's entourage had shown up to inspect the premises. The body of Alivda's victim struck them as a problem, immediately; two of them began canvassing people to find relatives to take charge of the clean up.

Alivda chuckled. "That's right, boys. Can't have Princess Luthan Dem H'Us seeing a dead body oozing blood."

"I need to see Princess Luthan," Sam said numbly.

"Really?" said Alivda. "Better stick with me, then." She tipped her head in the direction of the courtyard which was filling up with people trying to make contact with Luthan's forerunners. "Unless you want to compete with all the rabble who are here for the same reason."

Jack looked as if he had something to ask Alivda, but he kept silent. The warrior woman intimidated him, too, Sam guessed. She also noticed Jack was staring at Alivda with an unseemly fascination no proper Demish princess would tolerate. If he'd been her brother, not her servant, she'd have stepped on his toe to snap him out of it.

And Jack's only a boy! Sam thought angrily. Her recent experiences had taught her how simple-minded and fickle-hearted men really were in contrast to their heroic portrayal in the literature she loved so well, and it occurred to her, in a peevish moment, what unfair competition a women like Alivda was for women who weren't Vrellish inside. Sam couldn't imagine Alivda crying into her pillow for days over a broken heart. She probably didn't have any womanly feelings to be hurt. Which, apparently, was what men wanted. Or else they wanted to break girls hearts to make themselves feel important, which was even worse.

I am never going to care about another man if I live to be three hundred and ten! Sam promised herself. *I'm tired of being the stupid one who really cares.*

She considered the idea of learning how to toy with men, enjoy what they could give her, and then move on to the next thrill, but the trouble was she wouldn't enjoy a false relationship. For her, the whole joy of love lay in the depth and quality of her belief in it. *If what you love is porridge*, she thought sadly, feeling every throb in her shoulder like a condemnation from an ill-defined source, *then there is no use eating honey until it makes you ill. Really all the honey is good for is to dress the porridge up a little, now and then.*

Melancholy and in pain, she watched listlessly as preparations in the courtyard continued. Alivda rose to deal with the fore-runner in Luthan's livery when he came their way. Jack took advantage of her absence to edge closer to Sam and whisper, "Are you all right, Princess? You're looking pale."

"It is my broken heart," Sam said, miserably. "Oh, Jack! Maybe I'm just a fool who deserves to be trodden on for imag-ining anyone else really cares about anything but honey! Honey, honey, honey!"

"She's delirious!" Jack muttered in dismay.

Sam cast him a quelling look. "I'm fine," she said tartly. "Although I'd like to lie down. Don't warrior people with swords carry pain killers? *Klinoman* perhaps? My arm hurts."

"*Klin* will make you slack," Jack warned her. "Then you couldn't fight."

"I can't fight now!" she pointed out.

He nodded. "You could ask Princess Alivda if she has some."

"I'll suffer," Sam said grumpily.

Alivda came back looking pleased with herself. "Luthan will see us inside, when she arrives," she said, and added, "after you clean up."

Things happened quickly then. One of Luthan's forerunners took charge of Jack, and another escorted Sam and Alivda into the orphanage. The foyer, just inside the plain doors on the outside, was surprisingly nice. Whoever had designed it had an artistic eye for line and color, even if the materials used were cheap. Everything was painted a rich yellow-gold with an equal weight of trim and decoration done in Silver. The ornamentation suggested a rippling flow of water populated with playing, childish figures. Beyond the entrance, Sam saw hallways decorated in murals done by people with varying degrees of talent and in various stages of decay, many of them marked up or defaced. One mural was in the process of being painted over by a child equipped with a smock, a roller and a tray of yellow paint. Apart from the murals, the hallways were bleak with uncomfortably repetitious rows of glow-plastic lights overhead and rows of identical doors down either side. The place was two stories high and big enough to house three hundred rooms, at Sam's rough estimate, depending on how much of the space was taken up with shared facilities like the infirmary, where they were being taken.

At the infirmary, Sam's escort marched them past a room full of bedraggled people into a clinic where a slight, dark-haired woman with bird-sharp features and signs of commoner-style aging on her intense face, looked up from probing a festering wound in a child's calf to scowl at them.

"This prince has a cut that needs cleaning before we present him to Her Highness, Princess Luthan," said the forerunner, indicating Sam with a polite gesture.

"Mira! You're Mira, right!" Alivda exploded excitedly as she barged forward.

Mira straightened her back with a pained expression. "And you would be Diff," she guessed.

Alivda's pleasure turned hard. "Only Amel calls me Diff. No one else. And especially not a commoner, whether or not she's his so-called sister!"

"Of course," the weary-looking commoner said blandly. She put down the instrument in her hand, ignoring the patient on her examination table for the moment, and waved Sam over. "Let me see."

Sam obeyed with trepidation.

"You seamed this?" Mira asked after a brief inspection.

"Yes."

"Mm." Mira packed aloof disapproval into the syllable but did not explain herself. She called over an adolescent girl in the orphanage uniform of soft yellow pants and shirt with silver cuffs, lapels and hems. "Clean Prince...?"

"Samdan," Sam supplied.

"...Prince Samdan's wound and bind it for him."

"Do you have something for pain!" Sam asked in a panic, as Mira began to turn away.

The diminutive medic turned slowly back again. "Of course," she said, adding to her assistant, "give him a bottle of the Sevolite-safe analgesics and charge him for them."

The girl gestured to Sam. "This way, Your Highness."

"Shouldn't you look after highborns yourself?" Alivda challenged, with an edge to her manner that Sam didn't quite understand, given how excited she'd been about seeing Mira. "Aren't you the Sevolite expert?"

"A clean cut on a healthy arm hardly requires an expert's intervention," Mira told her.

Alivda looked at the child with the festering leg wound who lay waiting on Mira's examination table, as if involuntarily attracted to the proof of the child's greater need, although her lip wore a disgusted sneer.

"One of Prince Monitum's messengers informed me of the medical emergency on the Plaza," said Mira. "Tell Amel I am sorry I wasn't there. But I cannot be two places at once, and I am working for Prince Monitum as a forensic expert. This," she gestured to the child on the examination table, "is related. Prince Monitum recently liberated a whole den full of children in a section of the Twilight district at the edges of the lighting along the Ava's Way. The children were being used for flesh probing customers. Needless to say some of them are in bad shape. Tell Amel I'm patching them up for his orphanage. And you can tell him, as well, that I've left it up to Mona—my daughter— whether she wants to live here or on Fountain Court. And no, before you ask, she is no more his daughter than you are. He took an interest, that's all. He views her as his niece for my sake and the sake of my mother, Em. He loved Em a great deal." She sighed. "His memories of the past are always fresh. He lives them still."

Mira turned back to her work.

"I'm not your messenger!" Alivda said after a short, troubled silence, hurling the full weight of Gelack's status-laden pronouns at Mira's slight, bent back.

"Then don't tell him," Mira said coldly, without looking up, casting the 'him' appropriately for a commoner speaking of a Pureblood.

The sense of submerged and mysterious emotions under-
lying the exchange between Mira and Alivda held Sam so
spellbound, she barely noticed the attendant working ever so
carefully on her arm, until the girl handed her a bottle of pills
with instructions on them and withdrew with a respectful bow.

"Let's go!" Alivda said gruffly, and herded Sam out.

"This way," said the forerunner. "We'll have a seamstress
fix the cut in your shirt, Prince Samdan. That should be adequate.
Or perhaps we can loan you a jacket to cover it."

Sam just nodded. Alivda's ill humor engaged her emotional
radar.

"You're angry with Mira!" Sam blurted.

"She doesn't care if she breaks Amel's heart by leaving him,"
Alivda snarled, putting emphasis into the *pol*-case 'she' for Mira.
"She doesn't think she owes him a thing for taking risks to treat
her like a sister all these years. He's always hoped and expected
they could live together again when he had the power to protect
her. Now he can and she would rather work down here as a
commoner, serving a different prince!"

"But why would you want her to live with Amel when you
are jealous of her?" Sam asked.

Alivda stopped cold. She let Luthan's man get just far enough
ahead not to overhear what she said; then she leaned in near
enough to Sam that Sam had to lean back. "You're lucky I'm
a sucker for a story," Alivda hissed out between teeth that would
barely part. "Like why you smell like a Demish woman—despite
the cologne and the pants. Because if you were really a prince,
or a Vrellish woman for that matter, I would knock your head
off for that remark!"

I'm right, then, Sam thought with a gulp. She couldn't take
her eyes off Alivda's. It felt like being transfixed by two thin,
diamond javelins. All she could do was nod.

"And don't go sharing your opinions about me," Alivda
threatened. "Or you're dead. Nobody will blame me—not with
you carrying a sword. All I'll need are witnesses to vouch I killed
you fair and square!"

Sam's throat was completely dry. She nodded again, and tried
to swallow to make saliva flow. It wasn't until Alivda left that
she started to feel like herself again. The painkillers and a chance
to freshen up helped, too. By the time she, Alivda and Jack were
reunited in a pretty Silver Demish reception room in Luthan's
apartments on the second floor, Sam could cope with being near
Alivda once more. But she remained subdued.

Jack was clearly impressed by the room, but nervous about meeting Princess Luthan Dem H'Us. He kept licking his hand to slick his hair down. After the third time, Sam couldn't stand it anymore and snapped at him to stop. Why he should imagine hair held down in that fashion was preferable to hair sticking up was beyond her!

Alivda paced like a caged predator.

Finally the door was opened by a servant and Luthan was escorted in, flanked by two armed, highborn errants of her personal guard. Both were men, so naturally both of them immediately noticed Alivda, and kept noticing her, much to Sam's disgust.

Luthan was a whole other dimension of challenge to Sam's womanly pride. She was young, just sixteen, and the daughter of an important El Princess of the Inner Circle, which made her a potential candidate—at least in theory—to be a Golden Soul. And she certainly looked divine to Sam as she entered the little parlor in the midst of her entourage. Princess Luthan was wearing something casual by court standards, since she was out and about to do charitable work among commoners, but her costume was richer and more detailed in its embroidery than any Sam had ever owned. And her face was as clear and sweet as the icons of Amel passed around by the Children of Amel back on Clara's World. Except Luthan's beauty was entirely feminine, outclassing Sam in a new direction.

Alivda actually made an effort to be gracious. "Princess Luthan," she said. "I know you by reputation. Amel, who has been like a father to me since I was a toddler, has always spoken well of you."

Luthan raised both immaculate, bright yellow eyebrows. "Diff!" she exclaimed, in awe and shock, speaking in *rel*-peerage. "You're Diff! Aren't you! His baby dragon!"

"Only Amel calls her Diff!" Sam felt driven to clarify for Luthan's sake, seeing Alivda's jaw lock.

"I am Royalblood Alivda D'Ander D'Aur Barmi Lor'Vrel," Alivda introduced herself with her own, preferred string of credentials which lay claim to every ancestor who had held title to something worth ruling over. Then she grinned. "A bastard."

"I know who you are, of course, Royalbood Alivda," said Luthan, and proceeded to prove it in typically verbose Demish fashion. "You are the gift-child of Pureblood Ameron Lor'Vrel to his *cher'st* Highlord Ayrium, Liege Barmi, who is herself the gift-child of Prince D'Ander of Demora to your grandmother, the liege-killer, Perry D'Aur."

Luthan spoke to Alivda in *rel*-peerage, effortlessly mixing Demish and Vrellish preferences to favor the most polite interpretations such as through her choice of words like 'gift-child' over 'bastard.' She also followed Alivda's preference for the gender-free appellation of Royalblood to designate her birth rank, instead of the gendered, Demish preference for princess. In short, although Luthan's speech appeared to be nothing but a genealogical recitation, it conveyed her acceptance of the Vrellish aspects of her visitor's nature and firmly asserted their social equality despite the cultural disparities in behavior which separated Demish women from Vrellish ones. And she did it all without turning a hair or twitching an eyelid.

Luthan, Sam decided, was confident in her identity as a Silver Demish princess. She felt no shame at needing to rely on her male escort for assistance should Alivda attempt to intimidate her the way she had Sam, earlier. And Sam was jealous all over again.

Why do I always wind up in the middle? she despaired, looking from Luthan to Alivda and back again. *Neither one thing nor the other, and a failure at both as a consequence.*

The only sting in Luthan's address was her reference to Perry as 'liege killer.' And even that she rendered without flinching for fear of what it might provoke.

Fortunately, from Sam's point of view if no one else's, Alivda didn't seem to care.

"Nice to meet you," she told Luthan, with a bow. "But in fact I came here hoping to catch Amel apart from the flock of sycophants and opportunists bound to be sticking to him like feathers to honey in a windstorm now that he's been all but handed a hearth on Fountain Court. Court standing, *Okal Lumens* influence and eligible for marrying at last, with Ev'rel gone— it's a potent cocktail in the Demish scheme of things. Am I right?"

"And you, I suppose," Luthan answered her as smoothly as satin, "have come to court to save him from the opportunists who might take advantage of his good nature ahead of you?"

"I—" Alivda began, got the implied criticism seconds later than Sam had, and ended with a scowl. "Yes," she concluded, "if you like. But I have his best interests at heart. We've been looking out for each other, Amel and I, since I was two."

"From what I understand of your relationship," Luthan said coolly, "you have gotten him into more jams than you've gotten him out of again. You are also jealous of his lovers and his other friends."

"Nonsense!" Alivda declared with a quick, dismissive gesture. "My own grandmother is one of the lovers you refer to. Or was. They had a spat." Something about this appealed to her, making her grin.

Luthan was interested in this information. Sam could see her expression change when Alivda mentioned it. But she concealed it quickly, choosing to keep Alivda on the defensive. "Should I, then, dismiss as malicious rumor your alleged attempts to murder Ann of Rire?"

"Ann?" Alivda gave her clear, crisp laugh, and shrugged. "Well, Ann. That's another matter. But I was just a kid at the time. I swear she tried to kill me, too. Amel would never believe it, of course." She grinned. "He likes to think the best of both of us."

"How like him," said Luthan, in a curt tone. "So, if not to see me, why are you here?"

"To introduce Prince Samdan O'Pearl," Alivda said, with a bow in Sam's direction suitable for a Demish prince introducing another one, which was wrong in so many ways. "He's here to serve a term as your errant, but he got lost."

Thanks so much! Sam thought coldly at Alivda. *You brat!*

"Then I expect you haven't heard about the assassination attempt on Amel, on the Plaza, by a Demoran Purist?" Luthan remarked.

If she was out to test Alivda's feelings for Amel, she scored. The brash, Killing Reach warrior reacted as if someone had poured a bucket of ice water over her.

Although, of course, Sam told herself cynically, *it might be over nothing but her hopes of using him to rise to power.*

Sam herself suffered an inexplicable clenching in her chest until Luthan followed up with details.

"He's not hurt," Luthan assured them all. "But a nobleborn Luminary was stabbed protect—"

But Alivda had stopped listening. Without so much as a civil goodbye, she clapped her hand to her sword to keep it steady and bolted from the room like a *rel*-fighter shot from a battlewheel.

Luthan's errants made way for her, and Luthan did no more than wait until the stir was over before proceeding calmly with the business at hand.

"Welcome to Gelion, Prince Samdan," she said. "How is your twin sister? I heard about the sad business of her marriage. Men are so fickle! You know, of course, that it was your support of Princess Samanda's 'Light for Enlightenment' initiative that inspired me to ask you to court. Making *rel*-batteries available to commoners so they could study at night to improve themselves is so appropriate a way for Sevolites to benefit deserving dependants although it was a bit extreme of Princess Samanda to take to flight leathers, herself, in her enthusiasm, and there was the unfortunate business of your off-world collaborator's motives. But on the whole I blame Prince Habeman D'Mark of Diamond Palace for jilting her in her darkest hour. A personal rejection of such magnitude was the last thing she needed— I'm sure—after the humiliation of discovering her charitable project was a cover for a marketeering operation. Please do tell me how your sister is holding up under the strain, Prince Samdan."

Sam could only hold her breath. Luthan's praise for the scheme that had ruined her life was too hard to bear. "My sister," she stammered, when the silence grew awkward, "discovered a calling! She joined the Mountain Village Reverie to—to petition the Watching Dead to watch over Amel."

"Oh." Luthan said, startled. "I...hadn't realized the Messenger Cult of *Okal Lumens* had such a well-established hold in the remoter worlds."

"They don't call themselves servants of the Messenger on Clara's World," Sam said hurriedly, desperate to talk about anything except the details of her personal tragedy. "They call themselves Children of Amel, instead."

"How interesting," Luthan said, a little peevishly. She shifted her cloak at one shoulder. The cloak was woven of a delicate, translucent material, rich in complex braid. She gestured to one of her servants. "Prince Samdan O'Pearl will take Mona back to Amel for me. Give him Mira's letter and explain it to him."

"I'll need a signet of passage!" Sam was forced to admit, adding shame-faced, "I...left mine at home. By mistake."

"Well," Luthan said forgivingly, "it is your first time at court. I suspect things are rather less formal on Clara's World. I suppose we can provide you with a second one until the first can be recovered. But signets are valuable things, and I don't like the idea of leaving one in a household so recently duped by a con artist. Write a letter to your family, explaining, and I'll send an envoy to deliver it and fetch the signet back again. You must excuse me now, Prince Samdan. I came here to retire, privately, to recover from the shock of the assassination attempt against my good friend, Amel."

"Of course!" said Sam, fully aware of the authority of a Demish lady's protestations of emotional fatigue. She had used the ploy more than once to get out of a dreary situation and, given the gravity of the stimulus in this case, Luthan could well be telling the truth. She had a queasy feeling, herself, about the news of the assassination attempt against Amel, merging in her mind with the killing she had witnessed just outside the orphanage.

What a desperate life I am leading, Sam thought sadly. *What would mother think! And all my friends and family!*

"I am glad to hear His Immortality Amel survived unscathed," Sam said formally. "What is the empire coming to?"

"At least the assassin confined himself to an edged weapon," said Luthan. "Although, of course, that may have been no more than necessity given the trend toward increased security at all gates, following the Nersallian example. Court has been more and more suspitious about illegal weapons ever since the incident at Den Eva's where Liege Vrel was attacked with a flame thrower."

"Terrible business," Sam agreed, conversationally. "And how fortunate, given events on the Plaza, that Prince Amel is no less resilient than the liege of Vrel. Those who think he is a Soul of Light will be hard pressed to explain him surviving with body and soul intact, with one man stabbed defending him and the assailant a purist of *Okal Lumens*. A real Soul of Light would have died of shock."

"You are not, then, of your sister's persuasion concerning the divinity of Amel's soul?" Luthan asked.

"I was, once," said Sam. "But it all seemed less important, somehow, in the wake of the turmoil at home. And then I met him here, crossing the highborn docks, and he didn't exactly have the manners of a divine soul. I found him rude."

"If you inspired Amel to be discourteous, you are a man of rare talents," Luthan replied. "Prince Amel is a kind man, and a good friend. There have been times when I consider him my best friend, in fact. And I have long admired his good nature. But I do not consider him a Soul of Light. The whole idea seems...excessive. I mean, a Soul of Light is goodness incarnate.

A beacon. A treasure to inspire paladins to improve the world. Amel is—well, just Amel." She ended with a flustered laugh. "But such things will not be mine or yours to decide. Good cycle to you, Prince O'Pearl."

"Good cycle, Princess Luthan," said Sam, and remembered to bow her out of the room as a well-bred man should, but only when prompted by a glare from the herald.

Luthan's withdrawal removed the sense of occasion sustaining Sam and she looked longingly toward one of the plump, upholstered chairs so temptingly familiar and close at hand. But her travails of the day had only just begun.

"I am Jonnah," one of Luthan's servants introduced himself immediately, "herald, second class. I will brief you on your task."

First, he gave her a temporary signet of passage; then he made her sit down to write the letter home requesting the original signet. Sam feared her mother would recognize her hand writing. In the end, she convinced Herald Jonnah to let her dictate it out of consideration for her injured arm which was, indeed, painful.

Once the business concerning the signet was done, Jonnah presented her with a letter and a girl named Mona.

"This letter is from Mira," explained her tormentor. "It is for Prince Amel, explaining the medtech's decision to work here and her daughter Mona's decision to live with Prince Amel. Luthan met briefly with the medtech while you were being readied to receive her, although the wretched woman would not stop working on her urchins. Do convey to His Immortality Amel the personal sacrifice inherent in Her Highness subjecting herself to the sight of festering sores on small children."

Sam barely grasped the gist of all that the herald said. Instead, she stared at the child who met her eyes with a resolute look of sad determination.

Mona was about eight. A scrap of a thing dressed in plain clothes and a commoner's traveling cloak, with short black hair styled to frame her face. But her sense of self-possession put Sam to shame.

A commoner raised in the heartless city of UnderGelion, Sam thought. *And yet she has some faith to sustain her. I can see it in her eyes.*

"Do you understand, Prince Samdan?" asked the herald.

"Of course!" Sam sang out gamely, but she thought, with a touch of desperation, *Understand what?*

"On your way, then," said the herald, and followed up with some curt directions to Jack on whom to speak to on his master's behalf about arrangements when they had discharged their business and retired to Silver Hearth.

Then the herald and the rest of Luthan's people left them alone.

A long moment passed in silence as Jack waited for Sam to head off. Mona stood where she was, watching them both. Finally Jack cleared his throat.

"Shall we get started then, Your Highness?" he asked Sam.

"Alone?" she said, a bit shrilly. Her arm hurt. And being among Luthan's entourage for a short while had made her feel the warmth, once more, of civilized society. She wasn't quite prepared to give it up. "Surely," she said, "we'll be given an armed escort!"

Mona looked at Jack. Jack gave her a sheepish grin, excused himself and sidled up to Sam to whisper, "You are the escort, *Prince* Samdan," with a sidelong glance at Sam's sheathed sword.

"Oh," she said, feeling tired already, and more than a little scared. "Right."

Mona shouldered the bag of personal effects she had brought with her, walked up to Sam, executed a serviceable bow and looked straight up at her with eyes much too wise for a child. "Please, Your Highness," she said, in a steady voice laced with both longing and loss. "Take me to Amel on Fountain Court."

CHAPTER 6

Going Home

Blue Hearth

The errants guarding Lilac Pavilion came to attention as people bore down on their position in a tight knot surrounding Brother Ron's stretcher.

Amel pulled ahead with a bound. "Let them through to the med lab!" he ordered.

At the entrance the knot of bodies separated into those who followed Brother Ron inside, and those who stayed to hover protectively about Amel.

"It is good to have you back, my liege!" exclaimed one of the Dem'Vrellish errants.

The expectations bound up in the two, small words—my liege—bounced around Amel's head, amplified by the anxious looks on the men's faces. *They are nervous,* he realized. *Stranded here at court, without Ev'rel to keep them from each other's throats while they worry about their headless clans back home. The official D'Therd is a girl, on Demora, and D'Lekker is a little boy.*

For now, Amel confined his reaction to a nod as he went past his hearth errants and down the stairs, followed closely by his uninvited entourage.

Ev'rel's dignified old herald met them in the stately reception hall and gave a bow.

No, Amel thought, *not Ev'rel's herald. Mine.*

But he couldn't help being assailed by memories of Ev'rel as he looked around. He focused on *The Hundred Year Feast,* a large painting of ghostly figures seated around a table by a misty lake. The painting illustrated the story of two Golden Souls hosting a ghostly banquet convened to instruct a cast of Demish princes who had failed, in life, to unite under Golden leadership in common cause against a Vrellish foe. Amel remembered asking Ev'rel why she liked the painting when she had no use for Luminary moralizing.

For the irony, Ev'rel had said. *Because the Demish may remember—but they will never learn.*

Iarous returned to the reception room flanked by the Luminary abbess, Margaret, who was crying.

"The man who saved you on the Plaza," Iarous said. "I'm sorry, but he's dead."

Mira could have saved him, thought Amel. He looked at his Dem'Vrellish retainers. They had separated, like oil and water, into Lekkers and Therds. He thought about Brother Ron and Perry D'Aur. He looked at the picture on the wall again and thought about the Golden Souls of the hundred year feast, lecturing the spirits of proud princes not to squabble among themselves.

"I will not be Liege Dem'Vrel," he said slowly, like someone in a trance. He reached for an echo of the distant past, cleaner and stronger than the stewardship of recent occupants. He hoped Brother Ron could hear him if he'd settled in among the Watching Dead.

"I will be Liege Dem of the Blue Demish," Amel declared, "and this will be Blue Hearth again." He looked around him with a profound sense of how furious Ameron would be with him for this move, and was amazed to find he didn't care. "Therd and Lekker will be welcome in my oath as houses of Blue Dem."

Gasps went up from all eighteen Dem'Vrellish Sevolites assembled to welcome him.

"There will be some staffing changes, too," Amel flung out, high on the power to ride roughshod over people who had made his life uncomfortable under Ev'rel's rule. "I will give Herald Ryan the list. And Lerl is my new captain of errants." Lerl was a young nobleborn from the Lekker clan with much less experience than others present, but Amel trusted him and that was what mattered.

The senior Therd errant, D'Tan, who had been acting in the role of captain during Amel's absence from court, gave a start as if stung. He had been one of Kandrol's men, which put him at the top of Amel's list for dismissal even though he feared it would be taken as a sign of anti-Therd prejudice on his part. It might have been smart to appoint another Therd instead of Lerl Lekker, but it was too late to change his mind.

The dismissed man didn't wait to be asked to leave. He shouldered past his fellow errants with a reproachful glare and headed up the spiral stairs.

Good riddance! thought Amel. He was starting to see the up side of being in power.

"Lerl!" Amel called to the young errant he had just promoted to captain of errants after less than a year at court, and frowned. He was curiously bothered by the name Lerl. "Do you mind," he asked the young Lekker, "if I call you Larri, instead? It's a variation on your name, in FarHome usage, and...well, Lerl just sounds too much like Lurol, the name of the Reetion who was so eager to get back into my head while I was on Rire."

"Captain Larri Lekker is fine with me!" the young nobleborn exclaimed, still wide-eyed over his sudden good fortune.

Amel smiled sheepishly. But he didn't want to be reminded of Lurol every time he called for his captain of errants.

"Thanks," he said. "I will give Ryan my list of who stays and who goes. You and your errantry will help him manage the turnover. Those dismissed must be found work outside my hearth on Gelion if they are commoner, or provided with passage home if they are Sevolite. Give them honest references. Any questions?"

"No, Prince Amel," the newly renamed Larri Lekker answered excitedly.

"And one more last thing," Amel said. "I want all the new hires to be women. The only additional men I'll accept into the hearth will be their children and husbands if they've got them. Blue Hearth will harbor families from now on."

A couple of the men in the group perked up at this announcement, but the slightest head shake from Herald Ryan prevented them from voicing whatever hopes the new rules about family members had inspired.

Ameron's people looked thunderstruck.

"What are you still doing here?" Amel asked, remembering Ameron's curt words in the Blackwood Room.

Iarous answered for them. "I am here to offer you my services on Ameron's behalf," she announced. "Since you don't have a *gorarelpul* of your own to help you."

"So you can spy on me for Ameron?" Amel snapped, and immediately regretted being the cause of Iarous's hurt expression. The willowy *gorarelpul* was almost a friend.

"Forgive me, Iarous," Amel mended his manners but did not change his decision. "It is nothing personal. But I got enough of being watched, on Rire, to last me the rest of my life."

Iarous inclined her head. "Of course," she said. Then she gestured to the errants accompanying her and they filed out.

Amel stifled the urge to go after her and apologize. *I have every right to be master of my own hearth!* he thought. *And Ameron is not going to punish her for being sent home.*

Herald Ryan touched Amel's arm, and Amel turned to the sober old man who had never been anything but decent to him, even at the worst of times.

"If you are going to thin the household ranks," said the herald, "it is best done immediately. For morale's sake."

"Of course," Amel agreed. "Wait for me in the visiting lounge."

Ryan bowed and withdrew into the first room of the Throat.

Amel went to where the Luminary abbess, Margaret, stood with her head bowed. She seemed to sense his approach. When she looked up, their eyes met with a jolt of recognition for the grief they shared over Brother Ron. It felt natural to take her in his arms and she relaxed against him with a heartfelt sigh as her arms went around his back.

"Oh Amel, Amel! You must come home!" she breathed against his chest, as if they had known each other all their lives, although her choice of pronoun still proclaimed him a Soul of Light.

"To Demora, you mean?" he asked, speaking to the top of her hooded head, and squeezed her lightly before moving them apart. She had a remarkable face with a broad, intelligent forehead and large blue eyes the color of the Demoran sky. He didn't know what to do with the devotion those eyes offered him.

"Lady Abbess," he said kindly, "I cannot visit Demora. Not yet. I am finding my way here at court, and I need to be careful what messages I send about alliances until I understand the situation better, but I promise I will learn more about your order. I must find a way to honor..." His voice broke over the choice of word. "To try to deserve Brother Ron's sacrifice."

She made to explain something urgently, but an instinct warned him it would be too long and involved to get into in front of the errants so he raised a palm to stop her.

"Later," he said. "I promise. Right now, you and your paladins must go back to Golden Hearth or wherever else you are staying on the Plaza," he added, remembering not all Demorans got along with each other any more than the Lekkers got along with the Therds. "There is somewhere you can stay?" he asked. "Where you'll be safe?"

"I have means," she said. "But, oh—" she cried, and stared at him out of oceanic depth of meaning that he could not decode. "There is so much you need to know!" She lay her palm on Amel's chest with an odd little shiver. "It will be hard to leave."

"We'll talk soon," he said, and left at once, wondering where he was going to put the families of servants in the limited confines of the hearth, even though this was the least of his problems.

Herald Ryan stood waiting for him, working on a palm-sized pad of nervecloth encased in a block of sub-arbitorial Reetion crystronics that Amel had given him, years before, after Ev'rel rejected the hybrid innovation with a flare of impatience for his tinkering. It was the first time Amel had seen him use anything but his trusty notebook.

"Ryan?" Amel said, concerned. "You don't have to use that if you prefer—"

"Oh, no," the old man said, with a more relaxed smile than Amel remembered seeing on his sober face in all the years he had lived here under Ev'rel. "I have been entertaining myself with this since you gave it to me, but your late mother might have made it a talking point if she saw me change my ways. It was best to be consistent with your mother, and not particularly knowledgable about things beyond my sphere. But I've always taken in your little, spontaneous lessons about hybrid technologies, My Liege." Ryan smiled.

Amel was taken aback by the discovery of a whole new side to the sober, careful herald. He always thought Ryan was indulging him when he let him prattle on about some gadget or other he was taken with.

"Great," was all Amel managed to say. After an awkward pause, he delivered the list of personnel adjustments he had composed in his mind. Ryan used the touch-surface of the nervecloth pad to mark up and check the translation of the audio input into text.

"Use your judgment if you think I've made a mistake about anyone," Amel told his herald when he was done.

The older man pressed his lips together. "In fact," he said, "you may have already made an error, Immortality. By making Lerl...that is Larri Lekker, your captain of errants."

"Maybe," Amel said, in a guarded tone. "But only because I should have promoted another Therd. Sir Tanerd Therd, probably. He's capable, and more experienced." Amel heaved a troubled sigh. "I do have a Lekker prejudice, don't I?"

"Find another honor for Tanerd," Ryan advised.

Amel nodded and moved on to décor. "Sell off Ev'rel's collection of male statues. My brother Chad's effects should be sent to his daughter, Zind—including his collection of weapons! Get those off the walls in the Long Room and take some Blue Demish heirlooms out of storage, instead."

"Very good," said Ryan. "When would it be convenient to discuss invitations for your reception?"

Amel blinked at him. "My what?"

"The current lieges of the Avim's Oath are naturally eager to socialize with you before the Swearing," Ryan clarified with infinite patience.

"Oh," Amel said, coming down off the high he'd felt over reorganizing the household. "Won't that be difficult? I mean, with the change in staff."

"Staffing is one consideration, yes," said Ryan, and paused for Amel to arrive at the bigger one.

"But...Ameron's called the Swearing for two weeks from now, which doesn't leave us much time to campaign," Amel obliged him, like a good pupil.

"Perhaps Princess Luthan might help us with the loan of some temporary staff," Ryan suggested. "She has been very helpful during your absence from court. With her assistance I am sure we could arrange to host your initial reception here tomorrow night."

"So soon!" Amel exclaimed. He wanted time to mourn the losses he was racking up in his personal life: Perry, Erien, Mira and although he barely knew him, the unsettling death of Brother Ron.

"If the Council of Privilege concerning the Dragon-Lion Accord was not scheduled for tomorrow," said Ryan, "I would recommend holding your reception even sooner."

"Do what you think best," Amel conceded, making a circular gesture with his left hand. "As to seeing people individually, I'll just have to—"

He was interrupted by a ruckus from the direction of the pavilion at the top of the spiral stairs where errants stood guard against unwanted intruders, operating under the dictates of Sword Law.

"Highborn!" Larri's voice called down the stairs on a rising note of panic.

Tanerd Therd might have coped better, Amel noted. He also realized—with a sinking premonition of disaster—that he was the only highborn in residence after sending away Margaret and her paladins.

"Sword! I need a sword!" he heard himself saying in a voice as panicky as young Larri's. An errant thrust one into his hands and helped him strap it on quickly. Amel was horrified to find his hands were shaking. He took a deep breath, willing himself to be calm, and tore up the stairs to burst out of the newly renamed Blue Pavilion—still decorated in lilac motifs—to reinforce his nobleborn defenders.

The intruder was Zind Therd, flanked by Amel's disaffected errant, D'Tan.

Zind got straight to the point. "This," she said, pointing with her drawn sword, "is Lilac Hearth!"

"Why do you care, Zind?" Amel asked, holding his sword low. "It mattered to your father, I know, but the Knotted Strings is all you care about, and I can do more to help you there if you leave me a free hand here at court!"

Zind moved sideways, drawing Amel after her. "How?" she asked warily.

He raised his sword to the same level as hers, circling away from her. She was a *rel* sword. He was careful to maintain eye contact.

"It's too early to make specific promises," Amel told her.

"You could marry me," she said. "Or sire twenty highborns for us. I don't care which."

"Twenty!" Amel stopped circling and stood with his sword held across his body at chest height.

"The Knotted Strings need highborns," Zind told him unrepentantly.

"So..." he said, "ten for Therd and ten for Lekker?"

Zind made a rude noise.

"Thought not," Amel remarked and went back *en garde.* "Zind," he appealed to reason, "I need time to work out the details of any new deal with the Avim's Oath—the entire Avim's Oath."

Zind lunged. Amel fell back.

Instinct brought Amel's sword up in time to block a slash at his calf. He didn't think she wanted to kill him, but she might be quite happy to cripple him for a while. He moved sideways, away from her.

"What are you doing, Zind?" he asked.

"I want into Lilac Hearth," she told him. "To stay here, with you. To keep you from any more foolishness!"

"Ah!" He barely evaded her next attack. Sliding by him, her blade sliced through his flight leathers under his sword arm. The breath he snatched, in pain, stuck in his lungs.

She laughed. "Believe me," she told him. "I'm serious."

"So am I," said a deeper voice.

Amel wasn't sure if he was glad to see Vretla Vrel, or not.

Zind glared at Vretla, but she put down her sword. "We are not finished, Amel," she warned, jerked her head in D'Tan's direction and stomped off with the nobleborn retainer jogging after her.

"You have been avoiding me," Vretla told Amel, taking him by the arm.

"Temporarily," Amel assured her, slipping free. He still held his sword. His side stung. He could feel the wound starting to bleed, but he didn't feel weak—and Vretla wasn't giving him space to do more than back down the spiral stairs as she advanced. He was in no danger of tripping on anything unless the stairs had been cluttered with obstacles since he had last seen them. His memory for his immediate surroundings was effortless.

Vretla kept backing him down the Throat once they reached the floor of the reception room. He thought about making a break for it, but the look on her face and the sword in her hand made him doubt he had viable choices. He had no illusions about how long he'd last against Vretla. He kept his sword raised because it didn't feel like a good idea to lower it, but there was no way he was going to attack.

His nobleborn errants did nothing to intervene, either. One of them even ran ahead to open doors for them as they progressed down the Throat, with Amel walking backwards and Vretla going faster, room by room.

Do I know what I am doing? Amel thought, forcing down the rising panic in his gut.

"We're going to talk now, right?" he asked, halfway through the Long Room, lined with Chad D'Therd's collection of hand-to-hand weapons. Ryan had already got someone started on his orders, however, and he spotted a few blank spots on the walls. His side was hurting in earnest now.

"Sure," Vretla said, suddenly sheathing her sword without a break in her long stride. "When I've seamed your cut."

Gratefully, Amel threw his own sword onto the nearest couch and put a hand to where Zind's blade had sliced his flight leathers. It came away wet.

"Can't be very bad," Vretla remarked, "given the way you wince at splinters."

"I've got Family of Light nerve endings!" Amel protested, feeling riled. The cut wasn't bad but it did hurt, and her mockery made him angry.

"Bedroom," said Vretla, advancing relentlessly again. "We'll do it there."

"Vretla—" Amel scuttled backwards once more, and stumbled over a box of daggers. He hadn't forgotten it; it hadn't been there before Ryan starting taking down Chad's weapons.

Vretla pulled her seamer from her bright red vest.

"No!" Amel stopped. They were in Family Lounge, at the end of the Throat. Pictures of Ev'rel, Amel, his Dem'Vrellish half brothers, Chad and Lek, and their children—Zind, Princess Telly of Demora, Leksan and little Lars—lined one wall.

It's all about attitude, Amel told himself, thinking how Vretla would never have tried this with the late Chad D'Therd. *Don't act like someone she can bully, and she won't!*

"Oh come on!" Vretla insisted, brandishing her seamer. "Take your shirt and jacket off. It won't hurt for more than a second. Or did you want to stand there bleeding while we talk?"

"Talk?" he said warily.

"Of course! You will want something in return for giving me a child. Or two."

"One at a time or both at once?" Amel asked, feeling uncharitable.

Vretla just shrugged. "Whatever you feel up to, I suppose."

Amel couldn't help himself. He laughed.

"That's better!" she said, and waggled the seamer at him. "Get your clothes off and come lie down so I can stop the bleeding for you. This couch will do."

Amel pulled his flight jacket off and stopped, leaving the bloodied shirt beneath it stuck to his side where he'd been nicked by Zind's sword. The pain nagged. He told himself the wound was insignificant but the pain didn't care. It made him cross.

"Listen, Vretla," he said, and tossed the flight jacket onto a nearby chair. "I'm tired. I'll get an errant to fix the cut. Take a bath. Rest. And then we'll talk."

He did feel tired all at once. He was thinking about Perry. They would see each other again as liege and vassal, but it would never be like it was. She had made herself plain about the nature of their personal relationship. She didn't need a lover, not even one content to stand second or third in her affections. Or else she couldn't cope with his intensity. Was that also Mira's excuse, he wondered. But suddenly, the reasons didn't matter. It was over. Something powerful inside of him had gone dead.

Vretla advanced on him impatiently.

"Take off the—" she began to say, and stopped in surprise when he clamped a hand, with Pureblood strength, about her wrist.

"Vretla," he said firmly, "I've only just got back; been rejected by Erien; had someone try to kill me and another man die to stop him; disenfranchised the Dem'Vrellish in favor of a scattered bunch of Blue Demish nobleborns; and been attacked by my niece, Zind Therd." He paused for her to catch up. "I'm tired!"

"That reminds me." She drew back her other hand and punched him in the face, to his complete astonishment.

Amel reeled into the couch behind him, jaw hurting worse than the nick on his side that was busy ruining his shirt.

He shook off the shock and pushed himself up on his elbows, face coming up red with the impact. "What was that for!" he exclaimed at her, furious.

"Crossing swords with Zind before you've sired a child for me!" she yelled back. "You need a champion and I need an heir. Why are we wasting time?"

"Because I need to think about it!" Amel shouted.

"Good!" she said. "Then you've no real objection!"

She pounced with the spring of a big cat. He managed to grab her wrists, knowing that his strength served him best so long as he kept hold of her.

"You," she said between clenched teeth, wrestling with him awkwardly over the couch, "are the only one who has ever gotten me pregnant. I lost that child! I've been waiting a generation for the next one! And I'm not taking the risk of Zind or some even more Demish man-hoarder laying claim to you before I get what I need!"

"Ow!" Amel cried, as their tussle put her elbow into the cut on his side. Pain ignited his resentment over the undignified situation. He got a grip, and some leverage, and heaved Vretla clear of him.

She was up again before he'd pulled himself into a sitting position.

"If you want to fight," said Vretla, grinning at him, "fine!"

"Oh, no, Vretla, I—" Amel began to demur. But it was too late. She landed on him like a missile, winding him, hurting him and knocking him onto his back beneath her.

It's Vretla, Amel told himself. *Go still, make eye contact, get her to talk to me.* But his emotions were too churned up to rein in. He was being pushed around again, and he was sick of it!

Vretla's thighs clamped around his hips, pinning him, but she needed her hands to work on getting them both undressed. He twisted and punched her in the head. She rocked back with an excited yell. His hand hurt but he didn't care. He was nearly on his feet when she hit back, with a better instinct for rough-housing than he had and no less power. At least, if being Pure-blood to her Royalblood conferred an advantage in strength, it was far from evident to him. Amel tasted blood, and saw red.

He attacked her.

"Hah!" she cried, entertained, as she blocked his punch.

He shoulder-checked her into a side table. But she was less distracted by pain than he was and in seconds he was down on the floor again. She caught his wrists, obliging him to wrestle with her. Teeth gritted with the effort of resisting her, he felt her breath against his face and an answering rush of sexual anticipation zinged down his spine. He was furious with himself for the powerful feelings—so divorced from love. Fighting seemed to be a form of Vrellish foreplay his body understood despite his wishes. For a moment, he felt hopeless, even stupid. If she had noticed and changed tactics, become gentle, he might have yielded. Instead, her excitement got the better of her.

"If you want to be difficult—" Vretla ground out between her teeth, intoxicated by her feelings, "-I don't really need your cooperation!"

The threat lodged like a stone in Amel's gut. He was Vrellish enough, sexually, that she was probably right. He'd lost fights before with women as Vrellish as Vretla. But those were bad memories. Vretla was his friend! And he needed to believe in friends.

She was feverish with frustrated desire. She gave a cry like a wounded animal and heaved him up to smash him down again.

His head pounded. His side hurt. Blood mingled with the passionate bite of her kiss. Emotions washed over him like opposing tides.

Then Vretla was suddenly gone.

Amel sat up, wincing at the pain in his head, and saw Alivda watching Vretla scramble up off the floor. Both women looked murderously angry and Alivda had her hand on her sword. The thought of the two of them fighting flooded Amel with horror.

"No!" he cried, and scrambled up despite the pain plaguing him. He was shaking all over, head expanding and contracting in angry throbs, but he claimed their attention.

"No fighting!" Amel ordered. He turned his attention to Vretla. "Get out," he said as firmly as he knew how.

Her jaw locked. She looked furious but also troubled. Half of him wanted to tell her it was all right but it wasn't. He never wanted to be bullied again, by anyone.

Vretla blew air from her lungs, squared her shoulders and left without taking time to do more than snatch up her sword where she had deposited it earlier.

Alivda rushed to Amel's side as soon as the door was closed.

"You're hurt!" she cried. A quick check, and a wince from Amel, satisfied her that the cut was trivial. But she still said grimly, "Did Vretla do this? I'll kill her!"

"No!" He caught her hand and made her sit beside him. His head still hurt, but not too much. He considered explaining about the not-quite-duel with Zind, but decided against it. Instead he caught Alivda in his arms to hug her. "Good to see you," he whispered.

"When I heard someone tried to assassinate you, I felt ill," Alivda confessed. She drew back to look at him, her eyes laughing at her own distress. "Dumb, huh?"

"Absolutely!" Amel jerked clear, tore off his blood-soiled shirt, wadded it up and pitched it into the couch. "Why should anyone care about me?" he asked bitterly.

Alivda put her hands on her sleek hips and frowned at him. "Having a bad day, are we?"

"Diff!" he warned. "Don't patronize me!"

She raised both eyebrows. "And you can say that when you're the one calling me by a baby name!"

He sighed. "Do you want me to call you Alivda now you are grown up?"

She thought about it. "No. I like being Diff to you." She pivoted about to deposit herself on a couch, sword expertly managed and a leg dangling over an upholstered arm. "But anyone else who tries it will get dead."

"Bit extreme," he said.

She sat up straight on the cushions. "It's time for extreme measures!" Her eyes narrowed. "Ameron and Perry have no opportunities to offer, just warnings to 'wait' and 'be good.'" She folded her arms across the chest of her stylish flight leathers. "They can drop dead for all I care. I am claiming my own place in the world." She softened with a grin. "Beside you."

Just what I need! Amel despaired. But he couldn't bring himself to discourage her. She had always been trouble looking for a place to happen, but she had great potential as well, and she had a point about Perry and Ameron: neither her grandmother nor her sire had the temperament to teach her. Ameron found her alarming; Perry had resorted to locking her in a cage when Alivda was a toddler.

"I am going to be your champion!" declared Alivda. Then she spun on her heels and left.

"Wait!" Amel took a step after her, but Alivda was already out of earshot. He could run after her, but all his hurts raised a cacophony of objections, so he sat down on the couch to catch his breath. His head hurt and the nick on his side was bleeding sluggishly.

A servant came in and gasped at the sight of him sitting there, bare-chested and blood-smeared, feet planted well apart, hands dangling over his shins and his head down.

Amel got to his feet, surprised to hear a woman's voice in Blue Hearth. She was wearing a veil across her face, which was equally odd, but he recognized the wide, blue eyes. And there was no way she belonged in the clothes of a commoner.

"Lady Margaret," he said with a long-suffering sigh.

"I'm sorry, Immortality!" she exclaimed, rushing to his side. "But I must speak with you at once! About the succession on Demora. Oh, but you are hurt!" she interrupted herself with an edge of horror in her mounting distress. "Let me help!"

Helping might have been her intention, but she looked more apt to faint at the sight of Amel's injuries. He caught her under the elbow as she stumbled forward and lowered her to the couch.

She looked up at him where he knelt at her side. "Please!" she cried. "I must be near you!" Her eyes filled up with tears. "You are my life."

Amel sighed. "I don't want to find out how you will try to get in the next time," he said. "So maybe you are right. I can use the help of your paladins, as well, if only to convince Diff

I can be left alone from time to time." He stroked a lock of yellow hair from her forehead. "Are you and your order all right with my declaring myself liege of Blue Dem?"

"Political titles are irrelevant," she told him, staring into his face with a blissful look. "Soul of Light," she murmured.

"I...respect your beliefs," Amel managed, covering her hand with his own and thinking about Brother Ron. "Please respect my hesitance to share them. It would be such a huge responsibility and feel—well, pretentious."

She smiled as if he'd said the most beautiful thing imaginable, tears rising in her sky-bright eyes.

"I think I can get cleaned up myself," Amel said with a parting pat of her hand, and fled deeper down the Throat to Ev'rel's old room where he knew there was a bathroom and some first aid supplies.

He washed the cut in the shower. Afterwards, he got as far as holding a seamer over the sides of the open wound, but decided it wasn't necessary and put it down again, muttering, "I don't have to prove anything to anyone, including me."

A simple adhesive strip applied over a liquid sealant did the trick, plus a painkiller for his sore head. He dressed in soft lounging clothes and was getting ready to relax for what he felt was a well-deserved break from political pressures when he realized he was worried about getting out of sight of his sword, parked in a rack by the door.

Did Chad feel like this all the time? Amel wondered. *Never completely able to relax, knowing he might be called on at a moment's notice to defend the hearth?*

He felt better about the paladins moving in, then. And Diff. Although he worried about them at the same time. He was pretty sure Vretla wouldn't kill him, but was less sure how she'd feel about killing a Golden Demish man who tried to keep her out. And Alivda was still so young! A great fighter, of course. They had made it out of enough scrapes together in the last dozen years, for him to fully appreciate how Vrellish his baby dragon was inside. But he also remembered Di Mon saying how being young and Vrellish was a health hazard. And she was his friend Ayrium's daughter.

Amel walked over and lifted the borrowed sword out of its rack. *Tomorrow*, he thought, *I start lessons. I want to learn more about treating injured people, too.* Mira might still help him there if he could get up the courage to ask when she had chosen to

distance herself from him. He was just beginning to feel his way
around the edges of what might become of his relationship with
Mona, whose love was one of the few untarnished bright spots
in his life, when there was a sharp knock on the door.

"Pureblood Amel!" said the voice of Tanerd Therd, the errant
he probably should have appointed instead of Larri Lekker. Amel
noted Tanerd didn't call him 'my liege.'

"Yes?" Amel called back.

"You have a visitor," Tanerd said testily.

Amel was about to start strapping on the sword over his
lounging clothes when Tanerd added, "Sen Lekker."

"Sen!" Amel exclaimed, forgetting about the sword. Sen was
an old friend he hadn't seen in years, and the regent for House
Lekker's young heirs: seven-year-old Leksan and three-year-
old Lars. Amel hadn't seen his nephews since the death of their
father, although they had been very much at the center of his
and Erien's concern on Rire.

He burst out of Ev'rel's bedroom into Family Hall, where
Tanerd and another two errants were waiting for him. "Where
is she?" he demanded, looking around. "Where's Sen?"

"I asked her to wait," Tanerd said. "She has no business in
Family Hall."

"Go fetch her!" Amel said excitedly to the nearest Lekker
errant. "Bring her through!"

The man left with a grin and a willing nod.

"I don't want any interruptions!" Amel told the two remaining errants, eager to relax in the company of someone he could
trust and rely on. "Whoever arrives can wait. Give me an hour's
privacy!"

"With a Lekker?" Tanerd bristled. "When you've rejected Zind
D'Therd!"

"When Zind is ready to talk instead of fight I'll see her, too!"
Amel said in a voice strident enough to impress himself.

The Therd-clan errant blinked with surprise. "Yes, My Liege,"
he said begrudgingly.

I could take him! Amel thought and wondered why he should
consider it reassuring. Tanerd was, after all, his own errant.

He couldn't wait for Sen to come to him, and went to meet
her. He found her in the last room of Throat, on her way through
to Family Hall. She separated from her errant escort and came
to a sharp halt. As a nobleborn, she was not immune to wear
and time, but she still looked just the same, to him, as she had
the last time he'd seen her on Demora, years before.

"Amel," she said, suddenly breathless, and gave him her frank smile. "It has been too long."

"It has." He came forward to take her by the hands. "That will be all," he added to his errants.

Sen cast a sharp look in the direction of the door Tanerd had left by. "I was pleased to hear you put a Lekker in charge."

"And probably shouldn't have," Amel admitted, pulling her along. "It may have sent the wrong message. I never was partisan, you know, except where some wrong was at fault."

"Exactly," Sen said, following without releasing his hand. "We Lekkers were inevitably the ones in need of help. But we'll repay you now!"

Amel ducked back into Ev'rel's old bedroom and immediately wished he hadn't. Alone, it had been fine. But with Sen around he couldn't help thinking about Ev'rel, and nothing in the bedroom had been changed since her death. He knew exactly which drawer contained the scarves Ev'rel used to bind his hands in their ritual mitigation of her need to dominate him during sex. Memories of worse things she'd done squeezed him in an embrace of fear, arousal and pain-mangled love. It felt exactly like a clear dream coming on, but Lurol's mental surgery on Rire had done its job. The room invoked no more than memories.

Sen was saying something about the Therds and Lekkers never being one house despite Ev'rel's efforts of the last thirty years, when Amel looked away and pressed a hand over his eyes.

"What's wrong?" she demanded and the firm grip of her dry, steady hand on his arm broke Ev'rel's spell.

Amel shook his head. His body ached but that wasn't the problem. His anger had abandoned him, and all his emotional compasses were broken, their jagged edges piercing his heart.

Sen took him in her arms without a word. He hugged her, feeling he was home again, finally, in the sense he used to feel at home when visiting Perry on Barmi, or returning from a long flight to steal precious hours with Mira and Mona before checking in on Fountain Court. Even Lilac Hearth had felt like home sometimes when things were good between him and Ev'rel.

"Gods, you feel good," she said in a low voice. She wore a knife mounted in a sheath across her chest. It felt hard between them. She was full of a tension he had not suspected moments earlier, reminding him of the years they had shared as co-conspirators, rescuing a Lekker from some malice on the part of a Therd. They both knew Ev'rel had sent Sen away to Demora when she found out just how much her tough, bastard lieutenant cared for her meddling son. Ev'rel made Sen's exile a promotion to acting as her official representative on Demora because, like everything Ev'rel did in the realm of politics, it made parsimonious use of assets and promoted multiple agendas. Putting a Lekker as prominent as Sen in charge of managing politics on Demora was a way of keeping an eye on D'Therd's dynastic plans for his Golden Demish daughter. It was also typical of Ev'rel's efforts to maintain a balance of power between the rival clans.

Looking into Sen's face now, Amel imagined how hard it must have been for her to bring the proud Demorans to heel when she, herself, was nothing but a bastard in their eyes. He doubted Chad Therd would have helped much, either.

Grains of guilt about abandoning Sen to her fate, accumulated over the years, became a landslide in her presence. "The reason I kept my distance—" Amel began.

Sen pressed two fingers to his lips with her usual decisiveness. "It's what you always did, I know. If a woman made Ev'rel jealous, you left her alone. Otherwise bad things might happen to her."

A struggling desire to cast the details in a better light caught Amel's breath in his chest and worked the muscles of his throat. But in the end he simply said "Yes" in a faint voice.

Desperate to cast off the shadow of Ev'rel's obsession with him, he gave a strained laugh. "It wasn't only women, you know! She sent Tagar Therd to the other side of the empire because he spent too much time trying to teach me how to fence like a real man!"

"Tagar was in love with you," Sen said, deadpan.

"What?" Amel choked, ambushed by the angry, violent response he couldn't fight down whenever the concept of men and sex collided in his head.

Sen laughed. "Oh yes," she said. "Tagar was as boy-*sla* as the sky is gray on FarHome! He got caught at it on the station he was posted to, and fled to Killing Reach. I often wondered if he looked you up there."

Amel was busy reevaluating a hundred details of his interactions with the rugged bear of a FarHome *relsha* who had been so patient about giving him fencing lessons in his spare time. "I think he's flying for the Purple Alliance these days," he said, recalling a cryptic remark Perry had made years before, that suddenly made sense, and wondering how he could have been so dense. *Do I just not let myself imagine the unthinkable and miss the signs?* he wondered, flushing over his whole body with embarrassment. In other ways he was infamous for reading people's feelings even when they tried to hide them.

"I'm glad Tagar made out all right," Sen continued to make small talk, avoiding the two huge issues confronting them. "He was a decent human being, for a Therd."

"How do you feel about me making this Blue Hearth again?" Amel asked, deciding to plunge straight into the first challenge.

Sen looked around her, hand on the belt of her long FarHome skirt. "We Lekkers were never as obsessed with gaining status in the empire as the Therds," she said. "We'll have to see how it works out."

"I'll make it work!" he promised her.

The second issue was sex. They had come close many times during his sojourns on FarHome. It was Amel who refused to give in. He saw nothing Sen could gain by it that was worth the risk. He couldn't child-gift to any of the Dem'Vrel because Ev'rel would have used the child to challenge Ayrium's right to the title of liege Barmi. Besides, he had long realized it would have to be a case of none or many in the highborn-hungry Knotted Strings. Even Ev'rel, who hated pregnancy, had been obliged to have two children: one in marriage to Chad Therd's father, and one child-gifted to the Lekkers, in the Vrellish manner. Sex without children was possible, of course, but it had simply chilled Amel too thoroughly to imagine what Ev'rel would have done if she found out. Amel hadn't wanted to expose Sen to the dark, disturbed side of Ev'rel's nature.

But now Ev'rel was dead.

And I'm liege, Amel thought recklessly. The problem about children and Barmi still existed, but he wasn't going to let any child of his threaten Ayrium's right to Barmi II while he was liege Dem.

I can sleep with whoever I like! he thought, suddenly giddy with a sensation of personal freedom he had not anticipated as a perk of holding power.

Sen was watching him as if she could hear him think. She was a competent, practical woman. The smell of FarHome heather in her rough spun clothes told him she had not come from Demora, and the heather reminded him of Mira, who had altered it genetically so it could thrive in FarHome's dreary climate. The heather's success had enriched FarHome's poor soil, but the resulting population growth—a combination of immigration from across the Knotted Strings and a generation of peace—soon overtook the gains, resulting in a growing reliance on what the Dem'Vrel called the 'groceries.'

Shipped out from Demora, the groceries arrived in a cavalcade of freight ships every two weeks. Making sure the Demorans sent them was Sen's job, and for more than a decade she had coaxed and coerced reluctant Demorans into feeding her home world despite knowing the lion's share would go to the rival Therds.

Amel raised his palm to her cheek, his fingers trembling ever so slightly against her skin. "Sen..." he said.

She closed her eyes, covered his hand with hers and pressed it firmly against her cheek where his touch had been tentative. When she opened her eyes again, frank desire stared out of them. "I have wanted you half my life," she told Amel.

Taking her in his arms was like tumbling off a cliff.

"I don't know what this means," he whispered to her, desperately.

She answered him as practically as always. "I don't care."

They undressed each other in silence. He began slowly, exploring the emotional barrier they had built to prevent exactly this from happening. It was easy to desire her, but what he really wanted was the harvest of complex emotions stored up behind that barrier: feelings of trust and belonging. Instead, he couldn't shake a feeling of wrongness, and an incipient disappointment he could not define.

Sen found her own joy without much encouragement from him and he pushed the clouds of worry aside, smiling down at her beneath him where they had wound up, tangled in the blankets of Ev'rel's bed.

"You are sure?" he asked again, flushed and ready, but prepared to stop if she felt the same uncertainty he did.

She only reached for him and said, "Yes!"

The lovemaking went fine. When it was over, and she lay with her head on his chest, he studied the blissful expression on her lined face and ached with a peculiar jealousy to know the emotion so clearly alive in her. He tried to tell himself it was just the shock of the assassination attempt and all the other excitement surrounding his return, but he felt broken inside. He thought about Ann, far away on Rire, already pregnant with his child but separated from him by their different spheres.

He tried to imagine what Ev'rel would have said about this escapade, open even to the acid of her rebuke for the sake of the connection he had felt with her. But there was nothing but silence from the Watching Dead.

Sen shifted against him and he stroked her hair, still bound in its simple tie. He felt he should want to release it, and brush it, but he only felt miserable. Sen had always been discreet, he told himself. Maybe there would be no repercussions if he told her this could never happen again. Then they could go on as if this hadn't happened. Provided she wasn't pregnant. He hadn't been taking *ferni* for months. It just hadn't seemed necessary.

If she is pregnant, he thought unhappily, *I will have to child-gift to the Therds at once!*

Outside, in Family Hall, a child's voice cried, "But he'll see me! I know he'll see me!"

Mona! Amel realized, with a painful pang of empathy for the hope and uncertainty he heard in the child's voice. He sprang out of bed, dressing as fast as humanly possible.

With a pang of guilt for his numb heart, he paused long enough to squeeze Sen's hand where she was sitting up in bed, watching him. "Dress!" he said with a smile, and fled.

"We need to talk about Demora!" Sen called after him, but it was too late.

"Mona!" Amel cried as soon as he was in the hall. He couldn't see her. His errants must be keeping her in Family Lounge at the root of the Throat. A vivid memory of Mona as a toddler came back to him: a starving two-year-old clinging to her mother's leg. Mira had despised needing Amel's help. It was Mona who had proved able to receive his love. Amel saw Mira's mother, Em, in Mona, and it made him love her all the more. He had provided her with a Reetion education through toys and educational programming obtained from Ann. Only now was he learning this might be a liability for a bright child raised on Gelion, because in Gelack terms his precious Mona was just another commoner.

Amel burst into Family Lounge, causing half a dozen people to start and shift in response. His clothes were on, but hastily, his feet bare and his hair a feathery mop.

Mona stood with her back to Prince Samdan O'Pearl. She was fiercely defending her certainty of Amel's love to seven-year-old Leksan, who was being held from behind by Larri Lekker. Tanerd was there, as well.

On seeing Amel, Mona broke free of the incompetent O'Pearl with a shriek of joy. Amel dropped on a knee to receive the eight-year-old with an audible thump. As his arms closed around her, inhaling her sweet childish smell, his heart proved it was not as numb as he had feared. He clung to Mona as if she were life itself, tears springing to his eyes.

Still locked in Mona's innocent, enraptured embrace, Amel saw Leksan's face and knew he had wounded his nephew with the exuberance of his welcome for his foster child.

"But she's just a commoner!" protested Leksan, the hurt of rejection all too plain in his voice.

Amel settled Mona in his left arm and opened his right towards his nephew of roughly the same years, but so different an education. For a terrible moment, Amel feared he'd be rejected because of Mona. Leksan wavered. But his need was too great. Like a dam breaking, his locked muscles flowed into action and Amel absorbed a second thump against his chest.

"Mommy said I had to choose where to live, between you and her," Mona wept, oblivious to sharing Amel with Leksan as she clung and cried.

How like Mira! Amel thought, with involuntary fondness and familiar irritation. *To treat her like an adult, fair and square, despite the fact she's just a child!*

"My home is yours," Amel whispered to Mona, kissing her short, dark hair.

"I never thought we'd get here safely when we were on the docks!" Leksan declared, drawing back sooner than the girl had, but just as eager to claim his right to be loved. He was quivering with impatience at the limitations imposed on him by childhood. "I saw that Lorel, Erien, who killed my father!" The boy's dark eyes flashed as his mouth turned down. "I have to live long enough to kill him in a duel to disprove the bad things people say!" On a less manly note, he concluded, "You are going to make sure me and Lars get to grow up, aren't you Uncle Amel?"

"As if the Therds would kill children!" Tanerd complained indignantly, from the sidelines.

Sen's voice answered. "You have before," she said.

Everyone's attention snapped onto her so crisply it couldn't be solely for the sake of the remark, which was standard fare between the Lekkers and the Therds. Amel rose to his feet smoothly, a hand on the back of either child to keep them in his embrace as he turned. What he saw was Sen Lekker looking pleasantly disheveled in nothing but one of Ev'rel's luxurious dressing gowns. She was also, unmistakably, smug.

Tanerd's nostrils flared as he exclaimed, "Gods!"

"Tanerd!" Amel began.

It was too late. Tanerd drew his sword and laid it on the floor.

"Wait!" Amel nudged both children in the direction of Samdan O'Pearl for safekeeping, unsure of how Sen might receive Mona. He had to dodge bodies in the crowded room to follow Tanerd out the door, trying not to hear Larri muttering "Good riddance!" at his back.

Tanerd would not stop so Amel darted ahead of him and turned around.

"It isn't as bad as you think," Amel said firmly, flushed with embarrassment. He raised an entreating, outstretched hand. "Go if you must, but tell Zind it's not political. Tell her—"

Tanerd cocked a fist and swung.

Amel ducked. He rotated clear of Tanerd's next assault, sinking low as he did, and sprang up to block the nobleborn errant in the chest with his forearm, making him topple back.

"Tell Zind I am her liege as well, and I wait to learn how I can prove it to her!" Amel told Tanerd while the winded man had no choice but to give him his attention.

The next moment Tanerd had his breath back, scrambled up and fled from Blue Hearth, no doubt going straight to Zind Therd with the news Amel was sleeping with Sen Lekker.

Sen came up behind him and said, "I must speak with you about the Demoran succession."

Amel rounded on her irritably but the seriousness in her face stayed his illhumor. "Lady Margaret of the Messenger Order said the same thing."

Sen nodded. "I came here with her and her people. Amel, there is a squabble taking place on Demora between the royal lines of Vesta and Ander. You need to make sure the Anders win, for the sake of the Knotted Strings."

CHAPTER 7

Council of Privilege

"Your escort is ready," Princess Barbanna told Luthan, ending with a measured bow.

Luthan waved away the dressers finishing up her appearance and faced down her handler with a torrent of anguish in her heart.

"I'd like to have the new errant, Prince Samdan, among them," declared Luthan. It would be nice to know at least one of her attendants might sympathize, even a little. Prince Samdan came from a large, rustic family in an unfashionable district of Clara's World. Luthan imagined he had probably run barefoot through his backyard and splashed naked in a local swimming hole as a boy. She fancied it might give her strength to meet his eyes and see ordinary, natural feeling looking back at her.

Barbanna was puzzled by the request, but she gave the requisite dip again as she said, "I will see to it, Golden One."

Luthan frowned at the Demoran honorific. She had not pegged Barbanna for a Luminary of any sort.

She has probably promised Prince Oleander she will address me as a Golden Soul in exchange for him attending some reception or other she's promised to have him appear at, Luthan decided. It was embarrassing how good, practical Silver Demish got so excited about having someone more exotic than themselves to show off at a ball, as if they could never quite believe that they, themselves, were interesting enough. *It comes, I suppose, of our passion for Golden literature,* she thought, with a guilty twinge for her own lifelong love affair with the Golden Age canon. *Erien would think it was all nonsense.*

The next thought to pop into her mind was the question that had kept her awake for hours the night before: *will Erien come?*

As Ameron's named heir, Erien had the right to attend any Council of Privilege and any normal prince of Sevildom would naturally attend one as important as the meeting to resettle the Dragon-Lion Accord. But she also knew Erien could behave atypically.

It doesn't matter whether he comes or not, of course, Luthan scolded herself for the indulgence of thinking about Erien at all. *The feelings I imagine I have for him are nothing but a girlish crush, inspired by reading his letters to Tatt. I suppose he seemed exotic to me, living on a world as strange as Rire, which makes me no better than Barbanna lusting after the novelty of having Oleander come to dinner.*

Viewed in this light, love did not threaten Luthan's sense of responsibility to her house. In fact, now that Erien had proved to be an unattainable superior Sevolite instead of a houseless Highlord, she considered a hopeless and sentimental attachment to him perfectly within the repertoire of behavior for a well-bred Demish princess, whether she was about to be married or not. One needed a dream to dwell on. But she knew where her duty lay, and her love of literature did not extend to emulating the irresponsible heroines encountered there.

Amel was the only person to whom she might have confessed a recurring daydream in which Erien claimed her in defiance of the Dragon-Lion Accord, overcoming her protests with the force of his wild Vrellish passion, and winning her in a hair-raising duel with Horth Nersal. It was a messy scenario, prone to make her giggle at the very thought, but Amel would have understood. She was a little annoyed with him for avoiding her since his return to court.

I suppose he has important, princely things to do, now he is a liege in his own right, Luthan thought. She wasn't sure yet how she felt about him restoring the ancient name of Blue Hearth to the residence court had known as Lilac Hearth during Ev'rel's reign. On the one hand, it seemed a little rash; but on the other, even though it had been Lilac Hearth all her life, her Demish sense of history had always insisted it was really Blue Hearth named something else.

"All is ready," Barbanna said, returning to stand and look expectant just inside the door.

"Wait!" cried Luthan, stricken by a stab of panic involving the superimposition of Dorn Nersal, or his replacement, over the diagrams in Erien's sex manual. She cast about her frantically for some excuse. "I want to see myself."

With a look of repressed irritation, Barbanna gestured for two of Luthan's dressers to set up her full-length mirror so she could take a look.

Luthan faced the mirror determined to be objective about what she saw.

"A frightened child in a very costly gown," was the first thing she thought.

Turning a little this way and that, she imagined Erien describing her in a letter home to his Reetion foster father, Ranar: *The Princess Luthan Dem H'Us wore a pearled cap indicative of her virgin status, matched by a full-length overskirt and bodice. Rather than separate her Silver and Golden markers of inheritance, the two were densely interwoven on her skirt and bodice without creating any harsh lines of separation, which is probably a political statement in itself, given the Silver Demish goal of unification with the Goldens through economic and dynastic conquests.*

"Not to rush Your Divine Highness," Barbanna interrupted, laying on more flattery reserved for Golden Souls. "But you will soon be late."

Luthan gave a guilty start. "Of course!" She smiled at the dressers to convey her thanks for their artistry, knowing they took pride in their work even if the business was an ordinary one for the princess-liege of Silver Hearth.

Walking behind Barbanna to where her escort waited at the foot of the spiral stairs in the center of Silver Hearth, Luthan wondered for the thousandth time if Erien had thought of her at all when he appointed Dorn Nersal as the ambassador to Rire. In soft-headed moments, she liked to imagine he had done it to clear the field for his own suit, but she had done more than watch plays and read romantic poetry all her life, and the hard-headed aspects of her education in Demish genealogy, social etiquette and the practicalities of running a courtly household had left her quite capable of distinguishing the difference between fancy and fact. Her uncle, S'Reese H'Us, the real liege of Silver Hearth, wanted to introduce the blood of Horth Nersal into the ruling line of H'Us, and therefore Luthan was destined to have children by one of Horth Nersal's many sons and, if anything, Erien had done her a disservice by removing Dorn, who was at least courtly and civilized. She had no idea what sort of Vrellish lout she might wind up with instead.

At least it will be a temporary marriage, Luthan told herself to help screw up her courage as she sailed out of her dressing room. Vrellish abhorrence of monogamy and Demish rejection of anything less for their princess had arrived at this compromise back when Dorn had still been the designated groom. Luthan had made her peace with the arrangement and with Dorn's established *mekan'st*, Amy Lor'Vrel—who had since left court to join her beloved in his role of ambassador to Rire.

I am glad for them, Luthan insisted to herself without conviction. The truth was, she was bitterly jealous of them both.

Holding up her stiffly embroidered skirt by the tastefully integrated grips provided for this very purpose, Luthan climbed the spiral stairs leading to the Plaza above Fountain Court.

An escort of six errants closed around her inside Silver Pavilion. Luthan recognized Prince Samdan and knew, at once, how disappointed the displaced errant would be.

Too bad, she thought imperiously, smiling at the young provincial who looked thoroughly unappreciative of the honor bestowed on him so soon after his arrival at court, especially when he had demonstrated an addle-brained nature by leaving his signet of passage behind at home. Prince Samdan looked wrong-footed and out of place among her guard, which made Luthan feel better somehow.

They set off trailed by a party of ladies who would go no further than the end of Demlara's Walk, which connected the Plaza with the inner court of the Palace Sector. The need to present a suitably stately demeanor to all who had turned out to watch her passage occupied Luthan's attention until they reached the great doors leading into the Council of Privilege chamber. At this point, her heart failed her. She caught her breath, blinked at the spots before her eyes, and was grateful for the strength of an errant's hand on her elbow, steadying her.

With a glance of thanks for the anonymous errant, she went forward to take the lead as they entered the council room.

Instantly, her uncle H'Us was at her side to guide her toward her place, facing Ameron. The Demish side of the table rose to greet her. Horth's annoying brother, Eler, rose as well; so did Amel but Alivda remained seated.

Meaning what, exactly? Luthan wondered, studying Alivda's Demish looks, alarming beauty, and mannish attire. Her Uncle H'Us said Ameron's second daughter by his great love, Ayrium, was excellent proof of the hazards of having children here and there without benefit of defined rights. People even said Alivda was the reason Ameron had decided against further rolls of the genetic dice, since she combined Vrellish impulsiveness with Golden beauty and Lorel ambitions. Certainly it was well known

Ameron did not want Alivda at court. But here she was, sitting at Amel's side as if she were his heir or champion.

What are you playing at, my dear, foolish friend? Luthan thought protectively at Amel. He returned her a look of frank concern for her, instead.

Vretla Vrel was too busy boring her hot stare into Amel to bother about Luthan's arrival. Tatt Monitum half rose, with a friendly nod in Luthan's direction, achieving a comfortable compromise between Demish and Vrellish manners with typical Monatese aplomb. Horth Nersal remained seated. So did Ameron, but that was because he was Ava.

Finally, despite her better judgment, Luthan allowed herself to notice Erien. He was seated with the Vrellish on the opposite side of the table from herself and her uncle. Luthan's first, endearing impression was to note how young he looked. He was only seventeen, after all, even if he was mostly Vrellish. His face looked unnaturally pale in contrast to his simple, black clothes. At first, Luthan thought he was going to bolt up and bow like the princes of the two Golden factions and their seconds, but he froze instead, staring at her hard enough to make her blood boil up warmly in her cheeks.

It's nothing, she scolded herself. *Just his usual intense, disconcertingly Lorel regard.* But she couldn't stop her heart racing faster and was grateful to be able to sit and grip the arms of her stately chair.

To calm herself she looked at Amel, and suffered an unexpected flash of jealously for how casually he upstaged her just by being there. Here she was, in the flower of her youth, decked out in weighty statements of her importance, on the brink of womanhood—and he was pure and simply more breathtaking, dressed in a simple Blue Demish costume with tastefully minimal braid decorating the vest, Blue Demish liege marks on the collar of the loose shirt underneath it and a sword at his side in a light sheath. It wasn't just the way he looked. It was the way he sat there, breathing quietly, relaxed and poised, taking in everything at once and radiating a warm sense of presence for the benefit of anyone susceptible, like some uncanny Lorel work of art.

Luthan was a decent person, proud of the orphanage she had organized for Amel when he came to her about it years earlier, and the help she gave Tatt in researching the rights of commoners, which had made her party to the letters from Erien; but she knew Amel better than most people did, and in that moment she felt a chagrined inadequacy at the thought of competing with him for recognition by the Goldens as a divine soul. She knew far better than Amel how to make use of any luminary designation Demoran politics might see fit to drape about her slender shoulders, and told herself it was not mere ambition. After all, if she were acknowledged as a Golden Soul she could use the leverage to squeeze more support for the orphanage and Tatt's ministry out of rich, complacent Silver Demish only mildly concerned about the state of their souls, but greatly interested in having a divine presence grace their dinner parties. Would it be so wrong if, in the midst of such good works, she enjoyed the exercise of greater power? She dared not look at Erien as she thought such things. She suspected he would find her ambitions petty in comparison with his own grand designs about liberating the empire from its backwardness concerning bio-sciences—a prospect that sometimes frightened her despite her admiration of his intellect.

Amel noticed her attention and responded with one of his gentle but penetrating stares that always made her feel as if the troubled emotions she strove to hide were parading, naked, before him. Even his compassion for her, etched in subtle detail on his matchless face, was nothing but more unbearable proof of his spiritual superiority.

Luthan looked to her touchstone among her escorts, instead, and found Prince Samdan was also watching Amel. Then Ameron gestured and Luthan's entire escort was obliged to withdraw.

"We all know why we are here," Ameron opened the proceedings.

Luthan caught her breath, and took in the whole room again in a visual gulp. Her uncle, Prince H'Us, had left her to make his way back to his place at the Ava's right side; the prince acting as his second was seated next to him along the Demish side of the table, followed by Amel and the controversial Princess Alivda. Next came two sets of Golden Demish: the abbess Margaret whom Luthan had heard about concerning yesterday's attempt on Amel, accompanied by a paladin of the Messenger order; and Prince Oleander and Princess Chandra of House Vesta. Evidently Ameron had wisely deferred the question of which party should represent Golden Hearth until Demora saw fit to decide itself. Horth Nersal sat on Ameron's left, followed by Eler Nersal. The rest of the Vrellish came after them: first Tatt Monitum, then Erien and Vretla Vrel. It was significant how

Ameron had placed his vassals—Horth and Tatt—closer than his own heir, who commanded no fleets and ruled no tax-paying worlds.

"My son and heir, Erien," Ameron continued, without glancing in Erien's direction, "found it necessary to appoint Dorn Nersal ambassador to Rire on my behalf, making Horth's first-born unavailable to fulfill the terms of the three-child contract between the H'Usian princess-liege, Luthan Dem H'Us—" Ameron raised his hand to hold off objections from Prince H'Us. "That is, of course," he added solemnly, "a three-child contract to be enacted as a marriage in all senses understood by Demish custom, saving duration, with said marriage to expire upon the birth of the third child."

H'Us subsided with an uncomfortable grunt, aware of the disapproving stares of the Goldens, and chaffing at their un-voiced criticism. Luthan made a point of avoiding eye contact with El Prince Oleander for fear he might be getting misty-eyed on her behalf. She didn't think she could bear Golden pity right now. She was doing her duty by the Dragon-Lion Accord as a proud Silver Demish princess, not a half-Golden sacrifice to the whims of unfeeling exploiters.

Why, she thought fiercely, *even Amel's grandmother, the so-called 'sacrifice' herself, had been perfectly happy to come to court.* In all honesty, however, she had to add with a silent gulp of anxiety, *At first.*

She fixed her attention on the room itself, noticing its dark wooden panels and the high ceiling painted with art from different eras. Some of them were in need of restoration. She wondered if they were ignored out of negligence, or for fear of damaging them in an attempt to brighten their faded colors.

How faded will I be after three children with a husband I do not love? she asked herself involuntarily.

It was hard to hear properly over the roaring in her ears.

"I will recall Dorn if necessary," said Ameron, pinning Erien with a sharp look for fear he might object before he finished, "but only as a last resort. House Nersal, do you have another candidate to offer?"

Horth nodded. But it was Eler Nersal who spoke.

"We do," he said.

Eler levered his big, wide-shouldered frame out of his chair with surprising grace and bowed with the upper half of his body in no style Luthan recognized, but definitely in her direction.

"Your Majesty," Eler addressed Ameron once he had gained his full height, sword at his hip, and the honors of his fleet exploits and rank as arm commander of three battlewheels boldly displayed on his chest. "Myself."

"Eler!" Amel blurted, starting to his feet, a closed fist set down firmly on the table. "He's a womanizing troublemaker, Prince H'Us!" Amel appealed to Luthan's uncle in what was, for him, a positive tirade of negativity. "He sleeps with every woman who will have him, from barmaids to Vrellish peers to naive Demish women it amuses him to ruin!"

"Whereas your reputation with women is spotless," Ameron told Amel, deadpan.

Amel went white. Eler looked triumphant. Vretla was tactless enough to guffaw and add, with her horrible Vrellish vulgarity, "I've had them both, and I'd pick Amel any day, even judging solely on sheer stamina."

Eler gave her a cool look, eyes half-lidded, "I was hung over," he remarked.

Amel went a delicate shade of pink to the roots of his jet hair and the tips of his shapely fingers, and sat down. Alivda made a consoling gesture by patting the back of his hand as she struggled to repress a smirk.

Luthan watched Ameron frown, trying desperately not to think about Eler Nersal at all. She was half a breath from screaming and flying from the room in horror.

Blessedly, her Uncle H'Us came to her rescue.

"I, uh, appreciate House Nersal's offer," H'Us said as graciously as he could, with the air of a Demish gentleman taking Vrellish ignorance into account when attempting to communicate with them. "But the accord distinctly stipulates the groom must be directly descended from Horth Nersal by no more than one generation. Eler Nersal is Horth's full brother, but he is not Horth, nor is he Horth's son. So he does not qualify. Although we are, of course, duly honored by your offer, *Imsha* Eler."

Eler shrugged and sat down again, more loutishly than he had risen to claim Luthan as his bride.

"In fact," Prince H'Us continued, "we have decided we will accept only one substitution." He looked at Horth. "As signatory to the contract, it is your responsibility to stand in on behalf of your son and vassal, Dorn."

Luthan felt the blood drain out of her face. She tried, and failed, to imagine waking up with the fearsome liege of Nersal in her bed. There was something undeniably exciting about Liege Nersal, as a man, but whatever it was, it was rather more than Luthan had bargained for. Dorn she knew, and trusted not to frighten her. Horth Nersal was another matter.

"Horth can't go three or four years without gifting to the *kinf'stan*," Eler scoffed at the proposal. "He'll be challenged."

"Allowances might be made for, er, political necessity," H'Us sputtered, awkwardly, in response. Luthan could see he was as thrilled by the idea of capturing Horth's blood, in his own heir, as she was horrified.

All four of the Golden Demish present looked appalled.

Horth turned his head to study Luthan. "Is she a virgin?" he asked.

The Demish side of the table erupted in protest at the vulgar question, the Golden ones insisting Luthan should not be asked to endure such an affront—for which Luthan felt pathetically grateful to them—and the Silver ones bristling at the very idea she might be anything but virginal. Amel sprang to his feet to go to Luthan and was on the brink of helping her out of her chair, instead of merely decrying the need for her be rescued from such dreadful inquiries, when Ameron's voice rang from the walls, halting him and silencing everyone.

"Be still!" declared Ameron, angry at the shambles being made of his hard-won political match-making.

Luthan stole a quick glance at Erien in a second of unnatural calm, and saw he looked ill—which puzzled her. She knew he was friendly with Horth Nersal. Perhaps he was embarrassed for his friend? Or even, maybe, for her? *More likely he is sorry to have brought down his father's displeasure on him by making Dorn the Reetion ambassador*, she thought. But she couldn't quite believe it, and she couldn't quite take her eyes from Erien's face. When their eyes met, they locked.

Oh, Erien, she thought. *If it could only be you, instead.*

It was odd to be forced to remind herself that as a Pureblood and his father's heir, he was above her. She was accustomed to being viewed as the ultimate prize in the marriage game.

Ameron appeared to be preparing himself to tip-toe very carefully through the issues raised by Horth's remark, but the taciturn liege of Nersal spoke up to explain himself without being prompted.

"I do not bed virgins," Horth explained. "Get her some experience, first."

Luthan saw Erien wince. He broke eye contact with her to press his thumb and forefinger to the bridge of his nose. She had the eerie feeling he might be about to do or say something to make this all stop, but virgin or not, she lacked the naivety to hope for a miracle.

Luthan jerked to her feet, making a noise with her chair as she pushed it back. Amel was there to help her at once.

"Let me—" he began, but she shook her head, fighting to overcome her wounded pride.

Squeezing Amel's hand for courage, Luthan pointedly turned away from him to fix her gaze across the table on El Prince Oleander of Vesta and said, "I have decided I will accept your offer to compete with Amel for the right to be recognized by the Golden Emperor as a divine soul. But only if we leave at once!"

An imperious surge of strength sustained her when she saw— by the look on Prince H'Us's face—that her powerful uncle dared not contradict her. Even Ameron looked resigned in the face of the cultural *faux pas* he had seen unfold. They could salvage their accord and move the Demish and Vrellish closer, if they wanted—but without her!

It was El Prince Oleander who escorted her out of the Council of Privilege chamber. She found Prince Samdan and the rest of her escort waiting for her.

"May I bring them?" she asked Oleander.

"Just one," Oleander told her, kindly.

"Prince Samdan O'Pearl," she said, making her newest errant start, open his mouth, and close it again like a stupid fish. But she didn't trust any of the others. They belonged to her uncle.

Oleander nodded his acceptance. "We will see to all your needs beyond this one companion," he promised her.

Then the Goldens closed around them, pushing back her Silver escort, and they set off at a brisk pace for the highborn docks.

"Don't you need to collect things of your own from somewhere?" Luthan asked when she realized just how literally Oleander was taking her.

"Nothing else matters," the Vestal paladin said, giving her a look of deep pleasure and gratitude. "I have the only Golden treasure Gelion possesses in my care."

CHAPTER 8

Regrets

"And then Horth said—" Tatt struggled to pull himself together, tears of laughter in his eyes despite his mother's stern look. He waggled a hand in Erien's direction. "You tell her!" Tatt gasped.

"I have heard what Liege Nersal said," Tessitatt Monitum assured them both. "But is the Dragon-Lion Accord dead? Ameron and I had great hopes for it."

"Sorry," Tatt managed, and collapsed into a chair. "The accord is important, I know. But you have to admit it was funny. How did you ever manage to befriend that impossible man, Erien!"

"I don't blame Horth," Erien said stoically. "I blame myself."

Tessitatt shook her head. "Dorn was the right choice for ambassador." She yielded to a rare smile, shedding years of worry and responsibility. "And while it is incidental in comparison, you should have seen your half-sister Amy when she found out. It might have raised your spirits. She and Dorn will do a good job together on Rire."

Erien only frowned. He had come to Gelion determined to make a difference, and all he'd achieved so far was to drive away Amel and ruin Luthan's marriage plans; but he could not regret either. What he chafed at was the mad system of getting things done on Gelion. All he wanted was to create an academy of higher learning to start a process of systematic improvements in the empire, but there didn't seem a way to do it without playing power games he was ill-equipped to understand let alone succeed in. And for inexplicable reasons, irrelevant things to do with Luthan Dem H'Us kept popping into his head.

The three of them were talking in the library of Green Hearth, where little had changed since Di Mon's death on Monitum eleven years before, except that Tessitatt had added a life-sized portrait of her dead uncle to keep an eye on them. Di Mon looked out of it with his signature mixture of intellectual inquiry, emotional repression and lethal force.

What would Di Mon do? Erien asked himself. *How would he advise me to achieve the authority I need to resurrect the study of science?*

Tessitatt excused herself, saying she needed to confer with Ameron about what he expected of Monitum in dealing with the rupture of the Dragon-Lion Accord.

"Take off your sword and get comfortable," Tatt said to Erien. "We need to talk."

Erien hesitated. As Heir Lor'Vrel he ought to be spending more time in White Hearth where Ameron's staff of errants, secretaries and servants did everything they could to make him feel at home. On the brink of telling Tatt as much, he came out with the truth, instead. "I want to be left alone," said Erien.

"Pity," Tatt dangled his bait with a knowing smirk, "because I've learned things about the mess on Demora from that zealot who tried to kill Amel. Things about why Oleander Vesta is so interested in her."

Erien sat down.

Tatt slung his sword into a conveniently placed rack, and poured a glass of the notorious Monatese whiskey called Turquoise.

"I'll have one," said Erien.

Tatt gave his half-brother a look of mild astonishment, then handed over the drink in his hand and poured himself another.

"You needn't worry about Luthan," Tatt remarked as they settled down opposite each other in a pair of reading chairs under the silent supervision of Di Mon's portrait. "Demoran factions can have all the passion of a Vrellish brawl but it plays out in competitive poetry readings and beauty contests."

"Which was the assassination attempt on Amel: poetry reading or beauty contest?" asked Erien.

Tatt frowned. "Aberration."

"Are you sure?" Erien challenged. "Or are you assuming Golden Demish conflicts are harmless based on Vrellish prejudice?"

"Prejudice!" Tatt raised both eyebrows. "You forget, I'm Monatese. I have been known to read a book! Not often, I grant you, but my tutors were determined people." He leaned forward, grinning beneath his mop of wild brown hair. "Besides, they have some very digestible vids and historical simulations on Sanctuary, expressly designed for young fencers too impatient to turn pages." Tatt settled back in his armchair, nursing his drink with a casual air. "I know as much about the Golden Demish as anyone who isn't one of them."

"Documentaries stored on Sanctuary would probably date from the Golden Age of the empire," said Erien. "Making whatever you know half a millennium out of date."

"Demish cultures don't change fast," Tatt said. "Besides," he added as Erien prepared to launch into a debate on the subject, "we have more recent sources to rely on." Tatt winked. "Real political intelligence."

Of course, thought Erien. *He's liege of Monitum.* Tatt took his heritage so much for granted it was easy to forget the resources he commanded when he chose to draw on them.

"The Demoran schism is a simple dynastic affair at heart," Tatt told Erien. "The main players are three inner circle families: the Arbors, the Vestas and the Anders—or maybe just the Anders and Vestas these days since D'Ander married the last Arbor heiress to trump the Vesta claim to the Protectorship. Purists, like the Vestas, didn't like D'Ander because his father was Silver Demish. Silver princes like to take Golden brides. It doesn't go down well with the Golden princes."

"I know this," Erien said impatiently. Luthan was the product of another such union.

"Fine," Tatt pretended to take offense. "So tell me what you don't know, and I'll confine myself to those bits."

Erien sighed. "My apologies," he told Tatt, schooling himself to show patience and wishing he knew why he felt so irritable. "I'll confine my responses to appreciative nods, henceforth."

Tatt leaned forward in his chair, dangling his hands between his knees. From Erien's position, standing above him, Tatt's mop of hair looked like a fuzzy animal perched on his head, swaying as he gestured.

"Here's the précis," Tatt said. "The original Golden Age leaders were Arbors." His head bobbed to one side. "They were slowly displaced by the Vestas." His head bobbed the other way. "The latest upstarts are the Anders, who are actually a branch of the Arbor line. They are all so thoroughly inbred that most of them are half mad, and these days it is common for women to wind up as lieges because too many of the vigorous men have died defending Demora from Silver Demish encroachment on the challenge floor. So, despite a very serious obsession with Golden Demish purity, Demorans were reduced to using hybrids to fill critical roles, starting with D'Ander and now, apparently, reaching out to embrace another hybrid, with the Anders determined to have Amel, and the Vestas preferring Luthan because her mother was once heir to House Vesta."

"But Luthan is liege of the Silver Demish," Erien protested. "Why swear to her when the Goldens resist Silver encroachment?"

"She's princess-liege," corrected Tatt. "Maybe Oleander's betting he can marry her and displace Prince H'Us, or at least create a civil war. Getting her to defect to the Goldens, the way D'Ander did, would send a message of defiance, and she might even take some vassals with her. Today's Council of Privilege could become the stuff of legend on Demora: 'Virtuous daughter of Vesta flees attempt by Silver Hearth to marry her to a vile Vrellish Highlord, and escapes into the saintly protection of the brave Prince Oleander of the Vesta Order.' The Vestas have plenty of abbesses running reveries full of so-called 'weary sisters,' all eager and able to write up a storm of propaganda for the cause."

Luthan is a Vesta, thought Erien, *goddess of hearth and home.* He found the resonance apt and oddly mesmerizing.

"What does the title 'El' mean, exactly?" Erien asked. "You've used it a few times."

"It's a coveted designation entitling someone to be addressed in extra-lofty grammar, second only to the sort Demorans use for divine souls. Only Royalbloods or better are eligible for El honors, and they have to be descended from the Family of Light—now reduced to the Golden Emperor Fahild and possibly Amel, his great-grandson. Only an El prince can be Protector of Demora, and you can bet the Anders and Vestas are jockeying for that prize now Ev'rel's gone. They refused to appoint a protector during her reign as their liege, or perhaps she didn't let them. In any case, the prime candidates were both kids: D'Ander's son by the last heir of Arbor, and his half-sister's daughter by Chad Therd. The office of protector has been mothballed for a generation with Ev'rel pulling the puppet strings. Of course, ultimate authority still rests with the Golden Emperor—theoretically—but he hasn't even made a public appearance in decades, let alone attempted to influence policy. If he died they'd have to stuff him, because there is no other 100% Golden Demish being in the universe."

"I see," said Erien, sounding strained. "And is Luthan an El Princess?"

Tatt made a face. "Apparently. But only since the pressure to latch onto a suitable hybrid scared up an old scandal to do with Princess Chandra influencing Luthan's mother to accept a Silver Demish marriage on false pretenses: True love, broken hearts. You know, the usual stuff of Golden dramas."

"Stories," Erien said, a little harshly, "in which love is never enjoyed within marriages."

Tatt shrugged. "Well, that part makes sense to me. So there you have it."

Erien was longing for a sketch pad to start making diagrams. "Have what?" he asked, letting his frustration get the better of him. He didn't see how any of this told him much about what, if anything, might threaten Luthan.

Tatt looked surprised. "The cast of remaining El royalty!" exclaimed Tatt, in the tone of a disappointed tutor. "First, there's D'Ander's son, Dromedarius—"

Erien nearly choked on the sip of Turquoise in his mouth. "Who?"

"Dromedarius," Tatt repeated, looking puzzled by Erien's reaction. "Or Drom for short. Why?"

"It's a species of camel," said Erien. "In Latin."

"Camel," repeated Tatt, brow wrinkled in an effort to revive the scholarly side of his education. "I don't think I know about camels. It was some kind of beautiful, lithe creature I suppose."

"Hardly," Erien assured him dryly.

Tatt shrugged. "D'Ander was never the most literary of the Golden Demish. He may have picked it out of an old Earth book for the sound alone. I've heard he never even read the entire Ameron Biography, despite believing he was Ameron's secret paladin—minus the vows of celibacy, of course. You do know about the paladin orders?"

"A little," said Erien. "Please stick to the list of El royalty."

"Actually, I was getting to the next part," said Tatt. "About why an overzealous nut case might consider it his sacred duty to kill Amel. But I can see it is all starting to annoy you, so you have to promise not to huff and snort and fly off to Demora to tell the entire planet to give up the fundamental tenets of its cultural world view for the last thousand years and see reason. Demorans are terribly civilized, but they have been known to execute Lorels who insult their beliefs with too much rigor."

"Go ahead," Erien assured him. "I promise not to rush off to Demora to single-handedly insult every paladin on the planet, no matter how absurd their beliefs."

Tatt looked skeptical, but he gave in. "Riddle me this: what do you do if your whole way of life depends on the existence of a Golden Emperor who has no heir?"

"Change your political system to something sane, like holding an election," said Erien.

Tatt rolled his eyes. "Demorans, Erien. They're Demorans. Think *Okal Lumens*."

"I don't know!" Erien gave up in exasperation.

Tatt frowned. "Something about the Council of Privilege has got you rattled," he said. "You're not yourself. Drinking. And snapping like a bad tempered—"

"I should have done something to help Luthan," Erien said miserably.

"Like what?" Tatt asked.

Erien finished his Turquoise and refilled his glass.

"Pureblood or not," Tatt warned. "Turquoise is strong stuff. It comes with a built-in toxin to help the alcohol get the jump on highborn regenerative powers."

"Just finish the story," said Erien. "What has *Okal Lumens* got to do with an assassination attempt on Amel?"

"Apparently..." Tatt drawled, and toyed with his own drink a moment before cocking a wary look at Erien. "Promise you aren't going to do anything Vrellish, if I tell you?"

"Of course not," snapped Erien.

"Well," Tatt said. "Apparently there's a movement called the Order of the Messenger that's been growing in numbers for a decade or more, and is now intent on getting Amel officially declared as the heir of the Golden Emperor, himself."

Tatt waited. Erien failed to react as anticipated.

"I thought the idea of Amel being Golden Emperor would make you crazy!" Tatt confessed.

Erien shrugged. "I was already aware of D'Ander's belief in Amel as a Soul of Light," he said. "Why should it disturb me to know the idea has spread and gained political ambitions?" Then, slowly, his expression did change as a really offensive idea began to stir in the murky depths of whatever was bothering him. "Tatt, with all these factions...you don't think it's likely, do you, that any two or three of them might strike upon the idea of consolidating claims by marrying Luthan to Amel?"

Tatt laughed. "Erien, I expect every possible pairing off between the lot of them will be considered, at least once, by somebody!"

Erien was trying to find the idea of a marriage between Luthan and Amel impossible and not succeeding. *With Amel as Avim and possibly heir to the Golden Emperor, H'Us might even like it better than patching up the Dragon-Lion Accord, given Horth's bad manners today, from a Demish perspective.*

"About Amel..." Tatt said, probing cautiously. "If you don't want him sworn to you, it's fine with me! Except..." Tatt made a pained face, "you might have broken it to him a bit more gently, because we might need him now and then, at budget time. And I suspect he is feeling rejected, if I know Amel. Maybe even betrayed. He hasn't spoken to me since he found out I poached Mira for my ministry—and your academy, too, by the way! She's agreed to teach medicine for you if you get it going. Mother is skeptical." He grinned. "I promised her it wouldn't cost the Monatese anything in lost revenue for medical services, so you'd better make sure I'm right!" Tatt ended with a burst of laughter. "Oh gods!" he said, and erupted in chuckles again. "Amel could become the establishment around here, with you and I the ir-responsible troublemakers!"

Erien was not amused. "I am Heir Gelion," he said. "Surely that ought to be enough for respectability."

"Erien," Tatt sighed, setting a hand on his shoulder. "You are my brother and I love you. But I hope you know you can be clueless as a newborn about—"

Tessitatt came in wearing a strange look on her face. "It is Liege Vrel," she said. "She's asking for Erien. She says she wants to swear to him."

Tatt gave a jerk as if electrified. "Wow," was all he said. Then he punched Erien on the shoulder. "Don't mess this up, idiot! Find out how Amel's offended her, and give her whatever she asks for! Or tell her to swear to me and I will!"

CHAPTER 9

Liege of Blue Dem

A mob scene boiled around preparations for Luthan's departure for Demora outside a long-disused hangar complex on the highborn docks belonging to the Vestas. Amel stopped at the edges of it, surrounded by his entourage and still dressed in his improvised 'liege of Blue Dem' attire. Alivda stood at his left side with Margaret on his right, flanked by one of her paladins. Sen Lekker took charge of the hand of errants accompanying them and had them running interference to leave Amel unhindered by the pressing mob.

Amel wore a sword on his right hip. It was weighted more like a dancer's sword than a regular fencing weapon, but he found he was more confident using it than any of the other weapons he had found in D'Therd's collection.

I will never get through all this to speak with Luthan, he thought in frustration, looking at the churn of people ahead.

The Silver Demish were trying to stop Luthan the traditional way. Space had been cleared twice for duels, but so far Oleander was proving not every Golden paladin deserved the lame reputation attributed to the late Ava Delm's retainers since their ignominious defeat at the hands of Horth's father. One Silver prince was dead. Amel was certain Luthan would be upset if she knew about it, but he couldn't be sure she would change her mind even if she did. He didn't blame her for wanting to escape court after the debacle at the Council of Privilege.

Lady Margaret laid a hand on Amel's arm. "We will not get through, but we can find a way to talk with your friend, Princess Luthan, once we reach Demora."

Amel turned to her in exasperation. "I cannot leave now! Nothing's settled!"

"If she goes, you have to!" Sen urged him, shouldering her way past Margaret's paladin to Amel's side. "If you don't, the Therds and the Vestas will take the Golden Oath away from you, and the Knotted Strings will starve!"

Alivda was busy trying to catch a glimpse of Oleander through the crowd, where he stood waiting for the next challenger. "I could take him!" she declared. Amel turned to see her staring avariciously at Oleander: her nostrils pinched with excitement and her laser-blue eyes narrowed.

He pulled free of Margaret to turn Alivda around to face him. "Champions," he told her, "obey their lieges. So listen. You will not challenge Oleander just to get me a chance to speak with Luthan."

Alivda snorted. "I'm not afraid to spill Golden blood!"

"Diff!" Amel said sharply, squeezing her arms hard enough to make her look at him. "I said no."

He got her attention, but she only tapped him on the nose, wearing a smirk. "Bit late in life to start giving orders, Your Sweetness," she teased, using the nickname a PA acquaintance had invented for him.

"Either you are my vassal, or you are not," Amel told her, dead serious. "If you aren't, then go home."

She stared him down a moment, but they hadn't spent years sharing Amel's travels without her gaining an appreciation for when he really meant what he said.

"Liege it is, then," Alivda said, begrudgingly.

"Wait for me," Amel said, using his pliable, gentle voice again, and laid a hand on Alivda's arm for emphasis as he tipped his head to show her where he meant to go. He had just recognized Alivda's mother, Ayrium, in the midst of the milling crowd and realized that more than anyone else, it was Ayrium's support he had to have.

Alivda took care of deterring the paladins who tried to follow Amel. "I take his orders, you take mine!" she told Margaret's men, and squared herself away to face them if they tried to get past.

Will Ayrium swear to me? Amel asked himself with a sickening sense of dread as he approached his lifelong friend. He had never stopped to wonder whether Ayrium shared her mother, Perry's, goal of restoring Blue Hearth to its rightful place on Fountain Court. He knew Ameron didn't think it was practical, and Ameron's opinion mattered to his lover.

Ayrium was dressed in flight leathers with the badge of the Purple Alliance over her right breast: a silhouette of purple hills against a starry background.

"I've never seen you wearing a sword, before," she said when Amel stopped a pace ahead of her. "Or Blue Demish regalia. Mom would love the outfit," she acknowledged with a wan smile.

"She had better," Amel said, surprising himself at the anger in his voice.

Ayrium's beautiful, loving face developed a pained expression. "Oh, Amel! Mom had no right to lay down an ultimatum like—"

"She was right," he cut her off, unable to stomach pity. "What about you? Will you swear to me as liege of Blue Dem?"

"Once I would have, you know, without a second thought!" She shook her head, worry lines troubling her wide brow. "But Blue Dem isn't what I've come to talk to you about, Amel. I came when I realized Alivda had taken it into her head to join you. I've spoken to her father about it, and naturally this business of Blue Hearth came up, too. Ameron thinks you've lost your mind!" She bit her lip, anguish in her sympathetic stare. "I could beat Mom black and blue for putting you up to this! It's a lovely idea—but impossible!"

"What is Ameron's objection?" Amel asked. Knowing Ameron didn't believe he could pull it off had daunted him from the start, but it was too late to back down. He had made his decision.

Ayrium scuffed a foot on the hullsteel floor. "We talked about this when I first hooked up with Ameron. Not you being Liege Dem, explicitly, but the idea of untangling the title and land claims resulting from Perry's rebellion and bringing Barmi II back into the empire. It's messy, Amel. And the rest of the Blue Demish are scattered across the whole empire, except for Ilse Marin here at court. The Marins were fiercely loyal to Ev'rel, and the word is Ilse blames you for Ev'rel's death." She saw him flinch and winced about the eyes herself.

"So," he said, feeling wooden, "Ameron opposes your mother's dream of reintegrating the Blue Demish into the empire, and Ameron is your *cher'st*, while she's only your mother." His tone was stone cold, which was so unlike him it made her stare. Her back stiffened momentarily, then her lips pressed together and she let go of whatever harsh emotions he had stirred in her and took his hands in hers, threatening the reserve he hung onto like a shield to keep him strong. She was a little taller than him, and for the first time he resented it.

"It isn't as simple as who I love best, Amel," she said. "Ameron thinks the Silvers will never accept a Blue revival. He thinks the Purple Alliance will evolve best in isolation."

"It is true that Perry's rebellion has changed Barmi," Amel answered her levelly. "But the changes won't be lost by regaining the security of representation on Fountain Court. And I know it won't be easy reconciling the displaced on both sides of the original dispute. Ameron hasn't the time or the knack for in-tra-Demish diplomacy—but I do. Your PA has been struggling to survive for forty years under the shadow of a Silver Demish counterattack, without court protection and surrounded by the lawlessness of Killing Reach. Isn't that long enough?"

She gave him one of her old grins. "We get by."

His resolve wavered, leaving him desolate. "So I've done something stupid again, have I? By taking Perry at her word."

Ayrium lowered her eyes. When she raised them moments later a shadow had crossed her sunny soul. "You may be right about Ameron. The Silver Demish won't accept me swearing to him and he is politician enough to make a virtue of a necessity. He did study the Blue Demish situation before Amy was born, and he simply thinks it is too late to resurrect Blue Dem. So he asked me not to swear to you, yes."

Ameron asked her not to! Amel thought, and failed to take his next breath. Two seconds ticked by before the dry pain in his chest gave him the courage to be bold. *Fine,* he thought. *Ameron disagrees with me. Which of us understands the Demish better? Gold, Silver and Blue!*

"Ayrium," he said, marshalling the knowledge gleaned through years of being an invisible presence in the halls of power. "Ameron thinks the Demish are already too powerful. Therefore, he would rather leave them divided among themselves to keep them manageable. He also believes the Purple Alliance makes a useful buffer between Sevildom and Rire. And perhaps, until now, that's been true. But it's no longer in your interest. Change is coming. Horth has struck deals with the Reetions. Erien is determined to start educating Sevolites in the Lorel sciences. The next generation will see more disruption to the core prin-ciples of the empire than the last ten combined, and it is the Demish—with their fixation on tradition—who will be the most vulnerable. When that begins to happen, it will be Barmi II and the Knotted Strings who will have the versatility to see all

Demish through this crisis; but it will be the precious metal houses—Silver and Gold—who command the resources required. I must, therefore, have influence with them all. To salvage what is beautiful, to steer the transformation of what isn't, and—in general terms—to maximize the benefits of change with as little trauma as possible. I know this, in my heart, above and beyond whatever Perry wants. I have been learning it slowly, over the last two decades, visiting every corner of the universe as Ameron's envoy and Ev'rel's minion. I am the only one who has lived in every camp and knows it all. And if I cannot have happiness—not, at least, the simple-minded kind I thought I might have been able to look forward to, starting with some kind of true love—"

Ayrium smiled at this and would have stepped in to caress Amel's face with her hand, but he aborted her gesture by capturing her fingers in his own and holding her eyes with a steady stare. "If I can't have my fairy tale ending, I've decided to accept the responsibility of steering the bulk of the empire into the future as best I can. And to do it, I have to be Liege Dem, head of the original Demish house."

Ayrium was watching him with a blank look as he finished. "Amel?" she said, a crease of puzzlement stamped across her forehead.

"Still me," he told her, filled for a moment with a warmth he knew he couldn't afford to indulge. Pointedly, he let go and took a step back.

"What would it take," he asked her softly, "to be worthy of your oath?"

She inhaled, not sure she wanted to tread this ground with him, but she was thinking.

"Ships," she said at last. "And highborns to help us with our Vrellish pirate problems. Not in a generation, either. Right now. Lowered trade barriers with Rire, in the face of Monatese opposition. Acceptance of the Purple Alliance as a local confederacy, led by Barmi—which is without precedent and therefore will be almost impossible to convince the Silver and Golden Demish to allow. And last, but not least, a full-fledged planetary tribunal to settle all pre-rebellion claims on Barmi II, conducted and settled at the expense of Blue Hearth."

Amel nodded, unsurprised by any of the issues. "Understood," he told her. "But you left out getting the Silvers to formally acknowledge you as Liege Barmi and Amy as your heir."

Ayrium let out the breath she was holding. "Amy is the right person for the job," she told him. "Doubly so now that Dorn is securely hers, and ambassador to Rire as well as the son of the leader of the Bryllit Nersallians."

"Amy will succeed you as Liege Barmi," Amel promised. "And after that, her heirs by Dorn. Which makes perfect sense, you know, even from a traditional standpoint, since there is Blue Demish in house Nersal." He yielded to old, familiar feelings of belonging with a smile, troubled only slightly by jealousy for Dorn and Amy's happiness. "Half your lack of highborns might be dealt with by Amy and Dorn, alone, since I expect their family will be numerous enough to scandalize the Reetions with their two-child law."

Ayrium laughed, and then sobered. "Amy isn't without rivals, you know, even within the PA. It would be good to see her backed up by Blue Hearth on Fountain Court." She hesitated, and it wasn't hard for him to imagine she was thinking about Amy's father, who had remained reticent on the matter of his daughter's inheritance of Barmi II, and would continue to withhold his support so long as Perry's possession of the planet remained a sore spot with Silver Hearth. "If it could be managed," Ayrium concluded on a note of pessimism.

She touched Amel's face, sorry to hurt him, but forced to be practical. "I would need more than your word that you could deliver so much, with so little to work with. I'm sorry."

"You will have all of it, with the blessing of the leaders of the Silver and Golden Demish, before I ask for your oath again," he promised her.

She smiled with an air of indulgence. "Ships?" she said whimsically. "And instant highborns?"

He had no idea yet how to tackle any of this, but he said, "On my list," and grinned back.

Ayrium took his hand and gripped it tightly. "Ameron isn't necessarily opposed in principle, you know," she told him. "He just doesn't believe a Blue Demish revival is possible. Just don't try to poach any of his own vassals, and if you can't perform miracles..." She gave him a strained smile. "Go back to being the old Amel, again, please? Before you get yourself killed." She released his hand then and took a step back. "About Alivda—"

"She stays with me," he told her with finality.

Ayrium opened her mouth to plead, but they both knew the content of the argument and its refutation. Alivda might die in his service, but she was just as apt to kill herself in reckless frustration if she was not allowed some outlet worthy of her talents.

"*Ack rel*," Ayrium said after a long pause, and left him without the last embrace he longed for.

As he watched Ayrium walk away, Amel felt as if he was losing another sister in the cause of becoming a plausible Demish leader. Unexpectedly, the idea of himself as Ayrium's brother produced a backwash of aversion at the incestuous implications concerning his relationship with Perry D'Aur. He shook the idea off with a shudder. *Perry would be horrified!* he thought. His first impulse was to blame repressed anxieties concerning his relationship with Ev'rel. But the feeling lingered that perhaps, after all, Perry had been right to end their sexual relationship before launching him into the new life he was striving for, even if her desertion had left him bereft and alone.

As he stood struggling for emotional equilibrium, his entourage flowed around him, led by Alivda, and cloaked him with the security of their bodies once more.

"You will need Demora to fulfill that shopping list," Sen said, with a hard edge to her voice.

Amel turned his head to look at her, finding her jealousy of Ayrium endearing and simpleminded at the same time. "I will not forget the Knotted Strings in a rush to please Liege Barmi," he assured her. "At the same time, I suspect you may not be entirely satisfied by whatever I achieve on behalf of the Lekkers, since I want to please the Therds, as well. Nor can I win the Golden oath solely to exploit Demora's riches for the sake of FarHome and the Purple Alliance rebels. I will forge an alliance on real mutual interests, or I will not forge one at all."

Sen frowned. "And if you are forced to pick sides?"

"You would not say such things, nobleborn Lekker," Margaret defended Amel with flashing eyes, "if you understood what it meant to be a Soul of Light!"

"Don't push me farther than political necessity demands, Luminary!" Sen snapped back. "You don't know him! I do!"

The way she said it sent a thrill of impending doom over Amel's skin at the certainty Sen believed their tumble in Ev'rel's room meant more to him than it did. Why it didn't, he couldn't tell. But he was regretting it more each time Sen acted as if it empowered her above and beyond their old friendship out in the Knotted Strings.

Margaret looked so upset by Sen's attack that Amel couldn't help taking her under his arm where she seemed to fit so very well. "Sen, please," he said to his Lekker friend. "You don't have to share the religious beliefs of Luminaries to show respect for them."

"I'll respect them just fine," Sen said, with a glare for Margaret where she sheltered against Amel's chest. "If they can get you Demora's oath."

The resentment in Sen's voice surprised Amel. Margaret was on their side! Had Demoran slights over the years frayed her temper? Then Margaret stirred against his breast, trembling under his enfolding hand, and he remembered he had slept with Sen but had his arm around another woman who clearly viewed him with affection. He was used to stealing love where he could, and not having it publicly acknowledged. But he was slowly coming to the conclusion that to overlook the tensions between Margaret and Sen would be stupid. He was liege of something now in his own right, and no longer had to flit about the edges of power. Did that make all the difference? Was it really so simple and so disappointingly mercenary?

He drew away from Margaret, feeling wrong-footed about everything to do with women, and wishing he had abstained from allaying old frustrations with Sen, in Ev'rel's bed. What he'd shared with Ev'rel had been wrong in many ways, but still painfully real while where Sen was concerned his emotions seemed to have fallen deaf and dumb.

Margaret allowed herself to be set aside with a look of abject suffering Amel found all the more convincing because he believed she tried to hide it from him.

"He is a Soul of Light," Margaret confronted Sen with the conviction of a zealot. "And he will outshine the tinsel, Silver Demish princess."

Amel opened his mouth to protest Luthan was his dearest friend, and closed it again. If Demora swore to Luthan, he wasn't certain he could convince her to care about the importance of building bridges of understanding between all the Demish houses. He knew her well, and for all her heart-warming support for his orphanage and Tatt's Justice Ministry, she was not—at heart—a radical. She believed the Blue Demish were finished and the Silver Demish ought to govern the affairs of the Goldens.

But the Blue Demish, Amel realized in a moment of perfect clarity, *are not only the scattered trader clans like Marin and the family of Brother Ron. They are the Dem'Vrel in the Knotted Strings and*

Perry's Barmians. They are the Demish who have learned to survive change. And we need them!

"We must go to Demora," Amel said, with a decisiveness born of his epiphany. "And the sooner the better, because we have to be back in time for me to talk to the Dem'Vrel before the Swearing and make my case to Ayrium, as well!"

"Ten days to conquer the empire!" Alivda exclaimed, and drew her sword excitedly to thrust it up over her head with a blood-curdling yell.

"Ack rel!"

CHAPTER 10

Test of Souls

"But I thought I was going to fly with you," Luthan said hesitantly, as Oleander handed her over to a stranger dressed entirely in golden robes.

"This is an angel of the Inner Circle," Oleander said. "One of those drawn from the order of weary sisters pure enough to attend upon the person of the Golden Emperor himself. She has come here expressly to share the cockpit of your vessel with you on the way home."

"Oh," Luthan said, disappointed. Never in her sixteen short years of life had she flown in a *rel*-ship before, and the idea of doing it for the first time with Prince Oleander had somehow made it seem less daunting.

The next moment she remembered tales of angels sent to test the quality of souls and repeated herself with a whole new inflection. "Oh!"

Oleander squeezed her hand. "You will do fine."

Luthan hung on to his hand a moment too long. He smiled as he tugged away, briefly stroking her fingers with his own. His pale blue eyes were serene and composed, even though he was fresh from facing down half a dozen Silver Demish challengers in potentially lethal duels. At least, so Prince Samdan had let Luthan know, and it must have been something to see because he had looked a little green reporting it to her. And provincial or not, Samdan was at least a man. Luthan had been afraid to ask if anyone had been killed. She was in shock over her decision to leave and unable to face the idea it might be an irrevocable turning point in her life. She loved her Uncle H'Us, even though she was still too furious with him over the business at the Council of Privilege to speak to him or any of her male relatives right now. She believed in the Silver Demish way of life, which was solidly decent and respectable, even if it did need a bit of adjusting in some quarters.

So why, she thought desperately, *am I running away with the Goldens?*

"Come with me," the angel said, extending a slender arm from the folds of her shimmering gold toga, "and have no fear."

Easy for you to say, thought Luthan. *You aren't about to be proved a horrid fraud instead of a Golden Soul!*

But Luthan didn't shirk responsibilities and Oleander had fought for her. She was going to Demora.

Luthan suffered herself to be helped into a passenger seat of a sleek envoy craft with Prince Samdan on one side of her and the angel on the other. A pilot in Vesta livery slipped into the cockpit, at the front. Prince Oleander would be flying escort.

"What do you suppose will happen to my servant, Jack?" Prince Samdan asked, keeping his eyes forward. He had become terribly fidgety since finding out he would be flying with Luthan and the angel.

"Jack will be all right in Silver Hearth," Luthan said, glad to make small talk to dispel her nervousness. "Amel's herald asked for some people to replace the ones dismissed yesterday, so he might wind up helping there." Her heart had already begun to pound. The angel sat very still, with her hands in the sleeves of her golden robes. Her face was obscured by her cowl, but Luthan had glimpsed it earlier, and noticed she resembled Oleander, except that—unlike him—there was nothing distinct and impressive about her.

Bland, was the word that had sprung to Luthan's mind. Followed by, *Oh dear! Is that the sort of thing a Golden Soul would think about another person?*

Luthan's heart leapt into her throat as the ship started moving. Her hands tightened on the rests to either side.

Beside her, Prince Samdan said, "*Rel*-skimming isn't so bad, Princess Luthan. I've done it lots of times." He paused to nibble his lower lip before adding. "But I never thought I would be going to Demora in the same ship as an Inner Circle angel!"

"Don't worry," Luthan told him, as bravely as she could muster. "It is me she's here to test in soul touch."

"Let's hope so," said Samdan in a way that made Luthan wonder what so young and fresh-faced a prince could have to hide from an angel of the Golden Emperor.

*Whereas I...*Luthan thought, and stifled a moment of panic. Anxiety had wrung her with guilt over real and imagined peccadilloes before they were far enough away from Gelion to start reality skimming.

"Here goes," muttered Samdan, beside her, in a voice so high Luthan looked at him in surprise. Samdan was looking straight ahead, his smooth profile to Luthan and his body tense. Luthan wondered if his voice had broken yet, since his usual speaking voice—now she thought about it—was a bit forced, as if he was trying to sound more mature than he was. He was supposed to be twenty-one as she recalled, but some Demish were as slow to mature as the Vrellish were fast about growing up.

He's just a boy from a country demesne, Luthan berated herself, *and I've dragged him along into who knows what sort of strangeness just to have sympathetic company. His mother will hate me when she finds out!*

Most of all, though, she worried about the angel sitting next to her.

Between guilt and anxiety about being found wanting in soul touch, Luthan hardly noticed the ill effects of reality skimming itself. The change crept up on her gradually, weighing on her cell by cell, as if she hadn't slept enough the night before, and dampening the strength of her emotions. She held her breath, waiting for soul touch, but nothing extraordinary happened.

"How long will it take to reach Demora?" she asked after ten awkward minutes.

The pilot answered her from the front. "About four hours under skim, and double that maneuvering in slow space."

"Slow space?" asked Luthan.

"It's pilot's slang for non-skim transit," volunteered Samdan. "Some people call it slow space because it is so tedious covering distances that way, even if it's necessary."

"Oh," said Luthan, and settled back to attempt to clear her mind of all inappropriate thoughts. *Golden literature will be safest*, she thought, and proceeded to schedule herself a program of remembered plays and poems.

She was well into a mental recitation of *Princess Demora*, the tragic drama of the legendary woman for whom the world of the Golden Demish was named, which had the virtue of being over three hours long when performed in its unabridged form, when she began associating Erien with the forbidden lover of the classic tale. Like Luthan, Demora had received an odd gift from her admirer that she was at pains to hide, and as Luthan got to this part her mind drifted from the well-loved story into channels filled with the content of the Reetion sex manual Erien had given her.

How do couples get started! Luthan thought with dismay, recalling the pictures in the book. She had read about foreplay, of course, which bore some relation to the significant touches, long looks and chaste kisses of her own reference materials on the subject of love. But neither source answered crucial questions such as whether men would suffer some sort of internal damage if stopped halfway through, or what two people could possibly find to say to each other after indulging in such unimaginable gyrations with unfamiliar body parts.

She was innocent of experiencing soul touch until the angel beside her reacted with a start and a small, gentile gasp.

Luthan shut down both play and speculations about sex on her inner stage, to turn to the angel in horror. The woman's face was turned to stare across Luthan toward Samdan.

"What?" Samdan asked in alarm.

Luthan wasn't sure what Prince Samdan had been thinking, but judging by the flush on his face and the wide, dilated eyes of the angel who looked thoroughly shaken by whatever experience they had all shared, she suspected Samdan might be at least partially responsible for her own mental digression in the direction of arousing thoughts. Or was getting blamed for it, at least.

Nothing was said, and all three settled down quietly to wait the rest of the trip out.

–o—o—o–

"You're an angel?" Amel said stupidly, after being introduced to the woman in shimmering golden robes who had been assigned to fly with him to Demora.

"The Inner Circle lent one to each party," Margaret explained. "One for the Vestas, to test Luthan, and one for me, to test you." She laid a hand on Amel's arm. "You have heard about angels: the female counterparts of paladins who serve the emperor?"

"I've read about them, of course," Amel said, and seeing the serene eyes of the angel on him suddenly felt like an idiot for speaking about her in the third person. Swallowing down the rising sense of hilarity building up as he kept barging headlong through the stuff of Golden legend, he took a firm hold on his composure, tapped into his love of Golden literature and gave her as natural and earnest a bow as he knew how.

"I am at a loss to know how to properly acknowledge the honor you do me," he told the angel in the correct Demoran grammar. "But are you sure you want to risk soul touch on the trip out? I have experienced things no angel's wings should brush."

Oh, come off it, Amel! he chastised himself as soon as the words were out. *You sound like a bad play!*

But he didn't know what other store of wisdom to draw on for this occasion.

The angel smiled. She had a pale face framed in wisps of hair so gold they glittered like metal, but looked warm and soft. Her look was mild, her eyes so gentle Amel could have lost himself staring into them.

She said, "I am willing, if you are."

"You must accept," Margaret urged. "It is a prerequisite. You cannot be accepted as a candidate for recognition as a Divine Soul unless you are willing to fly with an angel."

"I have no objection on my own behalf," Amel told them both, and turned to Margaret with a concerned look. "I hope I do not let you down," he said, as he handed her his sword to stow. He was thinking about D'Ander, and how he had disappointed him the one and only time they had reality skimmed together.

Margaret gave the sword back to him with real reluctance. "I will not be flying with you," she said, and took the opportunity to press his hands in hers. "You are a Soul of Light," she assured him, with the same eerie confidence she always showed on this point. "I have no doubt."

With Margaret gone, Amel settled in his seat, stealing glances at the angel every few seconds. She never stirred or turned her head. The pilot called out a warning and the ship began to move.

"It doesn't always work, you know," Amel remarked as they picked up speed, headed for the surface up the highborn ramp. "Soul touch, I mean."

She said nothing. To distract himself, he looked around. There were no windows. All he could see was a glimpse of nervecloth screen in the pilot's cabin up front. There were no stars displayed. They were still underground.

With a sigh, Amel settled back and tried to relax. His head was a jumble of joys and terrors in which the unfamiliar business of defending Blue Hearth with a sword stood out, abetted by the sting of the cut along his ribs. Amel had suffered life-threatening injuries many times, including purposeful torture, and knew the hell of wallowing through hours too horrible to describe. In comparison, the salved nick was trivial. But it itched. He also had a finely tuned sense of his body in space, and the damaged part kept pointing out the insult it had suffered with all the self-centered outrage of an offended toddler. It bothered him to think the angel might pick up this level of discomfort over so insignificant a wound.

Erien wouldn't let it bother him, Amel thought, annoyed. His Reetion-raised brother seemed capable of deciding which stimuli to react to and which to ignore as deliberately as if he possessed the legendary powers of the Lorel adepts. But thinking about Erien only made him remember his brother's dismissive words about him to Ameron, and on the heels of that rejection came the hurt of Perry's and Mira's.

No, no and no! He denied the memories associated with each of them as they came flooding back. He had always known Mira needed more space. Why should it surprise him she preferred the orphanage compound to Blue Hearth? And Perry had always been a Blue Demish loyalist at heart. He knew Erien disliked him, too. It was nothing but his typical, dumb optimism to imagine that their shared experiences on Rire had earned him Erien's respect.

Why can't I be more like him? Amel berated himself as the movement of the ship lured him into a half-waking dream.

He was thinking about Erien fighting his way out of Lilac Hearth with Luthan's errants as their ship began to climb into space. Amel had spent most of that fight passed out on the floor once Branstatt had been forced to let go of him, but Amel let his imagination spin him a more active role. He was particularly sorry he had not killed Kandrol himself, so he took care of it personally in the replay. Next he brought to mind the fight between Erien and Horth Nersal outside his group home on Rire, but this time he didn't stop them with Reetion restraining foam. He waded in like a real Gelack highborn and they all sat down together afterwards in a comradely manner while the First Responders tended to their wounds.

The transition to reality skimming, once they cleared Gelion's challenge sphere in slow space, came about the time Amel began remembering the fencing lessons Tatt had tried to give him years before. He had learned even the most complicated sequences of moves with ease, and executed them with fluid grace. But he kept interpreting practice as a dance rehearsal, eventually making Tatt give up in despair. The definitive moment came when Tatt hit Amel in the chest hard enough to hurt, and Amel exclaimed in anger, "You didn't do that last time!" To which Tatt had replied, with a matching show of temper, "Of course not, Amel! That's the point!"

Amel had learned things from Tatt and other fencers over the years, but he was nowhere near Tatt's caliber of duelist. He was best at exploiting his powers of observation to evade attacks and dance away. "You have the aggressive instincts of a sleeping puppy!" Tatt had summed it up for him by the time their lessons drew to an end. Ayrium had tried as well, and Lek, and many of his friends across the empire. But he never kept at it for long, and he preferred not to wear a sword whenever possible. The truth was he just didn't like the idea of killing people and it wasn't something he could easily set aside.

Unless, he mused, *I could make myself imagine it was Jarl I was up against every time.* Jarl had been master of children in the sleazy den Amel was sold to at the age of ten, and of all the people who had hurt him in his life, his feelings toward this mean-spirited bully and killer of children were the most violent. Others he had understood too well or known too fleetingly to really hate. He hated what they did to him, instead. But Jarl he had beaten to a pulp with his bare hands when the opportunity had presented itself, six years after his stint in the UnderDocks.

And I would do it again, Amel thought bitterly, *even stark cold sane!* Arguably, he had been less than entirely in his right mind at the time.

Amel was reveling in the empowering idea of slapping Jarl's face on Zind in a blow by blow rematch of their fight outside Blue Hearth, in which he was winning for a change, when he felt a cool touch like the caress of a silken drape falling over the combat in his head and getting roughly entangled in the slashing swords.

The angel beside him gave a yelp.

Amel came to himself with a start and turned to see her staring at him, white faced.

"Sorry!" he cried, catching her cold hand as her eyes rolled up and she swooned in her flight harness.

CHAPTER 11

Red Hearth

Erien was trying to get drunk. At least he could reach no other conclusion despite the lack of a reasonable rationale. Why else would he be in a rough spacer's pub on the Plaza after Lights Down knocking back drinks?

His meeting with Vretla had been uneventful from his point of view, but Tatt's determination to get details had driven him out of Green Hearth. Vretla was prepared to swear to him for the price of a child or two, which he expected, and he'd told her he would have to think about it. What he actually kept thinking about, instead, was that he ought to have done something to help Luthan at the Council of Privilege, but he still didn't know what. Now she was gone and Amel had gone after her—a detail he found particularly vexing for no good reason he could pin down.

It wouldn't matter if I had something to work on, he thought. But Ameron wouldn't entertain ideas about his academy until after the upcoming Swearing.

He stared at the shiny surface of the bright red drink in his hand, called a Vrellish Lunge. As near as Erien could tell it was mostly gin mixed with something sweet and warmed to a sickly body temperature. He didn't like the taste, but it seemed to be what everyone was drinking in the Vrellish bar where he had wound up.

The bar was called the Red Tent, which was apt, because the whole thing was nothing more than exactly that, filled with seating surrounding a central hub. Servers came and went from the round room at the center ringed by a beaten-up, but obviously much prized, wooden bar. About a dozen patrons shared the space with Erien, drinking as listlessly as he was, except for a few Nersallians who sat rolling dice and gambling with each other as they munched on a pile of deep-fried protein snacks.

Erien was nearly finished his drink and wondering whether he could stomach another when a new customer strode in and woke up the bar. He was definitely Vrellish and, to judge by reactions, a new face at court. His bare chest was oiled. He wore leather flight pants and a pair of bright red suspenders barely wide enough for the crimson braid patterns embroidered on them. A sword hung at his right side and an odd-looking platform was strapped to one shoulder, reminding Erien of nothing so much as a perch for a bird of prey.

"Two drinks!" the half-naked newcomer proclaimed when he reached the weathered wooden bar. "One short, one tall."

It was polite, in courtly circles, for Sevolites addressing a commoner to reveal their birth rank by using a pronoun. The Red Vrellish stranger had not obliged, and it was clear the barman was afraid to guess, so Erien got up, thinking to help the commoner by engaging the very Vrellish-looking stranger in conversation that would reveal how Sevolite the man was.

Then the next surprise arrived. This one waddled into the bar on its hind legs, riveting everyone's attention. Even the Nersallians stopped rolling dice.

The thing had a long snout, large hairless hands and a soft belly. It took in the room with a bedraggled look, brightening the moment it spotted the Vrellish man.

"Vrazz!" it chirped with a twitch of its long, whiskered nose, dropped onto all fours and galloped up its friend's side to perch on the pad strapped to the man's shoulder.

'Vrazz,' if this was meant to be a name, lent a hand to help. Once the creature settled on the platform, it laid its snout down on the man's naked chest and drooped there like a wilted flower.

Erien had never seen a Tarkian grab rat, but it fit the description: about the size and weight of a two-year-old child, and covered in light gray fur except for the hands and snout, with a long prehensile tail and big ears.

"Is that a—" Erien began to ask, fascinated despite his own state of inebriation.

"Fip," said the man in the bright red suspenders, and gave his shoulder a bounce, causing the grab rat to bare its teeth and growl. "He's a little trip fatigued at the moment. Long flight in from Cold Rock. I'm Vras Vrel," he introduced himself in *rel-*

peerage, then noticed Erien's dark clothes and froze. "Are you Nersallian?" he asked in an accusing tone.

"No," said Erien. He was about to volunteer his identity when the stranger exclaimed, "Spiral Hall, then!" and embraced him, thrusting the dank smell of disgruntled grab rat into his nostrils momentarily, before standing back.

"Your Grace is a...Highlord?" the barman ventured, doubtless expecting the guess to be flattering, since the most likely explanation for Vras was that he came from Spiral Hall, where most of the residents were less than Highlord.

"Ah!" said Vras, with drunken good humor. "The Demish birth rank business! I know this." He paused to think for two seconds before continuing confidently. "I am what you call a Royalblood in your system. Or so my cousin, Vretla, tells me. We don't count percentiles in Red Reach. We get in our *rel* ships and sort each other out by who can fly hardest." He leaned an elbow on the bar to give his full attention to the barman. "And you are?"

The man took a step back clutching his dishcloth to his chest with both hands. Erien guessed he had never laid eyes on a Red Vrellish highborn before, except Vretla Vrel, who conducted herself more or less like any other peer of Fountain Court and was therefore considered reasonably civilized.

Vras snatched the dishcloth out of the barman's hands to flick him with it, saying, "Just like the last place! You stationers on Gelion are so unfriendly!"

"Vretla Vrel is your...cousin?" asked Erien, drawing Vras's attention to relieve the distress of the barman. He used the same uniquely Vrellish term for cousin that Vras had, which covered all but immediate relations who still smelled too much like family to be breeding partners. Ranar's research had determined that most Vrellish could explain how a relative was connected to them in more detail, if pressed, but a sibling's child and a mother's sister were all referred to individually as 'cousin,' or collectively as '*fem*-kin' if they were maternal relatives.

"I am Vretla's sword-heir," Vras explained himself, as his frank expression darkened. "Although I may have to challenge her myself the next time I see her! A Lor'Vrel, by the souls of my ancestors! She's offered her oath to a Lor'Vrel!" He made a noise in his throat. "She has lost her mind!"

"I...hadn't heard that Liege Vrel had sworn to anyone, yet," Erien said, carefully. "Only that she is exploring her options."

"Urr," Vras growled low in his throat. "Well, she won't swear to Ameron—not while he has the Silvers and the Blacks within his oath. It is all about rules with the Black Vrellish. And the Silvers are content to starve us over scribbles on paper. You!" He broke off to accost the barman. "Drinks, I said!"

The barman bobbed down behind the bar, produced two glasses, filled the first one all the way to the top and hesitated over the second.

"Half way!" Vras instructed, putting Fip down on the bar in front of the half-empty glass. "He's already tipsy, but it helps with the *rel*-fatigue."

The grab rat perked up enough to stick its snout into the glass, sniff and take an experimental lick with its long tongue.

The barman looked to Erien for rescue.

"Maybe you should give him his drink at one of the tables," Erien suggested.

But before Vras could answer, a new voice interjected from behind them, speaking in the accent of the Nersallian homeworld of Tark.

"I thought I smelled vermin," said one of the Nersallians who had been dicing earlier.

He followed up with a snatch for Fip's throat. The grab rat leaped off the bar and landed on Erien's chest to cling there with all four hands. A bad smell ensued as it emptied its bladder in terror.

"Fip is my friend!" Vras warned.

"Friend, is it!" exclaimed the Nersallian in disgust. "Red Vrellish are barking mad!"

Vras sprang away from the bar, looking much less drunk than he had when he'd swaggered in the door—until he bumped into a chair. He got himself under control again with a laugh, exclaiming, "And Nersallians are nothing but oversexed Demish!"

Erien might have intervened if he could have seen what happened next, but Fip wrapped his arms around his head in fright, obliging him to pry the creature off. In the struggle, Fip bit him on the hand. Then he plopped back onto the bar, scrambled behind it and let loose a volley of squat, unbreakable glasses at the back of the Nersallian's head, shrieking in a series of high-pitched yelps that might have been the grab rat version of a war cry.

The fight very quickly became a brawl. Vras was laying about him with a heavy chair, and had landed at least one good hit against his first opponent, but the Tarkian had friends who were ganging up on Vras and his vermin. One of them aimed a throwing dagger at Fip while the grab rat was busy taking aim at another Nersallian, and without thinking Erien shot out an arm to spoil the thrower's aim. The Nersallian retaliated with an iron-fisted punch, slamming Erien backwards into a table.

Erien stayed on his feet and was in position to block the next attack, having studied martial arts during his years on Rire. He landed a punch to the man's ribs, and heaved him clear far enough to buy the time to take a look around him.

Vras had his sword out and so did the leader of the Nersallians. Fip was hiding behind the bar and the rest of the assailants were standing clear to make room now the punch-up had escalated to a duel.

"Wait!" Erien shouted, holding out his arms. "There is no need for this! Vras Vrel and his grab rat are leaving, immediately, with me."

The leader of the Nersallians took a hard look at Erien in the less than bright light of the bar. His demeanor changed completely when he recognized him. "Heir Gelion?" he said, surprised.

Vras turned his sword towards Erien. "You!" he cried. "You're the Lor'Vrel Vretla's going to swear to!"

"Vretla hasn't sworn to me yet," Erien pointed out. "She's only thinking about it."

Vras noticed the wet patch on the front of Erien's shirt and lowered his sword, making a sympathetic face. "Fip?" he asked tentatively.

"I trust it will wash out," said Erien.

"Actually," Vras admitted, "it stains like bleach."

Erien sighed. "I have other shirts," he said patiently. Then he turned to the Nersallians, "Thank you for stopping this short of bloodshed."

"Just see he keeps that stinking pet of his out of our way!" the man complained, up-speaking Erien appropriately.

Fip made a dive off the bar onto Vras's shoulder.

"Why should I go anywhere with a Lor'Vrel?" Vras asked Erien excitedly, sword once again at the ready in his left hand.

"I want to help you and Fip," Erien assured him as reasonably as he could under the circumstances. The smell of Fip's pee was threatening to peel his sinuses and making his stomach rethink its reception of too many Vrellish Lunges.

"Why?" Vras asked suspiciously.

"I've heard about grab rats," said Erien. "But I have never met one. Fip seems remarkably intelligent."

"Not really," Vras disagreed, eliciting a whimper from the clawed and fanged creature on his shoulder. "Smarter than the average Nersallian, maybe, but I wouldn't say he's remarkably intelligent."

Fip raised his head enough to look right at Erien, made a patting gesture indicating his own chest, and said, "Zorry," in a thin, nasal voice.

"Until today, I hadn't realized rats can speak," Erien asked, in amazement.

"Not all of them can," Vras said proudly, and immediately stiffened with suspicion again. "Why are you interested?"

"Can we talk about this outside?" said Erien, uncomfortable with the way the Nersallians were glowering at them from their table, and wanting to change his clothes.

Vras sheathed his sword, pulled Fip off his shoulder into his arms and strode out. Erien followed.

They were barely clear before Vras spun around and said hotly, "You can't study Fip! So forget it!"

"I will not hurt Fip," Erien promised the volatile man in the red suspenders. "But given what I have just witnessed, something should be done to stop the Nersallians hunting Fip's kind for sport."

"Hah!" Vras barked a laugh. "Teach them not to hunt Red Vrellish in space, first. Then I might believe you could stop them killing grab rats for getting into their granaries on Tark!"

"And what is it the Red Vrellish do in space to make Nersallians treat them like grab rats?" Erien asked.

"Why am I even talking to you, Lor'Vrel?" exclaimed Vras. He threw up his hands as he spoke, obliging Fip to cling to his suspenders or fall.

A shape appeared out of the shadows between buildings on the Plaza. Erien became aware of it peripherally, his wits dulled by alcohol. A tingling feeling of threat rose on his neck. He looked, and saw a woman the same size and build as Vras wearing black leather trousers and a thigh-length vest worn open over an oiled chest as lean and muscular as a Vrellish man's, despite the suggestion of small, firm breasts. She had very short hair, a triangular head and a killer's eyes.

"He's Erien Lor'Vrel!" Vras told the woman, stabbing an arm in Erien's direction.

The woman cleared her sword.

"No, no!" Vras backpedaled, clamping a hand about her wrist. "He saved Fip."

The woman gave a snort that suggested to Erien that she was not as enamored of the grab rat as her male companion. But she sheathed her sword.

"Erien," Vras conducted introductions, "this is Sert. My twin sister."

The smell of Fip's pee was becoming increasingly revolting to Erien. "May I invite you both to White Hearth?" he said. "Where I can change and shower. I would like to know what your objection is to me as Vretla's liege, once I smell better."

Sert growled. At first Erien thought it was Fip, but the tone was too deep and the direction was wrong.

"I think he might be all right, after all," Vras said cheerfully. "He saved Fip." Turning to Erien, he said, "Come to Red Hearth when you're ready. We'll talk there."

Beside him, Sert moved and was gone like a swirl of smoke in the eerie glow of night lighting on the Plaza. Vras followed, jogging a few steps to catch up. Fip nearly fell off his shoulder and made a complaining sound.

"Sert!" Vras called after his sister. "Sert, will you slow down, I'm drunk!"

–o—o—o–

Erien showered and put on a fresh shirt in White Hearth. He didn't go back to the Plaza, but onto Fountain Court instead, through White Hearth's entrance hall. Red Hearth was two doors away, counter-clockwise past Green Hearth and Black Hearth. As he approached it, Erien realized he had never been inside it before and stopped a few paces short, wondering if he ought to be apprehensive. But his Reetion guardian, Ranar, had always thought well of the Red Vrellish, so Erien set aside his doubts and went to lay his hand upon the nervecloth panel on the door. It was interesting to him that the supposedly uncivilized Vrellish used nervecloth for this purpose when most other houses of Fountain Court preferred to post liveried guards or mount ornate knockers.

"It's open!" someone called from inside.

Erien pushed and the door opened onto a flurry of childish activity as half a dozen semi-naked boys and girls scattered into rooms off the Entrance Hall. A harried-looking woman wearing Vretla's colors emerged from their midst, pushing back disor-

dered hair to blink at Erien. She showed her age clearly enough
to be a commoner of thirty-five or a nobleborn twice as old.

"Oh," she said, seeing him, and straightened up. "Heir
Gelion!"

Erien suspected Red Hearth did not entertain many non-
Vrellish visitors. The scamps he had interrupted in some mischief
would be the children of Vretla's Spiral Hall vassals.

"This way, Immortality," said the harried child-minder. At
this point, a trio of armed errants appeared to back her up, but
seeing it was Erien they lost interest and left again. Clearly, he
was expected.

Intrigued, Erien followed his escort down Red Hearth's
Throat.

The first room was decked out in a neo-Monatese style,
complete with potted plants, nervecloth displays alternating
between people and spacescapes, and comfortable furniture
upholstered in shades that ranged from russet to crimson.

"The Red Room," the child-minder said, noting Erien's
interest. "This is where Vretla normally entertains court peers
and visitors, but she's asked me to take you through to Family Hall. I'm Nona, by the way. I'm what we'd call a Station
Master in Red Reach, but here I call myself Hearth Master." She
turned to smile at him. "I hope you aren't offended by my
grammar." She was addressing him in undifferenced *pol* to *rel*
pronouns, acknowledging his superiority without the addition
of differencing suffixes to measure the gap between them.

"No," Erien assured her, thinking about how interested Ranar
would be in Nona. Ranar believed most Red Reach stationers
had mixed blood due to the casual nature of sexual relations
between classes. "I'm grammatically flexible," he explained,
to be explicit.

"Me too," said Nona. "I can put on court clothes and mingle
with Demish servants on the Market Round as if I was one of
them." She laughed. "Vretla's not so good at fitting in at Demish
parties, let me tell you!"

"No," said Erien, noting that Nona and Liege Vrel were on
a first name basis. In a Demish household that would have been
extraordinary; here, he suspected it was normal.

More rooms followed, one of them filled with a jumble of
info-retrieval and display devices in various states of repair,
another one full of padded furniture and a third almost empty.

At the end of the Throat, where most hearths made a T-junc-
tion with Family Hall, Erien was shown into a big open space

without any rooms at all. The lighting was uneven. He could make out a layer of platforms and scaffolding lining the walls, studded with openings to cave-like niches. Spare clothes were hung here and there, bedding spilled out of sleeping spaces, and everything was decorated in trailing feathers, furry ornaments and strings of bright beads.

Vretla and her Red Reach cousins were lounging around a pit filled with steaming hot water. Steps led down into water that wasn't deep enough to swim in, and towels were stacked at the pool's edge on a configuration of movable blocks with padded tops, arrayed around the perimeter. Half a dozen house staff of both sexes sat on this arrangement of furniture chatting with each other and helping themselves to the refreshments. Sert was busy making out with one of the serving men. She broke off at Erien's arrival, rose and strapped on her sword again. The man pulled his clothing together with a sullen look over the interruption.

Clearly, thought Erien, *being on staff in Red Hearth comes with a different set of expectations than in a Demish residence.* Thinking of Tatt and his justice ministry, he wondered what the Vrellish did with commoners who declined their advances.

"Pureblood Erien," Nona announced their arrival.

Vretla hopped off a heap of waterproof pillows where she had been playing with Fip and stood with her feet apart and arms akimbo. She was wearing nothing but a loose drape over wet skin. Erien kept his eyes on her face.

"This is him," she introduced Erien to her company. "Pureblood Erien Lor'Vrel, Heir Gelion. What do you think of him as a possible l'liege?"

L'liege, Erien knew, was a collapsed form of the phrase 'liege of my liege.'

"Maybe," said Vras. "But I'd have to soul touch him to be sure." He folded his arms across his red suspenders. He still wore his sword, but he had shed the grab rat platform.

Sert walked around Erien, sniffing at him. After one circuit, she confronted Vretla with a disapproving look.

"Are you thinking with your head, cousin?" Sert asked.

"Yes, he's tasty," Vretla admitted. "But can't I think with my head and my appetite at the same time?"

The banter made Erien's jaw tighten in irritation. He was well aware of the Vrellish use of culinary terms to reference sex, and all too accustomed to female harassment in the Nersallian fleet where he had spent the last three years.

"I have thought about your demands regarding child-gifting," Erien told Vretla as neutrally as he could. "I will not produce a child I have no part in educating as it grows up. I understand this attitude is not a Vrellish one and you would expect to have sole custody, but I could not accept those conditions."

Both women took in Erien's statement with reserved looks. Vras looked impressed. "Woo!" he interjected into the silence that followed, and shook a hand as if to cool it off. "He talks straight, at least," Vras admitted. "For a Lor'Vrel."

"We are still getting to know each other," said Vretla in a slow, steady manner. "I think it unwise to make too many demands, on either side, too early."

Erien nodded, glad to shelve the topic for the time being.

"As I told you earlier," he said to Vretla, "I am not a conventional Sevolite. I spent my first seven years on Monitum, under Di Mon's tutelage, but I lived on Rire for the next seven. I am not interested in conventional Gelack politics. You and I were both Di Mon's pupils, and I share Di Mon's belief the Red Vrellish must remain a presence in empire politics. This might make us compatible. But why would you even consider swearing to me, when my position on Rire is well known, and you were one of those keen to invade the Reetion reaches not very long ago."

Vretla shrugged. "A great deal has changed since then," she said, in a sober tone. Her mood changed with a smile. She waved to an attendant and was swiftly helped out of her minimal covering and into a voluminous admiralty cloak with a high, winged collar and a built-in bodice, demonstrating a typically Vrellish lack of concern for the intermediate state of nakedness, except for her black thong. Erien was finding the atmosphere unsettling, and chose to avert his eyes.

"So," she said, startling Erien a little as she slung an arm about his shoulders. "Let us get to know each other."

Erien considered putting up with being manhandled, and decided if he gave in now it would only get worse later. He lifted Vretla's arm off his shoulder and stepped clear.

"Forgive me," he said politely, "but I am not comfortable with casual physical interactions. It is a personal preference, and not a sign of ill will. But I would rather we talked without touching."

The Vrellish trio exchanged looks.

They think I'm odd, Erien decided, but he could not help his reaction. He would not be pawed and if they insisted on trying they would find out how Vrellish he could be in a fight.

Vretla took a step back and stood looking at him with a thoughtful pout on her mouth. "As you wish," she said, civilly enough, although her tone was noticeably chillier.

Sert rumbled, "Lorel," under her breath, making it sound like a curse.

"I respect the reasons for your deep distrust of Lorel sciences," Erien told them all, noticing how Vretla's staff behaved very much like a part of the group, rather than remaining on the periphery, although thus far none except Nona had said anything to him. "I also appreciate how Reetion technologies must put you in mind of Lorel parallels, but technology itself does not commit atrocities. People do. One of the reasons I want to open an academy of sciences for Sevolites is to empower us all to make better informed decisions about the use of medicine, in particular, but other things as well. Including things like the visitor probe and Gelack conscience bonding."

Vretla absorbed what he said with a frown. Vras looked unhappy, and Sert continued to glower in a way that kept him ready to respond with violence if violence was offered. It was Nona who spoke up.

"Train Sevolites in the sciences?" Nona said, giving Erien every bit as dirty a look as Sert had. "Why? We like the way things run in Red Reach, Lorel."

Belatedly, Erien took note of the devices on her jacket symbolizing different kinds of work, or perhaps depicting levels of achievement in the trades represented.

"I would work with your people in whatever way was meaningful to them, of course," he told Nona, remembering what Ranar had conjectured about the importance of trade guilds run by Vrellish stationers.

"Well?" Vretla asked Nona.

Red Hearth's stationer mistress pursed her lips. "I don't know what to make of him," she said.

Vras broke the tension with a laugh. "So!" he said. "If we can't touch him, what do we do to relax?"

"We are a physical people," Vretla explained to Erien. "Food, games and invitations to share beds would usually occur at this stage in clan negotiations."

"What sort of games?" Erien ventured, but whatever response Vretla might have given him was swept away by the eruption of three errants, bursting out of Red Hearth's Throat at a run, waking sleepers in the surrounding enclaves with their shouts.

The first words Erien heard were "Raid!" and "Blue Hearth!"

Vretla, Vras and Sert were on alert. "Who attacked?" Vretla demanded.

"Zind Therd of the Knotted Strings!" she was answered.

The second Vrellish errant caught Vretla's arm to steady himself as he caught his breath. "Amel left two of his Golden Paladins as highborn defenders. One was out when the attack took place. Zind took down the second one."

The third errant was Monatese, dressed in Tatt's green livery. He arrived a few steps behind and addressed himself to Erien with a respectful bow. "Heir Gelion, my liege requests you join him at Blue Hearth to assist in the investigation."

"Of course," Erien said, but as he made to join the Monatese nobleborn, Vras Vrel and his grim twin, Sert, flowed around him.

"You are my liege-intended," Vretla explained their actions to Erien. "Let them attend on you," she smiled. "To take your measure."

Vras confirmed this analysis with a wide grin. Sert glared.

"Very well," said Erien, resigned. He thought of warning them not to act without consulting him, but remembered Ranar's tract on the Vrellish disposition and decided it would do more harm than good.

At least the grab rat stayed behind.

CHAPTER 12

Kidnapped

Tatt met Erien on Fountain Court in the mouth of the doors to Blue Hearth. Diplomat that he was, he did no more than blink at the two Vrellish highborns escorting him. "This way!" he said.

A couple of black-clad Nersallians prowled the entrance hall. Their heads turned like magnets tracking metal as the Vrellish duo went by. The Silver Demish were everywhere, putting the place in order, some of them servants and some of them sword-bearing princes attended by less Sevolite retainers. Erien's arrival stopped work cold as the Demish fixated on Vras and Sert, staring as if they had never seen a Red Vrellish highborn before.

Which is probably the case, Vretla excepted, thought Erien.

His very Vrellish followers appeared more amused than intimidated. Sert selected the most aggressive looking prince and stared back until the man broke eye contact in embarrassment.

"Ameron sent over a few princes to avoid further bloodshed before the Swearing," Tatt explained the presence of Ava's Oath vassals in Amel's hearth. "And he has jurisdiction, since Amel is still technically sworn to his heir. That would be you," he said, placing a finger firmly on the center of Erien's chest.

Erien frowned. He wasn't as politically naive as Tatt thought he was. He knew the grim rules of Sword Law and the dance of death they permitted. He even understood its larger significance on an anthropological level, thanks to Ranar. He simply didn't like it and never would. He couldn't help believing there had to be a saner way to permit competition between space-faring interests without risking all-out war.

"There was no breach of Sword Law in the raid," Tatt continued. "Zind defeated the highborn defender, and only then did she and her nobleborns subdue nobleborn resistance by Amel's errants." His usually mercurial expression turned murderous. "But it became my business once I learned a commoner was kidnapped along with Leksan Lekker. A girl called Mona. Mira's daughter."

Erien stopped. "Leksan and Mona were kidnapped?" he asked, alarmed.

Tatt nodded. "Zind is *de facto* D'Therd back home. I doubt the Therd clan in the Knotted Strings held with her father's decision to disinherit her in favor of his half-Demoran daughter when he started going Demish on the Dem'Vrel. I wouldn't be surprised if Zind didn't have much use for little Princess Telly, but be that as it may, she's bound to view herself as the lawful D'Therd in the renewed hostilities with the Lekkers. Word is she snatched the younger of the Lekker heirs before coming to court—probably wanted to use him as a bargaining chip—and with Amel gone, she seems to have decided to make it a matched set and took his older brother Leksan: the actual D'Lekker, at least in name. Sen Lekker acts as regent."

The dynastic details had little power to stir Erien compared with his Reetion outrage over the kidnapping! Leksan, Lars and Mona were children! He knew Gelacks didn't think about children in quite the way Reetions did. Sevolite children, in particular, were considered reincarnations of ancestors. But he couldn't help feeling shocked, and even betrayed.

Erien knew Zind! He did not want to believe she was responsible for what he saw around him when they emerged into the central reception hall, pierced by the symbolic spiral stairs leading up to the Plaza. It was here Zind would have entered.

"Amel's new captain of errants," Tatt said, with a nod in the direction of a wounded man being laid out on a stretcher by one of Amel's household staff. "And that's one of the Demoran paladins." He tipped his chin to indicate a kneeling figure in white robes. "He's doing penance for not being here when the raid occurred. His partner was killed trying to stop Zind. The servants say Zind sent nobleborns into Family Hall after the children while Zind and the paladin were fighting. We found one of Zind's there, as well, and two of Blue Hearth's errants. Mira's been patching up the wounded in the Blue Hearth med lab." He inhaled deeply. "There is one question of Sword Law unresolved, in that the nobleborns had no right to overpower Leksan, since he's highborn. They do seem to have done so before Zind arrived. Young Leksan fought and got injured. Mona stuck with him to treat the wound so they took her, too." Tatt scowled. "Errants are within their rights to gang up on an invading highborn who drops the shield of honor, and that definitely includes kidnapping a commoner child! I don't know about Leksan. I'm not even sure if the laws of the Ava's court or the Knotted Strings ought to apply!" He frowned. "Luthan would know." Tatt shook off his uncertainty. "There will have to be a Trial of Honor to clear it up, if Zind ever wants to be welcome again at court!"

Erien tried to make sense of the deaths and the mayhem, but all he could think about was young Leksan shouting vengeance at him for the death of his father.

"Where is Leksan's regent?" Erien asked.

"Sen Lekker? She's gone with Amel to Demora."

Like Luthan, Erien thought. It was disconcerting how the princess-liege of Silver Hearth kept popping into his head at the least excuse.

Mira came down the spiral stairs connecting the reception area with the Plaza, above, pulling off translucent gloves streaked in blood.

"The wounded will live," she said. She looked pinched and tired.

"Those would be the nobleborn guards who didn't try to stop Zind coming in, as is quite proper, but did try to stop her party on the way out when they saw she had the children with them," explained Tatt.

"They took your daughter," Erien said to Mira.

She looked surprised by his attention. "Ah," she said. "Of course—you are Reetion-raised. It slipped my mind." Her expression hardened. "I wouldn't have let them take her if I'd been here," she said. "I would have stopped it somehow: used my knowledge like a Lorel and got myself executed for it after, disgracing Amel." She paused to open a waste bag at her side and stuffed in the soiled gloves. "I should have kept Mona with me," she added in a bleak tone.

"You must be very worried about her," Erien insisted, in Reetion, to sidestep the issue of pronouns. He knew she understood the language because Amel had kept her connected with Reetion medical feeds and research venues throughout his envoy period.

Mira raised her head as if stung, and answered in stiffly proper Gelack. "I appreciate your views regarding commoners, Immortality," she said. "But I would be grateful if you addressed me as you should, in Gelack. It's simpler."

"I understand," Erien replied, obliging her.

"Amel must have introduced Mona to Leksan!" Mira erupted suddenly, her stoic facade cracking. "That's why she was with him when Zind invaded, not safe with the servants! And she doesn't know any better, herself, than to imagine she could be the friend of a Sevolite Royalblood, which is as much my fault as anyone's!" Her outrage crashed as abruptly as it had flared. She raised a hand to hold it over her eyes as she collected herself.

"Should we send for Amel?" Tatt asked Mira compassionately. "Fetch him back from Demora?"

And keep him away from Luthan, thought Erien.

"Oh, but that isn't necessary!" Vras volunteered unexpectedly, coming up beside Erien. "Erien is Amel's liege and therefore able to act for him in things like this!" He lay a hand on Mira's shoulder, bending over her. "My sister Sert and I have no love for child-stealers. We'll go with Erien to fetch your daughter back. And the Lekker boy."

Mira regarded the Red Reach highborn dubiously.

Erien considered the idea. He didn't like child-stealers either, and he owed Leksan something. He also suspected his credibility with the Vrellish was at stake here. They wanted an adventure to share with him.

"Liege Nersal is *brerelo* to Heir Gelion," said a woman in Nersallian black, who had been hovering at the periphery of the discussion. "Black Hearth could send an arm of the fleet into the Knotted Strings to punish the Dem'Vrel. We, too, disapprove of child thieves." She eyed Sert. "And man-rapers."

"Sert is nothing like our mother!" Vras rallied in his sister's defense, inserting himself between her and the meddling Nersallian.

"You're the product of a man-rape?" Tatt asked the twins, his eyebrows lifting and staying up, as if pinned, on his forehead.

"Our mother was the leader of a wild hunt," Vras admitted. "The one that seduced Vretla's father, Vackal, and kept him from court for so many years. And yes, it is well known she caught and killed our sire, Vras, who is my namesake, and was ha'brother to the liege of Clan Sert. Vretla avenged our sire when we were still infants and gave us to our father's clan to be named and raised."

The Nersallian woman gave Vras a look that suggested she understood why his villainous mother might have been tempted by his sire, but she followed up with a disdainful scowl. "Wild Hunts," she scoffed. "The Red Vrellish blame them for all their sins, but I wonder if they are as rare as Liege Vrel pretends. Too many Nersallian men go missing in Red Reach."

Sert muscled between Erien and Tatt to get at her accuser.

"Easy! Easy!" Tatt interposed himself between the two women, giving Vras and Erien a look that said: 'I could use help here!' Vras just scowled, showing his anti-Nersallian prejudice.

Erien only belatedly realized the proper Vrellish thing to do would be to flirt with one or both of the women to defuse the situation.

Instead, he announced, "I cannot take Nersallians into the Knotted Strings because they would expect to stay, and although I am Heir Gelion, this is an Avim's Oath problem; therefore, it would be politically unsound to involve the vassals of the Ava. But I will take the Vrellish to rescue the children."

Vras gave a whoop, forgetting his feelings about Nersallians sufficiently to slide an arm around the black-clad woman's waist and engage her in a celebratory kiss involving extensive body contact, which Erien suspected Ranar would interpret as Vrellish idiom for 'tough luck, but don't be a sore loser.' It took two seconds for the Nersallian to loosen up and settle for the con-solation prize. At least it certainly looked as if she would happily have made it up with Vras, if Sert hadn't reluctantly broken eye contact with Tatt to yank her brother out of the Nersallian's arms.

Both Vras and the Nersallian woman looked mildly intoxi-cated as they came apart.

Sex! Erien thought gloomily. *How can I hope to lead people who consider sexual overtures a normal part of every negotiation!*

"Do you keep your promises, Green Hearth?" Sert said to Tatt in a seductive tone.

"Maybe," Tatt said with a sloppy smile. "Check in with me when you get back."

Vras and Sert were both much more Vrellish than court hybrids, and the sexual side effects appeared to have taken Tatt and the Nersallian by surprise. Erien was feeling the effects of Vrellish pheromones in the air himself, and he didn't like it.

"Convey my thanks to Liege Nersal, if—indeed—he would have been willing to assist," he told the Nersallian woman, who had sobered up enough to execute a crisp salute. She took her leave with an air of military discipline.

"Meet us at Vretla's docks!" Vras told Erien, remembering he didn't like being touched in time to abort a friendly punch to the shoulder as he went past.

Sert was already heading off at a trot and Vras hurried to catch up with her.

"Whew!" Tatt exclaimed, giving himself a shake. His pupils were still dilated from the acute dose of Sert's sex appeal. "So that's what Red Reach women are like!" He grinned. "I hope we get more of them coming to court once you're their liege!"

"It remains to be seen if Vretla will swear to me," Erien cautioned.

Tatt paid him little heed. "You know, if what we just experienced is normal in Red Reach, Vretla might just be containing herself when she's at court!" He blew air hard enough to stir the mop of curly hair on his forehead. "Wonder what she's like on Cold Rock!" He gave himself a shake to dispel the fantasy and turned to Erien with a businesslike air, rubbing his hands together.

"So," Tatt said brightly, "let's suit up!"

"Not you, Tatt," said Erien. "I won't be responsible for putting your life at risk. Besides," he added, when Tatt made to protest, "this is Avim's Oath business, and Monitum is as much part of the Ava's Oath as the Nersallians."

"You're right about the Nersallians, I grant you," Tatt admitted. "Taking them into the Knotted Strings would be as good as declaring war. But me—"

"No," said Erien.

"Fine!" Tatt gave in, and looked around him unhappily. "I'll stay here, clean up and array charges against Zind in case she ever obliges us by turning up for her trial." He sighed, deflated. "Do you want me to inform Amel about what's happened?"

Erien considered this seriously. He liked the idea of dragging Amel back from Demora, but he suspected his motives were too personal to be honorable. And he did not want Amel interfering in his negotiations with Zind Therd.

"Not yet," he decided. "I'll send word to him once I have more information."

"Suit yourself!" Tatt said, a bit petulantly, and went off grumbling about the fun he was going to miss.

Erien stayed where he was in the midst of the mayhem caused by Zind Therd. He had liked Zind from the day they first met, when she had helped him to navigate the Lorel Stairs. Was it naïve to hope she had an explanation good enough to cover deaths and kidnapping?

Mira surprised him by reappearing at his elbow. "Immortality," she said, sticking to her own rules about showing deference. Her lips pressed together in a thin line as she waited for him to respond.

"Yes?" Erien encouraged her.

"Amel knows the Dem'Vrel," Mira said. "He might be better able to extract the children from Zind than a stranger, like yourself, backed up by Red Vrellish interlopers."

"You believe we should recall Amel from Demora, then?" Erien asked.

Mira looked uncomfortable. "Amel always wanted our relationship to be closer than I was comfortable with, but I do love him in my own way. As much as I love Mona."

She seemed to need someone's forgiveness for the stand she had made in leaving Amel's hearth. Erien was sure it wasn't his, but he said, "Of course."

"So I shouldn't ask you to send for Amel over this," Mira explained. "He's making a stand, at last, as a Sevolite, and he'll need Demora at his back to make it work. But Mona is just a little girl...."

"I will find her for you," Erien promised. "And Leksan Lekker as well."

Mira held her peace a moment, grimly. Erien prepared to leave.

"Don't chase them!" Mira blurted at the last moment, choosing English to deliver the order despite her earlier insistence on court propriety. "If you can't catch them at a way station, let them get all the way home unmolested before you try anything! If Zind has to run from the Vrellish, she'll sacrifice Mona!"

Erien turned to look at her.

"I assure you that I value your daughter as highly as my nephew Leksan, medtech Mira," said Erien, and left quickly.

−o—o—o−

Erien changed, again, in White Hearth, this time into his old Nersallian flight leathers. He left word for Ameron, saying Tatt could fill him in on the details. Then he left before anyone from the palace could interfere.

His first stop was the Market Round on the Palace Plain, where he made purchases and ordered them delivered to the personal docks of Vretla Vrel. He spent the next hour buying things small enough to fit in his duffle back. The shopkeepers pegged him for a Nersallian Highlord unless he asserted Pureblood grammar, which he was normally happy to let slip. But today the grammatical assumption his flight leathers inspired forced him to realize he needed new clothes. He couldn't fly into the Knotted Strings looking like one of Horth's highborns for the very reason he'd declined Nersallian. He found a shop on the second tier of the Market Round that sold leathers, and picked out a gray suit without too much fuss, under cover of a little grammatical subterfuge, until the time came to pay. At that point, because he had run out of honor chips buying other things, he had to use the signet of credit Ameron had given him.

The store clerk took one look at it and went white.

"O-one moment," the man stuttered, and disappeared into the back. Within moments, the store owner's entire family had appeared: a middle-aged man with generous laugh lines about his eyes; the man's wife, still draped in a tape measure with an embroidery needle tucked into her lapel; and a bright-eyed girl of about fourteen who stared at him as if he had stepped out of a Demish storybook.

"Heir Gelion," the man said, and bowed at the waist, inspiring similar obedience from his family.

"We are honored by your business," said the man's wife, when the family had straightened up again.

It was all terribly awkward for Erien, and telling them—truthfully—that he had Vretla Vrel and her cousins from Red Reach waiting for him on the docks did nothing to break the spell. The easiest way to escape proved to be agreeing to let them outfit him properly on his return to court, if they would finish the current transaction so he could get on his way.

Vretla had four deep-space landers ready and waiting when he reached her hangar on the highborn docks. He arrived at a jog, having dismissed the rented car used for the first leg of the trip across the docks. The short run felt necessary prior to closing himself up in a cockpit for a long haul.

Vretla was dressed in red flight leathers. Vras had traded Fip's shoulder pad for a red leather flight cloak with slits on either side for his arms. Sert was dressed in a black body suit with cutout designs tumbled down either side.

"Where is Fip?" Erien could not help asking, still curious to learn more about the limits of the creature's intellect.

"Parked with a *sha'st* in Spiral Hall," Vretla said with a chuckle. "She's paying for her pleasures."

"Fip doesn't like flying too often," explained Vras, and gestured. "This way."

The Vrellish lander was a flattened disk, its wings folded into housing on either side. *Designed for landing on cold rocks not green worlds,* thought Erien. A cold rock was spacer's idiom for an airless world.

"Are you sure we'll be able to land this on FarHome?" Erien asked, concerned.

"Sure!" Vras replied much too casually. "It can do atmosphere."

They entered the lander through a side hatch. Erien found himself in a space filled with padded Vrellish furniture blocks. The cockpit at the lander's core was a detachable *rel*-fighter, gripped in the space-tight embrace of the surrounding room.

Vras showed Erien how to detach the disk in a crisis to turn the cockpit into a stand-alone *rel*-fighter. "Of course it can be hard to find the disk again after a shake-up, even if it is signaling," said Vras. "Light only travels so fast," he added, with the distinct air of trotting out a maxim.

The interior of the disk was decorated in what the Demish might have called graffiti, although Erien suspected the Vrellish considered it art. The pictures covered a three-dimensional warren of padded furniture that could be reconfigured like a jungle gym and secured in place with clever locks. Given the general orientation of the passenger areas, Erien surmised that the lander was arranged to traverse space with the base of the disk facing forward, but a second set of niches were oriented for passengers to brace themselves when the lander flew edge-first with its wings deployed.

Natives of space, Erien recalled one of Ranar's comments about the Red Vrellish, looking at the furniture of the interior and imagining even the children on board calmly switching places for landing.

"We're taking landers to make it easier to set down on FarHome," Vras informed Erien. "That way there's no need to negotiate docking rights or secure a shuttle."

"I see," said Erien. He was bursting with questions—Ranar's glimpses of Red Vrellish lifestyles were restricted to the nobleborns of Spiral Hall on Gelion, and a single visit to the Red Vrellish meeting site called Cold Rock—but this was all the briefing he got.

Erien was still studying the controls when Vras left to get into his own lander. Vretla was already moving out. Overcoming his preference for thoroughness, Erien made a series of guesses and got his ship trundling after theirs, wishing he had insisted on using his own envoy class vessel, the *DragonClaw*, given to him by Horth. He felt sure he could have landed it anywhere the Vrellish had room to set down a lander.

It wasn't until they had cleared the surface of Gelion and were taxiing out beyond the planet's challenge sphere that Erien began to worry about the skis and winter gear he'd bought. He called Vretla on the radio before they lost the ability to communicate by voice.

"Did the supplies I ordered arrive?" he asked.

"What supplies?" was Vretla's bland reply.

"Things we may need on FarHome," Erien said, noticing Vretla had opened a channel to her cousins, as well, and wondering why. "I sent them ahead for you to load."

"Old Vrellish rule," Vretla drawled. "Flights don't turn back for what anyone leaves behind."

"We need those supplies!" insisted Erien. "People with Vrellish physiology have a lower ration of body fat than commoners or Demish Sevolites—and Zind has a mountain stronghold. I looked it up. They have snow this time of year. You'll need to dress for the weather, and—"

"She loaded the supplies," Vras interjected. "She's just teasing."

Erien listened to the three of them break out in a ripple of laughter, feeling nonplussed.

"Good idea by the way, Lor'Vrel," said Vretla. "I expect you have a plan for the long sticks with foot braces on them?"

"Skis," Erien began to explain, but Vretla had already shut their connection down to prepare for reality skimming.

Erien relaxed in his flight harness with a sigh. *I must remember to ask Ranar about Vrellish humor in my next letter so I'll know when they are making fun of me,* he thought.

Pilots had to clear the challenge radius surrounding any habitat before engaging skim. Failure to observe this universal rule was punishable by immediate attack by defending ward ships, and the loss of docking rights for the offending clan. Even the Vrellish behaved demurely until they cleared Gelion's challenge sphere.

But the moment they were under skim, all three of them shot off at four *skim'facs*—a punishing cruising pace for anyone in his right mind.

Erien hesitated only long enough to realize he was going to lose them on his long range telemetry if he didn't do likewise.

As he matched pace with the rest of his party, he caught a wash of exuberance that told him Vretla, Vras and Sert were in their element. He had never experienced anything like it before. Crack Nersallian pilots who cruised at four *skim'facs* did it to prove their endurance. But the Vrellish were simply having fun and their pleasure was almost seductive: an invitation to fly wild and hard, like a shout of self-assertion in the face of an indifferent universe. This, he realized, must be the allure of the wild hunt, in which a band of Vrellish flew their wits ragged. He had never understood the danger until now.

The Vrellish peaked at nearly five *skim'facs* and subsided to a cruising speed of three, like athletes settling into an easy jog. Erien found it harder to settle down. He had just experienced the legendary prowess of Red Reach highborns firsthand, and yet, in an empire founded on reality skimming, Vretla's people had stayed holed up in Red Reach for most of the Sevolite history, barely managing to maintain a presence at court as a bastion against Demish sprawl.

I could make a difference to them, Erien thought as he watched the three of them leap-frogging over each other.

As the trip progressed, other eccentricities showed up. Vras and Sert had a habit of slipping into wakelock to cruise within a single envelope: a feat of trust too profound to be treated as casually as conversation! Vretla and Vras also made a point of soul-touching him whenever they could, and he wondered if they felt his irritation as clearly as he felt Vretla's passion to exploit his potential as a sire, and Vras Vrel's open-hearted offer of friendship. Sert abstained, but now and then her leeriness leaked through when she sheered by a bit too close, testing his will rather than the honor of his soul.

It was nothing like flying with a disciplined Nersallian fighter hand, and Erien felt badgered by their attempts to assess his character via whiffs of the weird psychological effects of reality skimming.

He was relieved when Vretla signaled for them to regroup in time to make the jump out of the Reach of Gelion.

Once in the Knotted Strings, Vretla kept the other two in line, making a point of skirting way stations and keeping well clear of the ward ships buzzing around their challenge spheres. She even slowed down in the vicinity of the next two jumps, and let Erien take care of identifying them to the nobleborn ward ships on patrol. In both cases the Dem'Vrellish acknowledged Erien's newly learned shimmer dance for 'Heir Gelion' and let them pass.

Erien had kept an eye out for signs of Zind's party on his nervecloth ever since they'd entered the Knotted Strings. He couldn't help it, even though he knew it made no sense. For one thing, Zind's flight could have been any of the groups of blue or red dots he spotted traveling in the right general direction. For another, at the pace Vretla was setting, they had probably left Zind's party behind in the First Knott where they were already settling in on a way station for a twenty-four hour break. At least he hoped so, for Mona's sake. It took nearly thirty hours to make the trip from Gelion to FarHome at one *skim'fac*. Averaging three, like the Vrellish, it was still a ten-hour trip which was outside the bounds of nobleborn stamina. As a reference, Erien recalled that during his time in the Nersallian fleet, four hours had been the recommended maximum exposure for a single flight, even for highborn *rel*-sha flying ward duty. All in all, unless Zind was prepared to kill everyone who wasn't highborn and tax her own Highlord stamina, the pace Vretla had set would get them to FarHome days ahead of Zind, who would be obliged to stop along the way to let her captives rest.

Zind might have been willing to let Mona die, Erien had to admit, but he didn't want to believe it; and he tried to convince himself she wanted to keep the injured heir of the Lekker clan alive, as well. Leksan had been wounded in the struggle and reality skimming exacerbated injuries.

Take care of them, please! Erien wished, irrationally, at Zind Therd. If she did, it would say a lot about her character. *About her honor*, he admitted, still uncomfortable with the uniquely Gelack sense of this word that precluded some forms of murder while condoning others. But it was, at least, a concept Horth had taught him could be very real, and he suspected it was the same trait the Vrellish were looking for in him.

I must never lie to them, Erien promised himself, *or they will never trust me twice. I must never manipulate them, even if I think I'm right. Never act without their informed consent. That's the mistake too many like me have made. But I am Reetion trained, and Reetions know how to persuade.*

Instinct raised the hairs on the back of his neck before he realized he was processing an instinctive awareness of something changing on a patch of his nervecloth screen. Focusing on it, he realized the nervecloth had activated a delta patch to show him something taking place diametrically opposite the spot where the patch had manifested.

His three Vrellish escorts were already wheeling around to face the disturbance. Erien looped around to join them. As he came level, his screen filled with spatter streaked lights that spelled hell.

Ever since his first experience of combat in the Nersallian Fleet, Erien had found it hard to reconcile the chaotic horror of space warfare with the homey name Sevolites used for it. 'Shake-up' sounded more appropriate for a novelty drink or a dance craze.

Ranar said pilots used harmless words for reality skimming phenomena to tame them, but he doubted Ranar had ever been poised, as he was now, on the edge of a ball of frenetic lights slashing up space with their wakes as they struggled for control of a dull, steady glow at their center.

It's a freighter, Erien interpreted the scene: *its escort and defenders.*

He could tell by the magnitudes of each ship's displacement vectors that only nobleborns were engaged in the struggle, and could pick out which ships were cooperating with each other, but it was impossible to know what was at issue. He couldn't determine whether Zind and her pilots were in the fray.

A low groan of sheer frustration escaped him at the limitations inherent in *rel*-telemetry.

The Vrellish made the default assumption: pirates attacked freighters, therefore it was the freighter that deserved their help. Erien followed them with real reluctance, hating to be forced to guess which side to help.

The Vrellish shot through the fighting ships like living lightning, scattering those they did not dunk. 'Dunk,' like 'shake-up,' was much too benign a word. It described nothing less than time slip caused by perturbing another ship enough to make its pilot lose his grip on reality and absorb any unresolved time debt in the area.

Erien memorized where the dunked ships had disappeared and might, therefore, pop back into existence when the universe caught up with them again. If they did not reappear they would become Lost. No one knew whether that meant a lengthy time slip longer than a thousand years of reality skimming history had yet observed, or dissolving into nothingness. Either way, it amounted to falling between cracks in the stuff of the universe.

Two of the Vrellish made a second pass, with Erien and the third one assuming the role of anchors in a typical fish bowl attack, in which a few strong fighters waded in to disperse a greater number of weaker ones. An anchor's role was to prowl the edges of the action, poised to save his comrades from unforeseen hazards, and to pick off opponents who tried to run. But in this case neither Erien nor his companion attempted to stop any ships making a break for it.

When the hot lights of the shake up died down to blips of blue and red, transitioning slowly back to a typical defensive formation surrounding the freighter, Erien's fellow anchor hauled off far enough to make it safe and identified herself by dancing 'Liege Vrel' in vigorous pulses of receding reds, like the beat of a great heart against the infinite blackness of eternity.

The defenders signaled thanks, and extended an invitation to travel with them to the nearest port.

Erien never found out how Vretla intended to react, because one of the attackers popped out of time slip just as the freighter reached its position, setting off alarms in his brain stem. Erien was the first to react because he had been watching for one of the dunked ships to reappear. He saw the ship stutter on his nervecloth, blaze bright, and go for the freighter, choosing death over failure.

Erien sprang to intercept without thinking. A sensation as sickening as standing on the Flashing Floor whirled up as he squeezed—much too close—between the two vessels, blending his perceptions of the interacting pilots in a mad cocktail. He felt the panic of the freighter pilot and the hatred of the suicidal attacker. He tried to pull away, struggling against an unnatural paralysis of action in which a single instant of time seemed to stretched out ahead of him forever.

A strong jolt of something fierce snapped him out of it, and he was flying again enveloped in Sert's iron will. He couldn't explain how he knew it was her except that he had the eerie conviction he would see her sitting beside him, if he could only have turned his head.

Then he was flying on his own again, hands shaking on the controls of his cockpit and bathed in sweat. For a moment there was no one else in sight.

Sert shot clear of the debris spreading from the shattered freighter and Erien followed her, warnings sounding in his ears and sparkling in diamond pulses on the nervecloth lining of his cockpit. Debris, too dense to be puffed away by a *rel*-skimmer's intrusion field and too small to dodge, could shred a pilot when it manifested inside his ship. A tiny fragment announced itself with a loud ping as it ripped a hole in his nervecloth and bounced off the hullsteel behind, too small to see, but large enough to ricochet twice—without hitting him. If he had picked it up at a different angle, it could just as easily have shot straight through him. Fragments didn't manifest in hullsteel itself, but if a ship manifested around one during even a single, microsecond slice of shimmer, it diced with the pilot's survival.

Relsha told tales of hullsteel shards from a shattered ship that manifested in one stitch of shimmer, and due to a bizarre effect of time dilation, froze before the pilot's eyes, only to disappear in the next microsecond. In another variation on this tall tale, fragments were observed to travel a meter across the ship's interior between one stitch and the next, vanishing before they had the time to impact with the hull and be forced to match the ship's velocity. The physics of such stories were dubious: not because it was strictly impossible for a fragment to exist in one stitch and be gone in the next, but because *rel*-ships shimmered many times a second. Pilots never saw the hullsteel shard that almost killed them any more than they saw the one that did.

The event was over by the time Erien noticed it. There was no second ping on his inner hull, but he held his breath waiting for it until he had to breathe or pass out. Only then did he allow himself to realize he was not dead.

It was minutes later when he grasped that he and Sert were alone in space.

Sert signaled him to fly in a holding pattern once they were clear of the slowly expanding cloud of wreckage, and shot off to erupt into a spectacular shimmer display that had to be the *rel*-telemetry equivalent of sending up a flare.

It took a few tries, but eventually she was answered with an equally extravagant plume of reds and blues made tiny by distance.

Vras, Erien guessed. *Acting as a beacon*. Vras just have been waiting for his twin to reappear.

We've time slipped, Erien realized grimly; followed by a wash of relief at their escape.

He joined Sert as she and Vras executed a spinning dance around one another to celebrate their reunion.

Madness, Erien thought, watching them triple their *rel*-skimming exposure through sheer exuberance after what had to have been an ordeal for both of them. But he was also quietly impressed.

It took an hour to reach dock once Vras calmed down enough to lead the way, and twice as long afterwards to negotiate docking with the little way station, in the Second Knott of the Knotted Strings. Vretla was already holed up enjoying the gratitude of the resident Dem'Vrellish nobleborns, who turned out to be Lekkers.

Erien made it through the awkward proceedings required to accommodate his disk-shaped lander, feeling grainy and irritable with *rel*-fatigue. The berth was not the right shape and no one on the station had ever before had to deal with a Red Vrellish lander. Throughout the tedious procedure, Erien had to repress the urge to give orders rather than accept them from the fretful dock master, who clearly lacked experience with highborn travelers and seemed to hold conflicting attitudes about hosting four of them so unexpectedly. He veered between noxious enthusiasm and burst of terror, as if Erien and his Vrellish escort were exotic beasts instead of responsible *rel*-pilots.

Docked at last, Erien jerked out of his flight harness, planning to work off his post-flight edge with a few circuits around the disk section of his lander before dealing with the locals face to face.

What he saw when he slid out of the cockpit made him freeze.

The constructor-kit furniture of the cargo space was scored and strafed as if it had been clawed by a dozen wildcats with one claw apiece. The damage spread out in a fan. Some tiny projectiles had ended their flight by punching into a padded block; others had ended as smears against a hullsteel wall. Erien counted fourteen distinct tracks.

Clearly the matter speck that had manifested inside his cockpit hadn't been the only deadly passenger he'd picked up during one fateful stitch of shimmer very close to the freighter as it shattered. A quick look was all he needed to deduce that all the foreign particles had been taken on board at the same instant. A second wave would have shown a wider angle of dispersion than the first one, and unless a *rel*-ship was on very tight shimmer, like someone dancing a message, it skipped enough space between manifestations to get ahead of any less-than-light-speed explosion.

Erien reconstructed the snap shot in time of the particle cloud he'd manifested around, based on the tracks, and the resulting picture didn't jibe with the patterns of shattering hullsteel he'd learned about during his fleet tour under Horth. His best guess was that he had narrowly missed death at the hands of the freighter's cargo.

Hoping that at least one example might have been slowed down enough by a glancing collision with furniture to have survived intact, he began a systematic search of the floor. Fifteen minutes later, he held the answer to the puzzle between his thumb and forefinger.

It was a grain of oats: a protein-enriched variety with a distinctly yellow-golden color that was one of the hallmark exports of Demora.

He and the Vrellish had failed to prevent the loss of yet another shipment of what the Dem'Vrellish referred to as the 'groceries.' And if Tatt's analysis was right, it meant there would be more people going hungry on FarHome.

Erien emerged from his lander still holding the grain of oats.

"About time!" Vras greeted him, breaking off what looked like an animated conversation with the jittery dock master. They were surrounded by at least twenty people. Erien noticed one other disk-shaped vessel on the long, empty floor of the cargo dock, but that was all.

"What happened to the other two landers?" he asked, tucking the grain of oats into a pocket of his flight jacket. Some of the people in the clump of observers were paying him far more attention than he liked—and a disproportionate number of them were women.

"Sert and I shed ours when we went in to scatter the attackers," Vras explained. "And Vretla says the weather's too rough around the wreck to go fishing for them. So we'll be doubling up for the rest of the trip."

The dock master ventured to touch Vras on the elbow and shrank back as the Vrellish highborn turned around.

"S-so you will consider my offer, then? To stay with myself and my—"

"Daughter?" Vras asked, looking up to smile gamely at the nobleborn woman in flight attire watching him with pointed interest from behind her father. He sighed, making a face. "Vretla would skin me."

"Oh, but your liege—Vretla Vrel herself!" The dock master seemed to feel the need to say it out loud to convince himself. "She has already accepted our, uh, Vrellish hospitality."

Vras laughed. "Of course!" He cast a sparkling look of weakening willpower in the girl's direction. "But Vretla's not at risk of leaving behind gift-children nobody has bargained for!" Noticing Erien, Vras turned to him with his usual cheerful manner. "You might try Heir Gelion," he suggested helpfully. "He doesn't have a liege along to spoil his fun, and he's even more Sevolite than I am!"

Oh no! thought Erien, with a sinking feeling. Not even his fleet years had prepared him for the gene-hungry stares of women from a Sevolite-poor spacer culture like that of the Dem'Vrel, whose families relied on piloting prowess for their economic and military security.

"I would like private quarters," Erien said with greater force than he had meant, and grit his teeth as the clump of eager watchers sucked in their breath in disappointment.

"Of course!" the dock master capitulated with a bobbing bow. The rest began to move away in twos and threes, muttering to each other in undertones. Erien caught the word, 'Lorel.'

"Let me show you to your quarters, Immortality," the dock master told Erien, bowing again. "My daughter can take care of Heir Vrel."

Watching the young woman in flight leathers move in to do just that, Erien suspected he might yet discover how a Vrellish liege dealt with wayward male relatives before their stay was over.

He was glad to have other things to worry about himself, like the grain shipment. "Who attacked the freighter we saw shattered?" Erien asked the dock master as he fell in beside him.

"Pirates," his host assured him with a scowl. "At least that's what people say." He tipped his head to look up at Erien, hesitant to push his luck, but hungry for news of what went on in space. "Unless it's true what the *relsha* who were flying escort say. Did one of the attackers try to ram the *StarBoat*?"

"*StarBoat*," Erien said, smiling. It was common practice in Gelack to use English nouns as names, and while the words themselves meant nothing to the average Gelack-speaker, his foster parent Evert found the habit curiously endearing: a sort of unconscious genuflection in the direction of the shared Earthly heritage of Gelacks and Reetions. "Was that the freighter's name?" asked Erien.

The dock master licked his lips as he nodded. "She was inbound from Demora." He weighed his words with caution. "Could be pirates got her."

"But you suspect something more...premeditated?" Erien prompted.

The dock master had a rugged face and bent shoulders, with dark gray eyes sunk deep in folds of flesh as crinkly as worn flight leathers. Erien discerned a certain dignity about him now he was no longer scheming or fussing.

"Tell me what you suspect," Erien said. "I swear I will not implicate you as the source of the idea."

"Eh?" the man said, blinking at him.

"I won't tell anyone," Erien tried again in simpler diction.

The dock master sucked his lip a moment, thinking, glanced about him to either side, then laid a hand on Erien's leather-clad forearm and leaned toward him. "Pirates don't kill themselves to steal cargo!" he told Erien. "There's only one motive for suicide." He bared yellowing teeth to hiss the last word: "Hatred."

"Do you know who had cause to hate the *StarBoat*?" Erien asked.

"Therds," the aging nobleborn spat back at him. "If destroying *StarBoat* could keep food from the Lekkers. Or Lekkers, if the fight was about starving the Therds. It's always Therds against Lekkers and Lekkers against Therds. Always was and always will be now Ev'rel's blessed peace has died with her!"

My mother's peace, thought Erien. Given what a disaster Ev'rel had made of her personal life, it was strange to know she was remembered in the Knotted Strings as a peacemaker.

The dock master's grip tightened on Erien's arm. "I'm telling you this because you're her son. Maybe it was pirates—but if it was, a Therd or Lekker was tipping them off and paying them. Now I'll tell you something people don't think about much at court, Your Immortality. We aren't all Therds and Lekkers out here, and none of the rest of us wants them wrecking all we've gained these last two decades now your blessed mother's gone."

CHAPTER 13

Palace of the Golden Emperor

"If you really were as delicate as blown glass, you'd have expired of sheer boredom by now," Alivda said caustically.

Amel broke off his study of the faces surrounding them and looked up at her from his grand seat facing Luthan across the arrivals deck of the emperor's palace on Demora. "You can sit down if you like," he reminded her.

Alivda snorted her disdain for that idea. "What are we waiting for, exactly?" she demanded.

"I'm not sure," said Amel, which was technically true, although he did have an idea. He just didn't want to share it with Alivda for fear she would scoff at him for drawing on stories of the Golden Demish era.

"Huh!" Alivda huffed, and settled once again into strafing the assembled dignitaries with her stare.

Amel noticed Luthan's eyes on him and could not help smiling reassurance at her, even though he knew that if he managed to get himself acknowledged as a Soul of Light, his religious aura would outshine hers. But he had no quarrel with Luthan. Far from it! He considered her one of his best and dearest friends. He just needed to win more than she did.

Luthan smiled back at him tentatively. By her side, Prince Oleander knelt to speak to her, but they were too far away for Amel to overhear what he said. Meanwhile, the deck on which they waited continued to fill up with elaborately dressed people of unusual beauty, all of them blue-eyed and blond-haired, with delicate features and high, pale foreheads.

Amel had visited Demora during his envoy period and recognized the braid and motifs of the handful of top families. He had been noticing for some time that those who positioned themselves near Luthan were allies of the Vestas, while those who took up a position closer to him supported the Ander tradition of leadership.

This, Amel felt almost certain, was a Demoran variation on a pre-swearing reception: in this case, an opportunity for important people to express their support for one choice or the other, even though most of them were not entitled to enter the emperor's palace where the trials themselves would be conducted.

Unlike Alivda, whose impatience was palpable, Amel was enjoying the long wait as people continued to arrive and silently position themselves on the great marble slab of the arrivals deck with its ornate golden banisters. It was a spring day, the sky was blue and the air was fragrant with flowers from the emperor's gardens. The palace rose in golden splendor to Amel's right and lush lawns stretched away for acres all around them, populated with grazing creatures of Earth origin, such as rabbits, with a deer or two included. The arrivals came in horse-drawn carriages that crunched over a road paved in fine white pebbles. It was like a scene from the pages of Golden Age literature come to life.

"I wonder what Demoran rabbits taste like," Alivda grumbled under her breath at Amel's side.

He gave her a reproachful look. "Don't even think about it," he said. "They're considered the pets of the emperor."

"Mm," she said, and went back to looking people over. "Where's Princess Dela?"

Amel tensed at the mention of his adopted Demoran mother. He was sure she'd be late, and her arrival would break the spell of gossamer elegance surrounding them. But she had, indeed, adopted him years earlier, to give him a home base on Demora when he visited, and he considered her family.

He was also expecting Leif'lee'el, the widow of the late Prince Kantor of Ander, and their son, Dromedarius. Amel had met Leif for the first time only after her grief at D'Ander's death had unbalanced her delicate mind, but he knew young Dromedarius well because keeping the boy alive had been one of many secret projects he had shared with Mira.

Before she decided to leave me! Amel thought with an upwelling of fresh pain. He set his teeth, vexed by his maudlin feelings, but he still wanted to cry. Old fears surfaced, whispering that he was unable to establish real, lasting relationships and everything he thought was solid would keep turning out to be illusory. *No!* he attacked his doubts. *It was real, once. People change. I remember the past too clearly and it stops me from seeing who Mira has become—who she needs to be. I just have to move on and let her go.*

He did try to follow his own advice, but thinking about Mira made even a Demoran spring feel lonely.

"How did the soul touch test go?" Alivda asked him conversationally.

"Not well," Amel admitted. "I think I was reviewing my fight with Zind, and trying to make it come out better for me." He sighed. "I wish I had better instincts for fighting."

"Let me take care of the violence," she remarked, making him look at her.

Alivda, herself, never took her eyes off the people deployed across the arrivals deck as she talked with him. She had a crisp profile and the instincts of a killer.

Will you betray me when it matters? he asked himself, staring at her, and knew he would not tolerate disloyalty. Not this time. Not again. Ev'rel would have understood half of why he was so adamant, but the part she would never have grasped was the weight of responsibility that had settled in about him, like concrete, as his vision of leadership solidified out of the details he'd acquired flying here and there around the universe. He was going to have to change, as well, to be the leader he needed to be.

"I'm going to take a walk," Alivda declared.

Amel stopped her with a hand on her arm. "Shouldn't we stick to protocol?"

Alivda tipped her head toward Luthan on the other side of the deck. "The opposition's prissy escort, Prince Samdan, wandered off earlier. I want to check it out."

"Oh." Amel lowered his hand. The loss of contact felt eerily symbolic, and in a moment of inexplicable panic he caught at her again to make her wait.

"I do have an idea about what's going on," he said, suddenly feeling wrong about withholding his best guesses from her. "I'm not certain, but I think these people are declaring their position by where they stand."

"Figured as much," she said, but she gave him a smile that confirmed he had been right to share his hunch. "Try not to get assassinated while I'm gone?"

"Right," he said, relieved, although he could no better explain this emotion than his earlier doubts about her loyalty to him.

A commotion in the courtyard made them both look to see the arrival of a slightly road-weary coach manned by goggle-eyed footmen trying to take in everything at once.

"Dela," Amel said, steeling himself for embarrassment.

Alivda flashed him a wicked smile before she slipped away, drawing no more attention than one of the glittering attendants circulating among the dignitaries to supply them with amenities like sips of water out of golden cups or embroidered stools to sit on.

Amel watched Dela's carriage pull up at the foot of the long staircase. The horses drawing it looked tired. The coachman blew air out of puffed cheeks with the manners of a provincial rustic and looked about him as wide-eyed as the footmen still clinging to their places on the carriage. Three seconds passed before one of the palace attendants in the livery of the emperor came forward to help the new arrival out of her carriage.

El Princess Dela'an'ka'neen D'Arborette of Dee Manor was clumsy, plump and two shades too exuberant for the refined world of the Inner Circle she had been born into. Without the proper graces to enhance her prospects, she had been married off young to a country husband who gave her no happiness until he made the mistake of challenging Vretla Vrel on the grounds no woman could defeat a real man. Vretla had been acting as Amel's champion at the time, during his first official visit to Demora, and Dela settled the resulting legal entanglements by adopting him as her son.

The arrangement made Dela Amel's official family head on Demora, so it was no surprise to see her clambering out of her provincial carriage stamped with the modest heraldic claims of Dee Manor. Nor was it surprising that she was decked out in all the borrowed glories to which her adoptive relationship to Amel might possibly entitle her, exhibiting her usual lack of judgment when it came to the sensibilities of her more refined Inner Circle relatives.

Even Amel had to admit his claims to divine goodness looked tawdry plastered all over Dela's billowing dress, which only exaggerated her plumpness and placed unreasonable demands on her flawed skills in ladylike deportment.

She waded up the steps that so many of Demora's best and brightest had graced with the whisper of their feet over the last hour, causing the more delicate souls among those assembled to draw back when she nearly tripped by stepping on the hem of her dress as she reached the top.

"Soul of Divine Goodness!" Dela greeted Amel with open arms as he stepped forward to steady her. Tears shone in her large blue eyes beneath her towering coiffure, from which a few wisps of golden hair had escaped on either side. "I knew you were a Soul of Light the very first day we met!"

"Whether the Golden Emperor will recognize me as his spiritual peer remains to be decided, dear Mother," Amel greeted her kindly in Demoran idiom, holding onto her elbows. "And the very idea he might is too challenging for many here to countenance." He glanced up to catch El Prince Oleander frowning at him as he said this, and returned his attention to Dela. "We must respect their feelings and not be premature."

"Nonsense!" Dela cried, placing a soft hand along the side of Amel's face. "You have always been too good to be anything else but a Soul of Light, no matter what you've suffered!"

The reminder of his sordid background was an unwelcome one to Amel. She seemed to grasp as much and fell silent, letting him draw her back to his side of the landing deck to make room for the imminent arrival of the last, and most illustrious, families.

The matriarchs of Demora's two royal families, barring the Golden Emperor himself and Oleander's deferred claim through House Vesta, walked up the stairs side by side. One was the late D'Ander's half-sister and the other his widowed bride. Each woman was exquisitely dressed in a full-length gown of understated elegance proclaiming her widowhood. The only brightness about either of them were the banners of office across their chests. Behind each woman walked her sole surviving child: the handsome Prince Dromedarius dressed in fleet regalia; and the young Princess Tanith'ee'la whose family use name was Telly, arrayed in a virgin's pearly gown. But the parallels between the two matriarchs ended with this catalog.

D'Ander's widow, Leif, was as frail and insubstantial as a diaphanous scarf aflutter in a gentle breeze. She glided along with a dreamy air, a tiny smile locked onto her rosebud mouth. Halfway up the steps she stopped and looked around her with an air of incipient panic, as if the world had changed suddenly.

El Princess Tara'n'eel, widow of Chad Therd, half-sister of Kantor Ander on their mother's side and daughter of one of Oleander's relatives—also deceased—paused on the step beside

Leif, tiny cracks in her composure betraying her impatience with his sister-in-law's infirmity. Princess Tara was as robust as her brother D'Ander had been, although less outgoing in spirit and more somber.

A lioness, thought Amel, drawing on Earth imagery more legendary than even the emperor's palace on Demora.

He regretted the coolness in his relations with Tara, which was based on antipathy between the households of D'Ander's widow and that of the sister who had married his killer.

Not that Tara had a choice! Amel remembered. *D'Ander himself set the terms with Ev'rel before the duel he lost to Chad.*

Despite inauspicious beginnings, Tara had come to love her bold, accomplished husband from the uncivilized Knotted Strings, and that was the sin her brother's family could not forgive. Another obstacle had been D'Therd himself, who made it clear he wanted Amel to have nothing to do with his Demoran family.

Princess Telly had been her father's pride and joy. All D'Therd thought he needed was the optimum husband to ally her with, and his heirs would rule both Demora and the Knotted Strings. At least that had been D'Therd's plan, and no doubt he thought he had plenty of time to get on with it, since Telly was only fifteen when he died on Horth Nersal's sword. So much had happened to Amel since that duel it was odd to realize only a few months had passed.

This was the first time Amel had seen Telly since a brushing acquaintance at a formal event on Demora years earlier from which D'Therd had been unable to exclude him. Her face was slightly longer than it should have been, her forehead a touch wider, her mouth a little too firm and her complexion marred by a scattering of freckles across her nose and cheeks, but she had a hybrid vigor lacking in the more purely Golden beauties surrounding her. Her cloudy blue eyes connected with Amel's long enough for him to register a veiled resentment he had not detected in their earlier meeting when she was a child.

D'Therd must have set her against me as she grew up, Amel decided with regret. He liked her freckles and the natural way she wore her hair, in defiance of Demoran fashion.

Prince Drom came forward to take his mother's elbow and whispered something that restored Princess Leif to herself with a blink. Telly gobbled him up with her eyes as he attended to his infirm mother.

Interesting, thought Amel.

Prince Drom of Ander was a strikingly Golden man in his mid-twenties, and to look at him one would never guess he was any less robust than his father. But Amel had sat by his bedside through long hours of uncertainty about his survival in the aftermath of a simple cut or tumble, and been the intermediary between the family and Mira over the business of providing treatment for his disability. Mira's diagnosis, arrived at on the basis of blood samples Amel fetched to her, was a Sevolite version of hemophilia from too much Golden inbreeding. The young prince looked like his famous father, but he could not tolerate even a few minutes of reality skimming and the mere act of practicing swordplay would have been life-threatening.

Amel liked Drom a great deal. He had his mother's beauty and his father's spirit, leavened with a more naive idealism than D'Ander's, due to his sheltered existence enforced by regular stints of convalescence each time he rebelled against his limitations. For a short while, thanks to Mira, Drom had hoped to lead a normal life, but Amel had been forced to bring him the bad news his immune system was at risk of rejecting Mira's serum if he used it too frequently. It was emblematic of Drom's high spirits that his choice would have been to live a life of masculine rigor for however long he survived, but in the end his mother's horror at the thought of losing him had prevailed. Mira's drugs were carefully stored away for use in life-threatening emergencies, and Drom lived day to day, knowing that every time they saved him might be the last treatment he could tolerate. The disappointment had an oddly personal aspect for Amel because Mira had used his own healthy blood cells as the key component in the serum, making Amel both the savior and potential killer of D'Ander's physiologically crippled heir.

Drom returned Amel's smile gamely, but with skeptical concern. It was his mother who reached out with both her frail hands to capture one of Amel's in hers.

"My darling Kantor is so proud," the misty-eyed El Princess told Amel. Kantor had been the late D'Ander's given name, although she was the only one Amel ever heard use it. To everyone else he had always been D'Ander and always would be, even though the title had officially devolved upon his son, Drom. Princess Leif also had the disconcerting habit of referring to her husband in the present tense, because she believed she could commune with him among the Watching Dead. "Kantor always knew you were a Soul of Light," she told Amel, her pale eyes swimming in tears.

Amel didn't bother to repeat the cautions he had given Dela. There would be no point where Leif was concerned. He just smiled and thanked her, instead.

Tara and Telly were exchanging words with Luthan, but Amel strained his ears to hear without success.

"Welcome, friend," was all young Drom said to Amel, smiling in his sunny, brave way before turning his head to look to where Telly stood beside her mother, gazing back at him. The moment their eyes met, both young people looked away.

Gods, they're in love! Amel realized. *And they've got it all covered: Arbor, Ander and Vestas, with a bit of Therd blood thrown in to appease the Knotted Strings.* But if the Ander-Vesta feud was anything like the Therd-Lekker one, Amel could easily understand why the glances between the cousins were furtive.

The arrival of the two royal families concluded the ritual. A fresh batch of attendants came to help the lesser lights of high Demoran society to disperse, while preparing to escort the key players into the palace itself, where only those of the Inner Circle were allowed to step.

It was at this point Amel looked for Alivda, but he didn't see her.

–o—o—o–

Sam watched from the side of a manicured gravel road as a cartload of attractive young people in costumes filed past her, under the benign eye of three smiling guards, disappearing into a back door of the palace, where a bevy of older women waited to receive them. The cart they came in was a boxlike affair on wheels covered with a riot of windows, big and small, that were fastened with latches of every description. The sides of this strange vehicle—between windows—were decorated in a carnival theme, and it was fitted on top with the twin masks of tragedy and comedy, ancient as Earth itself, and gaily painted in myriad tiny scenes. The cart itself had no driver. Instead, a man in a harlequin's suit walked ahead with a remote control in his hand, like a child leading a pull toy, but without the string. The road he walked on was covered in white pea gravel and wound through a smooth lawn of green grass beneath a butter-yellow sun. The air was fragrant with the gift of nearby gardens and the day was neither hot nor cold.

Paradise, Sam had to concede despite a stubborn desire to uphold the honor of her less clement homeworld in Princess Reach. *Demora really is paradise.*

She had followed the cart's progress from its starting point in front of a row of pretty residences twenty minutes' walk down the gravel lane, and watched it disgorge its cargo of brightly dressed entertainers. She was so absorbed she never heard Alivda coming up behind her until the swordswoman spoke, nearly making Sam jump out of her skin.

"I've been up to the dorms," Alivda announced herself, standing a pace away from Sam with a hand hooked on her sword belt. "Did you know that there are practice rooms in the back yard that are open to the air with virtual walls that zap the water when it rains? I was told it never rains hard on Demora, but apparently you can count on a light sprinkling every few days." She looked up into the blue sky decorated with just the right scattering of thin white clouds. "Damn near perfect for a green world."

"I think it would get boring," said Sam, thinking loyally about Clara's World.

"You can cut out the boy act with the voice around me," Alivda said, sending a zing of fear down Sam's spine. "I'm also betting you can't use that sword to save your life," Alivda added, shifting in a way that raised the fine hairs on the back of Sam's neck. "Am I right?"

"Yes," Sam admitted, looking down. Her feet, encased in men's boots, looked suddenly ridiculous to her.

"Does Luthan know?" asked Alivda.

Sam shook her head. "There really is a Prince Samdan. He's my brother. I came in his place." She paused for two long seconds. "Are you going to tell her?"

"When and if it suits me to," Alivda said. "Running away from something, are you?"

"I haven't done anything *okal'a'ni*, or even dishonorable!" Sam rallied, stirred by offended pride.

Alivda rolled a shoulder to work out a kink. "Can't say the same myself," she drawled, making Sam's skin tingle with fear. "Nothing *okal'a'ni*, maybe—if you stick to the strict definition." She pierced Sam's heart with a laser stare. "But I don't always kill people fair and square. Not, at least, when nobody is there to tell."

"Oh," Sam said in a strangled tone. "Does Amel know?" she blurted without thinking, alarming herself with her recklessness. But once it had occurred to her to say it, she just couldn't pass up the quip.

Alivda gave her a swift reappraisal. "Are you threatening me, yokel?" she asked.

'Yokel' was one of the words used by courtiers to dismiss people who grew up in the safer, less sophisticated society of parochial Demish worlds. Pride resurrected Sam's courage, for good or ill.

"So Amel doesn't know you are dishonorable," Sam declared, "and you don't want him to find out. A good thing, too. Because if you didn't care about him, you'd be nothing but another murdering, ambitious bully without a soul to redeem!"

"Met a lot of us, have you?" Alivda asked her with a sneer.

Sam opened her mouth to assert that she certainly had, and thought better of it when she realized they had all been characters in poems and plays.

Alivda turned her attention back to the costumed performers as the last one vanished into the palace. "Did you find out what's up with them?"

"Yes!" said Sam, feeling herself on firmer ground. "Every Luminary knows about 'the gathered'. They are auditioning for the emperor because performing arts are all he lives for since he lost his dear wife and their daughter."

"Amel's grandmother," Alivda interjected, saw Sam was thrown off by it and prompted her impatiently to continue.

Sam obeyed her in a quiet voice. "The Golden Emperor Fahild sends out talent scouts across the planet. Those gathered are brought here to audition for him. If they pass inspection, they are enrolled in his academy of artists, and when they graduate they are sent out across the planet to perform in his name, as troops of the Emperor's Voice with the mission to uplift and improve the population."

"Interesting," said Alivda. She looked down the road toward the residences. Then she turned and walked off without a parting word.

Sam held her breath until she couldn't hear Alivda's boots on the gravel path anymore. *Oh!* she thought furiously, *I wish I had her back home with me on Clara's World! I would never ask her to a single ball, or lend her my horse, or take part in any of her charity events! And if we went out walking together I would find a way to push her into the creek!* Only belatedly, as the burning sensation of humiliation softened, did she realize how pathetic the worst threats she could imagine would have sounded to the cocky, sexy warrior.

CHAPTER 14

Socializing

Alivda reappeared as Amel was shown into the guest hall of the palace, side by side with Luthan and her entourage. Amel was preoccupied by the set of El Princess Tara's jaw as she and Leif'lee'el waited their turn on the arrival's deck outside.

"They are giving us precedence over local royalty," Amel greeted Alivda with a note of guilt in his voice.

"Good," she said. The attendant she had slid past to reach him shot an offended look at her; then dropped his eyes before the threat in her answering glare. "Some guards," she muttered.

"We're inside the security bubble," Amel explained, tearing his thoughts away from Drom and Telly's families. A quick glance to the side engaged Luthan's look of lofty disapproval for his bad manners, and he concluded hurriedly, "We'll talk later."

"No, we won't," said Alivda, "because I'm going to audition for the emperor."

"What!" he exclaimed in a whisper sharp enough to turn heads.

She patted his hand before she left. "I'm confident you can cope with whatever life-threatening trials over the correct use of forks you encounter here."

"That isn't—" Amel objected, but she was gone again before he said, "—the point."

"My," Dela remarked by his side, "is that little Diff? Your baby dragon?"

"Please don't call her Diff," Amel warned under his breath. "Or baby dragon. It's Alivda these days."

"Mmph," Dela harrumphed a bit too loudly. "She used to sound like such a charming child when you spoke about her. I'm afraid maturity has done her no good."

From Amel's other side, Lady Margaret leaned across him to shush Dela with two fingers pressed firmly over frowning lips.

Right, Amel thought. *Pay attention*. It shouldn't have been so hard; he was walking into the stuff of legend, the site of stories as old as the empire's history, the guest wing of the palace of the Golden Emperor.

Nothing inside came as a surprise.

On his right a row of pillars stood between him and a small sunken amphitheatre, with shallow steps leading down to the stage floor and back up again to a grassy shelf on the far side. Amel knew the rich, complex brown of the pillars, shot through with gold marbling, from their descriptions in poetry he loved, and had to repress the urge to walk over and touch one. The amphitheatre was bracketed in rows of cozy seats arrayed in arcs between the flights of shallow steps on either end. A tame waterfall occupied the entire back wall behind the grassy shelf, gliding down a wall of sparkling, golden stones. A model garden lay at the foot of the waterfall, complete with a park bench and a live rabbit nibbling the smooth grass.

"Spirit Park," Amel said absently, recalling scenes from Golden Age literature set in the very spot he was seeing for the first time with his own eyes. It was here that the spirits of the beloved dead and the great souls of history had visited heroines and heroes of the Golden canon. But in real life, the strip of indoor greenery looked too small and ordinary to support the weight of legend.

Amel looked to the left, next, and was equally disappointed by the arched entrances to eight apartments used by visiting El royalty and Golden Souls who sometimes stayed for decades when the business they came to conduct attenuated under the influence of Demora's fossilized protocols. They reminded him of Fountain Court: eight residences for contentious families engaged in power struggles and contained in a cultural airlock that defined the rules of engagement. It hardly mattered that those rules were designed to measure goodness instead of prowess on a challenge floor.

Don't people ever band together to get something really meaningful done? Amel wondered. He had always hoped friendship was the cure for competitive nastiness. Yet here he was, vying with Luthan Dem H'Us for the prize of being deemed a Divine Soul, so that one of them could claim the Demoran oath.

So enlightened of us, Amel thought with a heavy heart, as an attendant ushered himself, Dela and Margaret into their luxury apartment.

Dela said, "Ohhh!", and dashed across the big open living space to look into every room along the right wall, then headed for the gardens out the back.

Margaret folded her arms, favoring Dela's undignified behavior with a judgmental scowl. "She is hardly an asset," said the Luminary abbess. "Even though she is an El princess of the lesser branch of Arbor."

"I love her," Amel said simply, making Margaret flinch as if branded with a hot iron. He laughed to salve whatever wound he had inflicted and put an arm about Margaret's shoulders to reassure her. "When I was nothing but a black-haired hybrid, reviled for being plucked from the UnderDocks, she took me into her heart and adopted me as a son. How many *faux pas* does it take to use up credit like that?"

Margaret's large blue eyes warmed with tears as she received what he had deemed a light-hearted explanation of his tolerance. When she looked at him this way her eyes brimmed with meaning he could weigh, but not decipher, and he found himself noticing how comfortable it was to have her tucked up against his chest beneath a sheltering arm, the heat of their bodies combining and his heart instinctively speeding up to match the rhythm of her own. Her scent went to his head. The effect reached other places, as well, and he was suddenly embarrassed for fear she might realize she was stirring his infamous libido, an aspect of himself he wanted to keep firmly off stage on Demora.

Gently, Amel detached himself.

"I'm sorry," he said awkwardly, "I shouldn't be so...familiar with you. I keep forgetting that we hardly know each other."

"Of course," she said, as if she knew something he didn't, swallowed down her feelings, and gave him a brave smile.

Dela came running back with more strands of bright golden hair loose about her plump features, waving her arms in excitement. "You must come see the gardens!" she cried. "They're all connected!"

"Go ahead," Margaret said, clearly needing a moment of solitude to pull herself together. "I'll organize our things here."

Amel let Dela tow him across the spacious dining and lounging area with its own little sunken theatre space, and out a large

pair of crystal doors onto a patio bowered in the limbs of ancient trees.

A huge expanse of lawn spread out beyond, sprinkled with
tiny pink and purple flowers, and populated by herds of the
emperor's pet rabbits. Amel couldn't help thinking how welcome
the long-eared breeders would be on the tables of Knotted Strings
families, and wondered if Sen Lekker had ever thought of
harvesting a shipload.

"Where is Sen?" Amel asked Dela, realizing he hadn't seen
her since their arrival.

Dela halted, turned him to face her, and gave him a long,
searching look as if she feared he had suffered a bump on the
head.

"Oh," he remembered. "Of course, Sen's nobleborn, and only
El royalty—members of the Inner Circle families—are allowed
to attend on the emperor."

"Or serve him," Dela said gravely. "It is the greatest honor
a young El prince or princess can hope for, to be accepted as
a worker at the palace."

"And play commoner for a few years," Amel remarked with
a touch of scorn, and shook his head. "Yes, of course. Sorry,"
he added, recalling this had been the ritual of passage in which
Dela had failed, as a young girl, due to her less than refined
manners.

"The only people who aren't highborns in the palace are the
Voice of the Emperor performers," Dela added. "You know about
them. You've seen them perform at Dee Manor. Emperor Fahild
recruits them from all over the planet to audition, and then sends
them out across Demora to bring joy and teaching to all *Okal
Lumens*. It's sacred work on Demora to be a performing artist,
a poet, or—"

"Yes, yes," Amel assured her. "I remember, Dela."

She bit her lower lip, holding onto him to retain his attention. He was impatient to get past her. He wanted to stretch his
legs, and if he ambled a bit about the lawn he hoped he might
be able to spot Alivda, or find out which families had been put
into which apartments along the row. Would Luthan be next
door? Or would the Demorans have placed him beside Leif and
Drom because they supported him?

"I only want to be sure you understand your dancing and
poetry are assets in the competition," Dela told Amel. "Not things
to hide or be embarrassed about the way they are on Gelion.

Court Demish spoil the best things about Demoran culture by wanting to own or control them."

"Yes, I know," he reassured her, and gave her his full attention, even though he had spotted Alivda walking toward him through a fearless clump of grazing rabbits who barely moved to accommodate her. "I've performed on Demora before, you know," he reminded her, smiling. "At Dee Manor."

Dela nodded, and let him escape from her, still looking unconvinced that he understood her properly.

Amel sprinted through rabbits and flowering grass to meet Alivda.

"Still alive, I see," she greeted him with approval.

"We're in the first apartment," Amel said, pointing back behind him to where Dela was retreating into their garden. "Did you find out anything interesting, following Prince Samdan?"

Alivda chuckled, but didn't volunteer information about her encounter with the disconcertingly effeminate princeling from Clara's World, and Amel was not disposed to inquire.

"What I found out," she said, "is that there are still purists who think you're an abomination, and half the Royalbloods I've run into are dotty enough to get up to any cracked scheme they believe in, although I doubt the majority of them would have the grip to actually do anything. All the same, I wouldn't be entirely surprised if someone in the palace acting as a servant, or even one of the permanent dignitaries, thought it was his sacred duty to put a knife through your heart for leveraging your blood ties to the Golden Emperor to gain power. Apparently real Souls of Light would zone out at the mere thought of half the stuff you've survived with your sanity intact." She paused to reconsider. "Well, survived, at least."

"Diff!" he protested, and clipped her shoulder with a light punch. She defended herself in the same vein and poked him back, initiating a friendly tussle that was ended, abruptly, by the sound of a young woman clearing her throat and announcing herself with authority.

"Uncle Amel?" the voice declared. "My mother would like to see you in her garden at your earliest convenience."

Amel broke off to take in the sturdy form of Princess Telly. Her freckled face projected her father's stubborn confidence stiffened with a dash of regal hauteur, making Amel recall he knew almost nothing about her.

"Of course," he said, feeling oddly stupid.

Without so much as a twitch of her lips, Telly turned and marched off to what he presumed was the apartment she shared with her mother, and was surprised to see it was the one beside his.

"I'd better go," Amel said to Alivda.

"I suppose you can handle yourself all right with rank amateurs," she said gruffly. "Even if they do try to assassinate you. I just hope it's true Demorans don't go in much for poisoning. Guess it's not sufficiently dramatic, and the Watching Dead like a show if you're going to do something to honor them."

"You really think someone in there—some El prince or princess—is going to try to kill me with a sword?" Amel asked her, incredulous.

"Sword, knife, anything legitimate under *Okal Rel*," Alivda said complacently. "But never mind that—well, unless it's Oleander. He's dangerous. But he'll do it by the book so you'll have time to come get me if that happens. Now listen."

Amel was put out by her bossiness. He was twice her age and far more experienced in courtly proceedings, but it took him too long to piece through how best to put those particular facts to her. She had already seized him by one arm and was boring her bright blue stare into him.

"I'm going to cut to the chase and get myself in to see the Golden Emperor."

"Fahild? But—"

She pressed her fingers to his mouth and smiled at him. "What he says goes. All the rest of this is window dressing made up by his courtiers to spare him the effort of making up his own mind about anything."

Amel lowered her hand from his face with parental firmness. "Except he hasn't engaged in politics, personally, for—oh, let's see—nearly a hundred years? Not since the death of his daughter."

"Who was your grandmother," Alivda reminded him. "Making you Fahild's only living descendant."

"Which he knows already!" protested Amel, exasperated.

"Yeah," agreed Alivda, "but he probably thinks you're a jerk like your father, Delm. He hasn't had it explained to him by someone who knows you."

"Explained?" Amel sputtered. "Diff, Fahild is the sacred, living icon of *Okal Lumens*, and an old, old man, probably lost in his memories like a lot of Demorans over two hundred. What makes you think you can even get close enough to get his attention when—" He broke off and glared at her. "Don't you dare kill anyone. Not here!"

"No bodies!" she cried, raising both palms and putting on a sweet, harmless smile, as convincing as the grin of a cobra.

Amel frowned. "Don't do that," he told her. "It's creepy."

She patted his shoulder. "Miss me while I'm gone," she ordered. "And play your own angle like you don't have a second option, just in case I bomb."

Alivda trotted off across the lawn. Amel watched her until she disappeared around the back of the palace, rubbing his left temple slowly. Then he sighed, straightened his white-and-gold dress jacket and marched off to accept Princess Tara's invitation, thinking, *I already have a headache and the first day isn't over.*

CHAPTER 15

FarHome

"Don't you think it would be better if I flew with Vras?" Erien suggested, after Vretla explained she would fly his lander the rest of the way to FarHome, with him taking a passenger's berth in the disk section.

Vretla flashed him her feral grin. "Sert can't double up with anyone but Vras. So we're stuck with each other."

"Can't?" Erien asked suspiciously. "What do you mean?"

"Soul touch," Vretla said. "She fences passengers."

Fencing, in the context of soul touch, meant struggling for mental control of a *rel*-skimming ship. Strong pilots did it involuntarily. Erien had learned the hard way, with Horth, the only time he'd ever tried to fly his then-admiral somewhere.

"I see," Erien said, and paused. "What makes you think I'll be any easier to cope with as a passenger?"

Vretla shrugged. "I guess we'll see." She saw him hesitate and laughed. "Don't worry; I'll try not to think too much about what sturdy children you'll sire me after I'm sworn to you."

"Let's go," said Erien, feeling like a Reetion house cat rubbed the wrong way. *Which reminds me,* he thought to distract himself as he strapped into a passenger's berth, *I wonder how Horth is making out with the felines he brought home from Rire.*

Part of him wished Horth was there instead of Vretla and her people. He got along well with the taciturn Nersallian and appreciated his ingenuity. But there would have been no avoiding Black Hearth's expectation of a reward for taking out the *okal'a'ni,* and Erien still considered the jury out on that call. Zind was guilty of kidnapping, which was bad, but apart from that she had done nothing criminal in the eyes of *Okal Rel,* despite the death of the paladin, and he wanted to give her a chance to explain.

Vretla flew hard and true. Erien had expected the lack of controls under his hands to nag at his piloting instincts, but they were under skim for hours before he became aware of anything except a quiet sense of Vretla's competence.

He was dozing lightly, lulled by the confidence she projected while piloting, when he started sharing other feelings with her. At first they were mild erotic impulses of the kind he was used to repressing when they distracted him. But it wasn't long before Erien found himself in the midst of a half-waking dream.

A drum beat sounded deep inside him, keeping time with the blood pumping harder and faster through his arteries. Shapes moved in the darkness, intensely female and sexual, firing his senses with a primeval response he barely recognized as his, the same way Vrellish violence had surprised him in his struggle with D'Lekker.

Erien woke with a gasp and sat up in his restraints, soaked in sweat.

He exhaled, shifted to make himself comfortable in the passenger's berth, and scrubbed the tips of his fingers all along his hairline to defeat the sense his head was about to explode from the pressure his pounding heart exerted.

If Vretla had shared the experience, she revealed no hint of it to Erien. Nothing perturbed her piloting, and she said nothing to him about it when they set down at a space dock in Therd territory.

The dock town nestled at the foot of the mountain that harbored Zind's stronghold, sheltered in an alpine valley half-way up its craggy face. Vretla stood beside Erien, feet spread, and already shivering in her flight leathers as she sniffed the chilly air. Like most Vrellish, she would probably have been happier in a regulated habitat than on a naturally life-supporting planet, known as a green world. *Or a brown one, as Tatt put it,* thought Erien.

FarHome did look dismal compared to either Monitum or Rire, the two green worlds Erien had lived on while growing up.

The docking yards extended into a pier district on a chilly lake. The surrounding town of about forty thousand people looked poor and dull. Buildings were constructed of a cheap synthetics made from pulverized local rock, lending a gray cast to the uninspired architecture. Here and there amid the uniform banality a public building stood out, marked with the crest of Dem'Vrel that had been created by Ev'rel when she slammed the Knotted Strings together into one house to justify her foot-hold on Fountain Court. Erien spotted a public health facility, a taxation office and a food rations warehouse.

This is the mother I want to know better, he thought. She had seemed to care little for her Knotted Strings accomplishments, herself, viewing the work as little more than a necessary stepping stone on the way to becoming Ava. *But it isn't always what we value most about ourselves that best defines us*, Erien thought doggedly. There were ways in which he felt akin to his intellectually aloof mother with her isolated and intense attachments to people she could not do without. He badly wanted to displace his few memories of her, entangled as they were with her horrid obsession over Amel, with something he could feel safe acknowledging as an emotional resonance.

"This way," Vretla said, very nearly violating his space with a slap on the shoulder. She recovered awkwardly. "There's an inn on the wharf where we can rest. Sert and Vras will take care of the landers. You write a letter to Zind, asking to see her. I'll get it sent up to her."

She tromped off, beating her arms about her to keep warm.

Erien caught up, pulled off the winter coat he'd liberated from his luggage when they disembarked, and put it around her shoulders.

She started when he touched her.

"You need it more than I do," he told her, with a smile that was half shy and half domineering. "Lor'Vrel, you know. Higher percentage of body-fat than someone who is pure Vrellish."

"I'm one percent Lorel myself," she said curtly, and pulled ahead of him.

Clearly, something about him was bothering her.

Vretla settled their bill with the innkeeper and gave orders for his people to fetch what they needed from Vras and Sert at the docks. Then she commandeered a writing desk for Erien and prowled like a caged beast while he composed his letter asking Zind to meet with them.

"Let's see," she demanded when he was done, snatching the limp velum sheet from under his pen the moment he'd completed his signature, and before he could roll it up and seal it with a drop of his blood deposited in a prepared seal. Erien was aware Gelacks preferred velum to paper for official correspondence, and FarHome raised cattle so there would be no shortage or cow hide available. Of course, digital communications would have been much faster and perfectly viable given that neither reality skimming nor enclosing hullsteel structures were at issue. But Vretla had made it plain local custom permitted only intimates and vassals to freely communicate from a distance. Petitioners and mere acquaintances had to send letters under blood seals, whether they awaited the response from far away on Gelion or were camped out at the foot of Zind's mountain.

Vretla snapped Erien's letter taut and read it out loud, filling the writing alcove where the innkeeper had put them with her deep, throaty voice.

As acting liege of Amel, the heir to Ev'rel and therefore heir presumptive to all houses of Dem'Vrel, including the Therds and the Lekkers, I request a meeting with you to discuss your actions on Fountain Court in which you penetrated Blue Hearth (as Amel is currently referring to the court residence known, during Ev'rel's reign, as Lilac Hearth) and extracted two children. Ditatt Monitum's investigation came to the tentative conclusion you acted within Sword Law with regard to your assault on the Golden paladin, the only adult highborn resident at the time of your action; however I have been empowered by him, in his capacity as Minister of Justice, to investigate your abduction of the commoner girl, Mona. Information provided by Blue Hearth staff suggests you took Mona because Leksan Lekker was injured resisting your errants, and she has some training in medicine from her mother, Mira. I also wish to satisfy myself, on my own behalf and Amel's, that Leksan, the heir to the Lekker clan, is safe, and to speak with you regarding your intent in taking him.

Vretla rolled up the letter and handed it back to him.

"Too formal?" Erien asked her.

She pressed her lips together. "Sounds like it was written by a Lor'Vrel." Then she shrugged. "Might help. Therds like to think they are civilized."

"But you don't think they are?" Erien asked her.

She just grunted, a noise Erien was coming to recognize as Vretla's way of saying a remark was either too involved to get into, or not worth wasting words on. In this case, he suspected the former. As one of Ev'rel's chief vassals, Vretla was bound to know nearly as much about the two principal houses of the Dem'Vrel as Amel did.

"Do you believe Zind Therd is...honorable?" Erien asked, feeling peculiar to be concerned about a character trait he typically disparaged as primitive, simple-minded and badly in need of being superseded by a Reetion jurisprudence system. But it was all they had out here. "Do you trust her not to have us murdered?" he added, for clarity. "I mean, we are here—alone—in her territory."

"Us? Yes," Vretla said gruffly, with increasing impatience to be gone. "Not so sure about anyone named Lekker, even if he is a child."

She hustled Erien through finishing up the blood seal and disappeared with it, telling him not to expect a reply until the morning, at the earliest. "You're on your own until then," she said. "Vras and Sert won't be back until bedtime."

Erien settled down to peruse the few books and even fewer data disks available in the office alcove. One of the disks bore the Dem'Vrellish crest and proclaimed itself an address on the improvement of agricultural productivity, by Ev'rel, Liege of Dem'Vrel. He was trying to repair the disused media player to see what was on it, when a commotion in the common room outside got his attention.

He put the disk down and sprinted to investigate.

"So?!" Vretla was saying as Erien burst into the common room. "I only want him for the one night! Not to keep."

She was herding the innkeeper's son up the stairs. He was the pleasant youth who had taken charge of sending for their bags earlier, and Erien had gathered that the inn was run by his father and mother with the help of their son and few employees. A girl of about the same age as the innkeeper's son, who Erien had assumed to be one of the staff, now revealed herself to be his fiancée. She was clearly agitated, her head scarf disarrayed over her brown curls, as she struggled to free herself from the innkeeper's protective grasp.

"Stop her! Make her stop!" the girl cried, tears running down her face. She upspoke the culprit even in her distress, albeit without differencing suffixes. But even this much show of respect upset Erien. It was Vretla who was behaving badly here! The very idea that she thought she could pick a man and order him to her bedroom, which was clearly what was taking place, was a travesty of everything Erien had learned on Rire about civil rights. It made him ashamed to be Sevolite!

"Hush, Mardy," the innkeeper's wife admonished the hysterical girl. "Don't make her angry or it's you who will get hurt! She'll think you're challenging her."

"But we're engaged!" yhe girl sobbed, inconsolably. "And he's never—it's not right it should be her!"

The young man looked back over his shoulder at his distraught sweetheart with a worried, confused expression. The possibility of a Vrellish woman acting this way was clearly something all concerned knew to be possible, but Erien suspected the backwater town rarely entertained people quite as Vrellish as Vretla, even if she had been to FarHome once or twice before.

"She'll give him diseases!" the girl wailed.

She might have been correct, there. Ranar conjectured Red Reach stationers were the survivors of a thousand years of intense warfare between their immune systems and a host of venereal diseases for which Vrellish highborns were asymptomatic carriers. Their numbers were too low to develop much in the way of Sevolite-specific pathogens, but their patterns of travel and promiscuity kept lesser bugs in circulation among their station-bound sex partners, most of whom—if Ranar was correct in his assumptions—would prove to have some Sevolite DNA themselves, though below the threshold for nobleborn properties to manifest.

True or not, however, Erien was afraid Vretla Vrel would take offense; but she merely nudged the young man faster up the stairs and disappeared with him into the bedroom she had chosen for herself.

Erien put himself squarely in front of the hysterical girl and her future in-laws, and waited for Mardy to notice him.

"I will stop Liege Vrel from exploiting your fiancé," he promised her somberly, once she was able to take in what he said. "Wait here."

The girl went very still the moment she focused on him. When he'd finished speaking she sniffled and swallowed. "Wh-who are you?" she asked, up-speaking him in the same way she had addressed Vretla Vrel.

"Erien," he said. "Erien Lor'Vrel."

As the word 'Lor'Vrel' passed his lips, she caught her breath, pressing back into the arms of the innkeeper who held her tightly, looking grim-faced. His wife's face drained of blood.

Fine, Erien thought stoically, *now I have to prove to them a Lor'Vrel can be trusted, as well as uphold the boy's civil rights.*

It never occurred to him to note that the 'boy' concerned was probably a few years older than he was.

Erien bolted up the stairs. He didn't barge into the bedroom, however. He simply opened the door, walked in and bellowed in a commanding voice, "Vretla! Let the young man alone."

Vretla turned around with a dangerous, sinuous grace. Her eyes were half lidded. "Are you volunteering instead," she said, in a smoldering, lustful voice he almost didn't recognize as hers. Belatedly, he realized her impatience stemmed from the effects of their soul touch in the lander, which he thought she had escaped unscathed. But this only made him feel even more responsible for the current debacle.

"Go downstairs, now," he told the innkeeper's son.

Vretla had got no farther than removing the young man's belt and mussing up his hair. He snatched the belt off the floor and did as Erien said, still looking too thoroughly bemused to know whether he was merely astonished by the whole business or scared.

"I'm sorry," Erien told Vretla as the young man made his escape. "I know what happened. We...interacted, somehow—" He hesitated, but it felt perverse to pussyfoot around the matter in present company. "Erotically," he admitted, as clinically as possible. "It happened during the trip. Some sort of soul touch, I expect. I didn't realize it had troubled you, as well. I thought it was just me."

"Hardly," Vretla ground out in a rough voice. She bared her teeth in a grimace. "I ache," she said bitterly.

Erien tried not to think about the muscular anatomy of highborn Vrellish females he had no direct—but ample theoretical—knowledge of, based on Ranar's anthropological studies augmented by Mira's medical analyses that had been published via Reetion contacts over the years.

His own mouth felt dry, and his face was getting very hot.

"What's the matter with you?" Vretla asked, like a sword thrust, stalking closer across the pressed-stone floor. Her breathing was fast and deep. Her nostrils flared with every breath. "I thought, perhaps, that you were Lorel-cold. Or boy-*sla* even, being raised on Rire. But it's neither. You are Vrellish where it matters. And a healthy male."

"Vretla," he protested, backing up a step. "Don't. Please."

She growled low in her throat. And sprang at him.

The release of tension was exhilarating! Erien went down beneath her, protecting his throat reflexively with an upraised arm. Her legs tried to clamp around his but he flipped her over, drawing on his martial arts training. She was coiled steel in his grip. They wrestled for an advantage, her hot breath on his cheek, their bodies scrambling against each other. At first it was worse than the soul touch that caused all the trouble, but as the violence escalated the sexual tension between them began to drain.

Vretla freed herself with a vicious kick. On her feet, she heaved up the bed with a roar and hurled the whole thing at him, where he began to get up off the floor. He rolled against her legs, bringing them down on the broken frame of cheap synthetic material. They struggled up together, blocking and swinging in frantic turns. The fight was free form, less calculating than his sparring bouts with Horth in which he had taught the Nersallian leader all he could about Reetion martial arts in exchange for fencing lessons. It was different from his desperate struggle with D'Lekker, in Lilac Hearth, as well. He knew they were not trying to kill each other. He was less sure she would stop short of crippling him, and he needed to keep his wits about him.

Ten minutes later, the room in chaos, Vretla's cheek torn in a collision with a broken bed post and Erien's nose gushing copiously, they sat back to back against the mattress of the trashed bed and caught their breath, each of them groaning now and then as he or she tested out a painful body part to prove nothing was actually broken.

"This is all Amel's fault," Vretla said sourly, when her breathing was no longer ragged. "I would never have gotten into such a state if he hadn't gone all Demish princely on me when I needed his cooperation! I want a child!" she shouted to the indifferent corners of the universe, making Erien's ears ring. "What's so wrong with that," she concluded miserably.

"Nothing...is wrong...with it," Erien assured her, still panting with exertion. He laid his head back on the mattress. "Vretla, I don't mean to make you crazy. I am sorry. But this isn't...easy for me."

"Huh," Vretla grunted. "Am I too Vrellish for you? Some men like their women passive."

"No, it's not—" Erien began.

"You were three years in the Nersallian Fleet," Vretla interrupted roughly. "Am I that different from a Nersallian Highlord? They're Vrellish, too."

"Oh yes, I know!" he said, and laughed at his memories, swiping loose hair off his forehead and finding it sticky with blood: either his or Vretla's, he couldn't be sure. "Vretla," he said, feeling he owed her some sort of explanation. "I didn't sleep with any women while I was in fleet service."

She stiffened beside him, as if jolted with a shot of electricity, and pivoted to look at him. "For three years!" she exclaimed, astonished.

"Don't make it sound worse than it is!" he admonished her, sighed and pressed his hands over his face briefly, before he dared to continue. "My foster father, Di Mon, told me not to take the chance of getting any woman pregnant until I found out who I was. Then he died." He paused before correcting himself bleakly. "Actually, he killed himself."

Vretla was nodding. "Yes, yes, he had incurable regenerative cancer. It was a good end, under the circumstances."

"Maybe," Erien said begrudgingly. "Not for me, though. He never told me who I was, first. So I never...it got to be a habit, denying that part of me. And then there was the cultural dislocation of finishing my childhood on Rire."

"Wait!" Vretla hauled herself around, wincing, and settled with her legs crossed in front of her, staring at him. "Are you telling me you're still a virgin?!" she asked him, wide-eyed.

"You make it sound like a disease!" said Erien.

Vretla was speechless.

"I'm only seventeen!" he protested against her silent incredulity. When this failed to register with her, he narrowed his eyes. "Why? How old were you?"

She shook her head. "I don't know. When I was ten or eleven I got caught up with the wild hunt that my father, Vackal, fell in with; the one led by Vras and Sert's mother. I remember orgies. Vaguely. I remember recognizing, and avoiding, the smell of my own father. But I was overflown. I don't recall much before my days at court, as Di Mon's protégé. I remembered how to fly to Gelion, but not much more. I guess I must have left the hunt, alone, and gone to Fountain Court to find Di Mon. I think I recognized him when I saw him. Barely."

Erien tried to imagine what she'd lived through, stumbling away from a lifestyle that dissatisfied her toward something better that she could not quite remember.

"I see," was all he said, but silently he thanked Ranar and Di Mon for the fourteen good years of his own childhood.

At least, if nothing else, the confession of his shocking inexperience had made an impression on Vretla.

"Wow," she said, and waited a moment before adding, "so...are you Demish or Vrellish about sex? I mean, presuming you are going to, uh, you know, start. Eventually."

"I don't know," he admitted. "But I think I would like to be married. Not for the Demish reasons, necessarily, but something feels right about the idea of being with just one other person: a fellow parent and a partner. Of course, I don't know if it will happen." A nagging worry prodded him, urging him to put it into words before it slipped away, out of his conscious grasp. "What if I am too much like my mother? What if I don't need people, generally, but have the potential to become fixated on a few I need too much. I've had a hard time letting go of Di Mon," he admitted, with reluctance. "If I felt that way about a woman ..."

"Pick one who can fight back!" Vretla suggested.

Erien looked at her, trying to pin down his objections to getting the whole nonsense of virginity over and done with right now; but he only felt more miserable, like a starving man offered the wrong food.

Vretla sensed she wasn't gaining ground and gave up. "All right," she said, resigned to settle for a conversation. "I admit your mother was possessive about Amel. I've been thinking about it a lot since she died, and I've decided she was the reason that he never accepted my advances all those years he was Royal Envoy." She barked a laugh. "I suppose he thought he was protecting me!"

He was, Erien thought, but did not attempt to convince her because he did not want to share the things he knew but she did not.

"She shouldn't have been bedding her own son, of course," Vretla continued with the air of someone facing up to buried doubts. "But I can understand the temptation!" she erupted. "He makes me nuts! She was a good liege in other ways," she added in a sullen tone.

Erien found he needed to repress a smile, wondered why, and had to think about it to realize he was grateful to Vretla for her defense of the mother he would like to think well of.

"But that's beside the point," Vretla roused herself, again, to argue. "Ev'rel could be jealous," she said gruffly. "So what? It doesn't mean you will be like her! Look at Sert and Vras! They're both solid, and their mother was the leader of a wild hunt. Look at Amel, himself. He's nothing like his parents!"

Vretla fell silent then, brooding.

Erien wanted to thank her for trying to cheer him up. He thought about touching her shoulder, but he didn't want to stir up her interest in him, sexually. Instead he asked her gently, "What's the matter?"

"The Demish," Vretla muttered. "Amel's Demish. He is going to wind up married and I know what that means. Amel's got enough romantic nonsense swirling around his head to drown a ballroom full of virgin princesses; he'll stick to whichever simpering, blond infant they marry him to, and then I'll never have a child to be my heir." She gave him a wistful look, but one with little hope of help from a Lor'Vrellish quarter.

Erien felt bizarrely awkward, as if he was committing a crime of negligence in remaining aloof.

"Listen, Vretla," he said, and pointedly broke his own no-touch rule to lay a hand quietly on her nearest arm. "I know I'm not the easiest person for you and the other Vrellish to work with, but I have listened and I do understand. If you give me your oath at the Swearing, I will see to it you have your chance to bear a child."

She said nothing, but her relief and gratitude were plain. She would swear to him, now, he felt sure.

So why do I feel sad? Erien wondered, as the image of Luthan's face at the Council of Privilege popped into his head.

CHAPTER 16

Act of Kindness

Princess Telly waited impatiently for Amel to join her at the entrance to her mother's back garden, glaring at him resentfully with a frankness that accentuated the family resemblance between her and her half-sister, Zind Therd.

What have I ever done to you? Amel wondered, absorbing her nonverbal assault with an inward flinch. Whatever it was, he wondered if he should be worried about assassination attempts.

As he drew near, Telly pivoted with a swish of her pearly shawl and marched into the garden ahead of him, her bare shoulders just a little too wide for the cut of her delicate Demoran dress.

Amel put Telly out of his mind with an effort and concentrated on what El Princess Tara could possibly want from him.

Maybe she's the one whipping up purist zealots to have me killed, Amel conjectured. She had plenty of reason to be angry with him. Twice now, her life had been transformed by duels in which Amel had been the principal stake. In the first, Chad Therd had won her as his bride by killing her half-brother, D'Ander; and in the second, only months ago, she had lost her husband to the sword of Horth Nersal.

Tara stood waiting for Amel beside a wicker chair at the center of a leafy enclosure. He looked right and left, assessing the density of the artfully sculpted greenery that looked so perfectly natural it had to be the work of an expert, and wondered about eavesdropping devices and lurking fanatics.

"Amel."

His name dropped from Tara's lips like a stone—not a large one, a mere pebble—stripping him of all but their relationship as family, long neglected and recently inflamed by his role in the title challenge that had made her a widow.

He struggled to find something right to say about her loss but she spared him by speaking first. "My late husband, D'Therd, didn't like you. I expect the feeling was mutual. But I did not ask you here to discuss the past."

"As you wish," he said guardedly, and paused to glance around the leafy bower. "Are we alone?"

Her mouth glided into a polite smile, as tolerant as it was minimal. "If you mean, are others listening by one means or another...no. The palace is much like your Fountain Court: a political arena governed by Sword Law."

Which hadn't prevent Charous from trying to bug Lilac Hearth, in Ev'rel's day, Amel thought. Ameron had put a stop to it as soon as he found out, and if anyone but Amel had exposed her, he might have been forced to put her to death. Even worse, as Ameron's *gorarelpul* it would have been assumed Charous acted on his orders and her actions would have implicated him. On Fountain Court, the gains were seldom worth the risk of cheating. It was, moreover, difficult, because hullsteel complicated attempts to spy. Here, there was nothing but tradition to seal the privacy of the bower. *Of course*, Amel reminded himself, *tradition has great power on Demora.*

Tara gestured for him to be seated and he chose the wicker chair opposite hers. He watched as she sat down facing him, as stately as the approaching night.

"I find I have no appetite for small talk," she apologized

"Say what you need to," Amel encouraged her, settling a hand on his knee in an attentive posture, conscious of the sword at his hip. He was still not used to wearing one. "Whatever it is, I won't make it any more difficult for you than it has to be."

She nodded, looking sad and relieved. "I hope you understand that this divinity business is only a first step to attaining real power. My husband acted as Protector and Champion during your mother's reign as liege of the Avim's Oath, whether or not the Inner Circle would officially recognize him. They preferred to consider him my daughter's regent, presuming he picked her a suitable husband." She paused to consider her choice of words. "Things were never...good between the establishment on Demora and my late husband, and he did not tolerate dissension with much patience. His death has left something of a power vacuum in his wake and, as a consequence, whichever house of Fountain Court we swear to will not only determine whether we become part of the Avim's Oath or the Ava's Oath, but will likely determine who will reign here, as Protector." She paused and shifted slightly. "I don't believe there are any plausible candidates for Champion except Oleander, whose vocation has kept him out of politics...theoretically, at least." Her large, calm eyes lifted to meet his. "He might yet decide to marry and get back in the race. That would please the Inner Circle a great deal." She leaned forward. "It might, therefore, serve you to consider marrying into one of the royal families yourself. And for you, that would have to be mine. Unless you are prepared to wed a woman living in her memories."

"Leif," Amel said sadly.

"Do not misjudge me," Tara said, "I pity my sister-in-law, and her sickly son. But neither is a sound prospect for continuing the royal line."

"Are you proposing to me?" asked Amel, as simply as possible.

"No," she said and leaned back in her chair, drawing her shawl about her in a gesture reminiscent of an older woman. "I am offering you my daughter's hand in marriage."

"Telly?" Amel exclaimed, suddenly understanding the girl's ill-humor toward him. "I don't think she is interested."

"She is a child of fifteen," her mother said, as if this dealt with the objection, and looked up into the gently darkening sky, as if conscious her late husband might be listening among the Watching Dead. "Chad disliked you, it's true. But I knew my husband well, Prince Amel, and even more than he disliked you, he desired his descendants to rule over all he possessed: not just Demora, but all of the Knotted Strings, as well."

"With due respect for his accomplishments," Amel told her, "Chad never ruled over the whole of the Knotted Strings while he was D'Therd. Therd was only the largest of the houses sworn to Ev'rel as liege of Dem'Vrel. He was her heir, but never Liege Dem'Vrel himself."

"You favor the Lekkers," Tara said in her bland, diplomatic voice.

"Is that what D'Therd told you?" Amel asked. He found it difficult to call Chad Therd anything else, although it was no longer correct to call him that, even if it wasn't exactly clear whether that title should now devolve on Telly, as Chad had desired, or Zind, who was the more natural choice for the Knotted Strings.

"Will you consider the offer?" El Princess Tara asked him, declining to discuss the politics of the Knotted Strings. "If, of course, Oleander forces your hand with an offer to Luthan."

"I will," he said, and rose to leave. He debated whether to ask his next question, but decided there was nothing to be gained by withholding it. "I am surprised Prince Oleander hasn't offered to wed Telly, himself. If he wants to be Protector."

Tara rose as well, folding her shawl about her against a slight breeze. "My father was a Vesta, as you no doubt know. What you may not be aware of is that he was a friend of Oleander's when they were both young men. For this reason, I know more about the man than those to whom he has never been anything except a paladin, and what I know is this: Oleander disdains the act of procreation without love, and the Princess Luthan's mother was the only woman he toyed with loving before he took the paladin's vow. Oleander had to watch my half-brother, D'Ander, become everything he knew he should have been: champion, admiral and protector of Demora. Some people call Oleander a purist, but he isn't that simple. He didn't hate D'Ander for his Silver blood, and although he resisted him politically he only dueled him once—to oppose him becoming protector—and accepted the decision of the challenge floor. No, he would have followed Kantor with devoted zeal but for one character flaw. What Oleander hated my brother for was something Silver Demish men would find hard to believe, let alone someone of more Vrellish inclinations."

Amel wet his lips and shifted uncomfortably in his seat, suspecting she referred to him. Would Tara know about Sen, he wondered. Whether she did or didn't, he was relieved the 'highborns only' rule prevented Sen Lekker from accompanying him to the palace to complicate this ordeal.

"What Oleander hated D'Ander for," Tara explained, "was the way he carried on with women before he married Leif'lee'el. My brother was a heartbreaker, Amel. And a broken heart can mean a broken life for an El Princess. There was Ayrium, the bastard, to live down, as well. Oleander considered D'Ander thoroughly dishonorable where women were concerned. He had no better opinion of my husband, who had *mekan'stan* in the Knotted Strings. Which brings me to why I do not look to Oleander to resign his vocation to marry my Telly because, you see, my daughter unites both D'Ander's blood and that of my husband's—two bad men in Oleander's view of things. He could not bring himself to even think of marrying her. He is," she concluded, "a man of truly Golden sensibilities."

Amel had no clear impression how Tara felt about any of what she had just said, and it chilled him. She was too self-contained.

"Did you know D'Therd had other lovers?" Amel asked on impulse, troubled by her coolness, and immediately felt cruel for asking it. But a nagging sense of wrongness said he ought to know what her answer would be.

"My husband loved me," Tara told him primly. "And he never gave me cause for embarrassment while living here. As for the rest, he was a man worth forgiving."

"Yes," Amel said softly. "And thank you for your insight into Oleander."

She inclined her head. "Goodnight, Immortality Amel."

"Goodnight, El Princess Tara," he returned, hesitated briefly, and added, "May I leave through the inner doors?"

"Yes, of course," she agreed, without asking why.

The arrangement of the eight apartments with their dual openings reminded Amel of the set up on Gelion: the gardens were much like exiting through a pavilion onto the public Plaza, and the hall inside was like Fountain Court. What he wanted was a little time to think privately. And he knew he wouldn't get it if he went back the garden way, into his own apartment where Dela and Margaret would be struggling for dominance over household matters like assigning rooms and making do without the help of real servants.

Besides, the magic of the palace called to him, like a postponed date with awe, and he wanted a minute to soak it in.

Amel left El Princess Tara's apartment in an odd, disassociated mood that resonnated with the empty hall beyond. He stood still in the middle of the floor and looked around, anticipating a belated reaction to discovering himself in a setting that was half-myth to most of the Demish world. But nothing happened.

He had just had an offer of marriage too extraordinary to believe, made to him as casually as an offer of cakes and tea; he was in the palace of the Golden Emperor as an exalted guest, and all that moved within him were cold, marble thoughts of doubt and isolation.

Amel closed his eyes with a shudder, reminded of how he'd felt in bed with Sen Lekker.

The sound of a thin, lilting voice intruded. He opened his eyes. Around him loomed smooth, massive pillars that had stood sentinel over a thousand years of history, fading life by life into an echo. For a moment he believed he heard a ghost. Then he recognized the sound as the voice of Leif'lee'el, D'Ander's widow.

To his left, between the pillars and across the sunken amphitheatre, he saw two figures on the grass of Spirit Park. Above them, Leif was clinging to the rocky face of the wall, holding a one-sided conversation with the spirit of her dead husband, her arms wide and her face pressed to a cold golden boulder halfway up.

Amel's emotions sprang back to life with a bound.

Leif often wandered when she fell into one of her trances, but Amel had never before seen her climb a cliff to hug a rock! The frail El Princess, highest living descendant of the ancient houses of both Arbor and Ander, was dressed for bed in a long white nightgown, her hair and gown soaked by the water running down the sculpted cliff face of the golden wall. Her grip on the jutting bolder she clung to looked perilous, but she seemed so happy sharing fond domestic nothings with the soul of Kantor Ander that Amel was forced to wonder if she might not be better off falling to her death, to join him and end their separation. If her spirit was going to heal, he suspected it would have done so in the intervening years, and he was so touched by her indifference to her danger he could almost believe he sensed D'Ander's spirit in the rock, caressing her.

Prince Drom was on the grass of Spirit Park below his mother, trying to free himself of Telly so he could start the slippery climb that—given his condition—was extremely ill advised.

"Wait!" Amel cried, like a lance of sound cast across the amphitheatre. Then he broke into a sprint to reach the brave young man.

Telly had lost her shawl in the struggle to stop Drom climbing the wall, and had kicked off her high-heeled shoes to get a better grip on the grass. Her long hair was loose down her back and there were green stains on her evening gown from at least one fall. Undaunted by appearances, she hung onto D'Ander's gallant son with both hands and enough rigor that Drom was finding it impossible to disengage her without using more force than his upbringing allowed him to exert against a woman.

"Telly, please!" Drom was saying. "She'll fall!"

"She might survive the fall, Drom!" Telly pleaded in return, half-frantic with alarm. "You won't!"

Amel lost sight of them as he flew down the steps and across the stage of the amphitheatre. By the time he made it up the other side he was relieved to see Drom had taken Telly in his arms rather than wrestle with her. With the best route up the rock face already mapped in his mind, Amel paused only to shuck off his shoes before he began to climb.

Above him, he could hear Leif murmuring to her lost love as she pressed her face to the wet rock she clung to with her chilled hands. "Thank you, Kantor. Thank you for coming. It's been so long."

He was close enough to see her smile as she loosened one hand to reach out to an unseen face, her fingers molding to it as they moved. "Amel is here," she said, "to be recognized by the Emperor, just as you always knew he would be. Is that why you've come?"

Amel was just below her when Leif gave a soft cry, reached out and tried to climb higher after the departing spirit of her love. Her foot slipped. There was no way to catch her. No handholds on the glistening, golden rocks were good enough. Amel judged the distance, decided and launched himself off the cliff with just the right thrust to intercept Leif, who was falling limply in an arc that would see her landing headfirst if she fell alone.

He used his momentum like a dancer, spinning her in his arms as he gathered her up and schooled himself for the impact, feet first, with her legs held clear and her head cradled against him in his other arm.

They were nearly three body lengths up. He exhaled and relaxed, Leif passive in his arms; and enjoyed a beautiful moment of clarity in which he knew he had done all he could and it would be enough.

Still turning, they struck. Amel absorbed the impact through his legs with a grunt, curled around his passenger and rolled away from a fatal stone ornament on the grass that he had seen earlier. But Leif's weight had thrown him off enough to murder elegance, and he sprawled as they came to a halt.

Leif gently struggled free to sit up, shaken but wide-eyed with ecstasy. "Drom!" she cried to her son as he pulled her up. "I saw your father! And he still loves us both!"

"How can I thank you enough?" Drom asked Amel over his mother's shoulder as he held her to him like a father embracing his child.

Amel shook his head, thinking about D'Ander dying for him on the challenge floor. He got to his own feet very carefully, paying attention to every complaint as he moved. Highborn brains were well suspended in their skulls and he had calculated to avoid direct injury to his head. His muscles were less happy with him. But he was tentatively reassured by the even distribution of the stress. He was a little shaky, but apart from that, he had more or less gotten away with it.

So why was Telly staring at him in horror?

Amel patted himself wherever he couldn't see, to be sure he wasn't dying on his feet of damage too horrendous for his mind to grasp, but since he had never before had any luck tuning out his awareness of even the most dreadful wounds, he wasn't surprised to find his internal assessment confirmed. Amel decided Telly was just shocked to discover he was not as horrible as she had decided he was.

Telly tore her eyes from Amel to look at Drom and Leif. "Take her to your apartment!" she said. "I'll get help!"

The first step Amel took refocused him, acutely, on his left ankle. He took a tentative step and was forced to limp.

"Damn!" he muttered, remembering his left foot touching down sooner than his right one.

After a couple more steps, he decided it was not sprained, exactly. Just sore.

'Sore' was the medical term Amel was most comfortable with for dancing injuries of any sort. Sore meant it would hurt for a while and fix itself eventually, which, thanks to his regenerative physiology, was usually an adequate diagnosis.

Jaw locked against the pain, and favoring his left foot, Amel kept pace with Drom, thinking sadly of the love that empowered Leif to invoke her late husband so vividly. Whether she had drawn his spirit to her from the Watching Dead or constructed him in her imagination didn't matter. Either way, their love was still alive.

His own feelings for Perry, on the other hand, were embers in his heart. Their many years of intimacy left an indelible image there, but if he loved her still, he was no longer sure how. Certainly it wasn't as a lover. Even Ann seemed remote, far away on Rire and pregnant with the child she had cadged from him on personal grounds that, in retrospect, and given Erien's lecture on the subject, he now realized had been equally, if not predominantly, motivated by political goals. He didn't begrudge either woman her priorities. He didn't think he could respect a woman who cared about nothing in the whole world except love! But Leif made him realize he wanted more than he had.

He envied Drom and Leif, as well, as he listened to her telling him happily about her encounter with her husband's soul, touching his face with her delicate fingers as he carried her in his arms. Here, too, was love: a sharing that gave meaning to joys and solace in failures. Family bonds.

Why can't I have that? Amel wondered miserably as he limped along. *Do I expect too much? Or am I too afraid to trust my own judgment about people anymore? I was wrong about Ev'rel. Wrong about Mira. I am probably wrong to trust Alivda, too. She will do something I can't conscience, and I'll fail as a leader as I've failed in most everything else because I can't be the kind of person who puts success ahead of love.* It felt supremely unfair, and cruelly ironic, that he didn't even get to hang onto the love as a bobby prize.

For a moment, it felt as if he was on the Flashing Floor again, about to lose his grip, but he rallied at the thought that he was here to gain Demora, and other things depended on his success, too.

Margaret and Dela were arguing over sleeping arrangements as he hobbled in the door, trying not to notice his foot getting worse.

"If we aren't in the same room," Dela was insisting, worked into a passion, "how can we know if someone tries to kill him in the night!"

"Don't be preposterous!" Margaret countered.

Dela was the first to spot Amel as he arrived, but Margaret was the one who went sheet white as she turned to see what Dela was looking at and saw Amel recover from a stumble when he put too much weight on the sore foot.

Both women were at his side in time to catch the first few words of his less than polite curse, before he caught himself and tried to convert the whole thing into a concluding: "Uh, drat!"

Between the two of them, they all but carried him into a bedroom and settled him on the bed they'd been preparing, both talking at once.

"What happened to you!" exclaimed Margaret.

"Were you attacked?" Dela asked.

"Only by the ground of Spirit Park," Amel assured Dela, suffering an intense desire to hack off his agonizing foot. He forced himself to breath properly instead, and smiled. "I'm fine. It just hurts."

"It's worse than that!" Margaret exclaimed, pressing herself down into a soft, upholstered chair by his bedside. "You won't be able to dance!"

"Dance?" Amel swallowed down the painkiller pills Dela handed him, grateful she knew him well enough to offer relief without being asked.

Margaret looked miserable. "I was counting on your dancing to save us," she explained. "In the third trial."

"The first being soul touch by the angels?" Amel asked.

Margaret nodded.

"And the second?" he pursued, hoping her anxiety about it would prove unfounded.

"The trial of testimony," Margaret said with a sigh. "I've done what I could—sending people all over the empire to collect proof of your kindness. But that's the problem. The good you have done in your life is spread out, and very few of those who benefited have been willing to relate their tale to my missionaries, or come back with us to witness for you."

"What!" Amel exclaimed, tingling all over at the picture Margaret's words inspired of white-robed luminaries stalking his friends and acquaintances to get them to sing his praises in a manner deemed legitimate by Inner Circle standards.

"Your youthful experience was primarily at court," Margaret continued with a strained air, "and while what details I could retrieve made me weep with pride and sorrow for you, they aren't the sort of thing an Inner Circle jury...Oh, Amel!" she burst out in the midst of her struggle. "The Vestas have better resources, and Luthan's actions are so much easier to document! Even the orphanage you founded with her is most likely to go wholly to her credit since your role is shadowy. I've failed you!"

Amel's heart went out to her. It was Margaret who had pressed his case for candidacy as a Soul of Light, and to do it she'd been forced to use the means the jury recognized as legitimate to weigh his 'goodness.' The whole business still irked him—as if the weighing meant more than the thing it strove to measure, and reduced every genuine experience to fodder for a process that had less to do with goodness than with winning some artificial prize.

"Whatever you have managed, I am grateful for it," he told them both, seeing Dela was about to chime in with her own side of the story. "And discussing it further, tonight, won't make it any worse or better." He turned to Dela. "Get me an ice pack, or a bag of frozen food, extra pillows to put under my foot, and something to brace it with. Does the palace have a first aid department?"

"Um, not exactly...but..." Dela waggled a hand in his direction. "I'll get what you need."

"Thanks," he told her, lay back and closed his eyes, willing his pain off stage so he could think. "You are correct," he told Margaret, thinking about what Tara had told him about Oleander. "Neither of you should sleep in my room. Take one each, on either side. And go find a couple of palace volunteers, doing their stints as staff to the emperor, to sit vigil in the common area during the night as your chaperons. I don't want anyone able to report I am trifling with your reputation, or Dela's."

A throaty sound made him look up to see Margaret fighting tears of worshipful admiration.

He smiled as kindly as he could under the circumstances. "Go make the arrangements," he urged her. "Doing something always makes waiting easier. And who knows! My foot might be fixed by the time the trial of records finishes. How long is it scheduled for?"

She bit her lip, her smooth, wide forehead troubled. "Just tomorrow."

"Well then, I'll dance on my hands if I have to!" Amel said, and laughed, thinking how the talents he had treasured as a courtesan had been so inappropriate for a Sevolite prince on Gelion, but were finally valued here.

Where I won't be able to capitalize on them, he thought angrily, *because I got hurt, stupidly, being a good person off the record!* But he couldn't regret saving Leif'lee'el.

CHAPTER 17

Therd Keep

"You're sure about this?" Vretla asked Erien, watching Vras strap on his skis with glee.

"No," Erien admitted, as Sert took a few sliding steps, then halted to raise one ski-locked foot off the snow and set it down again.

"Huh," Vretla said, looking down at her own skis.

"It never occurred to me none of you had skied before," Erien admitted, and interrupted himself at the sight of Sert strapping on her sword. "No! It will be dangerous enough if you take a spill without getting tangled up with a sword."

Sert looked at him as if he were mad.

"Maybe we should go back down to the inn and send another message up the hill," Erien suggested.

Vretla narrowed her eyes against FarHome's dull, distant sun. "Diplomacy could take days." She paused. "Weeks." Her impatience was tangible. "And we won't make it past her people on the road. We could go cross-country," she admitted, studying the wilderness of stunted trees and deep snow flanking the single cleared road up to Therd Keep. "But I'd prefer to take my chances with a fast death than a slow one."

Erien thought that through and arrived at a picture of his very Vrellish companions shivering in their sleeping bags two days into a grueling climb. The road to Therd Keep lay in a narrow ravine that had been cut by a diverted waterfall now used to supply the town below with drinking water. The country on either side was rough and steep. Vrellish physiology and the terrain would not be the only obstacles, either. Zind's reply had warned them about guard stations manned with armed retainers who had orders to repulse Lekker encroachments with weapons fire if necessary.

"It would be unfair," her letter had told Erien, "to expect them to distinguish between dishonorable Lekker rabble and an honorable visitor from court, however important. Therefore you would be best advised, Immortality, to postpone your visit until such a time as I am able to guarantee Sword Law will prevail. As for the Lekker princes, be assured they are being well treated in my custody, even if I will use them as I must to curb their relatives' dishonorable greed. If you wish to challenge me for this, I will have to postpone the honor of engaging you or your champion, Vretla Vrel, until such time as I am at leisure to consider the importance of House Therd's court reputation."

Zind had said nothing at all about Mona in her letter, but that was probably because she lacked sufficient status, as a commoner, for Zind to bother mentioning her—or so Erien wanted to believe. He did not relish the idea of going back to Gelion with bad news for Mira about her daughter. Politically, he knew Mona's loss would put an end to any hope of mending his bridges with Amel, as well.

If that's what I want, Erien added to himself. He still wasn't sure. But whatever he wanted, in the end, regarding his relationship with his maternal half-brother, he didn't want Amel to have good cause to hate him for undertaking the children's rescue without involving him.

"I'm an expert skier," Erien told Vretla, looking down the steep but manageable path to the back of Therd Keep. "But you don't have to come with me. You can take the lander back to the docks and wait for me at the inn."

"These sticks slide on the snow," Vretla summarized, staring at the path ahead of them. "Use the poles to keep our balance. Watch you to learn." She put both poles into one hand to pull on a glove, then switched and did the same on the other side. "Seems straightforward."

Can they really learn just by watching me? Erien wondered. But there was no point discussing it. Vras and Sert were ready, as well. Waiting for him. None of them had their swords.

"About the swords..." Erien began, planning to explain he hoped it wouldn't come to any sort of duel.

"If she's honorable, she'll lend us new ones," explained Vras. "If not, it wouldn't matter," he ended up with a shrug.

"Go," Vretla said.

Erien shoved off.

The transition to pure action was exhilarating. He guessed the Vrellish felt the same, from the whoop of excitement behind him as they crested the first gentle mound on the route he'd mapped out using sensors to probe for faults in the snow cover or hidden hazards beneath it. Scruffy trees whipped by on either side. The air was crisp. Even FarHome's gray sky had a new appeal. They'd be down the hill in minutes, and if no one had spotted their lander setting down behind the cover he'd found, he didn't see why anyone would be looking out the back door of Zind's keep for unexpected visitors.

Erien dared to smile as the curving, gray wall of the back end of Therd Keep got closer and closer. Their approach ran alongside the wall, at the bottom. There would be space enough to slow and stop before they shot past. Then they could hide the skis, and figure out what to do next.

Then he heard Vras calling out, "Hey!" as Sert went past Erien like a bullet, crouched over her skis.

Not only do they learn by watching, Erien thought ruefully. *They experiment!*

Vras imitated his twin and shot past next. Vretla pulled up beside Erien, a little off balance for a moment as she adjusted speed, but recovered herself as adroitly as if she'd been doing this all her life.

"Di Mon used to say the Red Vrellish would rule the empire if we had the discipline to follow orders like Nersallians," Vretla said, sounding her age, which was twice Erien's. Then she crouched down with a soft whoop and went streaking after her younger cousins, determined to stay with them.

"Good luck for the empire, back luck for me," Erien muttered under his breath, before he took a deep breath and gave chase.

It was probably the shouting that attracted attention from the keep's wall. A small head poked out of a window.

Sert and Vras were already out of their skis, near the base of the gray wall, when Vretla and Erien arrived.

Vretla took charge. "Stay flat against the wall," she ordered, "and follow me around!"

"It's him!" a young voice shouted from high up. "It's the Lor'Vrel!"

Certain he was hearing Leksan's voice, Erien disobeyed Vretla to back up far enough to locate the source of the sound. He spotted three young faces staring down at him and broke out in an elated smile.

"Leksan!" he called up. Leksan, the biggest of the three, stood in the middle, leaning out the farthest. He was flanked by Mona and his little brother, Lars. Leksan was holding something in both hands.

"Leksan, don't!" Mona's higher voice pierced the air, and Leksan disappeared back inside, leaving the flower pot he'd been holding on the sill.

Erien stood directly below the children's window. He felt helpless, listening to the sound of a scuffle in the room above, and was not paying attention when little Lars took his brother's place and pushed the heavy pot off the sill, a look of intent concentration on his round, baby face as he did it.

The pot fell straight for Erien with damned decent aim for so young a child.

Vretla hit him first, from the side.

Erien went face down in the snow, the pot just nicking his head with a sharp spike of pain as it glanced off his skull.

He rolled over under Vretla, feeling blurry, with blood slicking his hair above one ear.

Her mouth closed over his, her body likewise tightening about him like a vice.

He pushed her back, spluttering, "I can breathe, thanks!"

"Oh," she said, chagrined. "Right."

. She snapped up and brushed herself down.

Zind's people were running around both ends of the keep to meet them, Zind herself in the lead.

Vras and Sert waited where they stood, Sert slightly behind and Vras prepared to handle the diplomacy.

Zind stalked up to Erien and Vretla looking big and thunderous, but not as surprised as she might have been.

"Erien Lor'Vrel, Heir Gelion," she said. "I see you are finding new ways to demonstrate your ignorance of protocol, these days, than bumbling up the Lorel Stairs unprepared."

"Your message warned me not to approach from the front of the keep," Erien said, calm again now his upset plans were disarrayed beyond all repair. "You didn't say anything against skiing down the hill behind."

"Negligent of me, Uncle Erien," she said, and produced an unfriendly smile. "Well, then, since you are here—come in, by all means." She turned her head to her second without waiting for an answer. "Take Heir Gelion to join the prisoners. I'll talk with Vretla. You see her kinsmen are entertained. Especially him," she tipped her head in Vras Vrel's direction.

"Zind!" Vretla began to object, and was cut off by the larger woman.

"Vretla, on a challenge floor you can probably take me, but you're on my turf here, uninvited, with a Red Vrellish male who could improve my fleet by half a dozen highborns in the next generation with no complications of blood rights involved." She gave Erien a thoughtful appraisal that seemed to imply, unlike this damned Heir Gelion, no less!

"Seems to me," Zind concluded, "it wouldn't do you any harm to be generous, under the circumstances."

"It's all right with me, really!" Vras assured his scowling liege, already busy chatting with a woman among Zind's guard who was armed both with a sword and a sidearm. "They seem like decent people despite the guns. Karol, here, says the Lekkers have tried to raid the keep twice, instead of agreeing to settle custody of the boys by the sword."

"They don't have an adult highborn champion to stand against me," Zind growled. "And they know they're in the wrong about the food, as well, so they don't want us to take our quarrel to Fountain Court."

Vretla rolled her eyes and waved a hand. "All right!" she gave in, and shot Vras a warning look. "Don't have too much fun, damn it! You have to be able to stand when it's time to leave."

"I'll mind him," Sert promised. Vras had already lost interest in his fem-kin in favor of Zind's female nobleborns. The discipline of Zind's group was likewise disintegrating. One of the men objected to the arrangement, perhaps offended at a girlfriend's sudden interest in the Red Vrellish stranger, and before Erien could blink twice fists were flying. At first Erien thought it was the men ganging up on Vras and Sert, but it quickly got too chaotic to be that simple, and he concluded some of the men were allying themselves with friends or sisters to help them get first dibs. Vras and Sert seemed to be enjoying themselves, and neither Vretla nor Zind looked worried about the brawl, either.

"Now we talk," Vretla told Zind, in a threatening voice. "And while we do, you'll see to it nothing happens to the Lor'Vrellish kid."

Kid, is it? Erien thought, feeling the hairs on the back of his neck bristle, and decided maybe she was right. He was out of his depth here, both strategically and culturally. *And I want to be l'liege of Red Vrel!* Erien despaired as he took one last look over his shoulder at the joyful brawl surrounding Vras Vrel before docilely following his all-male guard into the keep.

Horth's fleet training made him automatically size up his options for resistance. He imagined he could take the two Therd retainers escorting him. But Reetion logic countered the impulse. After all, they were taking him exactly where he wanted to be.

As he walked, he explored his head wound with careful fingers, and found it had already stopped bleeding. The headache it came with was the worst of the physical pain. Knowing it was four-year-old Lars, egged on by Leksan, who had tried to kill him, was much worse. On Rire, he had risked his life and Amel's to keep the secret of the late D'Lekker's shame. But was even that enough to compensate a child for taking a beloved parent away?

No, he realized, thinking about his own lingering resentment of Amel's failure to talk Di Mon out of suicide, even now he knew Amel had had no hope of changing Di Mon's mind.

Inside the keep, Erien's escort led him up worn stairs that seemed to go on forever. Some areas of the keep were in good repair, and he suspected if he had been allowed to explore, he would have found areas equipped with Nersallian engineering products and Monatese nervecloth screens. Twice he glimpsed unfinished upgrades that seemed to have been abandoned fairly recently.

He knew Therd Keep was not the center of his late brother D'Therd's base in the Knotted Strings. That was a port city far from here. The keep was Zind's stronghold in the middle of her personal fief, something she felt entitled to hold, regardless of her father's intentions for her Demoran half-sister. Once again, Erien sensed the latent instability Ev'rel's loss had caused in the Knotted Strings, and felt chagrined all over again for failing to unite with Amel to make sure her work here was preserved.

"We're here, Heir Gelion," the guard escorting him announced when they reached a locked door. He handled Erien's title as awkwardly as his partner did the nervecloth panel on the door as he poked and prodded it without eliciting more than a few error messages.

"Here," the first guard said, displacing him, and got the door open.

There is no lack of potential here, thought Erien. *Just a lack of resources and the education to make use of them.* But for the first time, the size of the task ahead of him if he wanted to revitalize the empire in a direction closer to what Rire had achieved raised goose bumps along his arms beneath his snow suit. He wondered if his mother, Ev'rel, had felt the same, and suffered the same flashes of impatience for the backwardness surrounding her. *And all she wanted was personal power,* Erien reminded himself. *Empowering others may prove more difficult, in the end. And if they misuse the power they gain, will that be my responsibility?* He could understand the temptation to progress slowly, holding tight to the reigns of progress. *The way Ameron wants to do it,* he guessed, feeling very young for the first time in his life, and very small in comparison to the surrounding universe.

"I'm sorry!" Leksan was shouting, hands fisted at his sides, as the door opened on a dramatic scene between him and Mona. The room itself was spare, but not punitively so in a culture where the lack of luxuries was commonplace. Cots were set against one wall; there was a bookcase; a rack of cubby holes, all empty now except for some extra bedclothes and pillows; a table with four chairs and a window seat. A few pots like the one dropped on Erien completed the furnishings, all of them holding plants that were sickly or dead. When in better repair, the chalkboard and fading Gelack characters on the wall suggested the room might have been a nursery. An open door revealed an unlighted back room with a low toilet and matching sink suitable for toddlers.

The main room was lighted electrically rather than with glow-plastic, which was further evidence of poverty in a Gelack culture. Glow-plastic, like the ubiquitous clean energy of *rel*-batteries, was charged by accompanying pilots on reality skimming flights, and the Knotted Strings was low on Sevolites.

Hence the scrabble outside over Vras, thought Erien, trying to be charitable. But he was still irked by the Gelack obsession for breeding up at all costs, despite its economic motivations—or maybe because of them.

Mona stood facing Leksan with the leg of a broken chair held cocked in one hand like a club. Her mouth was bleeding and although she held firm, she was crying. Little Lars sat on the window seat with his knees drawn up and his little arms wrapped around them. He was the first to recognize Erien, and shot up like a released spring shouting, "Leksan! Leksan!"

"It is all right," Erien told all three children firmly, as they turned as one to stare at him. "I won't hurt you." He indulged in a hurt expression as he touched his head where he knew it would look dramatic, coated in cooling blood. "I hope you won't make it necessary for me to defend myself, either."

"You missed, Lars," Leksan said out of the corner of his mouth, with a cynical expression.

Mona threw down the wooden chair leg dramatically. "You want me to forgive you for hitting me!" she railed at Leksan with all the confidence of a woman who knew she had the power, which registered loud and clear even without the in-accurate use of *rel*-peerage she applied to him. "You apologize to Heir Gelion for what you did!"

"Mona!" Leksan flared. "He killed my father!"

Mona turned on Erien with eyes blazing. "Did you, Erien?" she demanded in perfect Reetion.

Erien swallowed, disconcerted to encounter someone exactly like the kind of Knotted Strings citizen he dreamed of making possible one day through education, right there in the room, confronting him. "I—yes, I did," he admitted. "He was trying to kill me. I didn't mean to, but...I lost my temper."

Mona narrowed her dark eyes at him, projecting Mira's laser-like intelligence packaged in emotional overdrive that reminded him more of Amel, or perhaps the child's dead father.

And why not nurture over nature? thought Erien, annoyed with himself for dismissing Amel's influence just because it wasn't genetic. He had always disliked the Gelack penchant for genetic determinism.

"I know you," Mona told Erien, still talking in Reetion to exclude the Lekker children. "Amel told me about you. Amel told me about Leksan's father, too. He cared about both of you." She pursed her lips, making an internal diagnosis, then spoke with decision. "Reetions tell the truth," she said to Erien. "Tell Leksan what really happened. He deserves to know, doesn't he? Isn't that what you believe? Children deserve to be told the truth about what impacts them?"

Erien turned slightly at the sound of the door closing behind him. He sighed. Mona had him, cold. Leksan was nearly the same age he had been when Di Mon withheld his intention to kill himself, tipping his world into chaos. It was always lies he had despised, as a child. Lies he had to perpetuate on Rire, where lying was almost impossible. Secrets between Di Mon and Ranar he learned only when he was older. No matter how bad the truth, he had always wanted to know it all, so he could never again be blindsided. Just months ago, he had resented Amel for lies he told Mona to shield her from what might be coming. Now here he was, an adult, about to lie to a boy who'd lost his father.

I will tell him the truth, Erien thought. But as he stared into the warm, dark eyes of the boy so proudly defying him with vengeful anger, he saw a vulnerability deeper even than the boy's courage. *Most of the truth,* he amended.

Erien pulled over a chair and sat down in it. "I will tell you what happened," he told Leksan. "Then you can decide if you still need to kill me. But if you do, please wait until you're twenty-one to challenge, and I promise I will answer you under Sword Law."

Leksan's hurt and anger smoldered for a moment longer. His jaw shifted. He looked at Mona, winced at the sight of her bloody mouth, and said in a grudging voice, "All right. But don't doubt I will challenge you! Even if you are the Ava!"

"May the gods find the prospect much too boring!" Erien replied, with sincerity, and a swooping feeling of anxiety in the pit of his stomach at the very thought. Ameron was welcome to his throne.

"Tell me, then," demanded Leksan.

Erien looked down at his hands where they lay, relaxed, in his lap.

"D'Lekker, your father, was guarding Amel when I came to free him from Lilac Hearth."

"I told you Amel was being held prisoner!" Mona said from the sidelines. Leksan cast her a sullen look, but to Erien's surprise in the next moment he relented and moved closer to the oddly-reared commoner. Even more surprising, Mona put out her hand to take his and held it firmly. Erien tried not to conjecture on the meaning of the hand-holding. Threading just enough truth through the needle of repressed details to get this right was about all he could manage.

"Why was Ev'rel holding Amel prisoner?" Leksan asked slowly and intently.

"Politics," said Erien. "Amel told her I was the Throne Price to stop me and your father from dueling."

Leksan nodded eagerly. "About the Monatese understanding Reetions because they're both perverted," he said, with the innocence of childhood.

Erien bit back the rebuke on the tip of his tongue. *One thing at a time,* he told himself.

"Something like that," he admitted. "Your father and Tatt Monitum had clashed a few times, and D'Lekker wanted to provoke a challenge. But I was offended, too, and usurped the challenge."

Leksan nodded again. "Because you were raised by Di Mon, who was nothing like that," he said. "Di Mon was honorable."

Yes, because of Di Mon, thought Erien. *But not quite for those reasons.* He decided it was wisest not to answer directly.

"I was also raised by Ranar of Rire, who is what we call boy-*sla* and the Reetions call a homosexual," Erien said. "But I have never known a man more decent, intelligent and honorable. I wish I could have made your father, and the rest of Gelion, understand this without being prepared to duel, but I couldn't."

Leksan pouted. "You won," he said, and rallied. "But it was a fair fight. I even heard it said ..." He looked away, turning toward Mona.

"He heard D'Lekker went for you when it was over," Mona supplied. "Did he?"

"Anger can make men do things they wouldn't under normal circumstances," said Erien, determined not to lie outright about anything.

"I know my father had a temper," Leksan said, speaking to the floor between him and Mona. "But he never hurt my mother, or us. He was always...like summer, when he visited. He and Amel would take us on hay rides, or up in a *rel*-ship, sometimes. He gave me my first sword, and told me how important it was to be a Lekker. He made my mother laugh. And he...he loved us," the child concluded.

"I am sure that he did," Erien said with real pain.

"And he loved Amel!" Leksan flared again, more hotly.

"That too," agreed Erien, even more painfully.

Leksan's face screwed up in unspeakable misery. "But it is true, isn't it? He h-hurt him."

"Yes," admitted Erien.

Leksan let go of Mona's hand and turned to look toward the window which still stood open. Something dangerous and self-destructive moved in him. "I don't want to be someone who hurts people they love," he said boldly. Then he caught Mona's hand again and turned her toward him. "If I ever hit you again, for anything, promise you'll kill me."

"You won't," she assured him.

At the end of this avowal, the intensity of whatever had happened between the two children during their ordeal forced itself onto Erien's map of possible disasters despite himself.

"Excuse me for asking," he told the two children, "but isn't Mona going to come back to court to live with Amel?"

"I don't ever want to reality skim again," Mona told Erien gravely. "Not even to see Amel. He'll have to come here to visit me."

"I see." Actually Erien didn't, and was worried this would be a complication when the time came to leave, presuming Zind didn't decide to keep them all indefinitely.

"I'm going to marry her," Leksan declared. "Immediately. Even if we have to wait a few years to consummate it."

Little Lars trotted forward to intrude between them. "I can do the child-gifting for my liege-brother," he volunteered proudly.

"When you are old enough!" Leksan laughed, and mussed his brother's hair.

I will never get the hang of this, thought Erien. All he said, again, was, "I see."

"We'll swear to Amel, of course," Mona told Erien. "And you, as his l'liege."

"Actually—" Erien began to confess his misstep on that front, when the door behind them opened and Zind herself appeared.

"Satisfied with their condition?" she asked gruffly. "Good! Come with me."

She wouldn't explain anything until they were outside again in a light plane and in the air, with Zind in the pilot's seat.

"I figure you might be a lot like Ev'rel," Zind told him, keeping her eyes ahead. Her straightforward confidence and big build kept reminding him of her father, the late D'Therd, and he couldn't help liking her for it. He wasn't sorry Horth had won the duel, naturally, but he sometimes wished he'd had a chance to get to know Chad Therd better. After living his whole life as a question mark, it was hard to discover a mother and two half-brothers only to lose them immediately. He had Tatt, of course, on his father's side, and although he'd lost Di Mon he still had Ranar and his other Reetion parents. *And Amel,* he thought slowly, wondering why he so resisted thinking about Amel as his half-brother.

"Ev'rel was always sensible to deal with," Zind continued, banking right as she brought them down over an arm of the mountain and straightened out along the coastline. "All you had to do was figure out what she wanted and trade her for whatever you needed. What do you need, Heir Gelion?"

"Peace," said Erien, without needing to think. "Between you and the Lekkers."

Zind was silent for a long while. A settlement sprawled around the estuary of a mountain-fed river up ahead of them. It was nothing grand but it looked like a going concern, with signs of recent growth and industrial areas pressing outward along roads that fanned out and stopped at the base of the mountain.

"This plane runs on imported fuels that aren't good for the ecosphere," Zind began to talk again suddenly. "Taking you out in it is a decision, like everything else we do here. How much harm for how much good to strike the right balance for survival." She paused as they started to angle down over cultivated fields. "FarHome isn't much good at growing things," she said, as he took in the evidence. "We rely on imported fertilizers and fixers to grow Earthlife; on drugs and processing methods that make native plants digestible. Only a band of territory around the equator is habitable, as you must have discovered from space, and none of it is better than what you've seen. But FarHome is paradise in the Knotted Strings. Our only green world. And in the last generation, since Ev'rel gained Demora, it's become overpopulated and even more dependant on imports than usual. We've gained better Sevolites to fly for us, as well, but not as many as we should have because Amel would never child-gift to us. I don't like being dependant on Demora. I would like to have a highborn fleet and a hundred times more nobleborn freight pilots. I would like to have something to trade, as well," she added with a humorless laugh. "But never mind that. I could probably pull it all off, eventually, if we could just get rid of the Lekkers."

Oh no, thought Erien. Just when it had been starting to sound promising.

"See that city?" Zind said, nodding out the window again. "It supports three hundred thousand people, all but a few hundred of them commoners. And since the groceries stopped arriving every two weeks, half of them are going hungry and the weakest are starting to drop dead. What do I do about that, Erien? When it's the Lekkers who are stealing our groceries."

She swooped down over the city, low enough he could see the empty streets and lack of bustle at the space port docks. He saw empty parks on scraps of brown earth, old men sitting outside in chairs and women walking on the street, burdened with children. He saw lineups for rations being dispensed from a government building. When he had seen enough, she pulled up and turned back the way they'd come, silent again.

"What makes you think the Lekkers are to blame for the attacks on the supply ships from Demora?" asked Erien.

Zind snorted. "They've got food," she said. "Not where it would look too obvious. You can find Lekker cities on the surface that are also hurting. But they've got food in Lekker domes on cold rocks in the Second Knott, and even Lekkers in cities on FarHome get more relief than other clans. Sen Lekker claims she has stockpiled rations, but I think she's in league with the pirates, telling them where and when to find the transport ships, and sharing the booty. Or maybe there are no pirates, except the Lekkers."

"So you kidnapped their heirs, Leksan and Lars, to blackmail them?" asked Erien.

"That's right," Zind admitted with a sneer. "And if that doesn't work, I'll start killing the rest of them, as well. Until they are all dead."

"Rekindling the war that is responsible for your shortage of Sevolites," Erien pointed out.

Zind shrugged. "We have more and higher Sevs than them."

"But it's Sen Lekker who has the connections on Demora, isn't that right?" asked Erien. "Ev'rel appointed Sen as the Dem'Vrellish agent there, which wasn't a problem when your father was also a Demoran presence, via his marriage, but your relations with your half-sister, Princess Telly, aren't exactly cordial. Not when your father wanted her to be the next D'Therd—effectively deposing you." He looked out at the slate gray sky. "Though I must admit I can't see a Demoran princess thriving here."

They were in a clear patch, and Zind turned her head to look at him. "You want peace, you do this for me, Heir Gelion. You tell the Lekkers that if they don't stop this game with the groceries I'll kill their eight-year-old D'Lekker, and if that doesn't impress them I'll kill his four-year-old brother, as well. Then I'm coming after them."

"Unless?" Erien asked, walling off his rejection of the threat. He could not let himself believe she would do it, and still feel motivated to cooperate with her.

"Unless my people get fed—immediately. Before we find out what Sen Lekker has up her sleeve once she thinks we're weak enough to take out."

Erien thought of a dozen scenarios as they headed back to Therd Keep, but rejected eleven of them. He decided he would stay with the children to act as a human shield. Having a dead

Heir Gelion in the closet had to be viewed as a liability, even if Zind had shown none of her father's preoccupation with winning respect at court. The fleets of the Ava's Oath could deliver a worse sting than a social snub.

What he had to do was get a message to Amel on Demora to send the groceries through safely, as a starting point for negotiations with Zind and to ensure the safety of the kidnapped children. The messenger would have to be highborn and em- powered with his signet of passage backed up with his blood seal.

The hard part was deciding who to trust with the commission.

CHAPTER 18

Trial of Testimony

Oleander arrived the next morning to brief Luthan on the trial of testimony.

"You have nothing to worry about," he told her warmly. "What I do not already have thoroughly documented, I took the liberty of researching while on Gelion, and I had longer than Abbess Margaret to prepare. I also saw to it that not all of the envoys she sent out to gather testimony on Amel's good works were able to return. She may command a reverie, but not a fleet."

Luthan looked at him, standing before her so immaculate and civilized, and tried not to believe her ears.

"What is it, dear Luthan?" he asked, concerned.

"Tell me," she asked him breathlessly, "that you didn't kill anyone to stop them testifying for Amel!"

"Kill?" he stiffened. "Of course not!" His voice softened. "Delayed a little, is all. But how truly you are a Golden Soul, dear Luthan, to be concerned."

"I don't know if *concerned* is the proper word," Luthan said. "But I would find it insupportably absurd if people were murdered in the name of proving I was more divinely good than someone else!"

Oleander missed the point. He bowed to her, and told her with crushing sincerity, "But you are better than he will ever be."

Despite her pique, the words were good to hear.

And I don't want this just for myself, Luthan defended herself. *I want it for all the Silver-Golden hybrids like me, who have been told they aren't pure enough by Golden Demish relatives! And I want it so I can advise people with the proper authority.*

She had to ask herself, however, whether Amel being recognized as a Soul of Light wouldn't meet both objectives just
as well, without her.

The trials will decide, she thought. *That's what trials are for.
Deciding things.* But she couldn't help feeling a little grubby about
the whole affair.

"How did the trial of soul touch work out?" she asked nervously.

Oleander nailed Prince Samdan with a cold glare.

"He should not have traveled with you," Oleander said. "He
polluted the trial with unseemly emotions unfit for the soul of
an angel to share."

Luthan looked at Prince Samdan to hide her rising flush.
"Really?" she said in a squeaky voice, and cleared her throat.
"I thought it simply hadn't worked."

"You experienced nothing, of course," Oleander declared,
with a sage nod of his bullet-smooth head, his pale hair slicked
back and tightly bound behind. "I had guessed as much."

Luthan was dying to ask what the angel had picked up, but
decided not to push her luck. "Did Amel win the first trial?"
she asked instead.

"No." Oleander wore a sneer on his thin, perfect mouth. "His
angel picked up echoes of a martial mind."

"Really?" Luthan squeaked again, failing to reconcile the
description with her knowledge of the pathologically gentle
Amel.

"It is hard to know exactly what he was thinking about,"
Oleander clarified, "but the angel was convinced he was preoccupied with some sort of violence. Unfortunately," he added
in a brooding tone, "the judges were not all convinced your
angel's readings were due to the contamination of having a man
on board." He gave poor Prince Samdan another glare, making Luthan feel a twinge of guilt on behalf of the poor boy, who
had been her constant companion apart from his initial wan-
der around the palace grounds.

"C-couldn't the angel tell if the...unseemly thoughts were
male or female?" Luthan asked, struggling not to fidget. "If that
was the sort of unseemliness involved, of course."

"Do not trouble yourself with the uncertainties of imperfect
judges, El Luthan," her paladin advised her in a kindly voice.
"I know your soul is pure." He gestured grandly with a long
sweep of his arm, and for a moment Luthan was so taken with

the very idea of him standing there, in his glistening uniform, putting himself at her service, that she forgot to move.

The judges were already assembled in the amphitheatre when Luthan's party arrived. She counted twelve men and women, all thin and pale with sky-blue eyes and golden hair, each mantled in a richly embroidered robe. They were settled in the lowest row of seats on a set of twelve grand and comfortable couches. A glass samovar with golden fittings stood ready on the stage floor beside a long tray of flavored powders used to enliven the pale yellow tea inside. Behind the tea service stood two volunteer princesses in long golden skirts and high-necked blouses, waiting to act as servants.

There was no one else except the two royal families and Amel's party, comprising El Princess Dela—the only klutz ever born into the Inner Circle—and the literary magnate known as Lady Margaret. Margaret had given up her worldly position as an unmarried daughter of a regional Highlord to found the controversial Order of the Messenger, wielding her considerable influence as a renowned, living playwright, to bring the lobby for Amel's recognition to the current crisis of decision.

But isn't it odd how homespun and threadbare it all feels, thought Luthan, looking at the pale judges and the handful of unique but rather odd participants gathered for the trial of testimony. *If we were gathered on a Silver Demish world, we would have two hundred witnesses, all properly housed with their entourages, even if it were all for nothing but an ordinary wedding or a genotyping!*

Luthan avoided looking at Amel as Oleander seated her. A short silence followed until Oleander cleared his throat, prompting the first in the line of twelve judges to rise to his feet a bit unsteadily.

"Let the trial of testimony begin," the judge declared, and sat down again.

How rude! thought Luthan in surprise. *He did not even introduce himself!* On reflection, a small furrow planted itself on her baby-smooth brow as she decided she was probably supposed to know who he was and every one of his fellow judges, besides. She suspected the Demorans present did.

The woman next in line got up, and a long preamble followed, establishing the absolute authority of the Golden Emperor as the only being able to recognize another Pureblood as a Soul of Light and explaining that the judges of the trials could therefore do no more than recommend Amel should they see fit.

Recognition as a Golden Soul was not quite as exclusive, since it could be managed by unanimous vote at the gathering of Golden Souls held on Demora once a generation, but it was also within the prerogative of the Emperor himself at any time, and therefore the process would be much the same for Luthan as for Amel, should she win.

"We will, however, constrain ourselves to recommending only one candidate for divine recognition at these trials," the old El princess finally concluded, "out of respect for the grief of the Emperor for his beloved wife and daughter, whose loss wears upon him more with each passing year."

Or decade, I suppose, Luthan thought uncharitably. Fahild's wife and daughter had died within a few years of each other back when his grandson—Amel's father—was a child. Two generations had grown to adulthood by the slow clock of Demish maturation since that time: first Amel's father, Delm; and then Amel himself, the Emperor's last living descendant, who was nearly thirty-five. In fact, the more she thought about it, the more Luthan began to find Fahild's divine grief monstrous, instead of sentimentally sublime. *Because in the meantime he has left this limp collection of lame brains in charge!* she justified her lapse of reverence with a guilty pang. She also spared a glance over her shoulder at Oleander, who would have been running the whole show himself, by now, if he had been a Silver Demish prince of any kind!

Maybe even respect for tradition can be too much of a good thing, in the extreme, Luthan allowed, with a pang for the damage so thorny an idea inflicted on the tender spots in her young heart.

"Therefore, the role of this council of judges, which I am privileged to lead," the speaker droned on, still without introducing herself, "is solely to make a single recommendation to our Beloved Majesty in his Sacred Grief. This modest office, alone, do we claim. His Supreme Goodness, Fahild, may prove us in error when he is presented with our chosen candidate."

Finally! Luthan thought when the woman sat down.

Then disaster fell upon her!

Doubtless by using his paladin charm on Barbanna, Oleander had obtained her spiritual diary, the book a Luminary princess used to record her acts of goodness and admonish herself for her failings. Luthan listened in horror as Oleander produced it and began to read aloud, with lofty reverence, all the self-righteous congratulations bestowed upon her by her younger self as she presided over her servants' squabbles, chastised romantically intoxicated friends and ruled against what didn't suit her about Erien's Reetions as revealed to her in the letters Tatt had shared. Oleander was aware of her distress as this proceeded, and apologized for the trespass with a new and prettier turn of phrase each time it was his turn to rise and speak: praising her for her modesty, decrying the unfortunate necessity of exposing her inner beauty and assuring her of the deep respect it was engendering in their venerable audience, as Luthan grew more and more catatonic with shame.

But Oleander was correct about the impact on the audience, except for Amel's supporters, who looked at her with hot resentment rather than respect. Only Amel himself knew her well enough to guess it was not modesty that kept her eyes averted, but the discomfort of being confronted by her arrogant, childish morality. She didn't like looking up to find him watching her, because she saw not only disappointment but compassion in his warm gray eyes, and an unwelcome sense of comradeship— as if they were the only ones aware that the whole proceeding was absurd. She felt as if the two of them were in a morbid kind of soul touch, without benefit of reality skimming, in which his forgiveness was a curse. Once, when she caught his glance, the slight tightening at one corner of his mouth seemed to underscore her own thoughts, like a standing wave of communication, mind-to-mind: *how odd they know so little about what they strive to measure,* their silent communion resonated in her mind.

Despite the torment of listening to Oleander eulogizing her, listening to Abbess Margaret and El Princess Dela proclaim Amel's goodness was even harder for Luthan to endure.

Their case was piecemeal and badly framed. Both had collected crude statements from people who didn't matter to the judges and couldn't express themselves loftily. Dela sometimes got flustered and babbled, inspiring Amel to veil his face with a hand as he sat through gushing praises studded with too much rushing about like a paladin, on Amel's part, to match the fragile image of a Soul of Light thoroughly implanted in Demoran psyches. Margaret fared better, but it was clear to Luthan that despite her high breeding and commanding reputation as the author of great works, antagonism lay between her and the council over her push to get her order recognized as an official Luminary sect, and they were disinclined to give her what she wanted yet again.

After exhausting her collection of endorsements by the riff-raff of the empire, Margaret resorted to her own claim that she had identified Amel as the incarnation of the soul who had last graced the world in the person of Prince Faydoren of the Family of Light, a mythical hero of the Golden Age whose goodness was leavened by a lively strain of poetical genius and an affectionate zeal for the simple things of life.

A shocked silence followed her presentation of this unexpected presumption. Amel looked unprepared for it himself, and the state of ravaged modesty stamped on his expressive face matched the worst of Luthan's squirming discomforts earlier.

All eyes focused on Margaret as she drew breath to continue, a few of the judges only just waking up to an awareness something untoward was taking place.

"Yes, Amel is Faydoren!" cried Margaret, growing so agitated she nearly spilled her teacup by making the table shake where it touched her. "I proclaim it! And I know it as only I could know." She paused, and inhaled with a great shiver, swallowing before she could continue. Amel looked inclined to rise and pull her down, but wasn't quite sure he should.

"You all know me," Margaret said. "You know what powers of the spirit and the word are mine to claim. Believe, then, in my testimony, because what I know, I know by means immune to refutation by the mundane measures of this world. I know because he is my—"

For long seconds, Luthan had been aware of something not quite right in the looming stillness of the air above the amphitheatre and the waiting silence of the great hall beyond, as if something swift and alien was ruffling the edges of their old, aloof reserve.

The intrusion resolved into footsteps. Then, as Margaret struggled with herself to speak the final word of her surprising argument, a man appeared at the top of the steps above them.

A man with a bare chest, wearing red suspenders.

The Demorans reacted as if confronted by a spirit sprung to life out of a purgatory reserved for the most incorrigible of Vrellish souls. They froze, and stared like people about to drop dead of shock, except for one princess-judge who passed out with a gentle sigh.

The very Vrellish vision paused above them at the edge of the steps, his bare chest leanly muscled and lightly oiled, with solid red house braid confined to the width of the red suspenders slashing down his chest in two straight lines. He was black haired, sharp featured and gray eyed, dressed in worn flight pants and soft-soled shoes. Although completely out of place, he looked undaunted as he filled his chest with air and called out:

"Message from Erien for Amel!"

Amel stood and sat down again with a flinch, buckling toward the left as if his leg had given out on that side.

Two more Demorans fainted: a woman dressed in gold, standing beside the samovar, and a man on the council of judges. People were suddenly busy helping each other or containing their own surprise.

Oleander strode forward clearing his sword.

"Oh!" said the man on the marble edge of the steps leading down into the amphitheatre, and shrugged, clearing his own with a gesture as natural as exhalation.

"Dela! Stop them!" Amel cried, hissing in pain over whatever had gone wrong with his leg.

El Princess Dela rushed to obey, knocking over her chair and colliding with one of the delicate glass stands holding a samovar, whose minder shrieked as she fled up the stairs into Spirit Park to hide behind the stone bench.

Dela hurled herself between Oleander and the new arrival, her back to the Vrellish man. As Oleander advanced, she kept backing up until she bumped into the intruder's bare chest.

"Out of the way, you fool!" Oleander ground out in exasperation.

Dela gave an 'eep!' as the Vrellish man snagged her around the waist, squeezed her, and swung her aside, saying, "Later!" in a cheerful voice.

Looking flummoxed and offended, her hair falling loose about her plump features, Dela stood blinking at him, paralyzed.

Amel vaulted the table between him and the developing scene, landed on his right foot and hurried to take over, setting his left foot down ever so gingerly on the floor once he got his balance.

"No fighting until we've talked!" Amel declared, thrusting his arms out, palm forward, to either side.

The serving woman who had fled the toppled samovar chose this moment to act, snatched a long knife out of a hidden sheath in her bodice and hurled herself at Amel with a keening cry.

Oleander made no move to stop her and the Vrellish man looked utterly astonished by the whole affair.

Luthan rose in her seat, shouting "Amel!" at the top of her voice.

Amel pivoted in time to seize the amateur assassin by the wrist, but the intervention fouled his one-legged balance and they went down together in an ungainly muddle of thrashing limbs. Amel yelped once as her flailing struck his sore foot. The next moment Dromedarius was at Amel's side, taking control of the panting, frantic woman by grabbing her elbows from behind. She still held her knife.

"Don't cut Drom!" Amel appealed to the hysterical purist who was struggling and sobbing in the prince's grip.

"I had no idea Demorans were so volatile!" the Vrellish man remarked in astonishment.

"Who are you and what do you mean intruding here?" Oleander spat out at him in spiteful grammar.

"Vras, Heir Vrel," their alarming guest replied with matching arrogance. "And who are you, apart from someone eager to be dead?"

Luthan sat down for fear she, too, might pass out. Her heart was in her throat, and her head was spinning with fear someone was going to be killed. Acute pressure on her lips made her realize she was pressing her knuckles against her face, and she forced her hand down.

Amel had succeeded in climbing to his feet with a look of pain and irritation that redefined his beauty in a new, alarmingly aggressive way.

"May I introduce Paladin Oleander, Prince of Vesta," Amel addressed himself to Vras before turning, with a slight hop, to face down Oleander with the same ferocious courtesy. "Vras is sword-heir to Vretla Vrel of Red hearth. Since he is here to see me, I will deal with him. You may take up the offense with my champion, Alivda, if you so desire." He scowled. "Whenever she next sees fit to reappear."

Oleander's hatred for Amel boiled in his body's stiff posture as he swallowed the Pureblood address Amel forced on him.

"You are no Soul of Light!" Oleander's trained voice lanced out at Amel with ice daggers of certainty. "Abomination," he concluded in a lower register.

Drom came forward, his charge relinquished to Princess Telly, who had left her place beside her outraged mother to intervene.

"He is a Soul of Light!" El Prince Drom insisted, his bravery clear in the marks on his bare forearms, where bruises from
the woman's struggle with him were already coming up in
blotches of purple and red. His handsome young face grew
animated, light catching in his mane of golden curls. "He is
injured in the foot because he saved my mother's life last night,
thrusting himself from the cliff face of Spirit Park to envelope
her in his protection as she fell. She would have died, and most
likely myself with her—trying to help—if he had not been there.
The rigor to succeed in such a feat does not belittle the love
motivating it!"

"A stunt!" Oleander hurled back, his mouth marred by an
ugly sneer. "It is well known you and your mother favor him.
And I would not put it past your father's spirit to have lured
Princess Leif'lee'el up there in the first place just to give Amel
the chance to save her! Besides, we have nothing to prove it but
your word!"

"His ankle is sprained!" Drom cried, taken aback by
Oleander's cynicism.

"There are many other ways he could have injured his foot,"
Oleander dismissed the young man's protestation.

Luthan shot to her feet again. "Oleander!" she cried, making
him turn to her, his expression immediately kind and serene
again.

"Please!" she said, vibrating with fear he would fight Vras
or say more mean things about Amel. "Take me away from here.
I need to rest."

"I am your servant," Oleander said simply, and obeyed her.

They set off up the steps and across the brown, marbled floor
with Oleander hovering protectively at Luthan's elbow. After
the long hours of embarrassment, Luthan found his closeness
oppressive, even if there was a wild Red Vrellish man loose in
the palace, as well as a few unsuspected fanatics bent on killing
Amel.

"I do not understand how that Vrellish creature was permitted
to land on the planet, let alone enter the palace," Oleander said
tersely when they reached the door of her apartment. "I suppose
it must have to do with this Erien Lor'Vrel creature he claims
to represent, but he should not have been admitted if he came
as the envoy of Ameron himself! I must find out what happened.
Then I will return." He fixed her with his stern, pale eyes, and
she watched them melt with affection as he gazed at her. "It
is crucial I speak with you, privately."

"Me?" Luthan said, taking a step back. Her hand found the handles of the door behind her.

"I will return shortly," he promised her, and was gone.

Luthan went in and collapsed into the nearest chair in the common room. She was alone. The chaperons she'd asked to spend the night had left after she got up, and it was too early for them to set up their vigil again, to defend her reputation. *As if Prince Samdan could tempt me!* Luthan thought, in the midst of her turmoil, and felt even less of a Golden Soul than ever.

She thought of her nice rooms in Silver Hearth, her Uncle H'Us, all her servants and her many friends. Even Barbanna was looking good, and she felt sobs begin to rise in her throat.

Samdan burst in through the garden door. "Liege H'Us!" he cried breathlessly. "That Alivda person has smuggled herself into the palace as a performer, here to audition!" He dropped in front of her on both knees, his sword nearly catching under him before he remembered to deal with it. His eyes were big, with too much white showing around the dark blue irises. "Do you think she's going to try to kill the Golden Emperor?"

Luthan thought about the question seriously. "No," she said. "Never mind her. I think Prince Oleander is about to propose to me."

Samdan sat back on his legs. "Oh," he said. A funny look crossed his face that was all wrong for a man. "Congratulations?" he asked awkwardly.

Luthan leaned forward to take his hands, thinking clearly for the first time since the Council of Privilege. "I need you to arrange for me to talk, alone, with Amel. As soon as possible. The set for my dramatic reading will be built tonight by Oleander's people. We could meet there while we're supposed to be asleep. You aren't big for a man. We'll switch clothes and you can take my place, in my chamber. I'll return to your room when I come in and we can work out some trick for how we emerge in the morning. With luck we'll get one of the more absent-minded chaperons."

"But—" Samdan protested.

"Princess Luthan?" Oleander's voice preceded his gentle tap on the outer door.

"Coming!" she said, and rose, pulling Prince Samdan after her. He had soft hands, she thought, for a swordsman. "Go!" she hissed, giving him a little push. He went out through the garden doors.

CHAPTER 19

Discovery

Sam emerged, breathless, from the bower at the back of Luthan's apartments and took a few stumbling steps onto the smooth, flower-speckled lawn. It was dusk. Around her lay a vast and languid calm, even emptier of people than the palace at her back. The night was neither cold nor warm and nothing stirred the sweet air; but she shivered, wondering how a knight errant intruded on an enemy prince to deliver a message about a secret rendezvous. Standing on the lawn, empty as it was, made Sam feel exposed and she started at a sound from behind her, but it was only Luthan's voice greeting Oleander as he came in and closed the door.

Sam ran in the direction of Amel's apartment at the far end of the row, passing Telly and Drom who stood talking together at the back of his mother's rooms. Princess Tara's bower was empty, with no lights on in the common room beyond. Maybe she had gone to bed, or was looking for her missing daughter. Sam didn't care. A prickly feeling of danger made her dart into the empty bower and crouch, peering out at the twilight expanse of the lawn.

Moments later, Alivda came striding past from the direction of the stage entrance to the palace on its far side. She was dressed in a skin-tight costume with loops of silky tassels about the waist and shoulders. The failing light of day glided over the contours of her legs and arms as she walked.

Sam stared, pressed against an ancient tree trunk in Princess Tara's bower. In the stillness, she heard the faint sound of voices from Amel's back yard.

Alivda doubled back, disappearing from view.

Terrified she'd been spotted, but afraid to burst into the open, Sam squeezed between two trees. The hilt of her sword caught.

She paused to twist, and lifted it through. A wall of densely packed underbrush confronted her, but the plants were yielding, and she found that if she moved slowly and steadily she could gradually press her way through without making much noise at all. She even got a false sense of security from the press of leafy life surrounding her on all sides.

As she progressed, the sounds of conversation grew louder on the other side. She stopped when she was far enough through to catch slashes of color in the clothing of the people in Amel's garden.

"What is it?" Amel asked.

"I thought I heard something," another male voice replied, quick and light.

"What did you—oh!" This was in Princess Dela's voice. A sweep of golden tresses at a slanting angle suggested a fall, arrested before she hit the ground. Sam dared to move aside a single, giant leaf and saw Vras Vrel set the plump Demoran on her feet again, pause, and then suddenly pulled her close and cover her mouth with his own.

"Vras!" Amel exclaimed, in tandem with Lady Margaret's astonished, "Oh!"

Dela made a very different 'oh' sound as she and the alarming Vrellish man came apart.

"I've a weakness for soft, round women," Vras explained, with a touch of embarrassment. "My fem-kin say it isn't natural."

"Heir Vrel, sit there," Amel said bossily. "Dela, on the other side. Now tell me again, slowly. Erien is with Zind at Therd Keep because Mona and Leksan were kidnapped! But Erien thinks I'm more use to them here than there. Convince me, or I'm putting on flight leathers!"

Dela and Margaret's voices welled up in a chorus of protestations at the very idea of Amel leaving on the eve of the last trial.

"I can't dance anyway!" Amel retaliated. "And this contest has little to do with measuring the quality of our souls! Our ability to brag effectively, perhaps! Or maybe Oleander had it in the bag before we arrived! Mona and the boys need me more!"

"Think of Demora!" Lady Margaret cried, throwing herself against him in her distress. "If the Vestas win, they'll be reactionary and isolationist at the very time we need to strike a new deal with the empire! Think about the people who believe in you!"

"Are Demish women always this excitable?" Vras asked in a bewildered tone.

Watching to see how Amel would respond, Sam felt hands on her ribs from behind and gave a yelp. The next thing she knew, she was being manhandled through the trees, floundering to protect her face with her hands and gulping air.

Alivda mastered her easily, hurting her arm as she held it behind her. Sam forgot all about controlling the register of her voice. "Don't kill me!" she cried. "Luthan sent me!"

"Last I checked," growled Alivda, "that would make you a spy for the other side."

"No!" Sam began to cry, certain she was going to die. "She sent me—she wants to ask—"

Amel was giving her a funny look. "Prince Samdan's a...woman," he said, bemused.

Sam sobbed. She was worse than dead now. For the second time in her life, an attempt to do something extraordinary had only proved she was a fool. She was ready to die to end the humiliation.

Amel's voice was gentle, if impatient, as he told Alivda, "Let her go."

Alivda gave Sam a push. Strong hands caught her by the elbows and helped her sit at a bench with her back to the table attached to it. Only after she'd registered the security of wood beneath her did she realize she'd been helped by Amel. He pivoted on one foot to do it, and hopped back a step afterwards, his sprained left foot hovering just above the ground. Margaret was taking advantage of his injury to hold his left arm, but it was clear to Sam the abbess's help wasn't necessary. Even on one leg, Amel had excellent balance.

"What does Luthan want?" Amel asked.

There was just enough strain in his voice to detect, although whether due to the pain in his foot, the antics of the people surrounding him or his worry about the kidnapped children he'd referred to, Sam couldn't tell.

"She wants to see you, tonight," Sam said, her fear banished by a strange certainty he wouldn't let her be hurt. "To talk. She said Oleander might propose to her."

"Erien says Zind wants her groceries," Vras Vrel spoke up, alarming Sam for the sake of the contrast with Amel's mildly narcotic effect. "He says you can help the kids by making the Demorans send the food, under escort, so they'll get through to FarHome regardless of whether the Lekkers are in cahoots with the pirates who've been stealing them."

"The Lekkers!" Amel exclaimed. "They depend on Demoran tribute as much as the Therds. Why would Sen Lekker organize the theft of her own people's food?"

"Lekker docks are getting food despite the pirates," Vras explained.

Amel was silent for a moment; then he said very slowly, as if thinking out loud, "The pirate problem began after Ev'rel died." He paused. "Does Erien believes Sen, herself, is behind the raids?"

"The Lekker clan, anyway," Vras said. "We ran into one of the shake-ups ourselves, heading out. Erien snagged a handful of grains in the passenger section of his lander—yes," Vras answered Amel's look of alarm, "he had a close call. Anyway, he's worked with Zind to match his grains with stuff the Lekkers have, based on a Lorel analysis of some sort. He says he can tell if what the Lekkers are eating came from the same harvest as the grains he accidentally picked up. Sounds pretty far-fetched to me, but it made sense to Zind Therd. She even had the equipment he needs to do it. Some lab Ev'rel was helping her develop." Vras frowned. "I'm still not sure there's enough Vrel in that Lor'Vrel, but he soul-touches clean enough. And Vretla figures he'll give her a baby if you won't."

Baby? Sam thought, watching Amel absorb this detail with a thoughtful, bothered look. She tried to imagine Vretla Vrel being with Amel romantically, and was plagued by jarring images of unseemly skirmishes over candlelit dinners, resulting in a lot of broken tableware and a singed tablecloth.

Amel made up his mind with an inward snap that cleared the tension from his features, leaving him purposeful but oddly sad.

"I'll see Luthan," he told Sam. "And we'll organize what relief we can for Zind. Vras, it will be your job to see our offering makes it to its destination. Dela, you'll have to draw on our personal resources at Dee Manor and anything Margaret's order can provide. It won't be enough, but the official shipment has already gone. I can't command Demora to send more unless I win tomorrow. I'll also need to see Sen." He looked at Alivda, inviting her to offer her advice.

"Write her a letter," said Alivda. "Tell her what you will. But you're keeping your date with Luthan, and I'm keeping mine— with Fahild."

"You?" Margaret said, horrified. "You have met the Golden Emperor?"

"Sure!" Alivda grinned. "He's a lot like Amel in some ways, just more so. He saw me dance, and was impressed enough to give me the chance to tell him Amel taught me. And I begged him for a chance to tell him more about his great-grandson. He thinks you are just like your father, Delm, you know!" she told Amel. "Fahild's paladins won't go for a private chat, but the good news is they do what he says when he can be inspired to give a damn. So I'm here to change and to meet him again, for a longer conversation. That's what I came to tell you about."

Margaret was stunned.

Dela said in a squeaky voice, "You won't hurt him...will you?"

Alivda glared. "You have your orders, fat one!"

Dela went red, cried something aloud about protecting the Golden Emperor from abominations and would have got the worst of a clash with Alivda if Vras Vrel hadn't intervened.

"You have better things to do, warrior," he told Alivda, snagging Dela from the side and snugging her against him, careful to keep his sword arm free.

Alivda gave the Red Reach highborn a smoldering look and conceded his point with a grunt. Then she rounded on Sam. "Tell me how we're supposed to arrange this rendezvous with Princess Luthan?" she demanded.

By the time Sam had explained to Alivda about the prop room at the back of the set built on the amphitheatre for Luthan's performance tomorrow, she felt wrung out. Amel disappeared early in the process and returned at the end of it with a sealed note, followed by Drom dressed in outdoor clothes.

Amel was still hopping, with Margaret acting as a willing crutch. He detached himself from Margaret to sit beside Sam.

"Who are you really?" he asked. "And does Luthan know?"

"Please don't tell her!" Sam begged, tears springing up in her wide blue eyes. "I came because my brother wouldn't! To protect the honor of our house. And...to have something more interesting to do than to be a weary sister for the rest of my life."

"There's nothing wrong with having a vocation," Margaret said with an imperious sniff.

Sam kept her attention fixed on Amel's face as he took her hand, making her feel the two of them were the only people in the whole world. Anyone in her place would have felt the same way, she suspected. He had a knack of giving his attention wholly to the person he was focused on. "I won't tell Luthan,

yet, if you like," he promised Sam. "In fact, I think she needs
to keep thinking of you as a man at arms at her command. But
in return, I want you to do something for me as Prince Samdan
O'Pearl. If you are up to it."

Sam nodded. But it wasn't fair. She'd have agreed to duel
if he asked; she was so mesmerized by his new, solicitous attitude
toward her. *Maybe*, she thought, *he's only rude to men.*

"Drom will take you to the palace of the protector, where Sen
lives when she's working on Demora as the representative
for...my house," Amel concluded after an awkward pause. "I
want you to give her this letter. I want you to give it to her rather
than Drom. I don't believe she'd harm you, but she might think
she could use Drom as a hostage." He paused. "When she's read
it, she will either come with you to see me, or leave alone. If
she comes here, have her wait out the back of my apartment.
Do you understand?"

Sam nodded.

He pressed the letter into her hand. "Good. I'll tell Luthan
where you are."

He rose again without Margaret's help and hopped twice to
turn to Alivda. "Ready."

Alivda looked him over, then swooped to snatch him up into
her arms.

"Diff!" Amel protested. "I can walk!"

"You're too slow," she said. "And this way, if anyone stops
us, I'll say I'm carrying you to sit a while on the bench at Spirit
Park and contemplate something or other. Now stop squawking
or I'll be late for Fahild to sing your praises!"

"All right!" Amel gave in with as sigh, sliding his arm around
her shoulder for a better grip. He was as big as the woman who
held him, and possibly heavier, but as soon as his vexation gave
way to resignation there was something comfortable and ordinary about the two of them, together. They reminded Sam
of her relationship with her siblings as they tumbled up together
in the big manor house on Clara's World where she was born.

She's family to him, Sam realized, extraordinary as it was.

When Amel was gone, she pulled herself together and left
through the front doors with Prince Drom.

El Princess Telly caught up to them at the carriage just as
Drom was dithering about whether he should help Sam in, like
a woman, or continue to treat her like a man.

"Wherever Amel is sending you, I'm coming too!" Telly
declared and Drom didn't argue. *Wise man,* Sam thought.

CHAPTER 20

Innocence and Experience

Amel yielded to a little sigh as Alivda laid him down on a heap of folded curtains in the prop room Luthan had told them about. Alivda set a glow-plastic lamp at his back. Its light distorted her face with upward-cast shadows as she leaned down to say good-bye.

"Be good," she teased, and tapped him on the nose.

"Aren't you going to warn me this could be a trap?" he asked.

"I'm sure it is," she said, with an evil smirk. "But Princess Luthan doesn't scare me much."

Then she leaned down to kiss him, full on the mouth. The funny spasm of wrongness this invoked left Amel unable to react one way or another. Alivda gave no indication she had noticed, just chuckled low in her throat and was gone.

Amel detached his sword from its belt, drew it in case Oleander appeared instead of Luthan and laid the naked blade within easy reach of his left hand.

Why couldn't I be right-handed, like most Demish! he thought with a pang of sulky resentment for his Vrellish genes. *And be praised for my gallantry toward women, not how good I am in bed! I want to be a real Demish prince, damn it all!*

Discovering Sam was a woman had forced him to realize again how very Demish he was inside about the differences between women and men. He understood and respected the prowess of women like Alivda and Vretla, but he couldn't help feeling protective toward ones like Luthan and Sam. He wanted to marry someone he had warm, protective feelings toward, and raise a flock of children who would think of him as their manly Demish dad. Instead, he was caught up in a whirl of propositions and proposals he had to choose between based on political expediency, and was praised in settings as public as a Council of Privilege for his staying power in bed!

Then again, maybe I should stick to what I know, Amel told himself gloomily, gazing into the darkened corners of the room as he reviewed how badly he had messed up with Sen Lekker. He tried to feel sorry for her, but he was angry with Sen—and with Zind, too. *Those children had better be all right, Zind Therd,* he thought, unwilling to imagine a future in which they did not survive, beyond the certainty it would arouse a new potential for violence in him.

The wait soon began to drag. He was dozing lightly when a sound at the other end of the room made him sit up, automatically checking for his sword.

"Amel?" Luthan's voice said.

Amel relaxed with a smile. "Here."

She adapted quickly once drawn to the dim light by his voice. He watched her outline become better defined as she picked her way through the theatrical clutter to kneel at his side. She was dressed in a quilted robe with a wide sash, worn over a long nightdress. He wondered if her breasts were loose inside and rebuked himself. The scent of her filled his nose: a clean, female smell masked by the mild scent of baby powder. Her face looked child-sweet in the glow of his lamp, framed in a loose mass of golden hair. But she was agitated. Upset.

He leaned forward to grip her arm where she held it braced against the floor.

"What is it?" he asked, his concern for her as a dear friend overriding everything else.

"Oleander," she said softly. "He...proposed."

In the short silence that followed, Amel pictured how disastrous it would be to his campaign if she answered 'yes' to this proposal, and a knot formed in his stomach.

"He did it like a prince should, in a storybook," Luthan continued in a sturdier tone, a touch of abstraction in her young voice. "He told me he had loved my mother and been faithful to her all these years. He said he'd never slept with a woman and never would, unless she was his wife." She paused. "Do you think if you'd been raised on Demora, you could have lived to be eighty without having sex, even once, Amel?"

"Uh," he said, trying to imagine so different a life from the one he had led and consulting his body as an afterthought. "I'm...sure paladins are capable of more self-control than the average man," he said.

"And that ought to be wonderful!" Luthan exclaimed with a great sigh. "But—oh gods—I can't admire him for it when I don't want to be a virgin anymore myself! It's supposed to be this grand thing—saving myself for my true love—but instead I feel childish and vulnerable." She plucked at a fold of cloth beneath them. "How can I pick a husband when I've no idea..." She broke off in despair.

His heart went out to her. "I can see how it might be a burden," he said, striving to sound merely factual while it occurred to him he'd never been a virgin. He had gone from being only just aware of his emerging sexuality to-

He shook off comparisons that weren't useful.

"It's not such a big deal," he said. "I mean it won't seem that way, looking back when you're a grandmother."

"No," she agreed, smiling as well. "I suppose not." She paused. "You haven't mentioned the political dimension."

"I'm not feeling up to politics," Amel said, thinking about Sen and Mona. "Maybe I was dreaming when I thought I could be liege, on my own, without Erien's help."

"Oh, no," she said, in the heartfelt tones of a real friend.

His breath caught as she surged against him, alarmed by the softness of her dressing gown against his hands as he caught and held her. "Luthan..." he said huskily. She was filling his senses and he felt so alone. He didn't want her to know what it was doing to him physically, either.

"What do courtesans do to break in virgins?" she asked him in a breathless voice.

"What?!" he sputtered.

"In Den Eva's," she said, prying his fingers loose from her upper arm so she could settle in closer against his chest. "You used to train the novice girls there."

Amel's eyebrows lifted. "Luthan Dem H'Us," he said. "Where did you hear that?"

"From Tatt."

"Figures!" Amel growled. He shifted higher, letting her settle against his side, under his arm, instead of lying on top of him.

"How do you break in a virgin, humanely?" she asked.

He tipped his head to feel her hair against his cheek. "Luthan, it isn't a skill you have to learn," he said, thinking Horth Nersal's very Vrellish remark must be grating on her.

"Erien thinks it is," she said. "He gave me a book about it."

"He did what?!" Amel was still trying to make sense of the idea when Luthan shifted, put her arms around his chest inside his elbows, and brought her face very close to his.

"Kiss me, Amel," she said.

"Ohhh," he moaned softly, raising one knee as subtly as possible between them. "I don't think that would be a good—"

She put her lips to his lips as her hand slid haltingly down his side to his hip, and hovered there like a nervous bird. Her lips didn't move. The kiss was as innocent as the girl. But his senses swam in the warm, dizzy heat of his own response, and in the midst of damning himself for it he felt an equally powerful emotional surge.

He loved this girl-child, the same one he had seen grow up year by year on Fountain Court, and he knew she embraced life with a living heart. Surely she deserved more than the ossified love of a man like Oleander, more in love with his own power of self-control than the object of his denial! She deserved a prince, arriving in a blaze of glory in the final act. A man who could love her, body and soul! The very man he wanted to become!

And why not! he thought, heart thrumming with the glory of emotion moving in channels his experience with Sen had made him doubt he still possessed.

Ever so carefully, holding back the fire of his physical answer to the offer he doubted she meant quite as clearly as his body understood her to, he kissed her back gently, with the promise of future passion. He put his arms around her, felt her woodenness and schooled himself to go slow. He stroked her back. He breathed in her hair. He kissed the corners of her mouth. He gave her time to get in touch with her response. All his experience with women rested in his touch, moved in his breath, discovered the new quivers his maleness invoked in her body and coaxed them to thrive with tender skill.

"Oh, gods!" Luthan gasped, resisting him suddenly. "You are good at this!"

She sat back, her legs folded under her. Trembling. He let her escape, too grateful for the sweet affection swelling his chest to mind the ache of frustrated desire.

"I'm afraid, Amel," she confessed.

He shifted forward, forgetting his bad ankle, and winced at the pain he caused himself. "Luthan, I'm sorry, I shouldn't—"

"N-no," she stopped him, putting her hand to his mouth. "I'm not afraid of you. I'm afraid of Oleander. He reminded me how...you see I used to be afraid I would be cold. In bed. A-and unable to...I thought that might be why Erien gave me the book."

"Luthan," he said softly, lowering her hand. "Look at me."

She sniffed, bringing her big blue eyes up to meet his, hers luminous with unshed tears. He moved his hand against her waist and felt her inhale. "You aren't cold," he promised her.

Luthan nodded. "N-no," she said, looking a bit dizzy. "Thank you. I d-don't think...it's a problem. Anymore."

He could have licked her up like cream and asked for seconds. It made him feel old and despicable. He knew he could make her want him if she gave him the chance.

"What's wrong?" she asked.

"Nothing," he lied, and cleared a husky catch in his throat.

"You don't think Erien believed I needed help, do you?" Luthan asked. "I mean, that I couldn't learn naturally? Or was too...abstract about it all. Like Oleander."

"No," he said as kindly as he could, given the novel sense of jealously the question stirred. "I think Erien was trying to help in his own awkward fashion. But not because he thought you were frigid."

She smiled, looking bashful. Her cheeks dimpled. "Thank you for my first kiss. It was...very encouraging."

Oh gods, Amel thought. *Not her first!* But at least it reassured him that Erien had not really been interested. If he had been, he would certainly have at least kissed the girl by now!

"The pleasure was all mine," he told her, in a historical, dramatic dialect that made her giggle.

"Amel," she said, looking down at her hands resting in her lap. "I don't think I can marry Oleander. He's wonderful. I think my mother loved him and he loved her, but he's not for me. I mean, he is the sort of husband who would think about me all the time and take my handkerchief to hold against his face before a duel and all of that, but I want a real role to play in my own life, and babies, and—arguments," she concluded with certainty.

"You've got a good grasp of love, then," Amel told her, thinking of Perry with fondness for the first time since her ultimatum to him. "Especially the arguments. Neither Perry nor Ann would marry me, you know. Ann can't seem to get used to me being around. Whenever we're together too long she gets irritable. Perry simply doesn't need another man in her life. She's got Vrenn. Their arrangement doesn't preclude additional *mekan'stan*, but being the second or third man isn't what I want.

I want a wife, a family and a home. You feared you might be too invested in the idea of perfect love to tolerate its physical expression—well, I've been afraid, too. Afraid I can't feel love the way I would have been able to if I'd lived a different life." He paused to be sure she grasped what he was saying. "You've taught me otherwise."

She held her breath as she looked at him. Then the words came out in a tumultuous rush. "Oh, Amel. I do love you! You're my friend. I feel so safe with you. So comfortable. Teach me not to be stiff and frightened. Show me how to feel the things it says women can in Erien's book!"

A lump formed in his throat. "Luthan," he asked, "do you love Erien?"

Luthan drew herself up in a tight ball, knees drawn up inside her night clothes.

"I have a crush on Erien," she decided. "A little girl's crush. It doesn't involve all those oozings and explosions and contractions the book talks about." She set her chin on her knees. "But sometimes I think it sounds vulgar, the way love is described in the book. And I don't know if I want to have sex, at all."

Amel knew 'vulgar' sickeningly well himself, and wanted to keep that curtain in his mind firmly closed. "That book is no more use than Golden Demish dramas when it comes to making love," he told Luthan.

She frowned. "Erien wouldn't have given me inaccurate reference material."

"It's not inaccurate," Amel corrected, relaxing bit by bit the less they touched and the more they talked. "Consider eating," he proposed.

"Eating?" she said, puzzled.

"Mm. If you studied a Reetion book describing mastication, the digestive juices in your mouth and everything that happens after that, would it tell you anything about the taste of fresh applesauce? Or even what you, personally, liked to eat and what you didn't?"

Luthan regarded him with wary interest. "No."

"Well, there you go." He took her hands. "You won't have any trouble, Luthan. Not with a man you care about."

"I care about you," she said, and her pretty lips pouted, invoking memories of them against his. He wanted to kiss her again, hard. He wanted to seduce her, right now, before she changed her mind, because he knew it would mean a lot to her if they made love, and that in itself was an amazing fact. She might even mistake erotic feelings for love, and if she did, they might grow into real love. For them both.

"Luthan," he said, and had to pause to make his throat work properly. "Luthan, if you don't want to marry Oleander, would you consider—"

"Unhand her, you abomination!" Oleander's voice shook the backstage room.

"Stay clear!" Amel told Luthan, pushing her away from him. He had no time to grab his sword. It had gotten out of reach during his tryst with Luthan, and he only had one foot he could use.

He waited for Oleander's thrust, dodged and rolled, reasoning they would be more evenly matched in a wrestling competition on the floor. It was a close call. He struck Oleander's shins, wondering if he was still alive or already hit and too badly hurt to know, the way D'Therd's face had looked the second after Horth ran him through.

Oleander swayed, but didn't fall. Amel tried to surge up to grab the master paladin's sword hand, but his left foot let him down. He yelped.

Luthan screamed, "No you don't!" and a backdrop hung with satin curtains crashed down on them both.

Scrambling to his knees under the curtains, Amel heard Sam's voice cry, "Oh Luthan, I'm sorry, he found me!"

–o—o—o–

The ride to the Protector's Palace was an icy one. Telly had deduced Sam was female from an ill-advised courtesy of Drom's, and was convinced the two of them had been arranging to drive away together for illicit purposes.

"Trust you?" Telly lashed out. "Trust the son of a father with a reputation like the late Kantor Ander's?" She sat with her arms folded, studiously ignoring anything either Drom or Sam attempted to say. "I trusted you the last time you told me you would not do something foolhardy when you can't survive a bad bruise! And what did that get me? Sleepless nights wondering whether or not you were going to die with no means to even inquire after your health!"

"What do you want me to say, Telly!" Drom protested as they pulled up in front of the wide steps of the Protector's Palace, the wheels of their horse-drawn carriage crunching on the pea gravel lining the drive. An airship flew overhead; most likely a shuttle headed for a space station and from there the wider universe.

"Ask me to marry you, idiot!" Telly raved.

Drom sat back. "But your mother..."

"You are the son of a rebel," Telly said, narrowing her eyes at him above her freckled cheeks. "Make it a verb and rebel!"

"But your mother is my father's half-sister," Drom reminded her miserably. "We're too close in blood."

"Which is why we won't have any children," she said sturdily. "My father did nothing all my life but speculate about my children by some prize sire or another! Now he's gone and I'm going to have my own way. I am marrying you, no matter what my mother says, and not Amel!"

"I'll just...go deliver the letter," Sam ventured.

Drom cast her a distracted look. "Oh, yes." He paused a heartbeat, but even chivalry couldn't distract him from what he'd just heard, and his attention immediately reverted to Telly.

"You were planning to marry Amel?" he asked, hugely offended.

Neither paid any attention to Sam as Drom's footman helped her out of the carriage. She gave him a suspicious look. "Does everyone know I'm a woman, now?" she said.

"Of course not, Prince Samdan," the man said with a straight face.

Sam sighed, and trudged up the steps to go inside.

She didn't have to wait long to see Sen Lekker after telling the doorman that she'd been sent by Pureblood Prince Amel. The same woman returned, at once, to show her in.

"Have you seen Prince Amel?" Sam's guide asked as they walked side by side down a sober, wood-paneled hall. "Is he really as beautiful as people say?"

"Don't you have pictures?" Sam asked.

"Oh, yes! That is, people do," she admitted. "At least those sympathetic to the Messengers led by Abbess Margaret. But I wondered if seeing him is different from looking at his picture. Divine souls are supposed to radiate their goodness, you know. Not, of course, that I'm convinced he is a Soul of Light, myself. But wouldn't it be exciting if he was?"

Sam was too anxious about the task ahead of her to talk about the way she'd felt in Amel's company or what it might mean about the history of his soul.

I wonder how Jack is making out in Silver Hearth, she thought as she saw a servant go in carrying a tray of herbal teas, and felt curiously reassured to think of him waiting for her back on Gelion.

Sen Lekker didn't stand on ceremony. She came forward to greet Sam, ignoring the quietly steaming tea service set out on a table off to one side.

"Is Amel all right?" she asked immediately.

"Yes," Sam assured her, and produced the letter. "He asked me to give you this."

Sen took the letter eagerly but as she read it, her face grew stiff and cold.

"Friend," she said bleakly. She dropped the letter on the table, too stunned to care about her privacy, and Sam couldn't help sucking the words off the page, upside down. She read:

"Sen,
I've tried a dozen ways to say this. Nothing works. Forgive me if the net result is curt. I received word from Erien Lor'Vrel, in the Knotted Strings, that the Therds are suffering more than the Lekkers over the food shortage. Zind suspects you've made arrangements with the pirates and are purposefully starving her in preparation for another war in space. If it's a lie, I will protect you. If it isn't, I must act as liege of both the Lekkers and the Therds. Be innocent, please.
Your friend, Amel."

"I slept with him before we left Gelion!" Sen said. She made a harsh sound, deep in her throat, and brought a fist down on the letter where it lay upon her desk. Her lips twitched. She turned her head to stare off across the room toward the window, tension gathering in her face. "Tell him...thanks for the warning," she told Sam. She turned her head from the window as a new thought occurred to her. "Unless you're here to execute me."

Sam was still processing Sen's confession. "Me?" she said. "Uh, no. I work for Princess Luthan. I, uh—" For a moment she was terrified the hard, scrappy woman was going to force her into a fight. Then Sen Lekker's eyes crinkled and she merely sneered. "It might have worked, you know," she said. "If we'd moved faster. If I hadn't been reluctant to poison their food, instead of waiting for the shortages to weaken them. But poison and plague can so easily backfire, or attract the attention of Fountain Court." She gave a dull laugh. "The Nersallians might have braved the trip out to punish us for a moral lapse. They're keen to appropriate whatever belongs to those who drop the shield of honor too loudly."

"No," Sen sighed. "I was probably right to avoid plague or poison. Amel and that damned Lor'Vrel just didn't stay on Rire long enough. And now I'm ruined." She rose with a stoic courage Sam could not help but admire even as she marveled at the atrocities lurking in Sen Lekker's words. "We hate each other, you know, the Lekkers and the Therds. They hate us for being Lekkers and we hate them for being Therds. Amel never understood it and he never will. I hope it doesn't kill him in the end." She tapped her knuckles on the top of the table. "I suppose I'll never see Amel again, now."

Sen pulled herself together, straightened, and concluded. "Give him my regards. He's a damned good man. Nice to see he's toughening up, as well," she added with a glance down at the note. "Best destroy that," was her final advice to Sam. "If a Therd read it, they'd think he was being too good to me."

Then she turned and walked out of the room into an emptiness Sam could only guess at.

For a moment, all Sam could do was think about the note and how Amel had said nothing in it about the kidnapped children. She wondered what Sen might have done differently if the children had been mentioned. The thought made her uncomfortably aware of larger stakes and deeper schemes in motion about her than any she had ever conceived.

She hurried back to the carriage only to find it gone.

Have they eloped? she thought, bewildered. For a whole minute, she just stood and wondered. Then she looked around her, trying to remember the way they'd come, but she hadn't been paying attention to her surroundings on the way out. *I'll have to ask someone*, she decided.

In the end, it was an hour later than planned when she made it back to the palace. She arrived feeling tired, frustrated and eager for nothing but a bath and bed. It wasn't until Luthan greeted her with jittery excitement that she recalled she was to be part of Luthan's subterfuge for escaping the chaperons to meet with Amel.

"There you are Samdan!" Luthan said, already in her nightgown with a quilted dressing gown worn over it. "I want you to help me rehearse. I need a male lead to work with."

"Much better to get a good night's sleep," the still lovely, but centuries old chaperon told Luthan from where she was seated on a comfortable chair in the common room.

"We won't be long!" Luthan assured her, and busily swaddled both of them in flowing white robes for the piece she intended to recite. As she handed Sam her script she whispered instructions. "When we've rehearsed for ten minutes, we'll come together again to collect the scripts. You take them and give me your sword. Take a minute to strap it on over your robe now, so it will be prominent. If the chaperon says anything, just tell her a man at arms must be prepared for anything. When we've swapped props, you pretend to be me and go to my room while I walk out the door wearing the sword. I'll have to do it as I am, in my nightdress! There's no time to think of anything else. Amel might think we've cancelled and I must see him!"

Implausible as Luthan's plan seemed to Sam, it worked. Fifteen minutes later, she was alone in Luthan's room, tired, rattled and swordless. With a sigh, she shed her robe and boots and crawled into Luthan's bed, still fully dressed in the uniform of a Silver Demish errant.

She was sound asleep when the door to the room opened, letting in light from the common room and the tremulous voice of the old chaperon who still looked as youthful as a girl.

"El Princess Luthan?" the chaperon's voice inquired. "Prince Oleander is here in quite a state and says he has to speak with you, dear." She paused before confessing, "I don't know what to do about it."

That would make two of us! Sam thought in horror.

She cleared her throat and tried to sound muzzy with disturbed sleep. "Uh, tell him I...couldn't possibly...right now. In the morning, maybe? Yes."

"Luthan, forgive me!" Oleander's voice carried bold and clear over the protests of the startled chaperon who cried, in her quivering voice, "Oh, dear sir! You of all people! Oh dear! Oh dear!"

Sam lost track of the chaperon because Oleander kept advancing toward the bed.

"I cannot think, I cannot sleep," the Demoran paragon of manly virtues complained as he came toward her. "I cannot think of anything except how foolish I have been in postponing my leadership of Vesta, as its liege, and of Demora, as Protector, all these many years! Oh, Luthan, say you will accept me as your husband and begin the restoration of—what's this!"

Sam tried, but in her panic she didn't hide herself successfully under the raised sheet. Oleander had spotted something: a sock-covered foot, a slice of light blue trousers trimmed in silver, or a glimpse of her cropped, coppery blond hair that should have been golden and flowing instead.

The next thing Sam knew, her sheet had been ripped from her and she lay exposed in her errant's uniform, at the point of Oleander's sword.

The chaperon emitted a sound like air escaping an inflated pillow as she fainted.

Oleander remained where he stood, hand disconcertingly steady. "Where is Luthan? Tell me quickly or I'll kill you!"

He meant it and Sam wasn't ready to die.

"In the prop room at the back of tomorrow's set!" she blurted, volunteering no extra details.

Oleander made a face at the shrillness of her voice, but his thoughts were elsewhere. With a sneer of contempt for Sam's lack of manliness, he sheathed his sword and fled.

"Oh blessed Soul of Light—" Sam began to pray reflexively, and stopped cold when she realized the irony of praying to Amel under the circumstances, and she'd always meant Amel when she had used the phrase back on Clara's World.

Instead, Sam sprang out of bed. She was halfway across the floor of the guest hall before she realized she didn't have her boots on. She paused then, wondering if she should go back, and called for help instead.

"Help, help!" was all she thought to say. The words felt monstrous, bouncing around the brooding quiet of the pillared room, and she fell silent, suddenly more afraid of who might respond. With a gulp, she ran forward again.

She spotted Oleander from the top of the steps leading down to the floor of the amphitheatre as he disappeared into the back of Luthan's set.

"Oh no," she whimpered, took a gulp of air and tore down the stairs. Ten steps from the bottom she almost tripped over her feet, her heart was pounding so hard in fear.

The sounds of conflict reached her before she got inside. Luthan cried, "No, you don't!" with very unGolden vigor and something crashed.

Sam rushed in and halted at the sight of Luthan panting with excitement in her quilted dressing gown, and blurted, "Oh Luthan, I'm sorry, he found me!"

On the floor, two lumps crawled around under a toppled frame hung with thick, velvet curtains of snowy white. A sword tip jerked up through a break between the curtains at the end of an encumbered swing, and a sweet, familiar voice cried in pain. Red flowered in a white curtain even as it heaved with the movement of a cocked foot, followed by a crack of impact and Oleander's grunt.

Amel hurled back a long flap of curtain and got clear, on his knees. The other lump was moving as well. Amel pointed, "Luthan!" he ordered. "Give me that!"

She pulled down a pole used to lift up baskets of flowers and set them on hooks around the stage.

Amel halled the pole back as if he had been improvising with such weapons all his life, and swung as Oleander's head emerged.

At the same time, the walls of the prop room began to fall away around them, as if they were toys in a dollhouse being dismantled by a giant hand.

Breath caught in her throat, Sam spun to discover the amphitheatre was full of people. Dozens of them! Half of them were stage hands, dismantling the set. A few were royal guests, volunteer domestics and befuddled judges dressed in their night clothes. One was Alivda, ripping down the stairs from Spirit Park like a streak of blue, dressed in Amel's livery. Above her was a small knot of people in long robes packed closely around someone they shielded with their bodies.

And at the center of all the attention knelt Amel, still gripping the stage pole very competently in his hands; Luthan standing at his back in her dressing gown; and Oleander sprawled, bleeding from a gash across the temple.

Alivda drew her sword as she ran, heading straight for Oleander as the Golden prince began to move.

"No!" two voices cried in unison, with a similar lilt to the emotion packed into their matching abhorrence for bloodshed. One was Amel. The other was the man at the center of the protective knot.

Alivda confined herself to giving Oleander a shove with her boot, and went to pull Amel to his feet, instead. He was bleeding from a stab wound in his right calf.

"You!" Alivda ordered Sam. "Steady him!"

Sam obeyed robotically, fixated on the vision coming slowly down the stairs on the Spirit Park side of the amphitheatre. A door in the wall of the park stood open at its base, the fittings so ingeniously crafted it had not been visible when it was sealed. Sam saw flittering edges of a nervecloth projection rimming the door frame with a faint glow, which explained—in part—how the door had been concealed.

"Is that Amel? He's bleeding!" a liquid voice said with infinite compassion from the midst of the tight knot of Goldens.

Sam was able to glimpse a pale hand and long, golden robes before the Golden Emperor's attendants closed around him to sparet him from seeing Alivda put a seamer to Amel's calf.

Sam felt Amel tense. The next instant he gripped her arm so hard it hurt, as he uttered a muted sound that spoke of great pain blocked by greater will.

"Can't have you bleeding yourself faint for fear of a seamer, just now," Alivda said unapologetically as she stood up again. "It's just pain."

"Easy for you to say," Amel muttered darkly under his breath.

"Got someone for you to meet," she said as she took him away from Sam, draping a glorious theatrical cape about his shoulders as she did. "Looks good on you!" she declared.

Amel straightened up on his right leg despite the pain in his calf. He still couldn't put weight on the other leg. "What?" he asked, bewildered.

The cape she'd draped him in was part of the regalia for a Soul of Light from the Demoran Golden Age. Made of rich whites in three shades and of multiple materials, it stood high at the shoulders with jutting wings decorated in peacock feathers and a glittering array of story art worked in bejeweled embroidery. Heavy tassels hung at either side with gold fittings and soft baubles of synthetic fur softer than rabbit skins.

Alivda turned Amel toward the party moving slowly down the stairs and declared, like a Fountain Court herald, "Amel, grandson of Freya, daughter of the Golden Emperor, meet your grandmother's father—Fahild."

"Oh," Amel said, and went very still. Sam suspected he'd stopped breathing, but he put out a hand to one side for Luthan's, and she took it, moving close enough to support him on his right as Alivda was doing on his left. The glorious cloak hid his bloody leg.

Sam's eyes fixed on the Golden Emperor as he continued down the stairs, deflecting the panicky attempts of palace people to prevent him exposing himself to the sights revealed by the dismantling of the set. But even as she wondered at what she saw before her, she had time to note how intimate Amel and Luthan seemed to be.

Fahild stopped in front of Amel. He was tall and very pale. His eyes were too blue and his hair was the color of gold, but as light as air. Where Amel was fit and vigorous, his ancestor was as wasted as an invalid. Where Amel had strength, Fahild had only gentleness too deep and wide to bear his ineffectiveness in the world. He had withdrawn because he wasn't strong enough to use the power he possessed, Sam guessed. But he was everything the Golden Emperor was supposed to be. And his melting expression, as he looked at Amel, matched the unguarded love on Amel's face.

"It's...as if I know you!" Amel said, surprising himself with his own words, and laughed nervously.

Fahild spoke in a voice as thin as butterfly wings. "Forgive me for fearing disappointment, Amel Dem'Vrel, heir of my body and my spirit." He lifted long, limp fingers to touch Amel's cheek, thin as bone but infinitely graceful and as inoffensive as the touch of feathers. "True son of my lost daughter, and Soul of Light," the old, old man said, looking young again as the tears welled in his tired eyes. "Be my heir, and Demora's liege, and help us find our way in a new world."

Amel tightened his grip on Luthan's hand. "With Luthan," he said. "She, too, is a daughter Demora can be proud to claim."

Fahild turned his attention to Luthan, at Amel's side, noted their clasped hands, and smiled. "Let her children found our new dynasty of protectors," he said.

"Thank you," Amel got out, his eyes bright. "Thank you for everything. But how did you decide?" He looked at Alivda, just as Fahild did.

"D'Ander's granddaughter," the old Demoran said, and smiled indulgently, "not only dances well, she is wise beyond her years. She pointed out a Soul of Light needs hybrid vigor if he's going to cope with change. She has traveled with you, Amel, and the stories she had to tell were more than enough for any trial of testimony. She found those who had witnessed your bravery at the spirit wall, in saving Leif, and had them come to me: young Drom and Telly, who want nothing but each other in this world. The performance that cost you the use of your ankle was worth more than any dance. But I do beg the favor of watching you perform, someday, with your pupil here,"

Fahild said, beaming at Alivda. "I could not forgo a treat so spectacular, if you dance as well as she does."

"Better," Amel said, and got elbowed in the ribs by Alivda. But he was exploding with a joy that seemed able to hold all pain at bay. He turned to Luthan, took her in his arms, and said, "Princess Luthan Dem H'Us, Liege of the Silver Demish, Golden Soul and daughter of house Vesta of Demora, will you be my bride?"

"Yes!" she cried, and threw her arms about Amel, nearly knocking him over until she compensated, herself, for his injured legs.

In the gentile pandemonium that followed, Sam retreated to the sidelines to find herself a place to sit on one of the seats ringing the amphitheatre. It was five minutes before she realized Oleander had done the same, and was watching in bewildered devastation, nursing his bleeding head.

Amel detached himself from the developing festivities moments later to limp over, using Abbess Margaret as a living crutch. Sam noticed that Margaret looked as subdued as she felt, inside, and could easily guess why.

I suppose we all imagined we might be the one he would pick to reign at his side, she realized, watching Margaret's face. *How hard it is growing up!* But she was confident Margaret had to be twice as old as her, which meant she had achieved her state of sage disillusionment twice as fast. *That has to be worth something!* Sam hoped.

"Prince Oleander," Amel said respectfully. "I am sorry for our altercation in the theatre, earlier. And I need your help."

Oleander blinked at him, bewildered. "My...help?" he said.

"If you will give it to me," Amel said, gravely. "You are a remarkable man and a great paladin. I trust you will tell me now if you are my vassal or my enemy, and act with honor, either way."

For long seconds, Sam didn't know what to expect. Oleander was still armed and Amel was vulnerable. She braced for action, unsure what she'd do if it came to a life and death struggle for Amel's life.

Then, very slowly, Oleander moved from his seat to go down before Amel on one knee. "I will serve my Emperor," he said, "and my Emperor's heir."

Amel raised him, grasping his right forearm and holding onto it. "Listen, then," he said, and briefed Oleander on the situation in the Knotted Strings. "Go yourself to ensure the food reaches the hungry among House Therd, and to prevent the Therds retaliating against the Lekkers," Amel ordered when he was done. "The peace my mother built among the Dem'Vrel must not be ruined in a day by hate and greed. Take with you as many unmarried princes as you can spare," Amel continued seamlessly, although Sam failed to see why he should stipulate they be single unless he was concerned for their wives should the enterprise prove dangerous, which puzzled her.

"Go as Admiral of the Golden Demish fleet," Amel continued, "and Protector of Demora until Luthan's child is old enough to take your place; second in military rank, within the Avim's Oath, only to the Admiral of Blue Dem who is commander in chief of all my vassals."

Oleander narrowed his eyes. "Admiral of Blue Dem?"

"Alivda D'Ander D'Aur Lor'Vrel," Amel said, straight faced.

Oleander pondered. He glanced toward Fahild, where he stood chatting with Alivda and Luthan and saw Alivda make the sad, Golden Emperor laugh.

"You mean to unite the Demish under you," Oleander said, in a flash of insight, and fixed his frosted blue eyes on Amel again. "Spiritually where it can't be politically. It won't be easy."

"Nothing worthwhile ever is," Amel agreed. "And Oleander?" he added.

"Yes?"

Amel tightened his grip on the paladin's forearm. "Zind Therd needs a husband. If you're up to it."

The paladin blinked in astonishment. So did Sam, as Amel's stipulation about the princes being single fell into place and her jaw dropped with a soft-voiced gasp.

"Just a thought," Amel said, suddenly contrite. "But every marriage you can swing between your princes and the Dem'Vrel in the Knotted Strings will be a military asset when the day comes we need every highborn alive to save the empire." He yielded, in the end, to a grin. "And I think the women of the Knotted Strings might be an invigorating change for Demoran men."

"I will...remain open to new...possibilities," Oleander said. And frowned. "Take care of Luthan."

Amel said, "I will." And added, very seriously, "Her happiness means more than mine, to me."

CHAPTER 21

Back at Court

Amel entered the forward lounge of Blue Hearth, smiling as he striped off a pair of satin gloves with dangling folds of cloth at either wrist. The gloves were a gift from the Vestas. They had come with good news about Oleander's relief efforts on FarHome, and Amel was eager to ask Luthan if she thought the Blue Demish story braid decorating them could be taken as endorsement of his plan to resurrect the Blue Demish as a court power.

But he forgot the gloves the moment he saw Luthan standing by a sideboard in floods of tears. She stood with her hand over an open letter, so naturally Amel suspected it was to blame, and tried to get a look at it over her shoulder when he came to offer comfort.

She started guiltily.

"Oh, Amel!" she said, and dropped onto the nearest couch with her hands pressed to her face. "I'm horrid!"

Amel scanned the letter. It concerned Sam. Luthan's efforts to retrieve the lost signet of passage had flushed out the truth and the local liege was coming down hard on the adventurous Princess Samanda. Or at least, his wife was. Queen Garland of Jewel Country promised Luthan that Sam would never set foot outside the local abbey ever again, if Luthan would see fit to return her to their custody "for the sake of her poor, disgraced family who remain loyally fond of the wretched girl."

"I'm sorry," Amel said, feeling baffled. "I should have told you about Prince Samdan being Princess Samanda, but in all the excitement—" He stopped short. Luthan had lowered her hands and sat gazing up at him miserably. "It isn't the letter you're upset about," he realized.

Luthan bit her lower lip, struggling to control herself, then blurted, "It's Erien!"

"He's back?" Amel sat down beside her and took her hands in his. "Is he all right? What's happened?"

Luthan produced a handkerchief but it was pointless. Her nose kept running and her tears kept coming. "He...he's agreed to...to child-gift to Vretla!" Luthan burst into tears again. "To-night!"

Stunned, Amel put his arms around her. But no words came to help him.

"I'm sorry!" Luthan whimpered, her tears making spots on his silk shirt where she clung to him. "This is so unfair to you, Amel!" She pushed herself back, expression struggling for dignity.

He reached out to brush a golden curl from her face, feeling much older than his sixteen-year-old betrothed, and awkward. "You are in love with Erien," he said simply.

"I love you, too!" she insisted. "I just love you differently." She paused to swallow, narrowly averting a hiccup. "I'll get over this eventually. In ten years, maybe twenty. We should have at least a century to fall in love with each other!" she exclaimed in dire earnest.

"I hope it won't take quite that long," Amel said ruefully. His chest hurt and he felt jaded. *But I do love her,* he told himself, desperately reassured by the genuine pain he was suffering.

Luthan's expression changed, watching him. "I'm hurting you!" she cried.

"Hush," he said, taking her hand and letting her grow quiet as he stroked it, before prodding her gently with words. "Talk to me."

Luthan sniffed. "It wasn't until I heard Erien has agreed to child-gift to Vretla that I realized I was still secretly hoping for something to happen between us. And I don't want to be a bad wife! I want to be yours, Amel. I want to make it final." She raised wide blue eyes, pure and sweet and innocent, appealing to him. "Take me! Tonight! Rid me of my cumbersome virginity. I don't want to wait the months it takes to plan a Demish wedding! Teach me what I don't know about love between a man and a woman. Cure me of my childish ideas. Make me a woman, Amel! So I can leave this girlish love behind!"

A hideous bubble of laughter locked in Amel's throat as he listened to her, knowing she was pathetically earnest. For a moment he felt powerfully protective, more like a father than a lover. Then resentful. How dare she make this one more exercise in seduction for him! The next moment he was willing to oblige her, even cynically, if that was what it took to make her his.

"All right," he said, and leaned into a gentle kiss. Her mouth was yielding but impassive and tasted of salt tears. "I'll arrange it," he promised her. "Get Sam to act as your man-at-arms accomplice one more day. I'll get the directions to him, uh, her."

She collected herself to stare at him as if he had suddenly become strange and dangerous. "Tonight," she said breathlessly, and sprang up. "At the same time Erien...you know...with her!" Then she turned and fled.

It was long minutes before Amel rose, collected his gloves with the long floppy sleeves, and found Herald Ryan to dictate a letter of thanks to Oleander for the present. Setting up the date that night with Luthan was the next order of business. He sent for Jack to be his intermediary.

"At a place called Terrill's? On the Ava's Way?" Jack repeated when Amel had explained it all to him. "Get Her Highness Luthan there, with a hand of Blue Hearth errants for escort? And Prince Sam is to sooth Her Highness's jitters, is that it, then?"

"Yes," Amel said, and thought about Jack's plight instinctively, having been a commoner boy like him, in his early life. "It will be the last time Princess Samanda will be able to play Prince Samdan, by the way."

Jack blinked owlishly, looking out of his element in the clean, bright uniform of a Silver Hearth page.

"I heard you knew about him being a her, uh, I mean you-who-glow-with-the-goodness-of, uh..." Jack trailed off, shaken by his ignorance of how to address a Soul of Light properly in Demoran dialect, although he'd coped admirably in his first stab at a pronoun, addressing Amel as *bre'sevn*—someone seven courtly birth ranks his superior.

"Sit," Amel told Jack.

The boy did, shaking a little, his eyes on his exalted and alarming host as Amel crouched down in front of him. "Help us with this," Amel said in simple *rel*-to-*pol* address, still claiming superiority but without the weight of differencing suffixes, "and I'll make sure you have a place on Fountain Court whatever happens to Sam. I'll do what I can for her, as well."

Jack nodded, dumbstruck.

Amel gave an amused chuckle. "You don't need to be afraid of me, Jack! At your age, I was a commoner—just like you are!"

"Begging your pardon," Jack said with a little flare of courage, looking Amel over where he crouched before him dressed in tailored white clothes with one hand resting on the hilt of his sword. "But never quite like me. When you got hurt, you healed."

"Good point," Amel said, rising smoothly. His ankle gave a slight twinge but it didn't bother him. He reached out with a grin to rumple the boy's hair. "But I don't forget anything! Take what you want from the treat trays by the door on the way out."

Hours later, Amel had an unexpected visitor.

"Tatt!" Amel said, rising from a conference with Tanerd concerning Zind's terms for swearing to him. It felt wrong to be conducting business just an hour before his rendezvous with Luthan, but the Swearing had only been postponed by the news of his wedding, not forgotten, and he wanted all the Dem'Vrel in his oath. He'd been gratified to learn Oleander's mission to FarHome had made a favorable impression, and was dying to find out if the master paladin of Vesta had taken up his suggestion to woo Zind, but thus far it hadn't come up in the conversation.

The Goldens and the Dem'Vrel, Amel thought, *who'd have guessed! Oh, that would be me,* he congratulated himself. *Now all I've got to do is figure out how to manufacture full-grown highborns for Ayrium, and I've got it made!*

He had already reassured Ameron he had no designs on the Silver Demish oath, even if he was about to marry their princess-liege, which was why Tatt's appearance puzzled him.

Tanerd Therd bowed respectfully to Tatt as he took his leave, as one swordsman to another of superior reputation, reminding Amel that most Therds cared about court status.

"What can I do for you, Tatt?" Amel asked as soon as Tanerd closed the door behind him. He was conscious of the time. He had to leave within the next ten minutes unless he wanted to be late for his very special evening with Luthan. Alivda had gone ahead to make sure his old rival from Den Eva's, named Terrill, understood the need for discretion if he wanted to enjoy the generous fee Amel was paying him. Amel liked to patronize Terrill's for old times' sake, but he also knew Terrill too well to omit the stick while offering the carrot.

"I've come to consult you about love," Tatt said as he sailed in. "A friend of mine has a problem. He's lost his head over a woman, which is something that I," he grinned amiably, "being Vrellish, don't understand. So, how do you cure love?"

Amel was distracted by the sound of Margaret entering from the inward door of the receiving lounge, farther down the Throat.

"One does not cure love, Liege Monitum," the Demoran woman told Amel's visitor scathingly. "And as to mending a broken heart—how could one begin to advise you, when your very question presupposes one is speaking of a disease! Love," she paused to give Amel one of her melting looks, "gives life meaning."

"Yes, but being in love makes a person run a fever, drink too much and go pale at the mention of the woman's name," said Tatt, folding his arms across his chest. "Sounds like an ailment to me. Although perhaps I shouldn't be asking Amel. I don't think Amel's ever been in love, himself. He's more Vrellish that way."

Amel reacted as if stung, even though he knew Tatt meant it as a compliment. "I—" he faltered, thinking, *Have I?*

Margaret laid a hand on his arm, possessively. "Perhaps not in this life," she told Tatt with a mystic air, tears welling up gently in her rich blue eyes. "But his love is so boundless, any woman would be fulfilled merely to stand within its radius."

Amel had the odd sensation he was supposed to be sharing something spiritually with Margaret at a profound level. And felt vaguely guilty about failing to grasp exactly what it was he was supposed to feel.

"Uh, Tatt...and Margaret, please," he said lamely. "I have an appointment. Can we talk about this later?"

"Help me understand why being in love is so much worse than mere sexual frustration," Tatt said earnestly, "and I'll leave."

Margaret bristled at Tatt's casual reference to sex and excused herself. Amel watched her go, full of vague, puzzled feelings of inadequacy, rather as if he had arrived at the final act of a classic Demoran play unable to recall his lines.

"Being in love ..." Amel said, to refocus himself on making Tatt leave. "Uh, well. Being in love is different. I mean, it's wonderful to have a *mekan'st,* but that kind of love is for friends who lead separate lives. Being in love is about wanting one person to share your whole life with, from the biggest decisions to the smallest details. It's like finding your true home and going on an exotic adventure, both at the same time."

"So loving someone who doesn't love you back is like...being in exile and under house arrest?" Tatt conjectured.

Amel laughed despite himself. "What's worrying you, Tatt? A letter from Dorn, on Rire? I wouldn't worry about Amy ever leaving—"

"No!" Tatt took a deep breath as he extracted a piece of paper from his Monatese vest. "He may kill me for this, but I've got to tell you before he sees Vretla tonight, because she might just kill him if he's too lovesick to be useful to her!" The hand holding the paper drooped. "What's the worst he can do apart from challenge me to a duel?"

Amel took the folded paper from Tatt's and shook it open. The first thing he thought of was the artwork Ev'rel kept in her sketchbooks, because the hand was eerily similar. But Ev'rel never drew fully clothed, sixteen-year-old girls with their hair down.

"Erien has something of Ev'rel's style," Amel said after a moment.

Tatt frowned. "What do you mean?"

"Nothing," Amel said, with an odd, spasmodic shake of his head. "But Erien can't be in love with anyone. He's too Vrellish."

"I don't know," Tatt disagreed. "Erien may be Vrellish in some things, but he's never been very Vrellish about sex." He hesitated, decided and continued. "He's a virgin."

Amel blinked at him. "What?"

"I know, I know," said Tatt, "it sounds ridiculous. But turns out Di Mon told Erien to be careful about sex, and he took it very seriously." Tatt caught Amel's arm. "Do you love Luthan?"

"Yes!" Amel declared.

Tatt sighed. "Then I suppose I need you to do two things. One, tell me how to get someone out of love—because Erien's going to have to deal with child-gifting—and two, don't let the Demish swallow you up entirely."

"You're afraid I will forget my Vrellish friends?" Amel said, and shook his head. "Tatt, the Demish need me. And yes, I know, it's usually the Vrellish who think of themselves as the misunderstood minority in a Demish empire, but the Demish way of life is rooted in tradition. It's the source of their beauty and strength as well as their cruelty and weaknesses. And too much is changing, too fast for them: because of Rire, because of Erien, and maybe even the Nersallians under his leadership. That's why I'm becoming more Demish. To help. Not to scorn my Vrellish friends or deny what's Vrellish in me. Although in one way, I do want to be entirely Demish. I want to be married with a family. I don't know if being married will be the same as being in love, but I do love Luthan," Amel concluded firmly. "And I think, with her, I might just have a crack at all the rest."

Amel gave Tatt back the picture. "If Erien's attracted to her—well, he has good taste! But he's Vrellish. I will concede, since it is Erien, that I don't suspect him of self-interested motives, and I will even admit she has feelings for the starchy Reetion half-brother you and I share, albeit on opposite sides of our parentage. But Luthan won't accept half measures where she commits her heart. In the end, could Erien—or any Vrellish man—live up to the expectation of lifelong exclusivity?"

"Can you?" Tatt asked.

Amel thought of Perry and Ann. "There are other women I...love," he admitted, and tried to wipe out the pain with a smile. "But I am not essential to them. Being essential to someone else—that's the kind of love I want to earn!" He thrust his hands into his hair to distract himself, fluffing it up as he scrubbed his scalp. "Ack," he complained, and laughed. "Solve Erien's problem for him by all means, Tatt! But not with my betrothed." He forced a laugh. "And please, no curative den crawls for Erien! Find him a nice Monatese historian or a serious Nersallian engineer who will break him in respectfully and debate the meaning of it all with him afterwards!"

"Right," Tatt said harshly. "All before his appointment with Vretla, in two hours."

Amel was shivering inside. His cursed, inflexible empathy was screaming at him and he wanted to be deaf to it.

"You are wrong about Erien's feelings," Tatt said grimly. "I'm afraid he has come down with real, Demish love. And I'm worried." He paused. "I've read their literature. It kills people."

"Tatt—" Amel said hoarsely.

Tatt turned back on the brink of departure.

Don't do this, don't do this! an inner voice railed at Amel, unheeded. Erien's picture and Luthan's tears were haunting him.

"I'm meeting Luthan in one hour, at Terrill's," Amel told Tatt. "Room seven, upstairs. She was upset when she heard the news about Erien and Vretla. She wants to...well, this is his last chance. Understood? If Erien shows up, I'll give him the opportunity to make his feelings plain to her. If he doesn't, he's had it! And you can tell him this, too—if we trade partners tonight I'll have Vretla's oath into the bargain; Silver Hearth stays sworn to

Ameron, of course, and Luthan will still be the mother of my heirs on Demora even if Erien is the father. As for the rest of it, we both swear to Ameron, and that way neither one of us has to swear to the other. But on Fountain Court—I will be Avim. If he wants her that much...tell him to stop drawing pictures and prove it to her!"

–o—o—o–

Erien froze at the bottom of the stairs leading up to the second-storey landing of Terrill's wayside hotel. The place was shut down for the night and the empty floor of the pub at his back felt cavernous. He clutched a bottle of wine Tatt had forced upon him. His sword felt like a dead weight at his side and the jacket of his suit felt too tight.

Gazing up the staircase, he spotted Amel waiting at the top and felt nauseous. A fine line of sweat broke out alone his hairline. His hand ached where it gripped the bottle.

Amel came down the stairs silently, dressed in a silk shirt, dark pants and a short vest decorated in Blue Demish patterns. He, too, wore his sword, but the weapons were meaningless.

Erien felt horribly vulnerable.

"Did Tatt explain everything?" Amel asked, his face maddeningly composed and mature.

Erien nodded.

Amel looked at him a long time. Then he said, "I'm going to wait just long enough that I won't be late for Vretla if it turns out I'm going instead of you. If you don't come out by then, tomorrow we convene a Council of Privilege in which the two of you explain the change in marriage plans. And you *will* be marrying her."

Again, Erien nodded.

Amel scowled. "I'm not doing this for you," he said. He looked away quickly, to hide his expression, and Erien heard him mutter, "Maybe love is only able to bless idiot teenagers."

Beyond the harsh remark, Amel made no move to touch Erien, or to advise him. He just went to sit in the dark at a table.

Erien started up the stairs, feeling as if there were an infinite number of them, yet it seemed he reached room seven instantaneously. He stood before the closed door while he waited for his breathing to gentle and his heart to stop pounding, wishing he hadn't drunk half a bottle of Turquoise before Tatt showed up to tell him about Amel's strange offer.

He dared not think. He just put his hand on the door and pushed it open.

The room inside was comfortable but not luxurious. A big bed stood off to the right, balanced by a table on the other side for eating meals brought up from the kitchen. Luthan was in the private bathroom at the back.

"Amel!" she sang out, sounding nervous, and giggled. "Sam's waiting for me downstairs. Isn't it strange? Us getting together like this, here. Is Terrill's anything at all like Den Eva's? Oh dear, I shouldn't talk about your courtesan days anymore, should I? I don't know what's the matter with me, all I can do is babble away like a silly—"

She stepped out of the bathroom in a white nightgown with her hair down, looking just as Erien had imagined she would in the portrait he'd kept drawing, over and over.

"Oh," Luthan said, and her knees buckled.

Dropping the wine, Erien sprang forward to catch her. She gripped his arms, recovering before she passed out, and he helped her to the bed, holding her as she sat down on it. He sat beside her, letting her rest against him.

Feeling like a fool, more afraid of rejection than he had ever known he could be, Erien said abruptly, "I love you."

Luthan burst into tears. "Oh!" she said, and clung to him.

He put his arms about her back, one hands in golden tresses.

She pushed back suddenly, her eyes full of tears and her mouth tight with anger. "What did you mean by giving me such an awful book!"

He let her go, surprised. "I...wanted to help you understand."

"With anatomy lessons!" She shook her head. "Oh, Erien! I don't know anything about sex and I already know more about love than you do!"

"What's in the book is pretty much all I know about sex, myself," Erien confessed. It felt good to have it out in the open. "I'm no Amel," he admitted. "Sorry. I have never been comfortable with physical intimacy."

Luthan's face changed so dramatically he wasn't sure, at first, if it was good or bad. He feared her pity.

"Luthan, do you love me?" he asked when he could stand it no more. "Do you want me? I don't know what sort of husband I might make, but I do know I can't behave sanely concerning you. And I've arranged it all with Amel, through Tatt. Amel thinks we are in love."

"Are we?" Luthan asked, breathless.

"Are you?" he asked her, feeling giddy. His Pureblood physiology was burning through the dulling effects of the

Turquoise he had drunk earlier, leaving him defenseless against the blinding clarity of how badly he desired her.

She rustled in his arms, hiking up her nightgown to straddle him, and put her arms around his neck. "I love you, I love you, I love you!" she cried, kissing him between each iteration until his passion silenced her.

–o—o—o–

Sam paced up and down the empty pub floor of Terrill's, weaving around tables with chairs placed upside-down on top of them. Now and then, when she was close, she glanced at Amel where he sat listening to his internal clock tick off the minutes of his vigil. Amel had picked a spot equidistant from two nightlights where the gloom was thickest. It was too dark for Sam to decide if he looked sad or just distant.

A gentle thump from upstairs made him look up and remark, "He's dropped the wine bottle."

Sam drifted over, her eyes searching the ceiling. "How do you know?" she asked. It sounded odd speaking up to a Pureblood under such peculiar circumstances.

"Just guessing," he told her.

The silence continued a few minutes. Then something else went bump.

"H-he won't hurt her?" Sam asked nervously.

"No," Amel said with certainty. He leaned back and inhaled. "Luthan's received a letter from your liege's wife, Queen Garland D'Mark," he told Sam, "who thinks you ought to spend the rest of your life as a weary sister in the reverie devoted to...well, me, I gather." He sounded as tired of life, himself, as any weary sister.

"Oh," Sam said, her heart sinking. She fumbled a chair off the table Amel was sitting at and joined him.

"Such enthusiasm," Amel said dryly.

"It's not that I don't think it's worthwhile devoting myself to your order!" Sam assured him hurriedly. "My brother and I were early converts to the Children of Amel, you know—that's what we called the Messengers on Clara's World, and—"

He put his hand over hers on the table top, silencing her. "It's all right," he said, with the first glimmer of pleasure she'd seen in him this evening. "I told Jack I'd see what I could do for you," he told her. Then he got up. "Maybe you can put off the abbey by helping Luthan out but in skirts this time. Help her plan her wedding to Erien."

"W-where are you going?" she asked, wondering how she'd cope if Luthan screamed for help unexpectedly.

"Back to Fountain Court," he said, and grinned at her, the nightlights casting shadows on his face that made it seem more angular than usual. "I've got a date with someone who just might solve my problem of producing full-grown highborns for Ayrium."

"What?" Sam said, baffled.

"You'll be fine here," Amel consoled her. "If you need help, go find Alivda and Terrill. But be careful, she might be in bed with him. Be interesting to see who pays who, if that happens." He chuckled. "They might settle on calling it a friendly trans-action."

Sam's back kept getting stiffer as Amel talked, but by the time she had got up the steam to demand if he thought that was any way to talk to an unmarried Silver Demish princess, he was already walking away from her.

–o—o—o–

"Amel?!" Nona greeted him at the entrance of Red Hearth and tried to look past him, over his shoulder, as if she expected to see Erien arriving on his heels. It was the closest Amel had ever come to seeing a Red Reacher look awkward about anything where sex was concerned.

"Erien isn't coming," he told Nona. "He's getting married. I'm here, instead, to see Vretla about a deal."

"Oh," Nona said, and did a second take. "Oh!" she said, with more enthusiasm. "Come in, then."

Nona fled ahead of him down Red Hearth's Throat, but that was all right. He knew the way. He undid the lacing of his vest as he walked, and uncoupled his sword belt, wondering what the Demorans would think of their new Soul of Light walking into Vretla's lair, and thought, *Oh well.*

Vretla was lying on a floor mattress near the hot pool at the center of Red Hearth's big, open interior. A quick glance told Amel the surrounding space was thoroughly occupied by Vretla's vassals from Spiral Hall, watching from the shadows, but at least she had set up a canopy over her mattress as a concession to Erien's unVrellish sensibilities. The curtains were wine red, drawn back and bound with red cords.

Vretla rose, naked and glorious, from the nest beneath the canopy. Nona was still on her knees, interrupted in the act of relating the news of the substitution. She got up and took a few steps back.

Amel tossed aside his sword and took his vest off.

"It's been a while...Von," Vretla said in a burred voice, using his courtesan name.

"Avim Amel, actually," Amel corrected, starting on the buttons of his shirt.

She grinned. "If you prefer."

"I do," he said, asserting the one birth rank he had on her, and pulled his shirt off. Like the vest, his shirt was embroidered in Blue Demish motifs and he didn't want her tearing it. He was less concerned about his plain black pants getting damaged.

He took a step forward, and said, "Let's make you a baby."

Our titles are available at major book stores and local independent resellers who support Science Fiction and Fantasy readers like you.

EDGE Science Fiction
and Fantasy Publishing

Tesseract Books

Our titles are available at major book stores and local independent resellers who support Science Fiction and Fantasy readers like you.

Alphanauts by J. Brian Clarke (tp) - ISBN: 978-1-894063-14-2
Apparition Trail, The by Lisa Smedman (tp) - ISBN: 978-1-894063-22-7
As Fate Decrees by Denysé Bridger (tp) - ISBN: 978-1-894063-41-8
Avim's Oath (Part Six of the Okal Rel Saga) by Lynda Williams (pb)
   - ISBN: 978-1-894063-35-7

Black Chalice, The by Marie Jakober (hb) - ISBN: 978-1-894063-00-7
Blue Apes by Phyllis Gotlieb (pb) - ISBN: 978-1-895836-13-4
Blue Apes by Phyllis Gotlieb (hb) - ISBN: 978-1-895836-14-1

Children of Atwar, The by Heather Spears (pb) - ISBN: 978-0-88878-335-6
Cinco de Mayo by Michael J. Martineck (pb) - ISBN: 978-1-894063-39-5
Cinkarion - The Heart of Fire (Part Two of The Chronicles of the Karionin)
   by J. A. Cullum - (tp) - ISBN: 978-1-894063-21-0
Clan of the Dung-Sniffers by Lee Danielle Hubbard (pb) - ISBN: 978-1-894063-05-0
Claus Effect, The by David Nickle & Karl Schroeder (pb) - ISBN: 978-1-895836-34-9
Claus Effect, The by David Nickle & Karl Schroeder (hb) - ISBN: 978-1-895836-35-6
Courtesan Prince, The (Part One of the Okal Rel Saga) by Lynda Williams (tp)
   - ISBN: 978-1-894063-28-9

Dark Earth Dreams by Candas Dorsey & Roger Deegan (comes with a CD)
   - ISBN: 978-1-895836-05-9
Darkness of the God (Children of the Panther Part Two)
   by Amber Hayward (tp) - ISBN: 978-1-894063-44-9
Distant Signals by Andrew Weiner (tp) - ISBN: 978-0-88878-284-7
Dreams of an Unseen Planet by Teresa Plowright (tp) - ISBN: 978-0-88878-282-3
Dreams of the Sea (Part 1 of Tyranaël) by Élisabeth Vonarburg (tp)
   - ISBN: 978-1-895836-96-7
Dreams of the Sea (Part 1 of Tyranaël) by Élisabeth Vonarburg (hb)
   - ISBN: 978-1-895836-98-1
Druids by Barbara Galler-Smith and Josh Langston (tp)
   - ISBN: 978-1-894063-29-6

Eclipse by K. A. Bedford (tp) - ISBN: 978-1-894063-30-2
Even The Stones by Marie Jakober (tp) - ISBN: 978-1-894063-18-0
Evolve: Vampire Stories of the New Undead edited by Nancy Kilpatrick (tp)
   - ISBN: 978-1-894063-33-3

Far Arena (Part Five of the Okal Rel Saga) by Lynda Williams (tp)
   - ISBN: 978-1-894063-45-6
Fires of the Kindred by Robin Skelton (tp) - ISBN: 978-0-88878-271-7
Forbidden Cargo by Rebecca Rowe (tp) - ISBN: 978-1-894063-16-6

Game of Perfection, A (Part 2 of Tyranaël) by Élisabeth Vonarburg (tp)
  - ISBN: 978-1-894063-32-6
Gaslight Grimoire: Fantastic Tales of Sherlock Holmes
    edited by Jeff Campbell & Charles Prepolec (pb)
  - ISBN: 978-1-8964063-17-3
Gaslight Grotesque: Nightmare Tales of Sherlock Holmes
    edited by Jeff Campbell & Charles Prepolec (pb)
  - ISBN: 978-1-8964063-31-9
Green Music by Ursula Pflug (tp) - ISBN: 978-1-895836-75-2
Green Music by Ursula Pflug (hb) - ISBN: 978-1-895836-77-6

Healer, The (Children of the Panther Part One) by Amber Hayward (tp)
  - ISBN: 978-1-895836-89-9
Healer, The (Children of the Panther Part One) by Amber Hayward (hb)
  - ISBN: 978-1-895836-91-2
Hell Can Wait by Theodore Judson (tp) - ISBN: 978-1-978-1-894063-23-4
Hounds of Ash and other tales of Fool Wolf, The by Greg Keyes (pb)
  - ISBN: 978-1-894063-09-8
Hydrogen Steel by K. A. Bedford (tp) - ISBN: 978-1-894063-20-3

i-ROBOT Poetry by Jason Christie (tp) - ISBN: 978-1-894063-24-1
Immortal Quest by Alexandra MacKenzie (pb) - ISBN: 978-1-894063-46-3

Jackal Bird by Michael Barley (pb) - ISBN: 978-1-895836-07-3
Jackal Bird by Michael Barley (hb) - ISBN: 978-1-895836-11-0
JEMMA7729 by Phoebe Wray (tp) - ISBN: 978-1-894063-40-1

Keaen by Till Noever (tp) - ISBN: 978-1-894063-08-1
Keeper's Child by Leslie Davis (tp) - ISBN: 978-1-894063-01-2

Land/Space edited by Candas Jane Dorsey and Judy McCrosky (tp)
  - ISBN: 978-1-895836-90-5
Land/Space edited by Candas Jane Dorsey and Judy McCrosky (hb)
  - ISBN: 978-1-895836-92-9
Lyskarion: The Song of the Wind (Part One of The Chronicles of the Karionin)
    by J.A. Cullum (tp) - ISBN: 978-1-894063-02-9

Machine Sex and other stories by Candas Jane Dorsey (tp)
  - ISBN: 978-0-88878-278-6
Maërlande Chronicles, The by Élisabeth Vonarburg (pb)
  - ISBN: 978-0-88878-294-6
Moonfall by Heather Spears (pb) - ISBN: 978-0-88878-306-6

Of Wind and Sand by Sylvie Bérard (translated by Sheryl Curtis) (pb)
  - ISBN: 978-1-894063-19-7
On Spec: The First Five Years edited by On Spec (pb)
  - ISBN: 978-1-895836-08-0
On Spec: The First Five Years edited by On Spec (hb)
  - ISBN: 978-1-895836-12-7
Orbital Burn by K. A. Bedford (tp) - ISBN: 978-1-894063-10-4
Orbital Burn by K. A. Bedford (hb) - ISBN: 978-1-894063-12-8

Pallahaxi Tide by Michael Coney (pb) - ISBN: 978-0-88878-293-9
Passion Play by Sean Stewart (pb) - ISBN: 978-0-88878-314-1
Petrified World (Determine Your Destiny #1) by Piotr Brynczka (pb)
   - ISBN: 978-1-894063-11-1
Plague Saint by Rita Donovan, The (tp) - ISBN: 978-1-895836-28-8
Plague Saint by Rita Donovan, The (hb) - ISBN: 978-1-895836-29-5
Pock's World by Dave Duncan (tp) - ISBN: 978-1-894063-47-0
Pretenders (Part Three of the Okal Rel Saga) by Lynda Williams (pb)
   - ISBN: 978-1-894063-13-5

Reluctant Voyagers by Élisabeth Vonarburg (pb) - ISBN: 978-1-895836-09-7
Reluctant Voyagers by Élisabeth Vonarburg (hb) - ISBN: 978-1-895836-15-8
Resisting Adonis by Timothy J. Anderson (tp) - ISBN: 978-1-895836-84-4
Resisting Adonis by Timothy J. Anderson (hb) - ISBN: 978-1-895836-83-7
Righteous Anger (Part Two of the Okal Rel Saga) by Lynda Williams (tp)
   - ISBN: 897-1-894063-38-8

Silent City, The by Élisabeth Vonarburg (tp) - ISBN: 978-1-894063-07-4
Slow Engines of Time, The by Élisabeth Vonarburg (tp)
   - ISBN: 978-1-895836-30-1
Slow Engines of Time, The by Élisabeth Vonarburg (hb)
   - ISBN: 978-1-895836-31-8
Stealing Magic by Tanya Huff (tp) - ISBN: 978-1-894063-34-0
Strange Attractors by Tom Henighan (pb) - ISBN: 978-0-88878-312-7

Taming, The by Heather Spears (pb) - ISBN: 978-1-895836-23-3
Taming, The by Heather Spears (hb) - ISBN: 978-1-895836-24-0
Ten Monkeys, Ten Minutes by Peter Watts (tp) - ISBN: 978-1-895836-74-5
Ten Monkeys, Ten Minutes by Peter Watts (hb) - ISBN: 978-1-895836-76-9
Tesseracts 1 edited by Judith Merril (pb) - ISBN: 978-0-88878-279-3
Tesseracts 2 edited by Phyllis Gotlieb & Douglas Barbour (pb)
   - ISBN: 978-0-88878-270-0
Tesseracts 3 edited by Candas Jane Dorsey & Gerry Truscott (pb)
   - ISBN: 978-0-88878-290-8
Tesseracts 4 edited by Lorna Toolis & Michael Skeet (pb)
   - ISBN: 978-0-88878-322-6
Tesseracts 5 edited by Robert Runté & Yves Maynard (pb)
   - ISBN: 978-1-895836-25-7
Tesseracts 5 edited by Robert Runté & Yves Maynard (hb)
   - ISBN: 978-1-895836-26-4
Tesseracts 6 edited by Robert J. Sawyer & Carolyn Clink (pb)
   - ISBN: 978-1-895836-32-5
Tesseracts 6 edited by Robert J. Sawyer & Carolyn Clink (hb)
   - ISBN: 978-1-895836-33-2
Tesseracts 7 edited by Paula Johanson & Jean-Louis Trudel (tp)
   - ISBN: 978-1-895836-58-5
Tesseracts 7 edited by Paula Johanson & Jean-Louis Trudel (hb)
   - ISBN: 978-1-895836-59-2
Tesseracts 8 edited by John Clute & Candas Jane Dorsey (tp)
   - ISBN: 978-1-895836-61-5
Tesseracts 8 edited by John Clute & Candas Jane Dorsey (hb)
   - ISBN: 978-1-895836-62-2

Tesseracts Nine edited by Nalo Hopkinson and Geoff Ryman (tp)
 - ISBN: 978-1-894063-26-5
Tesseracts Ten: A Celebration of New Canadian Specuative Fiction
 edited by Robert Charles Wilson and Edo van Belkom (tp)
 - ISBN: 978-1-894063-36-4
Tesseracts Eleven: Amazing Canadian Speulative Fiction
 edited by Cory Doctorow and Holly Phillips (tp)
 - ISBN: 978-1-894063-03-6
Tesseracts Twelve: New Novellas of Canadian Fantastic Fiction
 edited by Claude Lalumière (pb)
 - ISBN: 978-1-894063-15-9
Tesseracts Thirteen: Chilling Tales from the Great White North
 edited by Nancy Kilpatrick and David Morrell (tp)
 - ISBN: 978-1-894063-25-8
Tesseracts 14: Strange Canadian Stories
 edited by John Robert Colombo and Brett Alexander Savory (tp)
 - ISBN: 978-1-894063-37-1
Tesseracts Q edited by Élisabeth Vonarburg & Jane Brierley (pb)
 - ISBN: 978-1-895836-21-9
Tesseracts Q edited by Élisabeth Vonarburg & Jane Brierley (hb)
 - ISBN: 978-1-895836-22-6
Throne Price by Lynda Williams and Alison Sinclair (tp)
 - ISBN: 978-1-894063-06-7
Time Machines Repaired Whie-U-Wait by K. A. Bedford (tp)
 - ISBN: 978-1-894063-42-5